Nicole Murphy has been a primary school teacher, bookstore owner and journalist. She grew up reading Tolkien, Lewis and Le Guin; spent her twenties discovering romance and lives her love of science fiction and fantasy through her involvement with the Conflux science fiction conventions. She lives with her husband in Queanbeyan, NSW. Visit her website: nicolermurphy.com

SECRET
ONES

NICOLE MURPHY
SECRET ONES

HARPER
Voyager

Harper *Voyager*
An imprint of HarperCollins *Publishers*

First published in Australia in 2010
by HarperCollins *Publishers* Australia Pty Limited
ABN 36 009 913 517
harpercollins.com.au

HarperCollins *Publishers*
25 Ryde Road, Pymble, Sydney, NSW 2073, Australia
31 View Road, Glenfield, Auckland 0627, New Zealand
A 53, Sector 57, Noida, UP, India
77–85 Fulham Palace Road, London, W6 8JB, United Kingdom
2 Bloor Street East, 20th floor, Toronto, Ontario M4W 1A8, Canada
10 East 53rd Street, New York NY 10022, USA

National Library of Australia Cataloguing-in-Publication entry:

Murphy, Nicole R
  The secret ones / Nicole R. Murphy.
  ISBN 978 0 7322 9161 7 (pbk.)
  Murphy, Nicole R. Dream of Asarlai ; bk. 1.
A823.4

Cover design by Natalie Winter
Cover images: Woman © Serge Krouglikoff/Corbis; all other images
  by shutterstock.com
Typeset in 10/12pt Sabon by Kirby Jones

To my husband Tim,
who believed in me when I didn't.

ASARLAI

There was a momentary feeling of pressure against her mind, then the stone door shimmered and disappeared. The woman who called herself Asarlai, meaning sorcerer, stepped into the stone chamber and looked around. This was an ancient place, forged centuries earlier out of the rock; used first as regular storage, it now hid things people would rather forget existed.

Her eyes skimmed over the forbidden objects stored on shelves and tables – knives, mirrors, books, cupboards, wands and hats. From each came a sense of darkness, of power that shouldn't be touched. Some were carved with sigils she didn't recognise. Others were stained with a reddish colour that she hoped was rust, not blood.

None of them had been moved. That, along with the mustiness of the air and the layer of dust that covered the shelves, the furniture and the floor told her that no one had been down here since she last had. She had covered her tracks well, and her work was undisturbed.

Her fingers tingled as she turned to study the black lacquered cabinet at the end of the room. She felt the anticipation building within her and took a deep breath

1

to remain calm. Today would be the day it all became hers. But there was still delicate work to be done.

With a wave of her hand the door to the chamber reappeared: solid, reassuring stone. No one would sneak up on her while she worked.

Asarlai walked down the long, thin room, the soles of her shoes slapping against the stone floor. She stopped and knelt in front of the cabinet and put a hand up to the gilt lock. It quivered and she nodded. The spell was still working. The lock was under such stress, it shouldn't take long to break it.

She pulled a long sliver of metal out from her sleeve and shook her head, disappointed that this required such a human skill as lock-picking. She slipped the metal into the keyhole and gently began to push it around. Finally, a click and a whir and then silence. Asarlai pulled the pick free and grasped one of the handles. She closed her eyes, took a deep breath, then opened her eyes and pulled.

There was a hesitation, just enough to make her wonder, begin to despair, then the ages gave way and the door opened.

Asarlai felt it straight away — blackness, fullness, power. It surrounded her, teased her, pulled at her and she leant back on her heels and closed her eyes, ready to bathe herself in the warmth. A warning rang in her mind and she shook her head to clear her thoughts. She didn't have time now. Once she was safe in her own laboratory, then she could enjoy.

There were five books in all, each bound in soft leather, some gilt, some carved. She reached in and pulled out the slimmest volume. Tracing a finger over the edges, she felt its desire to live again, and she smiled.

Asarlai took the rest of the books out and piled them up to one side, then closed and locked the cabinet again. It was highly unlikely anyone would come near this chamber and, if they did, they would studiously avoid even touching the cabinet, fearing the contamination. No one would know the books were free until she announced it.

She carried the books over to the door of the chamber, then turned back and made sure that her passage had left no trace and that the dust lay evenly over every surface. Then she opened the door, carried her booty outside and locked the room behind her. Hoisting the books into her arms, Asarlai began to make her way through the bardria building toward escape.

This was the moment she had dreaded. Over the years, she'd spent a great deal of time walking these corridors with books such as these, so it was a common sight. People waved, but generally no one stopped her — they were too busy about their own business. But if someone did decide today was the day to chat, and if someone who knew enough came close enough ...

Sweat formed on the back of her neck and she concentrated on keeping a relaxed face. No one would know how nervous she was.

She was more than halfway to the transfer room now, more than halfway to freedom. But her arms were starting to ache — somehow, these books were heavier than any she had ever carried.

She rounded a corner; there was a young man walking toward her. Sean Flaherty. Recently returned

3

from the family property in England. Moderate ability, moderate power. Asarlai relaxed. Sean didn't notice anything he didn't think was important, and she was less than important. For now.

But just as she passed him Asarlai stumbled. The books shifted in her arms and one slid and began to fall. She watched in horror, unable to do anything else.

Flaherty moved quickly and caught the book before it hit the floor. With a smile, he put it back on the top of the pile.

'Take care,' he said with a jaunty tilt of his head. Then he continued on his way.

Asarlai let go of the breath she'd been holding and started walking again. She saw people from a distance, but as she had hoped, she was unremarkable. She finally reached the transfer room of departure and it was empty. She stood in the middle, pictured her own laboratory and transferred.

The pull on her body, her senses, the force compelling her toward her destination was greater than she had ever known, yet her feet felt glued to the floor. For a moment she panicked: would the transfer be successful? Would she be caught between there and here and forever lost? But then it was over and she was standing in her laboratory, all five books in hand.

She hurried over to a bench and gently put the books down on the space she had prepared – carefully swept and then covered in a rich purple silk, the rightful resting place of such important tomes. She laid them out, side by side, then stepped back to look at them. Contentment overwhelmed her. Finally, after all these years, the forbidden teachings belonged to her. It was now time to rediscover, time to learn, time to educate, so that the gadda would multiply, and become what they were destined to be — lords of the earth.

CHAPTER ONE

'Celebrating something, Maggie?'

Maggie Shaunessy looked at the selection on the counter. Two bottles of the finest Champagne, crackers, cheese, strawberries, fresh bread and pâté. It certainly was a meal of celebration — she'd heard that morning that she'd received her Master of Education degree. But she wasn't going to let Harry Botherly know that. No matter how friendly he appeared, she didn't know his political leanings on humans and didn't want to find out through a scene at Sclossin's main supermarket. 'Does a girl need an excuse to spoil herself, Harry?'

He grinned. 'Not if it means you're going to spend up big at my store.'

The goods were quickly put in bags and paid for and she walked out of the store. As Maggie stepped from the warmth into the cold, she stopped and shifted the bags to one hand so she could throw her scarf around her throat and pull her beanie down around her ears.

When she'd come to Sclossin from Australia as a seventeen-year-old, she'd barely made it through her first winter, and swore she would never go outside in January again. But over the past decade, she'd come to appreciate the tingle of icy air against her skin — as long as she knew she would soon be warm again.

Star, I hated Sclossin, she thought as she strode down the pathway, nodding to the few others who were braving the threat of rain. It was so different from home. Winton was a country town: wide verandahed houses with tin roofs, swarms of flies in summer, frosts in winter. Sclossin was centuries old: stone buildings, wooden doors, green hedges in summer, fog-enclosed streets in winter.

Maggie walked to the end of the strip of shops and turned onto Bardria Street, moving away from the slowly-flowing waters of the creek that ran parallel to the main drag. To her left, the crenellated form of the Bardria, the home of the governing council of the gadda, loomed under the grey sky. In weather like this, she'd always fancied the building looked angry. In the infrequent bursts of sunshine they experienced, it became merely surly.

Next to the Bardria was the Sclossin Inn — the only place that humans were ever to be found at night in the town. Generally, the humans were happy for the people of Sclossin to govern themselves — it was part of an age-old charter with a medieval king that the modern political world of Ireland wasn't worried about. It had enabled the residents to ensure that only gadda lived and worked there.

However, business people and tourists were unavoidable — business for the times the human world couldn't be held back, tourists because Sclossin was a very pretty town. For the sake of keeping the secret, the inn was the only place humans could stay and if any of them realised that after their meal in the restaurant they found themselves oddly tired and inevitably went straight to bed — well, none had reported it.

When she'd arrived, Maggie hadn't seen the attractions of Sclossin, especially for humans. She herself was only there to do her first order study at the gadda school. Then she was going home, back to Australia and the human life that she'd been striving for.

Star, that had been a mistake. Her steps slowed as she remembered the years of trying to subdue her rapidly quickening power, while focussed on the adolescent goal of being just like everyone else. Coming from one of the richest families in Winton had helped; being smart, a bit dumpy and having to suddenly dash away when she felt her power building inside her hadn't.

Then there'd been her crush. What was his name? She chewed the inside of her cheek, and then smiled. Scott Campbell. The local football star and all-round hunk. When he'd chosen her to be his partner during chemistry in year eleven, she'd thought that meant her efforts were worth it, that she'd made an impact. Turned out he was thinking more of the impact her brains would have on his falling grades.

When finally her mother had sat down and talked about whether she might be cheating herself of the life she should have by refusing her heritage, Maggie had been forced to admit that trying to be human was stupid. She wasn't human. She was gadda. She was a member of a secret race with abilities and power that humans could only dream about.

Maggie had expected her year in Sclossin to be drudgery and horror – the only seventeen-year-old in a class of twelve-year-olds.

But then she'd met Ione – there for her second attempt at first order – and Maggie had found a close friendship like none she'd ever known. They'd got even closer when Jack was born, but their bond was cemented when Patrick, Ione's husband, died. Maggie had stepped in and kept the little family going until the worst of the grief was spent.

She'd also started to build a relationship with her father, long estranged. Over the years the large mansions, the foggy landscape, even the draughts in the old buildings had become very dear to her. She'd come to appreciate the gadda way enough to go on to second order, although her heart still belonged in the human world.

She turned to cross the road and, as she did, misjudged her step and put her foot into a puddle of water. It splashed up over her ankle boots and soaked her socks.

'Shit.' She pulled her foot from the water and stepped back up onto the path.

'Problem, Maggie?'

Maggie spun around to see Blair Callaghan grinning at her. She pulled a face at her old teacher. 'There are moments, just moments you know, when I hate Sclossin.'

'Well, if you'd kept up with your training like you should have, you'd be third order by now and you could probably dry your sock yourself.' The admonishment was spoken with a smile that took the heat from the words.

Blair was one of those people for whom it was impossible to see any other career choice but teacher. She, along with Ione, had been responsible for helping Maggie through that first hard year.

'Now, give me your groceries and then jump over the gutter onto the road.' Blair held out her hands.

Maggie handed the bags over and, as she did, noted that Blair seemed to have aged a great deal recently. Her once smooth skin was now harsher in texture and covered in myriad small lines, and there was grey scattered among the reddish-brown of her hair. It surprised Maggie – not only did she work with teachers, she'd grown up around them and had thought only the ones who didn't like the job aged. But then, she didn't know how old Blair was. Maybe she was much older than she appeared, and the years were finally catching up.

Maggie stepped over the puddle and turned to get her groceries, but Blair also stepped onto the road, undoubtedly helped by a subtle push of power. The two women walked across the deserted street together.

'This looks like the makings of a celebration,' Blair said.

Maggie made a snap decision. Unlike some of the teachers, who had made their Purist philosophy clear and had harangued Maggie for her desire to interact with human society, Blair had always been very considerate of Maggie's drive to continue her human studies. 'I am celebrating, actually. I've just completed my Master's degree. It's kinda like getting sixth order for humans.' Maggie jumped onto the footpath on the other side of the road, and took a quick glance up at

11

the building. The lights shone through the windows of the apartment she shared with Ione and her son Jack. It was like a beacon, speaking to her of warmth and dry socks.

She turned to watch Blair jump, and the older woman held out her bags with a smile. She'd been right — Blair either sympathised with her wish to work with humans or didn't care either way. 'Congratulations, Maggie. You must feel very proud of yourself.'

'I do.' Maggie took back her bags.

'I hope this means that you will now put the same level of dedication and concentration into reaching the real sixth order.'

Maggie laughed. 'You never let up, do you?'

'Not on students with potential,' Blair said. 'Speaking of which, tell Ione to give me a call. I've got a few ideas that just might break that blockage after all.'

Ione was quite a rarity in the gadda — she couldn't even pass first order. She'd made seven attempts at the test, had attended the gadda school twice and had had countless tutors. None of it mattered. The prognosis was that Ione had very little power, and very little natural ability. A talented person might have been able to work that level of power to pass the test, but Ione could not.

It was one of the great mysteries of the gadda. Ione's family, the Hammonds, were renowned for their talent and power and boasted more than their fair share of sixth orders. How could one of theirs not pass first?

Neither Ione nor her family were particularly concerned. They'd been more worried when Maggie, through her university studies, had introduced Ione to computers. The Hammonds didn't mind humans, but they couldn't see how doing such a human-centred job would be good for Ione.

Ione however had proven to have a talent for the technology, and now made her living as a self-employed database programmer.

Maggie shook her head and grinned at her old teacher.

'If I were you, Blair, I'd give up. Ione's going to be the one that got away.'

Blair shook her head. 'I can't. It's pathological, I'm afraid.' The two women smiled at each other. 'Enjoy your celebration.'

With yet another impulse, Maggie leant forward and kissed Blair on the cheek. 'Thank you,' she said. 'If you hadn't been such a good teacher, I doubt I would have survived the first year here.'

'You can do anything you set your mind to, Margaret Shaunessy. Now go. Party. Enjoy.' Blair waved her hand toward the building and then walked around Maggie and down the street to the shops.

As she watched Blair walk away, Maggie recalled her horrendous first day at the gadda school. It had started with history with Bart O'Hanlon and he'd spent the entire lesson explaining to the children how Maggie was the perfect example of everything that was wrong with the Humanist movement.

'The gadda are not human,' he'd barked out the first tenet of the Purist manifesto. 'Humans are a lesser life form, just as much use to us as dogs or birds or fish or horses. Actually, less use than fish or horses — at least you can eat one and use the other for travel.

Humans are nothing but a blight on this planet. To try to be one is foolish in the extreme, and I expect you will all show Miss Shaunessy the mistake she has made over the coming year.'

Maggie had walked into her next lesson – control with Blair Callaghan – shaking and wondering how much this teacher would hate her. However, Blair had treated Maggie as just another student – praise when it was deserved, censure on occasion but otherwise calm and polite. Her lessons had become Maggie's refuge, until with Ione's help she'd found her voice and stood up to the other teachers.

The fact she'd managed to outscore nearly every other child in the class and prove that she hadn't been defiled by her years living with humans had helped too.

Shaking the memories from her mind, Maggie used her shoulder to push open the door into the building. The apartment was on the second floor, and she made her way upstairs quickly.

She shifted the bags in her arms, used her elbow to bang on the door and frowned at Ione when she finally opened it. 'You took your time.' She stomped into the room, dumped the shopping on the dining table that stood at one end and slumped down on the lounge that stood at the other. She quickly whipped her boots and socks off.

'I hope that's not our Champagne you're thumping around.' Ione moved over to the table and opened the bag. 'Shame on you, Mags. Have you no sense of style?' She looked over her shoulder, saw Maggie pull the second sock off and drop it on the floor with the other one, and laughed. 'Been walking through the brook, have you?'

Maggie glared at her. 'Shut up and pour me a drink.' She picked up her wet things and took them to the washing machine. Then she went into her bedroom, cramped with a queen-sized bed, cupboards, desk and bookshelves. She stopped and looked at the desk. The hours she'd spent there at her laptop worrying her way through word after word to ensure that her research was as clear and concise as possible. It had all been worth it: time to celebrate. She grabbed another pair of socks, pulled them on and went back out to her friend.

Ione handed her a crystal glass full of Champagne and raised her own into the air. 'Here's to Ms Education 2010. May the caelleach never find out how you achieved it.'

Maggie rolled her eyes. 'Shit, Ione, stop making a big deal out of it. Are *you* planning to tell him? The people at the uni are keeping it quiet, my family isn't gonna blab. If he finds out I wrote a children's story with magic, and that's a big if, it won't be for ages. And anyway, you know I'll be able to talk him around. I even have the speech prepared. So stop worrying and drink up.' She lifted her glass and tapped it against Ione's. Then she downed the sweet Champagne, the bubbles tickling her nose.

'I hope you're right. Personally, I'm over rescuing you from Caelleach Cormac, especially since I'm beginning to suspect you enjoy it.' Ione put her glass down and started setting up the food on the table. She had a knack for making everything look pretty and inviting. There were colourful tubs of herbs growing on the sill in the kitchen, throw rugs and cushions in greens and pinks on the black lounge and beautiful embroidery on the handtowels in the bathroom.

Maggie screwed up her nose. 'It's not my fault he doesn't get me. And besides I wouldn't be an O'Hara if I wasn't pissing people off. Speaking of which, I wonder where Mum and Grandpa are.' Maggie looked at her watch.

'If they're going to be late, they'll just miss out on the drink.' Ione poured herself another glass.

A low, vibrating tone shifted the air around them: a request to transfer into the apartment. 'Speak of the devil,' Maggie said, putting her glass down as she silently gave permission.

She stood and faced the transfer spot in the middle of the room. It was important to have a dedicated place for transferring — appearing in the wrong spot could be fatal. The air went opaque and shivered and her grandfather appeared, a broad smile on his face.

John O'Hara was a large man, with a farmer's hands and a poet's eyes. His shoulders were beginning to stoop a little, his hair was white and his face heavily creased, but his voice held laughter and his eyes were still sharp enough to put hearts in a spin.

'Here's my girl!' John moved forward and wrapped his arms around Maggie. She returned the bear hug for a moment, but soon was having trouble breathing.

'Grandpa, breath, please,' she gasped.

John chuckled as he released her. 'Don't know my own strength.'

'I suppose it's not bad for an old bloke.'

16

John staggered back, as though he'd been struck.

'Maggie, you wound me,' he said. 'I hope you've got a good whiskey to soothe my damaged soul, Ione.'

'Have I ever not had a good whiskey for you? In fact, I discovered a terrific little distillery down near Leenane the other month, and I've been saving it for your next visit.'

'Bless you. Nice to know one of my favourite girls cares for my delicate health.' He went over to the table, sat down and reached for the cheese.

Maggie snorted. Her grandfather was on the wrong side of seventy, but he was as healthy as many men half his age.

'And where's Jack?' John popped a cracker topped with brie into his mouth, and looked around for the little boy. Ione's son had become as much a part of the O'Hara family as Ione herself over the years.

'Jack is at my sister's. He really doesn't need to see the debauchery that Maggie has planned for tonight.' Ione gave the whiskey to John.

'Nothing too debauched, please, Maggie. The family has a reputation to maintain, you know.'

'Hence the need for the debauchery.' Maggie had reached for her Champagne when another tone rang in the air, this one deep yet musical.

O'Hara's head whipped around. 'Why would the Sabhamir be coming over?'

Maggie couldn't hold back a shiver of fear. The Sabhamir was the protector of the gadda, the muscle of the bardria. His unexpected arrival was never good news.

'It's the story,' Ione said cheerfully. 'I've been telling her, John, the caelleach was always going to find out.'

'It can't be the story,' Maggie said, as much to convince herself as anyone else. 'He can't know about it. There's no way.' She closed her eyes and gave the signal for the Sabhamir to come into her home.

Before she had taken a breath, the Sabhamir stood on their transfer spot. Tall and dressed in unrelenting black, he looked what he was — the most powerful man alive.

'Margaret Shaunessy, you are summoned to appear before the bardria of the gadda,' he announced in a deep voice that seemed to vibrate right through Maggie. Then he bowed his head. 'John. Ione.'

Maggie stared at the Sabhamir, sure she had misheard. Why was she being called before the entire bardria? If it was the story, surely it would only be Caelleach Cormac wanting to see her.

'Sabhamir.' O'Hara stood and bowed. 'May I ask what this is regarding?'

'I'm afraid I'm not at liberty to say, John. However, you and Ione may accompany Ms Shaunessy, if you wish. I suspect she may welcome the support.'

'Yep, it's the story,' Ione said, quickly swallowing the Champagne left in her glass.

Maggie's stomach roiled, and all her excitement disappeared. It couldn't be, not the story, it couldn't be. Not the whole bardria.

John walked over to her and put his hand on her shoulder. No matter what she'd done, her grandfather would support her — and he was more than capable of standing up to the bardria. 'Is it the story?'

The Sabhamir raised a sculpted eyebrow. 'Let me put it this way, the bardria doesn't take any discussion of power with humans lightly.'

Maggie moaned. She was in trouble, much more trouble than she'd ever considered. 'I think I'm going to be sick.'

'Rubbish. The bardria are just being protective. You'll be fine.' John gave her shoulder a squeeze.

'If you wouldn't mind escorting Ione, I'll take Ms Shaunessy,' the Sabhamir said.

John leant forward. 'You'll be fine, Maggie. Just don't panic or start apologising all over the place.'

Maggie barely kept herself from calling out as John's hand left her shoulder. Don't panic? Hard, when she already had.

The Sabhamir stepped forward and held out his hand to her. Maggie looked up at him as she took hold and he helped her to her feet, wondering if he could feel her shaking. While his face remained passive, she was sure his eyes softened. He gave a short nod and she felt more confident. If the Sabhamir was on her side, it couldn't be that bad.

Without warning, they were transferring. Maggie felt the pull on every cell in her body, as it fought to remain where it should be, then the power took over and there was a sensation of rushing, busyness and nothingness, before she came back to herself, standing in a large room.

The Sabhamir walked behind her, taking a protective position. Maggie wasn't sure whether he was protecting her, or protecting the bardria *from* her.

She looked around, having never been in the bardria room before. The first thing that struck her was how plain it was — wooden floor, wood panelling three-quarters of the way up the wall, whitewashed panelling above. It was a simple room, and empty but for the two of them, yet she could feel the power in it. Judgements were made here; people's lives changed irrevocably, sometimes for the good, sometimes the bad.

In front of her was a long table with twenty chairs behind it. Each chair was the same size, made of the same wood. There was no sense that any seat gave distinction to its occupant, but she knew that this apparent equality wasn't the case. The representatives of the six original families were the real power of the bardria, led by the current caelleach, Horatio Cormac. He was a man renowned for being fair and just. Maggie's experience of him was of a man with little sense of humour and brimming with frustration.

Behind her were rows of chairs for an audience. She hoped they'd stay empty. If she was going to be humiliated, she didn't want dozens of gadda watching.

She tilted her head back to look at the famous first representation of the star of gulagh, the emblem of the gadda. The six-pointed star represented the original six families, the founders of the gadda and the orders and rules that all now followed. In the middle of the star was a heart, showing that emotion was at the centre of all the power the gadda wielded. The star sat in the middle of a glass ceiling, allowing the sun to light the room.

It gave a softness to the space that belied the darkness often dealt with here. This was where the bardria addressed the most dreadful of gadda crimes. Here people had their power stripped and were banished forever from the entire community. And the man behind her was responsible for enacting all sentences.

What would it be for her? Would she get an insignificant punishment? Or were the bardria so annoyed they would banish her? Surely what she had done wasn't so dreadful that they would cut off her powers, was it? Shit, what if this time she really had gone too far?

A door beyond the table swung open and Maggie jumped and squeaked. The Sabhamir nudged her and she looked over her shoulder at him. He gave her another small nod, and she relaxed. Yep, he's definitely on my side.

The bardria filed in, members of the most important families of the gadda, life-time appointees. Dressed in purple floor-length robes, each was marked with the level of skill he or she had reached — stripes for the gadda way, stars for the gadma way. They also had gold piping around the collars of their robes, and the symbol of the gadda on their breast, the sign they were councillors. Each walked to stand behind a chair. Once all were in position, they sat in unison.

Maggie quickly scanned the impassive faces. Those she knew favoured the Purist view of keeping the gadda and humans separate were looking at her with disdain, which she expected. The other half — the bardria was split fifty/fifty politically — kept their expressions blank. She couldn't tell if those people who normally supported her family would now support her.

She focussed on the man who sat in the centre – the caelleach, Horatio Cormac. Ultimately, he was the one she needed to impress. He was also likely to be the most annoyed about what she had done.

Cormac was nominally Humanist. Certainly, he'd been more than sympathetic to her grandfather and mother and had helped smooth things a number of times when John O'Hara's enthusiasm for humans got out of hand.

But he was also very much a traditionalist, and Maggie had realised within days of arriving in Sclossin that the caelleach wasn't happy she'd waited so long to come for her training. Nor did he like that once she passed first order, she went back to focussing on her human education. He'd had a heated discussion with her when she'd chosen to get her teacher's degree and work in public schools. He'd been so incensed by her introducing Ione to the world of computers that he'd screamed at her. The night she'd thrown a party in her and Ione's flat for the other teachers at her school, he'd ended up in the healer's wing with high blood pressure.

If he *had* found out about her story, then he'd probably be on the verge of a heart attack.

She watched Cormac look around the room, as if he could see who was present even though he was blind. She had often wondered just how much he could and couldn't see.

As the caelleach looked, two more people appeared in the room. One Maggie recognised immediately – the Ceamir, who ensured that gadda treated humans well and humans remained unsuspecting. The elderly woman was wearing a ceremonial robe of deep, rich red, the front of which hung from her hunched shoulders and dragged on the ground before her. No one knew how old the Ceamir was and no one was prepared to ask.

The man who had arrived with the old woman was dressed in a navy blue robe, and that told Maggie that he was the Firimir. It was his task to ensure that everyone who spoke to the bardria told the truth, and he did it by reading witnesses' minds. The sight of him in the room made her legs shake.

'Are we ready, Sabhamir?' Cormac said.

'Ms Shaunessy's grandfather and flatmate are coming, sir. They should be here –' The sound of a door opening interrupted the Sabhamir's speech. Maggie looked over her shoulder and saw John and Ione walk in.

'– now,' the Sabhamir finished.

John and Ione stopped beside Maggie and bowed to the table. 'Caelleach Cormac, councillors, greetings to you all. My heart burns with joy at being in Sclossin again,' John said.

'O'Hara. Ms Gorton.' Cormac bowed his head. 'Can I assume that you'll both wish to speak in Ms Shaunessy's defence?'

'Should it prove necessary, of course, but I doubt it will.' John bowed again, took Ione's arm and they sat down.

Maggie watched the caelleach's jaw tighten and almost shuddered. It wasn't looking good.

'Firimir, take your position,' he all but growled. The Firimir came over and stood behind Maggie. She was surprised to discover as he approached that he wasn't that much taller than she was — he had an aura of power that made him seem as tall as the Sabhamir.

The Firimir put his hands on either side of Maggie's head, and she felt a squeezing sensation against her brain before warmth enveloped her. All external noise and sights dimmed, and she was aware solely of the caelleach's face and voice.

'Margaret Shaunessy, you have been brought before the bardria because we are concerned that you do not understand the importance of keeping the truth of the gadda secret from the humans.' Cormac waved his hand and a pile of papers appeared. 'We have read this ... children's story, which we believe was part of — what is it called again?' He looked to one side of the table.

Another voice intruded on Maggie's consciousness. 'A Master's degree, Caelleach. A form of qualification among the humans.' The answer came from Helga Flaherty. She looked at Maggie and smiled.

And Maggie understood why she stood in front of the entire bardria. This wasn't just about the caelleach being annoyed at her again. It was part of the long-standing feud between the Flaherty and O'Hara families, one strongly Purist, the other committed to helping humans.

'We have read this story and it is disturbing, Ms Shaunessy. The name of a gadda is now irretrievably linked to a piece of writing about the use of power. I am at a loss as to how you could have considered this a good idea.'

Right now, so was Maggie. And boy, did she want to know how the bardria had got hold of it so quickly, not that this was the time to ask. She mentally reviewed her prepared speech, prayed that it would be enough for the Firimir, and began. 'Caelleach Cormac, councillors. My field of study in achieving my Master's degree was children's literature. Magic, as the humans call it, has always been a feature of writing for children. However, I felt that there wasn't enough writing about losing belief in magic. As you can see from having read my story, it deals with a child who comes to realise there is no such thing as magic and must learn to live happily in a world of humans. I contend that my story discourages belief in magic and could actually draw human minds away from the gadda, which we know is a good thing.' She smiled at the bardria members, knowing that keeping the gadda secret was one thing both ends of the political spectrum agreed on.

'I fail to see how having the name of a gadda linked to talk of "magic" is a good thing for us, regardless of the nature of that link,' Cormac said. 'You have completed the initial studies of our race, Ms Shaunessy, and in fact did it much more recently than anyone else here. Surely you have not already forgotten the lessons you learnt about what happens when humans associate gadda with what they call magic?'

Maggie winced. 'No, Caelleach, I have not forgotten. I do not believe that my case is similar to those tragedies.'

'I believe it is up to us to decide whether it is similar, Ms Shaunessy.' Cormac leant back in his chair. 'How many people will know about this story?'

'The staff at the university where I studied,' Maggie said. 'That is all.'

Cormac leant forward again, and Maggie realised she'd just scored a point for herself. 'And can these people be trusted not to speak of it?'

'I have asked them not to speak of it, or publish it, or let it be known. Its purpose was so I could achieve my degree, and further my education. I have no wish for it to go beyond that.'

'You asked them not to speak of it?' Helga Flaherty frowned. 'Could it be that you knew that it would not be a good idea for humans to find out about this? If so, why do it in the first place?'

Maggie scrambled quickly for an answer. She couldn't admit that Helga Flaherty was right, because that would be an admission of guilt. 'I chose this topic because it had not been pursued before and thus was more likely to be considered well by the people marking it,' she said. She noted confusion on the faces of some of the councillors, and wasn't sure if that was a good thing.

'If I might speak, Caelleach.' The Ceamir's soft voice floated through Maggie.

'Go ahead, Ceamir.'

'There is no doubting that Ms Shaunessy's name will now be linked with magic for a very long time, if not her entire lifetime, within that circle of people, and the association could certainly spread. However, I believe the impression will be that she is against magic, and therefore it would never be thought that she would have any interest in it herself. I think that if she stays visible in human society and minimises her contact with gadda for a while, there will be no suspicion about her and all will be well.'

Maggie felt her heart freeze. Oh shit, I'm going to be banished.

'What are you suggesting, Ceamir?' Cormac said.

'Ms Shaunessy should be sent home to Australia and banned from returning to Sclossin for, say, two years. By living and interacting with humans, something she has experience at, and limiting her contact to gadda to just her immediate family – all of whom pass very well as human – there will be little chance that the truth will be discovered.'

'And tell me how that is a punishment for her, Ceamir,' Helga Flaherty said. 'You return her to her family, allow her to do what she wants to do, and that punishes her?'

'Ms Shaunessy has lived here in Sclossin for ten years, ma'am. She has developed ties and links to this town, not the least of which are some close friendships. Not being able to see those people for two years will be a trial for her. And then there is the fact that, while living away from our community, she and her family will have to be circumspect about their use of their powers. If word of the story spreads, the O'Haras will need to live very human lives for a time.'

Delight flashed across Helga Flaherty's face. No doubt she was picturing John O'Hara hampered in using his power. 'I see the wisdom in your words, Ceamir. I believe you propose a suitable punishment, although I would add one caveat. I believe her father should also go to Australia with her, to ensure she remains connected to her gadda heritage.' Maggie's eyes widened, and she barely bit back a cry of *No*. 'Ms Shaunessy's development was hampered by her late arrival for training, which was no doubt encouraged by the O'Haras. There is still hope she can be taught our ways.'

Star above! thought Maggie. Her father, in Australia, near her mother, for two years? They'd kill each other long before that time was up.

'I believe that is a very suitable suggestion, Helga,' Cormac said. Maggie looked at him and he smiled at her. Damn, she thought. He had sensed her reaction and liked it. 'What say you, John O'Hara?'

John stood and bowed. 'I thank the councillors for their leniency toward my granddaughter, for I fear that her ill-conceived writing could have caused great difficulty for us all. As to Peter Shaunessy accompanying Maggie to Australia, he will not be welcome in my home.'

Helga frowned and opened her mouth but Cormac got in first. 'Fine. The bardria will assist Peter in finding a home nearby. Sabhamir?'

The protector nodded. 'It is a good solution, Caelleach.'

'Firimir?'

The Firimir removed his hands from Maggie's head. There was a pause, then the waft of wonderfully scented flowers flowed through the air. 'Margaret Shaunessy speaks truth.'

'Then it is decided — Margaret Shaunessy will be banned from all contact with citizens of Sclossin for the next two years, and must return to her family home in Australia within a week.'

Maggie watched the gavel hit the table with a resounding thud and tried to convince herself it could have been worse. She could have been banished. She could have been stripped of her power and sent out into the world, never to be gadda again.

This was what she'd always wanted, she told herself as she turned to John and Ione — to be human, and such she'd have to be for the next two years. But then she looked at Ione's pale face, and realised it wasn't what she wanted at all. She'd come to enjoy her dual life in Ireland — she could be as human as she liked during the day, and then come back to Sclossin each night and embrace the power that lit her life.

She had, she realised, found herself a very nice balance, which her foolishness had destroyed.

She smiled at Ione. 'That went well, I thought.' She tried to force gaiety into her voice and was sure she'd failed.

'Home, with both of you.' John took both girls by the arm. As a sixth-order oman, John had the power to transfer two people the short distance from the bardria building to the flat.

Once they were back in the loungeroom, Ione threw her arms around Maggie's neck. 'I can't believe they're making you leave,' she said. 'What am I supposed to do for the next two years?'

Maggie fought back tears. 'You've got Jack, and your programming. You'll be fine.'

'I told you.' Ione pulled back and slapped Maggie's arm, hard. 'When you told me the idea, what did I say?'

'"Don't do it, Mags. The caelleach will crucify you." You were right. It was stupid of me to think they wouldn't find out and, if they did, that they wouldn't care.' Maggie frowned. 'How the hell did they find out? It's obvious that the Flahertys are behind this.'

'They were watching you,' John said. 'Undoubtedly they've been spying on you from the moment you got here. A bit of power against a lock, a quick search of your lecturer's office and there you have it — one manuscript.'

'I didn't know. I mean, I know the Purists are against us, but to do this ...' Maggie went over and slumped on the lounge. She looked up at Ione and John. 'How do I explain this to the school? The children? I can't just pack up and leave my human life.'

'Illness, darling.' John came and sat next to her. 'You tell your principal that your mother has suddenly taken ill, and you have to go to Australia.'

'Why Siobhan?' Ione asked.

'Because she's not here,' John said, humour returning to the group. 'Now, when you get to Australia, we'll tell the authorities that you had a vicious break-up with a boyfriend and decided it was time to come home. Horrible thing to have happen just after Christmas, you know. You'll have to organise the paperwork to get into the educational system there, and in the meantime you can do something at the university. I've been told I need a personal assistant, maybe you can trial the position for me.'

'Working for you? That sounds like more than a reasonable punishment,' Ione said.

Maggie tried to smile. She knew they were both lightening the mood so she wouldn't be swamped in misery. She felt the effort was doomed to failure. She loved her life in Ireland. She loved the children in her year four class. She loved living with Ione and Jack.

John scoffed. 'She's going to have to play interference between her parents. *That* will be the cruel and unusual punishment.'

'Star above, Mum's gonna kill me,' Maggie said, and thought that it might not be such a bad idea.

Moments later Siobhan arrived, having been kept in Australia by her duties as one of Winton's GPs.

By the end of the retelling of Maggie's confrontation with the bardria, Siobhan was frowning. 'A shame your foolishness has to punish us all, Maggie.'

Maggie knew her mother was talking about Peter Shaunessy moving to Winton. She'd never lacked for knowledge of her mother's antipathy to her father. 'I'll keep him away from you. I'm sorry, Mum.'

'Here, Siobhan, have Maggie's drink as the beginning of her punishment.' Ione handed Siobhan a flute of Champagne with an evil grin.

'Not actually Maggie's glass, right?' Siobhan eyed the drink carefully.

'No, but the last of the bottle, so she's going to have to go fend for herself. Cheers.'

Maggie watched the glasses clinking with sadness and also a sense of dread. Somehow, she knew this was all going to come back at her, and not in a good way.

CHAPTER TWO

Lucas Valeroso looked at the selection on the table —
sandwiches, crackers, cheese, strawberries, fresh bread,
pâté, and flutes of Champagne. It all looked very
inviting, but he wasn't hungry. Instead, his mind and
body were focussed on controlling his nerves.

Nerves. He almost laughed. He was too old for
nerves. But then, he was about to receive the world's
pre-eminent physics prize, and that was worth a few
twinges of anxiety.

He went over to the bar, grabbed a glass of water
and turned to survey the crowd. The greatest scientists,
academics and business people in America, all here to
honour him and his work. For a moment, he basked
in the glory of that, the knowledge that he'd made it.
Then he acknowledged that they were probably all
here for the free food and booze, not him, and smiled
wryly.

The Julius Edgar Lilienfeld Prize was worth
$50,000, which was nice, but nicer was the recognition
of his work and his place as one of the best physicists
in the world. Not a bad achievement for a boy from
the ghetto, who'd made his way through a lot of his
adolescence in gangs, struggling just to survive. He

wished his boys could see him now, but then decided that wasn't worth it — they wouldn't understand what this moment meant for him and his career.

'Valeroso.'

He swung around and found himself face to face with Lee Suy Chin, his first boss. 'Professor Chin.' They shook hands.

'Well, I have to say I expected to be here with you one day, although I did expect it a few years earlier than this.' Chin had always been vocal in his belief in Lucas.

Lucas had thought so too, but then his past seemed to have a way of affecting his present. Normally in the form of one blackmailing little — he stopped the thought in its tracks. 'Life can be a bitch sometimes,' Lucas murmured, and Chin laughed.

'Well, you made it anyway, and it's a terrific little piece of research. My team's been going ape over it.'

'Thank you,' Lucas said. 'How are things at NJU?'

'A lot quieter since you left.' Chin laughed. 'I could never get over the number of things that would go wrong around you. Never your fault, of course.'

Lucas winced. He'd forgotten how weird things used to happen for no apparent reason. Light bulbs would explode, equipment would fall off the desk, and computers would mysteriously switch on and off. It hadn't happened for years, and he'd long ago put it down to coincidence. 'The poltergeist must have been bored.'

Chin shrugged. 'Well, you got here in the end, and I'm hoping you might consider coming back to the beginning. I've been asked to be vice-chancellor, so we need a new chair of physics. Sound like an idea?'

Shit, it sounded like a fantastic idea. A great career move. However, it wasn't quite what Lucas was interested in. 'Being chair doesn't give you much time in the lab.'

'True, it would curtail your research a little. But in terms of your long-term future, it could make you. Listen, have a think about it and call me in a couple of days.' Chin shook his hand and then went off to circulate.

Lucas tried to stop a huge grin and barely succeeded, smirking instead. The boy from the Bronx, a chair of physics while still in his mid-thirties. Unbelievable. The angry, scared kid who had only found contentment when deep in an experiment, now highly regarded and sought for positions of responsibility. It was almost enough to make a man believe that the good could win. Almost.

A bell rang, the signal that everyone should take their seats for the presentation. Lucas began to make his way to the table at the front and centre of the room, but as he walked through the crowd a small, round man with a fuzz of dark hair on the top of his head suddenly blocked his way.

Oh, shit, Lucas thought as Professor Hayden Smith-Jenkins turned his face up to the light. Head of the physics department at Carolina Tech and the only man to have persecuted Lucas because of his past.

Five years after learning the 'truth', the professor still wouldn't look at Lucas. He raised his nose higher in the air, turned and walked away.

And just like that, Lucas was reminded that he might be a brilliant physicist, but in some eyes he was a poor excuse for a human being. He made his way to his seat, his enjoyment of the day dissipated. The prize was given, he made his speech and his peers applauded him, but all he could do was wonder what they would do if they knew they were honouring an ex-con.

He knew he was expected to mingle, allow the guests their moment of joy in talking to the Julius Edgar Lilienfeld Fellow, but he was really bad at it. And now he wasn't in the mood to even pretend he didn't loathe it. He shook the minimum of hands, escaped and took himself back to the hotel. He packed and made his way to JFK to fly back to Chicago, there to lose himself again in his work, the only place he found any peace.

No peace this time. He couldn't stop thinking about how things had turned out for him at Carolina Tech.

He'd never told prospective employers about his juvenile record for theft and hijacking a car — as far as both society and he were concerned, he'd paid the price for his adolescent stupidity and he started his adult life with a clean slate.

When he'd arrived to teach at Caro Tech, it was to find the man who'd hired him had been replaced by Smith-Jenkins. His opening line — 'You don't look Hispanic' — had started their working relationship off badly.

Then Holly had arrived. She'd found him thanks to a report of his new job at their high school reunion.

'Well, look at you.' She'd whistled as she walked around him. 'Lucas Valeroso, a professor at university. What a scream.'

The students had gawked at the bleached blonde curls and very bright yellow dress. Lucas had been horrified. He hadn't seen Holly for seven years and had hoped never to again.

'Doing well for yourself. Much better than me.'

Lucas knew what was coming — during his student days, Holly had supported herself by blackmailing him, amongst other things.

This time he was a grown man, well-regarded in his field, and so he'd found the strength to tell her no.

He hadn't expected her to go to Smith-Jenkins. He really hadn't expected his boss to care about juvie crimes. She did. He did.

After months of being treated like a pariah — anti-discrimination laws meant Smith-Jenkins couldn't sack him — Lucas had quit.

He's spent the last few years both rebuilding after that hiccough in his career and hiding from Holly.

As he sat next to the gleaming silver platform that represented his current research, it occurred to Lucas that the publicity from winning the award might draw Holly to him again.

He began to pray it wouldn't.

CHAPTER THREE

When the party was over and Maggie's family had returned to Australia, Maggie had regained her good mood. There was nothing she could do to change the bardria's decision and for tonight her focus would be on celebrating her achievement and enjoying Ione's company.

Kitty's Star Bar was a hive of activity. A few small groups of day-drinkers remained, greying heads bent over pints of cloudy dark liquor as they attempted to solve the problems of the world. Younger people were three deep at the bar, ready to get their night started, and the dance floor was half full.

Maggie and Ione shook the doorman's hand as they went in. Maggie felt the pulse of his power against her palm and there was a twinge of sadness. For the next two years, she'd only feel this mark of the gadda from her family.

With Champagne still buzzing through their system, the women happily ignored the crush at the bar to hit the dance floor. The latest gadda tunes pumped through the air, while balls of light danced and weaved around and between the dancers. Maggie loved dancing and soon lost herself in the music, uncaring that Ione quickly found herself a partner for some fun in a dark corner of the bar.

After a couple of dances, Maggie decided it was time to refresh her alcohol quotient, and made her way over to the bar, now less busy. She squeezed in between a couple of women and signalled the barman.

'Great to see you, Maggie,' Simon said as he wiped the counter in front of her. 'The usual?'

'Actually, I'll have a martini, thanks,' she said.

Simon cocked an eyebrow. 'Getting on the hard stuff a bit early, aren't you?'

'Hey, I'm young, and I don't have to work tomorrow, so party on.'

'That's what I like to hear.' He mixed the drink and Maggie carefully carried it from the bar. She stood beside the dance floor, tapping her foot and sipping on the drink while she watched the lights flash from colour to colour and weave between people's legs. The lights could be conjured to react to a multitude of things — the beat of the music, people's power, even the amount of alcohol sold. Tonight it seemed it was gender. Specifically, the lights seemed to be hovering around the men's faces, lighting every plane and curve.

Maggie wondered if that meant Kitty was looking for husband number four or if she just wanted to perve. Whatever the reason, Maggie was grateful.

As she watched, the lights shone on the sharp angles of a male face she had never seen before. That was odd — Sclossin was such a small town, you soon knew everyone around your age. A visitor, she decided. Whoever he was, he certainly knew how to move. Cute too — she didn't normally go for guys with red hair, but his was rich and deep, and his bearing was king-like.

She caught his eye and smiled; he smiled back and the night started looking even better. He left the dance floor and made his way over to her and she was pleased to see his body seemed to match his face — nice height, slim build but muscular.

'I hope you're dancing,' he said, his eyes moving over her. 'It would be a tragedy for the most beautiful woman in the room to not be.'

Up close, his eyes were a brilliant light blue and his lips, while thin, curved nicely. And that slight streak of arrogance was attractive too. 'I could be persuaded.' She stirred the olive around and fluttered her eyelashes at him.

'Then persuaded you shall be.' Her mystery man put his hand out, not so much as a request to join him but as a demand.

Wow, Maggie thought, talk about your typical romantic hero. If he puts this level of intensity into his lovemaking ...

She put the glass down on a table behind her and took his hand. Their power met and heat swirled in her belly as his desire touched hers. Oh yes, she thought as he led her onto the dance floor. It was going to be a fun night.

There was just enough conversation to find out his name was Sean and he was from Sclossin, but had been working on his father's property in England for the past five years, explaining why she didn't know him.

Then conversation wasn't important any more, and the priority became looking, teasing, touching — first the arm, then the hip, then their bodies drew together, moving in unison.

Their hips meshed and a thrill ran through Maggie as she felt his erection. Her nipples tightened – his smile became wolfish. With perfect timing, a slow song began and they wrapped their arms around each other, and ground their bodies together until Maggie was sure her blood was boiling, she felt so hot.

Sean moved his mouth close to hers, until their breath was mingling, and whispered, 'We don't really want to spend the rest of the night here, do we?'

'Absolutely not.' Maggie brushed her lower lip against his while squashing her breasts into his chest. Her nipples were so sensitive they sent a jolt of pleasure through her body to pool in her groin. She grabbed Sean's hand and pulled him out of the pub.

The cold air outside hit her and she stumbled. Her mind cleared, and a little voice wondered if maybe ... then Sean pulled her to him and kissed her, and all thoughts left her mind. Her power rose and met his, his arousal washing over her with a flood of sensation. His mouth pressed hers open and then his tongue was stroking in and out, stoking the fire within.

Nothing mattered other than getting him home, where she could release all the pleasure his touch promised. She pulled back, gasping. 'I live just around the corner.'

'Good,' he said and kissed her again. One of the great things about being gadda was how your power spoke to your partner's during sex – no need for spoken directions or guessing what turned the other on: you could feel it. Something else she'd miss out on for the next two years.

At the door to the flat, she had a moment of concern – what if Ione was home? But then, Ione would be the last person to care what Maggie was doing. And Jack was away, so noise wasn't an issue.

They barely made it into Maggie's room before they started undressing each other. Sean kissed her and tugged on her nipples. The kiss was nice, the tug not so much. He just needs guidance, Maggie thought, and pulled his mouth down to her breasts, giving him a push of power to show she liked it.

Sean took to it enthusiastically and Maggie gasped and moaned her delight.

Then, too quickly for her liking he was pushing inside her, filling her wetness. It felt so good she forgave him his haste. They moved together, and Maggie felt her climax coming closer and closer.

But then Sean strained, cried out, and he pumped into her one last time. Oh, shit no, Maggie thought; her body was so ready, so desperate for release. His power washed over her, highlighting the intensity of his orgasm and the lack of hers.

Sean lifted his head and smiled down at her. 'Wow,' he whispered. 'Just ... wow.'

Maggie smiled, even as her body raged its disappointment. Settle down, she told her flaming nerve-endings.

She relaxed, wondering what he'd do. Perhaps he could go again, or go down on her, or maybe he'd be even more inventive?

She dismissed the first possibility when he pulled out of her. She remained calm as he spoke the words to ensure his sperm did not impregnate her — gadda had no need to practise safe sex otherwise, as infections and viruses were no match for their healing skills — and then cuddled her into his arms.

She kissed his shoulder, and pressed her clitoris against his hip, keeping the furious pulse of her desire alive.

Sean held her and stroked her back, and his emotions started to register as his power melded into hers. Her anticipation faltered then gave way to frustration as it dawned on her that he wasn't going to do anything to make her feel just as good. Not a bloody thing. She opened her mouth to tell him to get on with it but he stopped her words with a kiss.

'Unfortunately I have to go, I've got a meeting in the morning. But once that's over I'll come and take you out for lunch. This is the beginning of something wonderful, Margaret.'

'It's Maggie. And wonderful?' Maggie could barely believe what she was hearing. She could read the blossoming rightness and power within him — he had spoken the truth: he did feel that they had formed a special link.

'I knew you felt the same.' He kissed her again, got out of bed, and got dressed. Maggie raised herself onto one elbow and watched him with disbelief. How could he not know that she hadn't orgasmed? Or did he know but not care? She had had a handful of lovers in the past nine years and never had any of them left her without an orgasm.

Sean blew her one more kiss and then he was gone. Maggie flopped back onto the bed. He wasn't worth the effort, she decided, even as his certainty moved within her. She'd tell him so when he came to get her for lunch and within a week she'd be back in Australia and not have to worry about selfish Sean ever again.

Her body began to quiver with rage. Shame he didn't finished the job, she thought. She'd take care of it herself, if she wasn't far too angry to concentrate. Nice of him to make it so clear at the beginning that he was a total jerk — it saved her expending any time on him.

Maggie rolled over, punched her pillow and tried to relax. Then she rolled to the other side. Then she flopped onto her back and threw the doona off, scowling at the ceiling. Then she was back onto her side again and snuggling into the cover's comforting warmth. Soon, her body calmed, her mind stopped plotting ways to make Sean pay and eventually, she fell asleep.

CHAPTER FOUR

As dusk grew, the shadows in Lucas's apartment lengthened. Lucas squinted to see through the gathering gloom. He should get up to put a light on, but the experiment was going so well.

He lay on a trolley underneath a large metal platform, big enough to be a bed, and made the final adjustments to his latest attempt at a teleporter. After turning a screw to adjust two bits of metal until they were the perfect distance apart, he pushed himself out, rolling on the wooden floor until he was clear of the structure. He stood, pulled a car key from the pocket of his jeans and placed it in the middle of the platform.

Lucas walked over to the kitchen counter, which was covered with bits of wire and metal, screws and various tools. In the middle of the mess sat a computer screen and keyboard. He keyed in some instructions aimed at tricking the atoms making up the key into 'believing' they were in another place, and then turned around to inspect the platform. It began to shake, very gently. Lucas took a step closer, focussing his attention on the key. Was it starting to waver? Yes? No? He hoped to see it bleed into transparency as its particles started to reconfigure in the new location.

It should disappear and reappear on a matching platform on the other side of the room. He drew in a deep breath. Then the shaking increased and the platform began to rock.

'Shit.' Lucas typed furiously, trying to shut the apparatus down before it blew a fuse … but it was too late. There was a pop and darkness descended.

Silence reigned and he became aware of how late it was, aware of the cold seeping into his body. Better get the power back on. When he'd replaced the blown fuse and come back in from the landing, he turned on the gas heater, picked up a screwdriver and began dismantling the platform. Dr Warren, the old quack who'd gotten him fascinated with science, would have been horrified to see Lucas dismantling an experiment. If at first you don't succeed, try, try again, was Dr Warren's maxim. Lucas had added to it: after the tenth attempt, however, pull the fucking thing apart and start again.

Now his concentration had been broken, his body decided it was free to complain about the long hours. His neck began to ache, his back became stiff and his stomach growled alarmingly. He checked the time on his computer. He'd just worked twelve-and-a-half hours non-stop. No wonder he felt like shit.

He grabbed a dinner from the freezer and noted he only had two left. He put the dinner in the microwave that stood on top of the fridge and started heating it. He moved over to his main computer and called up his diary. He added *cook* to the free two-hour slot on Thursday morning, then sat back and considered his calendar.

Most of his available time was taken up with teaching and marking. He knew passing on his love for physics to future scientists was a valuable thing to do, but he was starting to get over it.

The ringing phone interrupted his reverie.

'Hello. Lucas Valeroso.'

'Lucas, glad to get hold of you. It's John O'Hara here, from Winton University, Australia.'

Lucas's mind whirled into action. Winton was a world-class tertiary institution with an internationally renowned science faculty. John O'Hara had begun his own academic career as a talented chemist. 'Professor O'Hara, an honour, sir. I read your report in the latest edition of *Quemular*. Fascinating stuff.'

Instead of preening, as experience had taught Lucas most academics would, John O'Hara scoffed. 'Piece of fluff. Only wrote it as a favour to the editor. He needed a filler.'

Lucas lifted an eyebrow. If the man considered a well-researched and -written paper like that a piece of fluff, he would be a hard taskmaster. 'What can I do for you, Professor?'

'Well, Doctor, I want to offer you a position here at Winton.'

Lucas nodded. This made offer number thirteen. Everyone wanted the current Julius Edgar Lilienfeld Fellow. It would be interesting to see what this job offer was. 'Tell me more.'

'Research, Valeroso. Pure and simple. Don't want you wasting your time in the classroom.'

Sweet Jesus. Was the man a mindreader? 'No teaching at all?'

O'Hara snorted. 'You're not a teacher, you're a scientist. You need a place where your creativity can run free, where you have time to explore and discover.'

Lucas was beginning to like John O'Hara. 'I've heard good things about your science faculty.'

'Of course you have. I've worked bloody hard to build up my science staff. And it's going to get better.'

It might not be as good a career move as his other offers, but it was everything he actually wanted. A smile spread across Lucas's face, but he tried to keep his tone business-like. 'Can you e-mail me through a contract?' He gave O'Hara his e-mail address.

'Absolutely.'

'I'll read it, and then call you back.'

O'Hara gave his number in Australia and then hung up. Lucas finished his now-cold dinner and waited for the contract to arrive.

After printing it out and reading it, he realised he had to go with his gut instinct. He called John O'Hara.

'You've got yourself a researcher,' Lucas said, after O'Hara answered. 'When do you want me?'

'ASAP. I'll fix up the visa and when it's OK I'll book you some flights. Shouldn't take more than a couple of weeks. In the meantime, I'll organise for your belongings to be packed and shipped over, so they'll be here when you arrive, if you don't mind being without them for a while over there. We'll put you up at a hotel there as well while you wait, if you don't have family to stay with.'

Lucas looked wistfully at his apartment. The two platforms, one near the kitchen, the other standing where his bed would pull down. There was a lot of work he could do in two weeks. But then, it would be better to be able to start as soon as he got to Australia. 'A hotel will be fine. I'll need to give notice here, and I've got some classes so I'll be able to keep busy enough and not miss my research.' Not too much, anyway.

'Terrific. Pack lots of shorts and T-shirts, my boy. It's summer over here and you're going to love it.'

As he hung up, Lucas thought that he might just love it, at that.

CHAPTER FIVE

When Maggie woke, sunlight was streaming in the window. She got up, pulled on some underwear, a pair of jeans and a jumper and stumbled out of the bedroom. Ione was already up, sitting at the dining table and scoffing down a breakfast of sausages, eggs and mushrooms.

Maggie leant against the wall and smiled at the sure sign that Ione had got lucky the night before. Her body was so slender, it always required refuelling after vigorous exercise. Right now, Maggie could understand the need.

'Any left?'

Ione looked up and frowned. 'You aren't much into fry-ups.'

'Well, you're not the only one who needs refuelling.' Maggie wandered into the kitchen and checked the fridge. No eggs or mushrooms left, but the sausages sure smelt good. She put a couple on, then made herself a coffee and went back into the dining room.

'Hmm, so someone well and truly celebrated last night, did they?' Ione leant her elbows on the table. 'Tell me everything. I want details.'

'You're a perve.' Maggie sat and took a sip of the coffee. 'Not much to tell really. His name is Sean, he's just back from managing his father's property in England and we had a nice time, for a while.'

Ione frowned. 'What do you mean?'

'He came, I didn't, and he didn't address the inconsistency.'

'What?' Ione's back straightened and her eyes blazed. 'Not a single twiddle of the knob?'

Maggie rolled her eyes. 'No, not even. So when Master Sean comes back to pick me up for lunch, he's going to get it with both barrels, since I didn't get the chance last night.'

'Hang on.' Ione suddenly banged the counter. 'Sean, just back from his father's estate in England? He wasn't about my height, with red hair and pale blue eyes, was he?'

'Exactly. Why, did you have your eye on him last night?'

'Oh, fuck, Maggie. Fuck, fuck, fuck.' Ione jumped up and ran to the bookshelves.

Maggie put her coffee down. 'Ione, do you know who he is?'

Ione's fingers grabbed at a hefty tome, which Maggie recognised as an old edition of the gadda cultural record, *People of the Gulagh*. 'If it's who I think it is, you just shagged a Flaherty.'

'What?' Maggie shrieked, jumping to her feet. 'No, no, I couldn't have, I'd know. There's no way I'd fuck a Flaherty.'

'I think you did and, what's more, he's the long-awaited heir.' Ione turned her attention to the pages of her book, fluttering through them at top speed. 'Here.'

She handed the book over to Maggie and pointed at someone in the Flaherty family portrait.

'Oh, fuck.' Maggie sank down on the couch with a moan. Last night's loser Lothario was there, next to his grandfather, a teenaged version of his smirk playing round his lips.

Ione shuddered. 'One thing for certain, we can't let your grandfather find out about this. It needs to stay between us.'

'And everyone who saw the two of us leave Kitty's together last night,' Maggie said. 'I can't believe no one told me who he was.'

'Could they have thought you were acting out over the bardria?' Ione shook her head. 'I'm so sorry I didn't see you. I should have checked before I left. Well, there's a good thing about the non-contact order. No one can tell your family.'

'Except Dad, if he finds out.' Maggie moaned and buried her face in her hands. Of course he would find out. 'Maybe I should just tell them myself.'

'That would probably be the best bet. After all, the other part of this equation is whether *Sean* knew who *you* were. He *could* be making a play to join the feud. I don't know if he's as Purist as his dad ...'

'Crap!' Maggie sat up. 'Is this linked to the story? Did he seduce me on purpose?'

'If I were you, I'd hightail it over to Australia quick smart,' Ione said.

'Crap. Shit. Bloody hell.' She had no choice. If she was to avoid Sean's arrival and get away from whatever Purist plot was currently underway, she needed to get to Australia. That meant calling her grandfather.

She went to the phone, wishing she had power enough to speak to him mentally long distance. A phone call could be answered by her mother, and she'd prefer to tell Siobhan about this latest catastrophe face to face. She looked at the clock, calculated the time difference and decided to try the university first — it wasn't uncommon for her grandfather to still be there in the evening.

He answered on the third ring. 'John O'Hara.'

'Grandpa, it's Maggie. Can you come over?'

'Now?'

'Yes. Sorry. It's important.'

'OK.' He put the phone down. Maggie turned to make sure that Ione wasn't standing in the middle of the room and then John appeared.

'What is it, darlin'?'

'I think it's the Purists again.' She took a deep breath. Admitting to a one-night stand to your family was never an easy thing to do. 'Last night, I met a guy at Kitty's and we came back here. This morning, Ione identified him. I slept with Sean Flaherty.'

'Oswald's boy?' Maggie nodded. 'How is that possible?'

'He's been in England for the past five years, so I didn't know who he was.'

'Does he know who you are?'

'I don't know. I don't think so.'

'He would now,' Ione said. 'You think he hasn't told anyone? He'll find out he shagged Maggie Shaunessy, just like we did.'

'Assuming he didn't know last night,' John said. 'It's a bit coincidental that you'd sleep with the

Flaherty heir, scion of one of the most Purist families around, the day they manage to get you kicked out of Sclossin.'

'That's what I thought,' Maggie said. 'He said he'd come to take me out to lunch, but Grandpa I can't —'

'Of course not.' John nodded. 'We need to get you to Australia. You're obviously not safe here. You need to call your principal, tell them that your mother's ill and that you're leaving now. I'll contact Cormac, tell him we've decided to get you to Winton sooner rather than later. He'll be so relieved, he won't ask why. Io, darlin, it's a lot to ask but —'

'I'll handle Sean.' She grinned. 'I'm sure I'll enjoy it.'

'Get someone over to be with you. One of your sixth-order uncles. I understand Sean isn't so powerful himself, so the force will intimidate him,' John said.

'Gotcha.' Ione winked.

Maggie stared at them, wondering how they could be so calm when it seemed her life was spiralling out of control. John looked at her and frowned.

'Phone call, Mags.'

Her principal was all sympathy and support and Maggie hung up feeling like a worm for having lied to her. She turned around to see John sitting on the couch.

'The caelleach is more than happy, and wishes you a safe trip. Ione's in your room, to help you pack.'

'Thank you, Grandpa.' Maggie kissed his cheek, and then went into her bedroom.

Seeing Ione standing by her bed, an empty suitcase lying open on top of the quilt, brought home what was happening. Tears pricked her eyes. This was it. She wouldn't see Ione for another two years.

She saw flashes of their friendship, and how important it had been in the hard times. Maggie's homesickness when she first came to Sclossin; her dad's resentment of Maggie's studies and Ione's grief when her husband Patrick died.

And now Maggie's stupid little story was separating them, and last night's mistake meant they wouldn't have time to really say goodbye. Shit, Jack wasn't even here.

Ione understood and the two girls met in the middle of the room for a crushing hug. 'It will be OK,' Ione whispered in her ear. 'Your family will understand, and you know how much you've missed Winton.'

Maggie nodded and kissed Ione on her cheek but the sorrow didn't abate. They packed the suitcase — just what would be expected for a quick trip home — and Maggie carried it out into the loungeroom.

John stood and gave Ione a hug. 'Take care, and don't push Sean too far. Tell him and get him out the door.'

'I can't guarantee I won't have a bit of fun with him, John.'

'Don't risk it, Ione. You can't trust these Purists.' John gave her a gentle shake. Then he looked at Maggie. 'Ready?'

'Yes.' She looked at Ione. 'No.' She burst into tears, put the case down and flung her arms around her friend. 'I'm going to miss you so much.'

'And I you.' Ione hugged her back. 'I'll think of you every day.'

Maggie pulled herself away and, sniffing, picked up her suitcase. Then John took her by the arm and they transferred.

Seconds later, she stood in the doorway of her grandfather's house, looked out over the town, and allowed all the scents of Winton to flow into her. Dust, expected after a long period without rain. The tang of animals, the sour smell of diesel engines from the farmers' four-wheel drives. Heat. It was amazing that heat had a smell, but Maggie had to swear it did. It was musky, thick, and sweet. Sclossin was about the same size as Winton and just as rural, but it didn't have the rich, hearty smell of hot Australian dirt.

She felt sweat form at the back of her neck and start to drip down her spine as she stepped onto the red paving that ran the length of the back of the house. Hopefully, her classroom would be air-conditioned — it would be a while before she was comfortable with an Australian summer again.

Her grandfather's Spanish-style home, arches and white-wash and red roof, stood on the top of a hill overlooking the town. The slopes were covered with an olive grove, her mother's pride and joy. At the bottom of the hill, paddocks separated the olives from the playing fields and buildings of the university. The town spread out from the university, taking up much more room than Maggie remembered.

Overall, the view was one of success and expansion. She was looking forward to exploring Winton after ten years away.

'I need to go fetch your mother,' John said. 'I'll pop back to the university and wander over to her office.

Won't be long!' He gave her a squeeze then walked back into the house. She barely felt the stirring of power as he left.

Maggie wandered inside. The kitchen had been remodelled again and was a concoction of steel and stone, very modern and clean looking. She opened the fridge and saw John had prepared a lasagne for dinner. Fantastic. An open bottle of wine caught her eye and she reached for it but checked herself. No, best to do this on a clear head.

She wandered down the hall and pushed open the first door on the left. Her grandfather's study was a riot of paper and books, with a narrow but clearly discernible trail to the overladen desk. She smiled and closed the door carefully — what looked like chaos made great sense in her grandfather's mind, and none of the piles should be disturbed.

The door opposite led to her mother's room; the remodelling had continued in here. The bed was low to the floor, the mattress sitting in the middle of a black platform, and there were black and white patterns on the sheeting and the curtains. The only colour was the red feature wall behind the bed. The new look really suits Mum, Maggie thought.

The next door along opened into her room. She took a deep breath and then pushed it, wondering what her mother had done here. The answer was nothing, and she was glad. It had been years since she'd spent more than a few weeks in this room. She wanted to redecorate herself.

She stepped into the room and looked around. She had long ago taken the pop-star posters down, but it still resonated with her teenage self. The girl who had lived in this room had dreamed of one day being a brilliant teacher. Well, she'd managed the teacher part; the brilliance however was definitely in question.

The room was quite plain. The single bed had a red and gold striped cover that matched the curtains. The walls and carpet were beige, her desk and shelves a light wood veneer.

She sat down on the bed and the springs creaked. A new bed was obviously priority number one. She lay down and stared up at the ceiling. On this narrow mattress she had dreamed of one day being attractive, even desirable. It seemed she had achieved that as well, although whether she was attracting the right men was now a matter of opinion. She had also wished not to be gadda. And I almost achieved that this week, Maggie thought with a grimace.

The sound of a motor seeped into her consciousness, and wheels squealed on the gravel outside. Maggie took a deep breath and let it out. Time to face the inquisition.

She got to the loungeroom just as the front door opened. Siobhan was first in the room, dressed immaculately in a cream suit with a pink shirt, her hair pulled back into a bun — the perfect outfit for a trusted and respected country doctor. She stopped at the sight of her daughter and raised an eyebrow.

'So, your grandfather wouldn't tell me what's going on, and I cannot believe you could have stuffed up again, not in such a short time.'

Maggie tried to smile and failed miserably. 'Oh, you can when you're as talented at making mistakes as I am.'

John followed his daughter into the house, closing the door behind him. 'Well, off you go,' he said.

It would have been nice to at least play at being glad to see me, Maggie thought as she watched her family take their seats. But then, they weren't big on dishonesty. That was why she was here.

'Mum, I think I may have done something really, really dumb, but in my own defence, I didn't know it was dumb at the time. If I had known, I wouldn't have done it.'

Siobhan didn't say anything, just continued to look at Maggie. She could tell the whole story without interruption.

'After you guys left yesterday, Ione and I went to Kitty's and there was this guy there. He was really cute and we had a great time, so I took him back to the flat.' This was harder than telling her grandfather.

'It wasn't until this morning, talking to Ione, that I realised who he was. Anyway, the man I slept with is Sean Flaherty.'

For a moment Siobhan's face was blank, and Maggie wondered whether this time, she had gone too far. But then her mother laughed.

'Oh, Maggie, we've missed you.' She jumped up and gave her daughter a hug.

'OK,' Maggie said, hugging her back, not sure what it all meant.

'This isn't a joke, Siobhan,' John said. 'The Purists seem to be targeting Maggie.'

'But just imagine the look on her face when she realised who she'd taken to bed,' Siobhan said, laughing. Then she frowned at Maggie. 'Not that I condone one-night stands, honey. This is exactly the sort of mess that often ensues. But I bet your heart attack this morning was something to see.'

John smiled. 'That's true.' He looked at Maggie and began to laugh. 'I bet you feel a right eejit.'

'That's one word,' Maggie said, relief flooding through her. 'And you'll be pleased to know that he was a dud root.'

'Not a surprise, he is a Flaherty,' John said. They all laughed and Maggie seized her grandfather in a hug.

'Right, now that's done, onto the next problem,' he said. 'You can't just appear here, Maggie. This isn't Sclossin. You know the old codgers down at the Royal watch every car that goes in and out of this town, and if they don't see us leave and come back with you ...'

'They can't possibly see everything,' Maggie scoffed.

'Yes, they can,' Siobhan said firmly. 'I've got to get back to work, Dad. Bloody BAS. You'll have to do the sneak.'

'Hmmm.' John looked at his watch. 'Perfect timing. There's a train that arrives in Tamworth in an hour.'

Siobhan went first, sauntering out to the car to make sure the coast was clear. Then she signalled and Maggie ran from the house, scrambling into the back of the station wagon and lying down. She felt the *thump* as her bags appeared next to her. John came out and stopped to throw a blanket over everything (including Maggie). The engine kicked over and they started toward the town.

If Maggie had felt hot before, she was soon perspiring madly, sweat dripping from her nose. She opened her mouth to ask if the air-conditioning could be turned up, then remembered and sent the request mentally instead.

'*You need practice at that*,' came her grandfather's reply, clear as a bell in her mind. '*And it's on as high as it can go, it'll just take a while.*'

Maggie gritted her teeth. This is punishment beyond the sin. To take her mind off it, she tried to follow the path of the car in her imagination. The road from their home down into the town wound a little up and down the hill, before straightening as it ran along the side of the university. A left-hand turn took them onto the main street. Then the car swerved gently and came to a stop.

'Thanks for the lift, Dad,' she heard Siobhan say. 'Give Maggie my love when you see her, and tell her she can get stuck into that bottle of wine that's open in the fridge when you get home.'

'*Love you too, Mum*,' Maggie sent. The door opened and the car rocked, then it slammed shut.

'*I know, darling*,' she heard in her head. The car pulled away from the kerb again.

The trip continued uneventfully for the next hour or so. Maggie moved and stretched, but she wasn't game to take the blanket off, just in case a passing driver or truckie should spot her.

Finally, John pulled off the road. 'I think you can get into the front now. We'll head back to Winton.'

Maggie threw off the blanket, and climbed over the back and then the front seat, leaning forward to put her face directly in front of the air-conditioning vent. 'Thank you. I thought I was going to suffocate back there.'

'Let that be a lesson to you. Think through the likely consequences of actions *before* you commit to them.'

Maggie leant over and pressed a kiss to his cheek. 'I do love you, Grandpa.'

'Don't think you can kiss your way into my good books, young woman,' John said with a smile. Then he turned the car around and they drove back toward Winton.

The countryside was summer brown and some paddocks were bare. 'It looks so dry, Grandpa.'

'It'll come good, darlin. All things move in cycles, and in the end there is balance.'

She nodded, leant back and let the cool air wash over her.

'You know, your timing is pretty terrible,' John said. 'I'm in the midst of organising a move from America.'

'A move of what?' Maggie closed her eyes and let the sway of the car soothe her.

'*Who.* I've managed to secure the current Julius Edgar Lilienfeld Fellow.'

'Who?'

John sighed. 'Can't one of you follow the news?'

'Was it in the news?'

'*I* read about it.'

'In *Chemist's Monthly*, no doubt.'

'Physics, actually. I can't believe I'm bringing one of the greatest minds of this generation to Winton and neither my daughter nor my granddaughter cares.'

'We do care, Grandpa. See?' Maggie clapped her hands. 'Yay.'

'Oh, can it,' John grumbled.

They re-entered the outskirts of Winton, and Maggie sat up again to have a good look around. It hasn't changed, she decided. Sure, the old federation brick buildings had a new coat of paint and the general population seemed younger thanks to the university but deep down, the town hadn't changed. Maclean's Haberdashery still had terribly old-fashioned plaid clothing in the window. John Thompson still leant against the doorway of his pharmacy, chatting to a customer. Bill Retton's beaten up old ute was parked as it always was in the third space from the corner, directly in front of the Royal's front door.

Familiarity swept over Maggie and with it came comfort. She hadn't realised until this moment how much she had missed Winton.

Then the car stopped, and she focussed on the street lights that hadn't been here last time she was in town. OK, maybe it had changed a little, she thought.

The Main Street shops, which had once taken up just one block of the road through town, now sprawled over two. Most of that space was taken by a new shopping centre, complete with a major department store, cinema and huge supermarket, which provided weekend work for the university's students. But Casey's, the town's original grocery shop, seemed as busy as ever. It's a sign, she thought, that people will never stop wanting a little personal attention.

As she sailed past old landmarks and recent additions, and recognised suddenly grown-up faces on the streets, Maggie realised her family had been right — this was really the only way she could have come home to Winton. She smiled and waved at old friends at almost every corner.

Then the houses became neater than she remembered; the woodwork painted in decorative schemes, the gardens laid out to precise plans. Winton had become a popular town to live in.

The car turned a corner and a large brick tower loomed: the first sign of the university. Stone gates, breaking a tall metal fence, guarded the corner of the next block. Behind the fence, she could see manicured lawns and clipped hedges leading up to a former stately old mansion, now the stately old administration block. Behind it rose the university proper: a magnificent stone building in the manner of the great universities of the world; it had archways that seemed to be carved out of time rather than sandstone, long shaded walkways and vines scrambling for purchase on pillars and between windows. Only the light colour of the mortar and the still sharply cornered blocks revealed that this building was only thirty years old. Maggie smiled. It had been hugely expensive, but her grandfather had stated that his university was going to look like a centre of learning for the ages, not a space laboratory.

Of course, he had soon realised the need for laboratories. The car zoomed past the glass and steel dome that housed the university's prized science faculty. Beyond it was the obligatory cricket oval, and then the first of the student colleges.

Soon, the buildings gave way to farmland, the university's agricultural wing. Maggie didn't know a great deal about cattle but thought the cows that grazed by the fence seemed particularly healthy. Then they were up the hill and her grandfather was pulling back into the driveway.

'Now, your mother was planning on working late tonight on the paperwork, so if you don't mind we'll leave the welcoming ceremony until tomorrow night,' John said as they go out of the car.

'Not at all, Grandpa.'

'Good. Now, lasagne?'

'Yum.' Maggie linked her arm in his and walked into the house, hopeful she'd enjoy her new life in Australia.

CHAPTER SIX

'Time for the ceremony.' John's voice rose from the basement.

Maggie took a deep breath as she stood. It had been a long time since she'd done a gadda ceremony. She hoped she didn't make a mistake.

'Sorry we couldn't do this last night,' Siobhan said as they went downstairs.

'That's OK,' Maggie said. 'Somehow it seems better like this. I feel like I have Australia back in my soul.'

As they walked into the basement, John moved to the centre of the room, where a star of gulagh was painted on the floor. He crouched down and placed a hand over it. A light blue glow coloured his skin. He lifted his hand and the star came with it, as though glued to his hand, revealing rich dark soil beneath it. He put the star on a table by the wall, then stood on one edge of the bare earth.

'Take the side opposite me, please, Maggie.'

Maggie did so, and Siobhan walked over, a small glass bottle in her hand. When Siobhan unstoppered the bottle, Maggie caught the distinctive smell of musk, lavender and olive oil from the pink liquid within. At once she remembered the essence of her childhood:

happiness, laughter, love. Her mother had created this potion for her at her birth and no other gadda had the same scent.

Siobhan held the bottle out to John and he smeared some of the potion across his forehead. Siobhan offered the bottle to Maggie and she repeated her grandfather's actions.

Siobhan anointed herself as well then stoppered the bottle. John held his arm out at shoulder height, his hand flat, palm down and parallel to the ground. Siobhan put her hand on top of his, and Maggie's went on top of both. The moment her palm touched her mother's knuckles, she felt her family's power flow into her. She closed her eyes and allowed the warmth to rush through her body.

Her grandfather spoke the ritual – their ceremony of renewal. 'In the name of all the O'Hara, past, present and future, I welcome Margaret Kathleen Shaunessy back to my home, the place of her heart.' Maggie felt the power pulling at her hand. Slowly, she, Siobhan and John crouched down until the pile of hands touched the dirt. She felt a spurt of love flow into her: her grandfather's welcome.

I was so lucky to grow up here, she thought. Living in Winton, she had been to school with humans and was already aware that with her brains, she was different from her gadda peers, who she encountered on holidays with her Shaunessy relatives. When she was nearly twelve she had announced she wasn't going to Ireland to begin the traditional training. John hadn't batted an eyelid.

'You do what you need to do to be happy, Maggie girl. But don't leave it too long. You'll begin to suffer for refusing your inheritance,' was all he said. And when her father, Peter, demanded she go to Ireland to study, her grandfather had stood up to him – not that she'd needed him to, even then.

She smiled at John. He really hadn't aged in her absence. She knew he was getting old but she wasn't ready to face the idea of losing him. He seemed to understand the train of her thoughts because he winked at her. Then they stood and John lifted his hand from the bottom and placed it on Maggie's.

Then Siobhan spoke. 'In the name of all the O'Hara, past, present and future, I welcome Margaret Kathleen Shaunessy back to my home, the place of her heart.' Again, they crouched down and, as the hands touched the dirt, Siobhan's warm love and acceptance rolled over her daughter.

Siobhan had accepted Maggie's decision not to study in Ireland, even though it brought her into further conflict with the man she had once loved. And when Maggie began to suffer, both from denying her heritage and from an unrequited schoolgirl crush, Siobhan had continued supporting her.

After a couple of years of teenage angst, Maggie had realised that popular Scott Campbell wasn't going to really notice his plump, studious classmate, no matter how much help she was with late homework. Then Siobhan had persuaded her that she could only figure out who she really was by becoming fully gadda. Once she was true to herself, her star would shine and no one worthy would be able to resist her.

Maggie smiled. Mothers. They were always right. She caught Siobhan's eye. For a moment she read concern there, then Siobhan smiled and Maggie felt a pulse of power flood through her. Again, they stood and Siobhan put her hand on top of the stack.

Then it was Maggie's turn. 'I, Margaret Kathleen Shaunessy, thank you for the welcome to this, my home, the place of my heart.' Then they crouched again. When Maggie's palm lay on the earth, she felt the invisible star of gulagh tattooed on her chest flare as the land welcomed her back. A tear sprang to her eyes. She loved Ireland, it was her heritage, but Australia was home. Then they stood and she placed her hand over her mother's again.

They walked in a circle, three times clockwise, three times widdershins. Then, in unison, they dropped their hands to their sides.

John nodded. 'Welcome home, Maggie girl.'

Maggie nodded, tears welling in her eyes. She had just performed her first gadda ceremony at home. It brought such a rush of joy to her that she could find no other answer than to fling her arms around her mother and her grandfather and hug them tight.

'Now, we've got business to discuss.' John folded his arms over his chest. 'What are we going to do about getting you a job?'

'I'll contact the education department tomorrow and get the paperwork to get registered in New South Wales,' Maggie said. 'That might take a few weeks — I'll probably miss term one. But that means I can have a holiday. I deserve one.'

'And what if you can't register?' John said. 'You transferred back here — legally, you're not in the country. What if they need a passport or something to prove that you're here?'

Maggie frowned. 'Why would they need that? I'm an Australian. Sure, I'll need to prove my qualifications, since they're Irish, but why would they need proof I entered the country legally?'

'You need to be prepared, Maggie. Maybe it might be worthwhile to have Ione book you a flight, and we can whiz you back to Sclossin and then have you fly back to Australia.'

'If that's what I have to do, I will, but I'm sure you're worried about nothing.'

'Well, we'll see what you find out tomorrow. In the meantime, there's that PA position I told you about.'

Maggie spun around to her mother. 'I should have a holiday, don't you think?'

'Holiday?' John scoffed. 'From what?'

'I've been working hard, and studying hard. It wouldn't be good to overwork me, would it?' She stuck out her lip and silently begged her mother to agree.

Siobhan grinned. 'I think a bit of work would be OK. Mornings with your grandfather, afternoons relaxing.'

'I do need the help, cushla.'

Maggie looked at her grandfather, then at her mother who nodded. 'He does. His secretary left at the end of last year and the administration's starting to get on top of him. Just until you get your teaching stuff settled, Maggie.'

'Just the mornings.' Maggie frowned at her grandfather. 'I mean it, Grandpa. I'll come down at nine, I finish at midday and I won't do anything else. Understand?'

'Star shine on ya, Maggie.' He kissed her cheek. Maggie had the distinct impression she'd just been had.

CHAPTER SEVEN

John O'Hara is as good as his word, Lucas thought, watching the removalists pack up his life. He turned and looked at the boxes, all lined up, realising that only a quarter of them held personal belongings: the rest contained his research papers and apparatus. He took a moment to wonder if that was a good or bad thing. Then he shrugged the strange melancholy from him. You don't go forward by standing still.

He grabbed his two suitcases. They contained not only all the clothing he owned, but also his notes and the hard drives from his computers. He wouldn't trust these to just anyone.

He went downstairs to hail a cab for the journey to the hotel. A female voice, sweet as pie, purred in his ear: 'You look like you're going somewhere.'

Damn. Of all the goddamn timing. Five minutes later and he would have been gone. He turned around and stared at the woman who'd almost ruined his life. Once, he'd considered her everything a heterosexual man could want: devious, intelligent and hard-headed. But then he'd met Dr Warren in juvie, and been introduced to the discipline and structure of science. And by the time he walked out of the detention facility at eighteen, Holly Faulkner hadn't been that important any more.

He glared down at her. 'What do you want, Holly?'

She smiled. 'First, I want a kiss from my old buddy.'

For a moment he considered telling her to go to hell, but he knew that wasn't a wise move. He managed not to roll his eyes as he bent down and pressed a kiss to her cheek. A floral perfume wafted up into his face, so strong it made his nose itch and his eyes sting. He was left with the taste of her caked-on foundation on his lips. 'I'd love to chat, but I don't have time.'

'We'll share a cab and chat.' She turned to the street and lifted her arm.

A taxi screeched to a halt and he put his suitcases in the trunk and sat in the back next to Holly. The familiar passivity had washed up past his knees now. He always ended up swamped in it around her.

'Where to, darling?' She smiled at him.

'The Capital Inn.' The taxi driver nodded and the car began to move.

'You're going to stay in a hotel in town? I don't understand, Lucas. You didn't lose your apartment, did you? Are you ... in trouble again?'

Frustration and desperation rose within him, though he was still paralysed. 'How much do you want, Holly?'

Holly pouted. 'Lucas, you've become so harsh. All those hours bent over your chemicals working doesn't suit you at all.'

He leant back against the seat and watched the Chicago streetscape pass by. He didn't bother correcting her misunderstanding of his work. He would be silent until she spoke her piece.

She sighed. 'You don't play any more, Lucas. All work and no play. And I remember you used to be so good at playing.' She reached over and put her hand on his leg.

He continued ignoring her.

'Oh, all right.' She pulled her hand away and slumped back into the seat. Her tailored overcoat slid enough for him to see her stocking-clad knee peeping out from under a fine woollen suit skirt. Her ankle boots, he had noted, were very high-heeled and probably expensive. He looked away. 'My friend James has come up with a brilliant idea for a business. He wants to develop and sell robot pet carers. Isn't that brilliant? The robot will sit out in the backyard and play with your dog, provide it with food and water when it needs and even clean up after it. Have you heard of a more darling idea?'

He couldn't remain silent any longer. 'Shit, Holly, it was bad enough when you wanted me to break the law –' he looked at the driver, who was ignoring them both '– but at least then your ideas were sensible.'

She pouted. 'James says it's a real goer.'

'Since he hasn't built the damn robot yet, how would he know?' The frown grew on her face and he decided to calm down. He couldn't afford to upset her. 'Besides, I'm not a roboticist. I can't help you.'

'Oh, I think you can, Lucas.' She smiled. 'Didn't I read that you've just won some prize? Fifty grand, wasn't it?'

Lucas felt sick. 'That's research money.'

'And I think it would be a very good idea for you to research this robot. Just think of the good it would do for all those people worried about their pets. You do want your work to do good for the world, don't you?'

Lucas clenched his teeth. 'I have to account for that money, Holly. Every cent. If they find I've been using it on a stupid idea like a robot pet feeder —'

Holly leant closer and he forced himself not to move away. 'It would seem to me, Lucas, that with all this money to spend on your research, you'd have plenty of your own money free for other things.'

God, he wanted to tell her to go to hell. But what if she found John O'Hara, and what if the Australian turned out to be just as prejudiced as Smith-Jenkins? 'How much do you want, Holly?'

She flopped back into the seat. 'Twenty grand. And a name. Someone who does actually know robots and can help us.'

He mentally reviewed his financial situation. It wasn't a problem of finding the money — he'd grown up poor, he'd learnt early in his career to save a buffer in case things went bad — but it would take time to access it.

The idea of giving Holly money made him feel ill, but the idea of losing the opportunity in Australia was worse. 'It will take me a couple of weeks to get the money together.'

'Thank you.' She smiled, then reached into her purse and pulled out a business card. 'Here's where you can send the cheque.'

He took hold of the cardboard, stared at the pink dogs dotted around the outside and wondered when he would stop paying for the past.

'Now, a name of a roboticist.'

'Sorry, Holly, don't know any.'

'What, not one? What the hell kind of tin-pot institutions have you been teaching at?'

None of the universities he'd worked at qualified as tin-pot institutions but there was no point arguing it with her. 'Much as I would like to help you, Holly, and you know how obliging I am, I can't. Sorry.' He shrugged and began to silently pray that she would be prepared to give up.

She tilted her head a little and looked up at him with an expression that a puppy would be proud of. 'Not even a name? Someone I can study up on.'

Shit. He frowned as he searched his memory — who was the robotics guy in that article in the *AJS*? 'Try Glenn Thundercloud. I think he's at Philadelphia Tech.'

'There, that wasn't so hard, was it?' She patted his arm. 'You know, I've been thinking about the old neighbourhood. We were such a pair of rogues, weren't we? And now here we are, all legit.'

Lucas thought she only had one foot in the camp of legitimacy. If that. 'I don't think about it much.'

'Really? How can you not? Often when it's dark and I hear sirens wailing or I see some story on TV about a bloke bashing someone, I think of your old man.' Holly shuddered.

'He isn't worth wasting your time on.' Lucas folded his arms across his chest. He could feel his jaw tightening, his body tensing and prayed again that Holly would leave him alone so he could relax and enjoy this new adventure.

'Do you still have the scars? You know, those scars are such a turn-on, Lucas. Women like a survivor, a man tough enough to stick around.' As she spoke, Holly touched the back of his neck, right where one of the scars was.

Lucas shied away from her. For a long time after getting out of prison, he'd considered having plastic surgery. Then he'd decided the scars would be a reminder that he should never treat another person the way Ricky Valeroso had treated him.

He looked out the window and saw they were nearing the hotel. He allowed himself to give a little sigh. Not long until he was free of Holly and perhaps for good. After all, she'd find it hard to trace him in Australia.

'Why don't we celebrate our reunion? I remember how you like it.' Holly squeezed the top of his thigh.

As suddenly as that, his anger slipped its reins. He shrugged her touch away and turned to face her. 'I'd rather spend eternity facing a hundred hours a week of stupid students then one day in your company.' His voice rose in volume and, as he almost screamed the last words, the taxi screeched to a halt. Lucas flew forward, bounced off the seat and cannoned into Holly, pushing her down onto the floor.

He sat up and looked around. The taxi was in the middle of the road. Behind them, several cars tooted their horns. The taxi driver, muttering 'what the fuck's, leant out his window and gave them the finger while he revved up to move forward to the kerb.

Colour leached out of Lucas's face. Fuck. It had happened again – he would get emotional, and something would go wrong. Almost as if Chin's words had brought the weirdness back. He shivered, but forced himself to remain calm. He just had to act casually.

'Can't you drive better than that?' Holly demanded, yanking herself back up onto the seat.

'Fuck you, lady.' The taxi driver's voice trembled. Lucas opened the door and jumped out, slamming it in Holly's face.

By the time he'd retrieved his bags and closed the trunk, Holly was out of the car and facing him.

'You know better than to treat me like that, Lucas Valeroso.' The words hissed between chemically whitened teeth.

'I'm done, Holly. I don't give a fuck.' Lucas pushed past her and marched into the hotel lobby. At the back of his mind, he knew he shouldn't have said that, but he couldn't get his anger under control.

He heard her heels clacking after him. 'Do you really want to piss me off, Lucas?'

There was no one at the desk. Lucas put his suitcases down, pushed the bell and then folded his arms across his chest.

Holly leant on the counter and glared up at him. 'You can't afford to fuck with me, Valeroso.'

Lucas stared at the wall in front of him. 'I've given you a name. I'll give you your twenty grand –'

'Make it thirty.' He spun to face her, and she smiled. 'I told you not to fuck with me.'

'Fine. Thirty.'

'In a week, Lucas. Or I'll be back.'

'Of course you will.' Lucas turned back to the desk, his body shaking.

Holly started to walk away, but stopped. 'You never said why you're staying in a hotel.'

Why the hell would anyone move from his or her apartment to a hotel? 'Fumigation. Rats.'

'Eww.' Holly shuddered then she turned and walked away.

'Good afternoon, sir, and welcome to the Capital Inn.'

Lucas forced himself to focus on the receptionist. 'Good afternoon.' He reached into his pocket for his ID but stopped when his phone rang.

He pulled it out and saw it was John O'Hara. 'Have to take this, excuse me.' He hit the button. 'Hello?'

'Lucas. John O'Hara here. Sorry to bother you, but we've had a bit of a hiccough with the visa.'

With the sound of Holly's voice still ringing in his ear, it wasn't hard for Lucas to work out what the hiccough was. 'I was under the impression my juvenile records were sealed.'

'Not for immigration purposes, I'm afraid.'

Fuck. Fuck, fuck, fuck. 'Well, thank you for the opportunity, Professor O'Hara, I —'

'Hang on. This doesn't mean you're not coming. I've had a chat to the folks at immigration, and they reckon that if we go with a temporary business visa for two years, and with character references, it should all be fine. Is there anyone you can nominate who can speak for you?'

For a moment, Lucas couldn't speak. O'Hara knew the truth, and he didn't care. 'Um, I guess the head of the board of the prize committee would. And my current boss, and my first as well — Suy Lee Chin, from New Jersey University.'

'Excellent, excellent. If you can text me their names and contact details, and let them know to expect a call from the Australian embassy, then we'll get right onto it.'

'Professor O'Hara —'

'John.'

'John.' Lucas took a deep breath and released it. 'I just wanted to say that —'

'Not a problem, my boy. Just wait until you meet some of my staff — your crime isn't the worst on our books. I don't care about the past, Lucas. I want your future to be here in Winton.'

Lucas hung up the phone with a smile. Things were looking much, much better.

CHAPTER EIGHT

Maggie pushed her chair back from the kitchen table and sighed. She was working her way through text book orders for the science department and it was boring her to tears.

She stared at the pile of papers, then at the clock. 10 am. Grandpa wanted this sorted this afternoon, she didn't have time to stop. But it was so *dull*.

As if in answer to her unspoken complaint, there was a knock at the door. Maggie jumped up and almost ran through the house. She flung the door open. Then all her happiness fled.

'Dad.' Her mouth gaped. Peter Shaunessy stood at the front door, his handsomeness hidden by a flushed face and narrowed eyes. His blond hair was plastered sweatily to his head and his shirt to his chest.

'I cannot believe that I just endured all that human transportation, just because my daughter doesn't know how to use the brains nature supposedly gave her.' He glared at her.

She quaked for a moment. She probably should have found a minute to break the news of her sentence — *his* sentence — to him herself. But bugger him! she thought. About time *he* was the one doing the travelling to see *her*.

'Nice to see you too, Dad.' She turned and walked through the house to get him a cool drink.

'Margaret, don't walk away from me.'

'I'm getting you a drink,' she called over her shoulder.

Peter followed her and watched as she got water from the fridge and poured them each a glassful. Her father took a sip and then looked around.

'It's changed,' he said.

'Well, you haven't been here since you ran out when I was a baby,' Maggie snapped back. Peter winced and Maggie realised she was being a bitch. 'I'm sorry, Dad.'

'Me too. But my god, Maggie, if it weren't for your stupid story, I'd be home in my nice warm house in my very cold town. I hate this place, Maggie. You have to understand that it doesn't put me in the best of moods.'

'True. I'm sorry that you've been forced over here for such a long time.'

Peter sighed and pushed a hand through his hair. 'I can't figure it out, Maggie. I mean, you're intelligent enough, and you're practised at keeping gadda secrets from humans, and then you go and do this.'

'I'm sorry.' She put her glass down and gave her father a hug. He hesitated for a moment, then hugged her back.

'I know you are.' He pulled back and looked at her. 'But I'm not happy, Maggie.'

'Fair enough.' She picked up her drink again. 'Have you got somewhere to live yet?'

'A townhouse in Station Street. It's nice enough, but it needs some redecorating. I'm hoping you can help me.'

Maggie nodded. 'We can go into Tamworth, there are some good shops there. I need to get some stuff for my room; the stores here don't have much.'

'I need to go to the bank as well, get some things set up.'

'We can do that.' Guilt threatened to overwhelm her. Peter was really getting the wrong end of all this. Being here in Winton would affect his work with the bardria in Sclossin, as well as the running of his property. Shaunessy cattle were renowned throughout Ireland.

The front door opened and closed and Siobhan called out. 'Hi, Mags. Time for a cuppa with your poor old mammy?'

'Oh, shit,' Maggie murmured, putting her glass down.

'Calm down. Your mother and I can be civil,' Peter said.

Siobhan stepped into the kitchen and then stopped. Her face went blank. 'I was going to ask if your guest wanted to stay for lunch.'

'It's all right, Siobhan, I was just leaving.' Peter nodded at his ex-wife.

Oh god, Maggie thought. Watching the waves of enmity that washed over her parents, it was hard to believe that once they had been passionately in love. Or perhaps only hatred like this could grow from love.

'I'll see you to the door, Dad.' Maggie led her father past Siobhan and to the front door. There, she kissed his cheek. 'I'll take you to Tamworth tomorrow, OK?'

'That'll be grand. I'm staying at the Royal, until the townhouse's furnished. I hope you'll have lunch with me as well. We need to discuss how this is all going to work.' He kissed her cheek and got into his hire car. Maggie waved him off then walked back to the kitchen to find her mother frowning.

'Sorry, Mum. It won't happen again.' Maggie sighed. 'He's giving up a whole lot because of my stupidity, more than the rest of us are. Go easy on him.'

A pause, then Siobhan nodded. 'Just keep him away from me.'

Maggie flicked the kettle on, wondering how she was going to survive the next two years.

Shopping always makes you feel better, Maggie thought as she and her father drove into Winton at the end of a productive day on the Tamworth retail strip. Peter had rented one of the new townhouses on the outskirts of Winton and, after they looked at it, they had gone into Tamworth to buy furniture. Two beds, one for him and one for her when she stayed over, tables, chairs, lounge suite, bookcases and electrical appliances.

She'd also bought the same bed for her bedroom at home, since it made sense to have the same mattress to sleep on, as well as new curtains, bedspreads and linen – all very lush, 500 count cotton and silk, in a thousand shades of blue and gold.

Peter frowned as she piled it up on the counter. 'Isn't that a bit lavish?'

'That's me, Dad, Ms Lavish 2010.' She waggled her head. 'I'm all decadence and sensuality.'

Her father had sighed. His taste was more austere – his furnishings were in dark, heavy wood; and the linen and upholstery were classic stripes or crisp white with piping. But she understood his need to attempt to recreate the feel of his Sclossin house here.

That conversation had been pretty much the only one they'd had throughout the day. She understood why he was keeping his distance, although it still hurt. During her ten years in Sclossin they had become quite close, despite his abandonment of her and his opposition to her human work and study. It felt as though they were beginning their reconciliation over again, and it was her fault. Maggie swore that she would think through the consequences of her actions more thoroughly in the future.

Once back in Winton, they sat at the bar of the Royal, lunch ordered, and sipped on cool glasses of sauvignon blanc.

'I think the townhouse will look really nice once we put it all together,' Maggie said. 'I'll come down first thing, and by tomorrow night it should be really homey.'

'I'm looking forward to that,' Peter said. 'The hotel is comfortable enough, but nothing is better than having a home.'

'Which room will you use as your office?' Maggie used the accepted code for talking about a gadda laboratory in public.

'I was thinking the one at the back: it's only got the one window to block out.' Peter took a sip of the drink. 'Ah, if there's one thing the Aussies do well, it's wine.'

'I think you'll find we do a few other things well too. Like cricket, rugby league, rugby union —'

'I'm Irish, not English,' Peter cut in. 'I'm on your side.'

Maggie smiled, glad to see their easiness starting to return.

A voice interrupted them. 'Well, hello, beautiful.'

Maggie frowned as she turned. Who the fuck? His hair had darkened and his body filled out, but it was Scott Campbell. Still good looking: the crinkles around his eyes added character to his chiselled face.

'Hello, Scott.' God. Did Mum tell him where I'd be? For some reason Siobhan thought dating a local would help convince the bardria she was serious about the sentence. Maggie couldn't quite see the connection herself.

Scott put a hand on the back of her stool and smiled down at her. This close, she could smell soil and grass and sweat on him — a manly smell that she would have found very attractive, if she had known it could go somewhere. Sex between humans and gadda was dangerous for the former and a bit numb for the latter. A girl really got used to feeling a mystical connection in the sack. Maggie bit her tongue to keep from giggling. 'I've been hoping to catch up with you. Nice to see you home, Brains. You're looking good.' He checked her out, sliding his hand down between her body and the back of her seat.

Maggie sat forward and winced. 'Scott, this is my father, Peter.' Hopefully knowing *who's* listening will make him behave, Maggie thought. 'Dad, this is Scott Campbell. He's an old school friend.'

'Yeah, sure, heard you were in town, Mr Shaunessy.' Scott leant over and held out his hand to Peter. Peter stood to shake it, but dropped it abruptly when Scott added, 'Does this mean you and Dr S are getting back together?'

Maggie stared up at him. Her memories of Scott didn't include him being a boor and a lech.

'I wanted to come and see Maggie settle into her new life,' Peter said smoothly as he sat back down.

'Hopefully you'll see her settled into some other things as well,' Scott said cheerfully. His fingers brushed the back of Maggie's neck and sent a shiver down her spine. Not a good one.

'If you don't mind, Scott, my father and I are having lunch together,' she said coolly.

'Sure, not a problem. I'll call you tomorrow and we'll arrange a time to catch up. Nice to meet you, Mr Shaunessy.' He sauntered off toward the end of the bar, where a group of men were gathering, their dirty and sweat-stained clothes proclaiming the end of a working day.

'Can you believe Mum wants me to go out with that?' Maggie took a big swig from her wine glass.

'Why on earth would she want that?' Peter looked as though he'd never heard worse news.

'She thinks it would be a good idea to go out with a hu— local for a bit,' Maggie corrected herself quickly.

'Well, fine, but him?' Peter sniffed.

'He wasn't so bad when we were kids, Dad. In fact, I had a huge crush on him when I left Winton.'

'So that's who you put off your training for.' Peter shook his head. 'Your taste in men is interesting, to say the least. Especially considering who your latest conquest was.'

Maggie moaned. 'I'd hoped you wouldn't hear of that.'

'Why? I think it would be a good thing if you and Sean got together.'

Maggie stared at Peter, aghast. 'He's a Purist!'

Peter flushed. 'Well, yes, but –'

'We've had this argument again and again, and I'm sick of it. I'm a Humanist. Always have been, always will be. If you can't accept that –'

'Hush.' Peter put his hand on hers while his eyes flicked around the bar. He leant forward and spoke softly. 'I know you are, Maggie. I wasn't referring to the Purist versus Humanist feud. I was referring to how it became personal between the O'Hara and Flaherty clans. It occurred to me that if the personal aspect was ended, then there might be progress in bringing the political opinions together.'

Maggie frowned. She knew the story of how the personal feud started. When Maggie's grandmother had chosen John O'Hara, self-confessed supporter of humans, over Oswald Flaherty, scion of one of the original six houses and as anti-human as any gadda, it had blown their philosophical differences to extremes. During her grandmother's life, nothing much had happened, but since her death the feud had slowly been ramping up, with Oswald determined to make John pay.

However, even if a relationship with Sean eased Oswald's anger, she couldn't see how it would bridge the gap between the two families' beliefs.

'Dad, I'm sorry, but even if I did think it could end the feud, nothing could convince me to give Sean

Flaherty a shot. He is selfish, egotistical and concerned only with his own gratification. Literally.'

'Margaret.' The flush in her father's cheeks deepened. 'There's no need for that.'

'Sorry, Dad, but that's the way it is. I know you're friends with the Flaherty and I know you admire him, but his son is not worthy of my time or attention.'

Peter sighed. 'If you don't love him, you don't love him. A relationship is hard enough, let alone trying it with someone you don't love.'

The question that Maggie always wanted to ask was right there — had he loved her mother? Why hadn't their love been enough to keep him here? But she held back. The truth was, she didn't want to hear the answer.

CHAPTER NINE

Two weeks later, Lucas flew from Chicago to Los Angeles and from there to Australia. As the plane flew over Sydney, he looked hopefully down at the country that would be his home for several years to come.

Customs was a breeze, and then he was on a shuttle bus that ran him the few kilometres over to the domestic terminal, where he would catch his next flight.

He looked around him with interest. It all looked familiar, yet foreign.

After locating the gate he was flying from, he bought the local paper, sat in a coffee shop, and tried his first Australian coffee. It wasn't too bad – not quite milky enough for his taste, but drinkable. Then he looked through the paper. The main story was on whether the long-running drought might be breakable after all, what with recent increased rainfall – and destructive floods – across many of the affected areas. He tried to imagine an entire city underwater and shuddered.

He turned the page: interest rates, climate change, underage drinking, and the latest pop group to hit the charts – Australians and Americans weren't that far apart in terms of what interested them. Even the TV guide didn't seem that different.

The sports pages, however; that was where the real differences lay. He finally found a football report but it only dealt with one team, and there was no mention of the New York Jets. He'd have to rely on the internet unless he fell madly in love with cricket, whatever that was.

His flight was called, and he picked up his bag and made his way over to the gate. The plane was a thirty-seater, almost full. He found himself next to a tall, red-headed man. Lucky the guy was slim — his own wide shoulders were taking up more than his fair share of room.

The man, who had the window seat, looked up and smiled at Lucas as he sat and stowed his bag under the seat in front of him. 'Good day to ye.'

'Hey.' Lucas pulled his seatbelt across and did it up, then he smiled at his companion. 'You're a long way from home.'

'You too. American, right?'

'New York. The Bronx, actually. Where in Ireland are you from?'

'A tiny village, you wouldn't have heard of it. It's in County Leitrim, beautiful country. My name's Sean Flaherty.' Sean held out his hand.

Lucas took it and as he did so, a shock ran up his arm. 'Oh, sorry: static.' He pulled his hand back, even though he didn't believe his words. That was weird. 'Lucas Valeroso.'

Sean froze for a second, but the smiling Irish eyes were back almost immediately. 'Valeroso, you say. That's an interesting name. Where does it come from?'

There was something in Sean's eye, a flicker, which had all Lucas's hackles up. 'From my stepfather. Hispanic.'

'Right. And why are you flying up to Tamworth today, Lucas?'

'Work.' Lucas decided to shut down this conversation. 'Well, it's nice to meet you but I'm afraid I'm going to have to be unsociable and get some sleep on this flight.' He leant his seat back and closed his eyes.

Luckily, Sean took the hint and didn't speak any more, but Lucas felt the man's head turn his way time after time on the forty-five minute flight. Behind his closed eyes, his mind was spinning. Why had he felt so suddenly protective of himself? What was it about Sean Flaherty that he didn't like?

The flight was otherwise smooth and they landed in Tamworth with the sun high in the sky. Lucas stepped from the aeroplane door onto the stair and the heat of the sun hit him; his skin registered a light burning sensation very quickly. He took a deep breath – the air smelt clean, fresh and green.

The air-conditioned terminal was no more than a single room with a track for luggage and a couple of hire-car booths.

An older man, balding but with surprisingly young skin and bright eyes came toward him. 'Lucas, my boy, how wonderful to finally have you here. I'm John O'Hara.' O'Hara lifted his hand toward Lucas but stopped when something over Lucas's shoulder caught his eye. He frowned.

Lucas looked and saw Sean Flaherty behind him. He saw Lucas and nodded, then his eyes slipped to

Lucas's companion. He stopped, his mouth twisted, and then he nodded his head. He looked at Lucas and winked, on his way to collect his luggage.

Lucas looked back to O'Hara, who had dropped his hand. O'Hara closed his eyes and was still for a moment, then opened them and smiled at Lucas. 'Sorry about that. Senior moment, you know. Now, let's get your luggage and I'll take you out to Winton. You'll love it.'

Lucas nodded, smiled, and swore silently that John O'Hara had never had a senior moment in his life. There was a history between the two men he'd just met, and it wasn't a good one. Lucas didn't like the idea he seemed to be walking into something. He'd better find out what was going on before he committed to staying.

He waited until they had the luggage in O'Hara's car and were on the road. 'Do you know Sean Flaherty?'

O'Hara looked out at the road ahead. 'It would seem you do.'

'I met him on the plane. He's not a problem, is he?'

'Not for you. He'll probably cause a few ructions in my family, but he'll be on his way back to Ireland soon enough.' O'Hara flicked a glance at Lucas. 'Did he say anything to you on the plane?'

'No.' Lucas had nothing to gain by getting involved. 'I slept practically the whole way.'

'Well, I hope you're well rested. Unfortunately, we have the staff welcome function tonight. I'll understand if you only come briefly, but you do have to make an appearance. You'll have plenty of time in the next couple of days to rest if you need.'

Lucas nodded. 'That sounds fine.' He sat back and enjoyed the trip through the Australian countryside. Wide swathes of yellow-gold, dotted with cattle and sheep, interspersed with stands of bush – eucalypts, shrubs, flowers. The whole impression was of a bucolic – if very dry – paradise.

O'Hara took him directly to his new apartment, in a building across the road from the university. 'I'd like to stay and help you settle in, but this time of the year's one of the worst for paperwork. I'll see you tonight.' And O'Hara took off with a cheery wave.

The apartment was basic – one bedroom and furnished – but there was room to add personal touches.

Not that he had any.

Overall, it would be a comfortable enough place, until he got to know the town and decided where he wanted to settle.

In the meantime, after twenty-four hours of travelling, and facing the staff function that night, he needed to stretch his legs.

Lucas walked across the road and into the university grounds. The main building looked fresh and solid, and its graceful lines would age beautifully. The science building just screamed current research. Beyond that he passed the sporting fields and then paddocks (which he had to own looked much like the sports area; he was used to more bleachers and markings and goal posts).

Beyond the fields was a hill, on which grew rows of green trees. A plantation, but he was too far away to see what type. At the top of the hill the sun lit up a long, low, white house. That'll be where the richest family in town lives, Lucas thought. They always picked the best spot. Perhaps O'Hara himself.

He decided to walk across the fields, check out the plantation, and head back home. By then, he'd probably be ready for a real nap.

They were olive trees. He paused at the fence. This was undoubtedly private land. But the cool shade was inviting, and as long as he didn't touch the trees …

You can take the boy from crime, but you can't take the crime from the boy, he told himself with a grin, as he jumped over the fence and walked into the grove. Scents hit him, musty and sweet, and he stopped and closed his eyes to allow the experience to seep in.

'Hey, you, ya can't come in ere!'

Crap, he thought. He opened his eyes and saw an old man trundling toward him. His back was bent, his hands shook and his face was flushed a florid red.

The man stopped just out of reach and frowned. 'Didja hear me? Ya can't come in ere.'

'I'm sorry, I didn't realise this was private land.' Lucas smiled. 'I was just after a bit of shade before walking back to the university.'

The man's eyes narrowed. 'A Yank. Shoulda known. Think you rule the bloody world.'

His vehemence was almost palpable. 'My apologies; it won't happen again.'

'Just make sure it doesn't, cos normally I carry a gun, and I'm not –'

'Hello, what's going on here?' Another voice broke in. Lucas turned and saw a gorgeous woman walk toward them. Golden hair fell around a lovely face. She had terrific curves too.

The woman placed herself in between the two of them, her back to Lucas. 'Is there anything the matter, Jeff?'

'This Yank was trespassin.'

'Oh, I'm sure he didn't mean to.' She looked over her shoulder and smiled at Lucas.

She was stunning, light and happiness, and her smile hit Lucas right where it counted. God bless you, John O'Hara, he thought as he smiled back. To his delight, her smile deepened, became no less friendly but a lot more interesting. Jeff looked at them, grunted in frustration and stamped off, tossing a warning not to touch a single leaf on them trees back at them as he went.

The woman looked properly at Lucas, then smiled and said, 'You've got permission to come any time, Dr Valeroso,' before nodding one last time and stepping behind a tree in the direction of the low white house.

Lucas turned and made his way back to town, considering the clues to her identity. She was from the house at the top of the hill, he guessed. And she knew who he was, and he hadn't met anyone in town, so she had to have some sort of connection with the university. And that probably meant she'd be at the function tonight. So he'd see her again. Soon.

He was really going to enjoy working at Winton University.

So that was Lucas Valeroso, Maggie thought. He wasn't at all what she'd expected. Grandpa had raved about his dedication, his relentless work ethic, and she'd been picturing a bit of a dork. She was surprised that he was the most attractive man she'd ever seen.

He really shouldn't have been – there was something genuinely harsh about him. But the sharp angles of his face, the black hair brushed back from his forehead, his strong nose and his hard body were offset by lush lips and blue eyes.

Yep, he was gorgeous, *and* a world-renowned scientist. Shame he wasn't gadda, or she'd be dragging him back up the hill. She was years off having the sort of control she'd need to have sex with a human, to control her power during orgasm. Still, Lucas Valeroso sure looked worth the effort.

As Maggie stepped onto the pavement surrounding the house, Siobhan appeared at the door. 'Can you come in here and help me, please?' Her icy tones were ominous.

'What's wrong?'

'You have a visitor, and another is expected.' She nodded over her shoulder.

Maggie walked past her to the kitchen door and stopped.

'Sabhamir.'

'Margaret.' The protector of the gadda nodded. On the table in front of him was a cup of tea and a plate with biscuit crumbs. Her grandfather sat next to him.

'Why are you here?' Maggie went over to lean on the table across from her visitor, her legs suddenly weak. 'They haven't decided to banish me, have they?' She looked at her grandfather, who to her horror avoided her gaze.

The Sabhamir smiled, and relief washed through Maggie. 'Not at all. No, I'm here because part of the sentence passed on you is about to be broken and I need to ensure that you know nothing about it.'

Maggie frowned and looked at her mother. Siobhan looked less than impressed. 'I still don't understand. Is this something about Dad?'

'No, this is about Sean Flaherty.'

'What?' Maggie tried to focus; her thoughts began to align. 'What has he done?'

The Sabhamir nodded at John. 'Your grandfather saw him at Tamworth airport earlier today. We're assuming he's making his way here, considering your ... encounter.' The Sabhamir kept his face blank. 'Did you know he was coming here?'

'Shit, no. He's coming here?'

'We believe so. Ione says that when he went to your flat to pick you up for lunch he was quite insistent that you be together. He said you were, ah, *soulmates*.'

'Shit, shit, shit, shit, shit.' Maggie slumped into a chair. She stared at the Sabhamir. 'It was just that one night.'

The Sabhamir quirked an eyebrow. 'Do you want to tell him so yourself?'

She waved her hands in front of her. 'Oh no, no way, I don't want to see him. I just want him out of my life.'

'Maggie.' Siobhan put her hand on her daughter's shoulder. 'I know that he's a Flaherty, and we're worried about the Purists, but I think you need to face Sean yourself. The boy has broken the directive of the bardria and has spent a day on a plane in order to see you. He clearly thinks there's something between you, and I doubt that sort of devotion will be broken by even the Sabhamir. The only one who can make him see sense is you.'

Maggie tried to think of an argument against Siobhan's, and couldn't. 'Damn.'

'Margaret.' Maggie turned her attention to the Sabhamir. 'I need to know that you weren't aware that Sean was coming to Winton to see you.'

Maggie realised the extent of the danger. She looked the Sabhamir full in the face and said calmly, 'I had no knowledge that Sean Flaherty was coming to Australia. I did not ask him to, I did not encourage him to. I have had no contact with him since the night before I left Sclossin and I will defend my innocence in this.'

The corner of the Sabhamir's mouth twitched. 'A little more dramatic than necessary, but I shall report your words to the bardria, with my own judgement of your innocence. Now, we just have to wait for Sean to turn up. I don't suppose there are more of these biscuits?' He looked hopefully at Siobhan and Maggie remembered that he wasn't much older than she was.

'I'm not sure I want it said that I bribed you for my daughter's sake,' Siobhan said, with a grin.

He waved his hand in the air. 'No one would begrudge a hard-working man a break after travelling all the way from Sclossin to Australia.' Everyone laughed.

A knock at the door stopped the Sabhamir. All eyes turned to Maggie. She stood, took a deep breath, and whispered, 'I'm not sure I can do this.'

'Come on.' Siobhan took her hand, and led her to the loungeroom. She let go when they stood in the middle of the room. 'Stay calm, and try to be gentle with the boy. This could be for real.' Then she went over and opened the door.

'Mrs Shaunessy, a delight to finally meet you. I see where Margaret gets her beauty. My name is Sean Flaherty, and I've come to put an end to the feud between our families.'

Maggie shivered. His voice resonated with truth. He really believed what he was saying.

'Come in, Sean.' Siobhan stepped aside. Sean took a couple of steps forward but stopped when he saw Maggie.

'Margaret, darling.' He rushed forward.

Maggie put her hands in front of her, and took a couple of steps back. 'Hold it right there, Sean.' He continued toward her.

He wasn't going to stop. Maggie panicked. She reached deep, grabbed hold of her power and pulled on it. Hurriedly recalling words for a shield, she let the energy loose. She felt something hard spread from her hands mere seconds before Sean ran into it.

He stumbled backward, swearing. Maggie put a foot behind her to balance herself from the impact. She dropped the shield and stared in amazement. She'd never practised it much during her second-order training as she hadn't seen the need for it. It surprised her that she was so good at it.

'What was that for?' Sean pressed his hand against his nose while he glared at her.

'I'm sorry, did I hurt you?' She didn't like him, but disfiguring him wasn't her intention.

He lifted his hand away and looked at it. 'Just a

bump, I think. But I don't understand why you would shield yourself from me.'

'Because you weren't listening to me.'

'Listening to what?'

'Sean, you shouldn't be here.'

He frowned. 'Why not? Where should I be, if not with you?'

Maggie let out a breath. 'Sean, I think you've got the wrong impression about us. I'm not interested in a relationship with you.'

She watched expressions flit across his face — confusion, hurt, thoughtfulness. He looked over his shoulder, back at her and then his voice sounded in her head. '*Margaret, darling* –'

She shook her head. 'No, Sean, no mental communication. If you have something to say, say it aloud.'

He looked over his shoulder again — at Siobhan — and then took a step toward Maggie. 'Can we talk in private?'

'There's nothing to be said that can't be said in front of my mother.'

His lips thinned. 'Darling, I don't think that's the case. I think there are things that you don't feel free to say in front of your family.'

'Such as?'

'That you love me. That you want to be with me.'

Frustration began to build. 'Sean, I'm sorry, but I don't love you. I don't want to be with you. I don't want a relationship with you and not because of the family feud. There's nothing between us.'

'That night –'

'Was a one-off. That's it. It was a mistake.'

He reeled back, as if she had struck him. 'You can't think that.'

'How can you think that we have some sort of fated connection after just one entirely substandard night in the sack?'

'Ah.' He smiled, and Maggie felt she'd said the wrong thing. 'If you're concerned that I might think less of you because you picked me up in a nightclub, then —'

'Oh, for crying out loud. As if I give a fuck what you think of me.'

'Maggie.' Siobhan's cool tone washed over her, reminding her she was supposed to be considerate of Sean's feelings. Why should she be, when he wasn't considerate of hers?

'I tried.' Maggie looked over Sean's shoulder at her mother. 'I can't make him see sense.'

'Sean.' Siobhan walked around to stand next to Maggie. 'Maggie has made up her mind, and it won't be changed. You'd best return to Sclossin and —'

'No.' Sean shook his head vehemently. 'I will not leave Margaret alone here, to be poisoned against me.'

'Time to bring in the big guns,' Siobhan said, turning and waving her hand. Maggie knew the moment the Sabhamir stepped into the room — Sean's already pale skin lost the rest of its colour and his mouth gaped open.

'Sabhamir.'

'Sean.' The protector of the gadda stood between Maggie and Sean. 'John O'Hara summoned me here when he realised you were about to contravene an order of the bardria.'

Sean pulled himself straight, and looked the Sabhamir in the eye. Maggie had to admit that took guts. 'The order does not apply to me. I am family, or I will be.'

'The only person in Sclossin given permission to travel to Winton on Ms Shaunessy's behalf was her father. You were granted no such permission.'

'Then give it to me now. I know the bardria will, if I apply to them.'

'Then apply to them. In the meantime, you will return to Sclossin.'

'I can't.' Sean smiled. 'I only bought a one-way ticket.'

'Consider me the return leg.' The Sabhamir looked at Siobhan. 'Will it cause a problem if I transfer him back?'

'We can deal with it,' she said.

'Good.' He turned to Maggie. 'You're sure?'

Maggie looked around him. 'Sean, please accept that I didn't mean to hurt you, but that I can't be with you.'

'Margaret, don't let them do this to us.'

She looked at the Sabhamir. 'I'm sure.'

He bowed his head, turned and touched Sean's arm and they were gone.

Siobhan opened her arms and Maggie walked into them, her face turned to the floor.

'It will be all right, Mags. The Sabhamir will make sure Sean gets the message, and he won't bother you again.'

'How could he feel like that?' Maggie shook her head. 'I don't understand.'

'Don't let it concern you, darlin.' John's voice came from behind her. 'It's over.' He patted her shoulder. 'Now *you* need to get ready for the party tonight, and *I* have work to do on campus, so I'll see you both later.' He kissed them and then left.

'I think we deserve a drink after that.' Siobhan gave Maggie a squeeze and then directed her down the hall to the kitchen.

Maggie slumped at the table and stared down at its polished surface. What the hell else could go wrong in her life? To think, just a short time ago, she'd been excited about meeting the entirely attractive Lucas Valeroso.

Now, that was a much better topic of discussion. 'I came across Jeff trying to heavy Lucas Valeroso in the olive grove. I think I managed to save Grandpa's American star without any damage done. Jeff really is like a bulldog.'

'I'm glad to hear that.' Siobhan put more tea and biscuits on the table and sat down. 'So, what is Dr Valeroso like? I'd put money on pasty skin, fizzy blond hair and knock-knees.'

Maggie grinned. 'Try over six foot, jet-black hair and gorgeous.'

'Really?' Siobhan smiled.

'Yes, amazing — and human. Bugger.' Maggie took a sip of tea.

'Hmmm. If he's that yummy, I might give him a go.'

Maggie almost spat the mouthful of tea out. 'You can't.'

'I'm fourth order, darling. I can handle it.'

A vision of her mother and Lucas together crossed her mind and Maggie shivered. 'I'm sure he's not your type, Mum. I've heard his head is always buried in either books or his experiments.'

'He's young and, so you say, gorgeous. He's anyone's type.'

'Oh, I wouldn't say he was that good-looking.' Liar. 'A bit brutal, really.' In that granite-hewn, totally hot way. 'I'm sure at second glance, there's nothing to him.' Please, please, don't let that be true.

Siobhan put her cup down. 'Maggie, be careful. You've already played with one too many fires lately.'

Maggie felt colour rise in her cheeks. 'I'm well aware that I need to keep things clean for a while. Although you were the one who said it would help me keep clear of the gadda if I had a fling with a human.'

'Maggie, I considered Scott a safe bet because I was quite sure you wouldn't be attracted to him and so could easily finish the relationship without being hurt. I didn't think Scott would care much either – another score for him. But if you really like this Lucas, and then have to end things because he is human and it won't work ...'

Yet again Siobhan had a point that Maggie didn't like. 'I can flirt a bit, can't I?'

'If you want to lead the man on, then sure!'

'Dammit.'

Siobhan kissed her cheek.

'It will all work out, Maggie, and two years isn't so long.'

Right now, it felt like eternity.

CHAPTER TEN

Lucas leant against the wall, studied the crowd of tuxedoed men and gowned women before him, and wondered how he managed to get himself talked into these things. He hated social engagements; he hated them even more when he only knew the host. But then he remembered the pot at the end of his rainbow, and smiled.

After the meeting in the grove, he'd gone back into town and had lunch at a café. The waitress was more than willing to have a chat. He'd learnt that the girl was Maggie Shaunessy, John O'Hara's granddaughter.

Getting involved with the chancellor's grand-daughter seemed doomed to failure, but she was so beautiful, and so warm. No harm in spending a bit of time with her, surely?

So here he was, actually wearing a tie, goddamn it, on a hot Australian February night, waiting for a woman he'd glimpsed for a few minutes to make an appearance.

In the meantime, he was watching the university staff.

John O'Hara's comment about his crime not being the worst on the books intrigued him. He'd always considered a carjacking at knifepoint a heinous thing to do. What had some of these other people done?

They were an eclectic mix — young and old, male and female, and a multitude of nationalities. There were many more Asians here than he'd seen at any university in America, as well as people who seemed Middle Eastern or African.

The group nearest him consisted of an older man wearing a leather jacket that somehow worked with his extravagant mane of silver hair, a young woman wearing a white hijab over a deep blue silk dress and a middle-aged woman in a bright red sari. The three of them were involved in a serious discussion, from which words such as *lexical semantics*, *phraseology* and *discourse analysis* floated to him.

Linguists, he decided. And an interesting group — the differing language backgrounds of the lecturers would undoubtedly add to the students' experience.

'Dr Valeroso?'

Lucas turned toward the speaker and saw an old man with a tuft of white hair sticking up from the top of his head and the rest curling around his ears. 'Frank Testori, mythological studies. Welcome to our happy little family.'

Lucas reached out to shake the offered hand. This man was either going to be a complete fruit loop, or brilliant. 'Pleasure to meet you, Professor Testori.'

'Please, Frank. Every time I hear the word "Professor", I keep looking for my doctorate supervisor. You know the kind: a little fuzzy around the edges but sharp as a tack about his subject.'

Lucas managed not to laugh. 'Frank. I'm afraid I've not read up on mythology lately. What's your speciality?'

'Cross-cultural similarities. I find it fascinating that cultures that are so diverse can come up with such similar stories. For example, the Jewish creation myth is also found in Indigenous Australian and South American mythology. Now, how do you think that could be?'

'Isn't there a theory that the Atlanteans spread all this sort of stuff around the world?'

Frank nodded enthusiastically, the tuft of hair on his head bobbing. 'Yes, the Atlanteans: fascinating story. My favourite theory relating to the Atlanteans is that they were in fact aliens. Now, you're a physicist, Dr Valeroso. Do you think it possible that a race that could travel through space would not have the technology of electronics and computers? We have found no evidence of electronics from the time they were supposedly here on Earth, so how could they be aliens?'

Lucas thought, He *is* brilliant. He had been right: O'Hara didn't hire run-of-the-mill academics. 'I don't know many of us prepared to consider anything beyond our own fields of study.'

Testori snorted. 'You'd have to be stupid not to realise that no subject can be studied in isolation.'

Lucas laughed. 'Indeed. And I hope physics can provide you with all the mythbusting you need!'

'Mythbusting! Yes, yes: that's perfect. Lovely to meet you, and welcome.' And Testori turned and hurried away.

Lucas leant back against the wall, smiling. If the rest of the staff was half as entertaining and intelligent as Testori, he was going to enjoy it here.

His eyes focussed on a young woman who stood in the middle of a group of older men. Glorious golden hair was twisted up around her head. Her halter-neck black jersey dress, its hem just sweeping the tops of her feet, enhanced the rich curves of her body. Jackpot, he thought.

She turned and their gazes caught. She walked over, moving gracefully even though he was watching so closely.

'Dr Valeroso.' Her smile was as sunny as it had been that afternoon, although it lacked the heat he'd liked. 'I'm pleased to see you survived the encounter with the grove's protector.'

He bowed his head. 'Thank you for saving me.'

'I'm sure you're quite capable of saving yourself.'

'But always nice to have someone else make the effort, don't you think?'

'Sometimes, you have no choice.' A shadow passed over her face and Lucas wondered what bad memory he'd just dredged up.

She shook her head and the smile resumed. 'I hope you've managed to settle in.'

'To my accommodation, yes. I haven't seen my laboratory yet, but I'm looking forward to it.' He didn't like how businessy this conversation was.

'If there's anything you need, let me know. I'm working as the chancellor's PA at the moment.'

He wondered if there was a reason O'Hara had hired his granddaughter to work for him. 'At the moment? Isn't that what you normally do?'

'No.' Another shadow. 'I'm just helping him out until I can get some paperwork sorted out – for both of us! I teach primary school. I think in the States that's elementary school.'

'Then you're a fellow educator.' Lucas was desperate to find a connection. He'd been so sure there was something between them during their first meeting.

'Except you're abandoning the chalkboard.' The lightness that had entered her tone gave him hope.

'Not by choice, I assure you. I'm allergic, you see.'

'What, to students or the chalk?'

'Um, both?'

She laughed, a thrilling sound that played over his body like music.

'Actually, I think it's the marking I'm allergic to,' Lucas continued.

'How can it be? That's my favourite part – hours bent over a desk, red pen in hand, wondering just how to tell someone they got it wrong without ruining their fragile self-esteem.'

'Are we supposed to worry about their self-esteem?'

She laughed again. 'Lucas Valeroso, that's just too bad.'

'Really? I'm trying very hard to be good.'

'Oh, I'm sure you are.'

And there it was, that attraction that had so instantly drawn him. When her eyes sparkled like that, Lucas felt as though anything were possible. 'Perhaps you can help me with that, Ms Shaunessy.'

'Please, call me Maggie.' She held her hand out. He reached for it, expecting to feel a thrill at the first touch of skin on skin. The shaft of energy that ran up Lucas's arm surprised him with its intensity.

He knew she felt it too, because her eyes went so dark his stomach dropped into his shoes with arousal. Then she released him, and he fought back the disappointment. 'We're thrilled you decided to come here, Dr Valeroso.'

The ice in her voice threw him. What had he done to piss her off? 'I'm not sure I had much of a choice. I think Chancellor O'Hara decided I was coming here, and that was it.'

'Once he sets his mind on something, it does tend to happen,' she said. 'I need to keep circulating.' She looked at him, and he fancied she was trying to read his mind. Then, with a nod, she walked away.

Damn, damn and double damn, Lucas thought. He'd really stuffed that up, somehow. Then he remembered the shock he'd received when he shook that aeroplane guy's hand — a shock exactly like he'd just felt with Maggie. And Flaherty was involved with the O'Haras somehow. Something strange was going on around here. Good. He quite liked a good mystery, especially when the heroine was smart and gorgeous.

There was no longer any reason to hang around. Time to catch up on some sleep.

'He's what?' John O'Hara almost screamed the words. Siobhan frowned; they were within earshot of the party.

'Lucas Valeroso is gadda. Surely you noticed.' Maggie looked from one to the other. 'When you shook his hand.'

'Can't say that I did. Shake his hand, I mean. Wait here.' And O'Hara walked away.

Maggie looked at her mother, who shrugged. 'I haven't had a chance to approach him yet. Not very sociable, is he?'

'He's perfectly easy to talk to, one on one.' Maggie began to pace up and down the grand hall. Never in all her living days would she forget the moment when she shook the hand of the world's pre-eminent (and possibly yummiest) rising physicist – and realised he wasn't human.

'I have to say, your taste in men is improving, Maggie.'

Maggie spared her mother a scornful glance. 'You can talk, Ms Divorcee.'

'Your father is an idiot and a misogynist, that is true, but he is attractive. No one can deny that.'

John reappeared, forestalling Maggie's response. 'She's right. I caught him sneaking off to bed and shook his hand: the man is gadda. And I don't think he knows it. We need to confer with the bardria. Come.'

They rushed through their goodbyes and left the party in the capable hands of John's vice chancellor. Once they'd zipped up the hill courtesy of the campus security guard and his mini-van, O'Hara led them through the house and opened the door to the cellar.

A dim red glow lit the darkness below. John threw his arm out, stopping the women. 'Stay here.' He started down the steps slowly. Siobhan and Maggie looked at each other, then followed him.

A message hovered in the air over the star of gulagh. The red letters dripped as though they were bleeding. It read: *Stay away from the humans.*

Maggie wrapped her arms around her waist, a chill running through her. Who would come up with such a thing?

'Who's this one from?' Siobhan said.

'This one?' Maggie stared at her mother. John ignored both of them.

'Siobhan, some oil of cloves, please.'

Siobhan crossed her arms. 'I think you should call the Sabhamir.'

John shook his head. 'No need to involve the bardria over Purist idiocy. I'll extract some essence, work out who is doing it and warn them off.'

Siobhan shook her head and muttered, 'Stubborn old man,' but she went over to the cupboard under the stairs and rummaged for the oil, which she found and took to her father.

'Girls, stand back. Siobhan, have your shield ready.'

Siobhan took Maggie by the arm and put her behind her in the far corner.

'Mum, what do you mean *this one?*' Maggie whispered.

'Hush. Your grandfather needs to concentrate.' Maggie looked over her mother's shoulder and watched her grandfather pour a couple of drops of the clove oil onto his hands. He rubbed them over his palms and up his arms a little. Then he stepped forward until his toes were right next to the star. He leant back and stretched his arms out.

Maggie realised the clove oil was to protect him from the power of the star in use but, even so, this extraction was a risky thing to try. She squeezed her hands together and pressed closer to her mother.

As her grandfather's fingers started to pass over the top of the star, the message flickered. John quickly pulled back. He tapped his chin, studying the message.

'Dad, just call the Sabhamir,' Siobhan said.

'No, I can do this.' He turned and walked over to his bench. He picked up a knife made of gleaming silver with jewels worked into the handle. He poured some of the clove oil onto the knife, then wiped it over the entire weapon with a cloth. Then he went back, this time standing some distance from the star.

He lifted his hand with the knife extended and started to push it toward the message. As the blade passed over the star, there was a soft hiss. John stopped just as the tip was about to touch the message.

'That should have split it,' he muttered as he reached toward the star with his other hand. The hand holding the knife shook with the effort of keeping the weapon still. Slowly, his free hand moved up to level with the knife, then along it, so close that Maggie thought he must be cutting himself.

This time, his hand passed over the star, but just when his finger was about to touch the last letter, the message flared and then disappeared.

'Damn.' John stepped into the star. 'I almost had it.'

'I told you we should have got the Sabhamir.' Siobhan walked over to the star and bent to touch it.

'You're probably right as always, Shevvy, but it's too late now.'

'Not too late for an explanation, I hope,' Maggie said. 'What the hell do you mean *this one*? Has this happened before?'

John and Siobhan looked at each other. Siobhan spoke. 'We didn't want to worry you darling –'

'No, cos having me discover it like this is much better. Stop making excuses and tell me.'

'It's been happening for a few months,' Siobhan said. 'Once a week or so, we'll get a message saying we should stay away from humans, or that if we don't return to Sclossin there'll be trouble, or –'

'Trouble like what happened to me?' Maggie said. Siobhan looked at John with a frown.

'Do you think that maybe the Purists thought that if they revealed what Maggie had done, we'd be told to return to Sclossin?'

'It's possible.' John scratched his chin. 'Perhaps their plan was to use it to blackmail us, but unfortunately the caelleach got to it first. It would seem that whatever the Purists are planning, they are increasing the intensity.'

'So, what now?' Siobhan said. 'I say report it to the Sabhamir anyway.' Maggie nodded.

'Of course.' John looked around the laboratory. 'I'll have a chat to him about it. In the meantime, we need to be careful. I don't want you two girls to go anywhere apart from your jobs. You aren't to spend any time alone with humans outside of work. Siobhan, I want you to put a simple lock over your surgery, just enough to give you warning if a gadda enters using his or her power. I'm going to put a lock over the house and over the chancellory and the science block. That'll cover Lucas's laboratory too, just in case he gets embroiled in all this. We also need to tell Peter what's going on, so he can protect you when you're with him, Mags.' John's face was set in stern lines. It was clear he wasn't going to negotiate any of this.

Maggie wondered when life would return to normal.

CHAPTER ELEVEN

As she let herself in to have dinner with Peter, Maggie was amazed how much her father's townhouse in Winton felt like the Shaunessy farmhouse outside of Sclossin — traditional and yet homey. He'd certainly settled in over the past few weeks.

'Hi, Dad!' she called out, putting her purse on the hall table.

'In here, Maggie,' he called from the room they'd set up as his laboratory. Maggie walked down the hall to join him. He'd done a lot of work, and it now had the aura of power that all gadda laboratories had. The window had been covered up, and a large bookcase, holding books and jars and earthernware containers, placed in front of it. Along the wall opposite the door was a waist-high bench, with more jars, a mortar and pestle and a recipe-book stand. In the corner was a comfortable chair. The carpet had been removed and a star of gulagh painted on the cement slab beneath.

Peter was standing at the bench, studying a book open on the stand.

'Whatcha doing?' Maggie asked, pulling the door closed behind her. No one ever left the door of a gadda laboratory open.

'I'm looking at some of the prescribed activities for learning control for the third-order test.' Peter turned a page. 'There are quite a lot of outdoor activities, which we won't be able to do here in Winton. They'll have to wait until you're allowed back in Sclossin. But there seem to be enough minute control activities for you to practise indoors for the next couple of years. That will probably be good for you, since your fine control has never been that strong. You need to develop it if you wish to go past third order.'

Maggie rolled her eyes. 'Assuming I even get that far.' She sat down in the chair.

Peter turned and frowned at her. 'Why wouldn't you? Your mother and I are both fourth order — she could probably have passed fifth if she'd wanted to — both my parents were fourths and your grandfather is sixth. In fact, with your intelligence and the special skills you've developed in the human world, you could possibly even consider the gadma way.'

'*No* way.' Maggie shook her head fiercely. The gadma way was a specialised study of gadda power and, while it could bring many rewards, it demanded a great deal to achieve them. 'Only complete crackpots or power-hungry idiots try the gadma way. It can kill you. Besides, Ione can't even pass first and her family is renowned for producing sixths, so genetics aren't everything.'

Peter sighed. 'You have passed first and second — and what's more did that easily. You could go much further, if you wanted to.'

'I promise I'll make a good fist of third, but I'm not going to consider anything else. Now, in an effort to change the subject, Grandpa would like to speak with you.' She threw it out there, sure it would stop the conversation cold. In fact, she was ready for several minutes of pleading and explanation as her father tried to avoid her other family.

'Wonderful.' Peter turned, closed the book and put it away. 'I've been hoping I'd have a chance to catch up with him sooner rather than later.'

Maggie slumped back in the chair. 'Really?'

Peter looked at her and raised an eyebrow. 'I don't have any problems with your grandfather, Maggie. I have great respect for him.'

Just not what he does, Maggie thought as she pulled her mobile phone out of her pocket. She put in a quick call to John, who promised to be straight over. Then she smiled at her father. 'Shall we have a drink while we wait for him?'

Peter nodded and they made their way into the kitchen. It was the only room her father hadn't re-decorated. It looked thoroughly modern and thoroughly human.

Peter poured them each a glass of wine, as well as one for John, and they took them into the combined lounge–dining room. Here it was back to pure Sclossin – old, much-polished wood and brass.

Moments later the doorbell rang, and Maggie went and let her grandfather in. John walked into the loungeroom and stopped, looking around.

'Marvellous,' he said. 'A piece of the old country come to life. Siobhan is much too willing to adopt Australian customs in furnishing, like her mother was, and I've got no say.' Then he smiled and held his hand out. 'Peter, welcome back to Winton. The town's changed a great deal, hasn't it?'

Maggie couldn't believe that her grandfather had brought up Peter's absence so unabashedly, but her father didn't seem to mind. He stood, crossed the room and touched the back of his hand to John's in the gadda way. 'Good to see you, John. The town's certainly grown a great deal, and the university looks fantastic. The science block is just as you imagined it would be.'

'I hope you'll pop in to see Adrian Laquotte while you're here. He'd love to take you through the herd.'

'I certainly planned to.'

'I'm sorry.' Maggie looked from one man to the other. 'What are you talking about?'

'You knew we were using your father's herd as stock for the university,' John said.

'No, I did not.' Maggie stared at her father. Why would he be doing anything to help humans?

'Adrian wanted to see if he could develop a cow that was tough enough for Australian conditions, yet was still a good milk producer, so he's been using semen from my bulls.' Peter shrugged. 'Drink, John? All I have is wine, I'm afraid. I just can't come at this Guinness in a can.'

'You get used to it when it's all you can get.' The two men walked over to sit down at the dining table, as though nothing was out of the ordinary.

Maggie marched over and stood at the end, her hands on her hips, glaring at them both. She couldn't believe they'd been in contact, working together, all this time and she hadn't known about it. 'Why didn't I know this?'

John grimaced and Peter said dryly, 'I'd imagine there wasn't a chance to tell you without your mother being around.'

For the first time, Maggie considered how her mother's bitterness toward her ex might have clouded Maggie's own relationship with her father. It wasn't a pretty picture.

'What about when I was in Sclossin?'

Peter sighed. 'I tried, Maggie. Repeatedly, but the moment you hear the words *Purist* or *Humanist*, you explode into emotionalism and it's impossible to make you understand. I admit I gave up – I preferred to have some semblance of a peaceful relationship with you than keep fighting what seemed an unwinnable battle.'

'Then make me understand now.' Maggie hoped she was open-minded enough to handle whatever her father was about to say.

'I can see the positives on both sides. I agree that the more gadda and humans interact, the more the secret is put at risk. At the same time, I can see how our powers can help humans, so I make decisions for each individual circumstance. I don't have a blanket position. When your grandfather approached me about the problems with dairy stock here, I could see that I could help without too much risk. However, your study was risky, particularly when you brought humans into Sclossin, and that's why I opposed it. Do you see?'

Maggie did, and felt a sense of shame wash over her. It seemed a very sensible way of being, and she couldn't believe she'd so resolutely labelled him as Purist.

'I do. I'm sorry, Dad.'

Peter smiled, held out his hand and Maggie walked over and took it, pressing a kiss to his forehead. Peter gave her hand a squeeze, and then looked at John. 'Now, you had something to talk to me about?'

'Yes, Peter, there are some recent events we should discuss,' John said. 'The first actually I think Maggie should tell you, unless you know why she came to Australia so suddenly.' John looked at Maggie.

'Oh yes, I heard.' Peter also looked at Maggie and she slumped down into a chair and took a huge slug of wine. 'According to Oswald, Sean's quite adamant that you two should be together.'

'So we've heard.' John quickly told Peter about Sean's aborted attempt to speak to Maggie. Maggie kept drinking her wine, her face flaming.

At the end, Peter was shaking his head. 'Well, I'll certainly try to make clear to Oswald that there's nothing to it as far as Maggie's concerned.' Then he frowned. 'Oswald never mentioned that Sean came here. I'm surprised.'

'Perhaps he's embarrassed by his failure,' John said. Maggie looked up to see the two men exchange a glance and, to her surprise, her grandfather was the first to look away. 'Yes. Well, that's not all.' John then described the message and explained it had happened before. Peter's face was pale by the end of the telling.

'You should have called the Sabhamir,' he said.

'I know, I stuffed up. We have to deal with it. However, there's another thing which further complicates matters. It would seem we have an unknown gadda here in Winton.'

'What?' Peter's shout seemed to shock even him. He took a deep breath and released it. 'What do you mean?'

John explained what had happened with Lucas. 'I wanted to let you know so that you wouldn't be surprised if you met him, but I also hoped you might recognise him — or perhaps have a clue as to his heritage. You know more of the gadda than I do.'

'This is something else you should tell the bardria,' Peter said.

'I will, but first I am investigating it myself.'

'He could well be what he seems — someone who doesn't know that he's gadda,' Maggie said.

'Until we know for certain, we all need to keep an eye on him. Peter, can you see what you can find out? None of my contacts in Sclossin know anything.'

Peter nodded. 'I'll get in touch with some friends at the bardria.'

She found it hard to believe Lucas was dangerous or malevolent, but then she'd certainly proven no good judge of men lately.

'Would it help if I spent some time with Lucas?' Maggie said.

'Absolutely not,' her father said firmly.

'That's not a bad idea, Mags,' her grandfather said calmly.

'And if he is out to hurt her?' Peter said.

'I don't think he is,' Maggie said. 'I can go and see him now, get him to come up to the house for dinner tomorrow night. He can't do anything to me in the middle of Winton, and once we've got him in the house we can all control him if we need to.'

'I don't like it,' Peter said.

'I do. Go do it, Mags. If you're not back here in half an hour, we'll come after him and blow the consequences.'

Maggie gave them both a kiss and then left, hoping her hunch about Lucas was right.

Lucas sat at his dining table, hands wrapped around a steaming cup of coffee, while he thought through his options. He'd set up the lab that O'Hara had assigned to him, and it was a perfect working environment – situated in the basement of the science block so he shouldn't be disturbed when the students started in a week or so, yet close to everything he needed. And the rest of the staff was normal – at least he hadn't experienced that strange sensation he had felt when he shook hands with the plane guy and Maggie – not to mention O'Hara himself.

He'd been surprised when O'Hara caught him at the door during his escape from the staff function.

'I didn't get the chance to talk to you tonight and I just wanted to make sure everything's fine,' the older man had said. His words and tone were casual, but the focus in his eyes was not.

'Fine,' Lucas said, improvising until he knew what the rules were. He'd much rather be blunt and ask exactly what was going on, but it wasn't time for that.

O'Hara nodded and held his hand out. 'Well, good night then, Lucas.' Lucas stared at the outstretched hand for a moment, knowing what was going to happen. Sure enough, the moment he grasped it, that strange tingling. He looked at O'Hara who nodded as if he noticed nothing. They hadn't seen each other since.

Lucas took a sip of his coffee. Were the benefits of this job worth the unexplained phenomena and the eccentric cast of characters?

There was a knock on his door. He spilt some coffee and then grimaced. God, he was jumpy. Perhaps that was the answer: he was feeling stressed. He put the cup down and went over to the door, throwing it open to reveal Maggie Shaunessy's smiling face.

'Hi. I'm not bothering you, am I?'

In many ways, Lucas thought. She was wearing something short and cottony and smelt like peaches. 'Not at all. What can I do for you?' He leant against the doorframe and crossed his arms over his chest, making it clear he wouldn't ask her in.

'I was hoping we could meet for dinner tomorrow night. I so want to talk to you about the work you're doing. It's not every day you get to pick the brain of the world's latest acknowledged genius.' She smiled.

Maybe a meal with her would provide answers. And if not, then at least a night spent looking at her wouldn't be such a bad thing. 'Sure. Meet you at the Royal at eight?'

Disappointment flickered in her eyes; he almost laughed. No way, missy, I'm not having dinner with you in more intimate circumstances, he thought.

'Sure, I'll see you then.' She turned and walked away.

Lucas closed the door. Hopefully, he had imagined the tingles and the glances. He decided there was nothing to worry about, other than how soon he could get Maggie Shaunessy into his bed. Feeling happier, he went into the kitchen to begin dinner.

CHAPTER TWELVE

Maggie stood in front of her cupboard and considered what to wear for dinner with Lucas. Her first choice was something from the sexier end of her wardrobe, wanting to impress Lucas physically as much as he impressed her, but then she wasn't sure that was such a good idea for a dinner at which she was playing spy.

In the end, she opted for simple high-waisted pants and suede, low-wedge shoes – and a fitted red top with a neckline just low enough. She pulled her hair up in a boring ponytail, but put her best perfume in the hollow behind her ears.

She walked out into the kitchen and pirouetted for her mother. 'How do I look?'

'Like Mata Hari.' Siobhan rolled her eyes. 'I can't believe I'm with your father on this. I don't think you should go until we know more about him.'

'Dad will be in the restaurant, so I'll be safe enough and, if he is working for the Flahertys, he won't be game to do anything in public. If he isn't, then he probably doesn't want to hurt me.'

'Ah, here you are.' John strode into the room. 'Good news. Peter's friend has come through. As expected, there's no record of a Lucas Valeroso, or of a man matching his description, being banished. Lucas does not know that he's gadda.'

'There, you see?' Maggie appealed to her mother, while her excitement grew. It appeared that Lucas wasn't one of the bad guys, and that meant she could consider other possibilities, such as just how good he might really be.

Siobhan rolled her eyes again but said no more, and Maggie walked down the hallway toward the front door, grabbing the car keys from the hall table as she did.

As she stepped into the loungeroom, the phone rang. Her heart gave a thud. Surely Lucas wasn't calling to pull out of the dinner. 'I'll get it,' she called out and she picked up the receiver.

'Hello, Maggie speaking.'

'Margaret, darling, thank goodness I caught you.' Maggie almost dropped the phone when Sean's tones oozed into her ear.

'What are you doing?' She hissed. 'You're not allowed to call here. And why *would* you?'

'Hush, darling, it's OK. I'm working on the bardria to give us a dispensation, considering everything. But darling, I had to call. I have to warn you. There's this man. I met him on the plane, coming up to see you. His name's Lucas Valeroso, and he's gadda, but no one I know has ever heard of him. Darling, you have to be careful. Avoid him, he could well be dangerous.'

So, Sean didn't know who Lucas was. Did that mean Lucas wasn't part of the Purist plan? 'Yes.'

'Good girl,' Sean said. 'And don't you worry, we'll get this whole thing with the bardria sorted out and then you and I can explain things to your family together. They'll understand, once they see how happy we are. I'll go now, so you don't have to fret. I love you.' And then he hung up before she could even consider whether to respond.

Maggie put the phone down and walked slowly back to the kitchen. She sat down at the table and stared at her grandfather.

'Cushla, what is it?' He put his hand on hers.

'It was Sean. He knows about Lucas and he's talking about it. In Sclossin.'

'Bloody hell.' John got up and began to pace up and down the room. 'I'd hoped they hadn't actually touched on the flight. Damn.'

'Why damn?' Maggie said. 'This is a good thing. Sean said he doesn't know Lucas, none of his friends do. It means Lucas isn't part of whatever Sean and his father are doing.'

John stopped and looked at her, but his eyes weren't focussed. He blinked, and then smiled at her. 'You're right, Maggie. This is a good thing. It means all you need to try and work out tonight is whether Lucas knows he's gadda or not.'

When Maggie walked into the restaurant at the Royal, Lucas was waiting for her. He was dressed casually in a pair of slacks and a thin pullover that did great things for his chest. Good enough to eat, she thought. It certainly revived her spirits.

Lucas stood as she approached the table and his expression was controlled, which was disappointing.

She pulled out the chair opposite him and they sat at the same time. A waiter came over straight away, so

Maggie had something to do while she considered how to start the conversation.

'White wine, thanks,' she said with a smile. Then she looked across the table to see Lucas lift a glass of water to his mouth. Great, he's a health nut, she thought. Well, I suppose you don't look that good just from teaching physics. 'And I'll have a Thai chicken salad.' There, that should make him a little more impressed with her.

'Steak, rare, with salad, hold the fries,' he told the waiter. Then he looked at Maggie. 'So, you wanted to pick my brain?'

Oh shit, Maggie thought. She needed to get her thoughts in order. 'I'm interested in how you got into physics, and what you're going to be working on here at Winton.' She poured herself a glass of water and hoped the wine would be there soon.

Lucas looked at her for a moment, as if judging her. Then he answered. 'Teleportation,' he said.

Maggie spat her water across the table. She stared at Lucas in horror. Did that mean he knew he was gadda, and he was joking with her, referring to the fictional equivalent of transferring? Or was the joke at his expense, that he was trying to invent a machine to do something he had the potential to do himself?

'I can see you're in the *it's impossible* school,' Lucas said.

'Um, no.' If the bardria ever found out about this, they'd not be so concerned about children's books. 'So why that?'

He shrugged. 'Well, when you've got free research time, you might as well go for the big things.'

'Bloody hell.' Maggie stared at him. 'That's ... how long have you been working on it?'

'Several years in my spare time. I'm looking forward to getting a proper crack at it now, though.'

The wine arrived and she took a sip, sighing as the cold tartness slid down her throat. 'Nothing like a cold drink on a hot day, wouldn't you say?' She smiled at Lucas and was pleased to see his eyes fixed on her lips.

'I can see I'm going to like it here,' he said, looking into her eyes. Disappointment filled her; there was no tell-tale heat there. 'I can't get over how hot this country is. Not that America isn't hot in places – New York can be stifling – but this whole place gives an impression of heat.'

'I know what you mean. I've just spent ten years in Ireland, and the only impression you get there is *cold*.' She gave a fake shiver. 'But then you get used to it and it just works for the place.'

'So you got your qualifications there?'

She nodded. 'NUI. I just completed my Master's degree.'

'Congratulations. Will you go onto your doctorate?

'Oh, I'm going to take a break from studying.' Please don't ask why, she thought, taking another sip. 'So, didn't I read once about some scientists here in Oz working on teleportation?'

'I'm looking forward to getting in touch with them to see where they're up to,' Lucas said. 'I'm surprised by your interest. I wouldn't have thought there was much call for physics in the lower grades.'

Shit, crap, damn. 'I'm, um, considering moving up into high school and I can't quite decide between teaching English or science. I was quite good at science myself, and I've always maintained an interest.'

'Not surprising, considering who your grandfather is.'

She nodded, glad the on-the-spot lie had managed to work so well. 'Maybe I could come and have a look at your lab, see how a real scientist works to help me make up my mind?' Under the table, she crossed her fingers. If he bought it, she'd have what her grandfather wanted — good access to Lucas.

'Sure. I wanted to ask you a few things anyway, as the chancellor's PA.'

Maggie smiled at him as their dinner arrived. Things were going extremely well, she thought.

'So, when does the school year start for you?'

She blinked, then frowned. 'It depends on how quickly I hear about my registration. Probably after Easter.'

'So your decision to move back to Australia was a sudden one, was it?'

She recalled her grandfather's suggested excuse. 'Bad break-up.' She put some of the salad into her mouth and almost sighed as the spices danced over her tongue.

'You must have been upset when your boyfriend followed you, then.'

Maggie gulped, the food went down the wrong way and there followed a terrible moment of coughing and choking. Lucas got up and she waved him away as she got herself under control. He sat down, watching her with concern as she picked up the wine and took a large swig to wash down the mouthful.

'Sorry about that,' she finally said with a weak smile. 'So, you were saying something about your work?'

'Actually, I asked if you were upset when Sean Flaherty followed you here from Ireland.'

No way! I'm supposed to be the interrogator! She decided to come out all guns blazing. 'He is not my boyfriend, just a mistake that refuses to go away. But he will, you better believe that.'

Lucas smiled, and her breath caught in her throat. 'Oh, I believe you, and I'm glad to hear it,' he said.

Maggie's heart began to pound at a million miles an hour. Oh star above, she thought, I'm in big trouble.

Lucas let himself into his apartment, pleased with how the evening had gone. He was quite convinced that Maggie meant it when she said that Sean Flaherty wasn't in her life any more.

That didn't explain the physical reaction he'd had to both of them and to John O'Hara, but overall, things were coming along nicely. Certainly, the buzz between him and Maggie was growing each time they met. He hoped he'd solve the mystery soon, and for the good. He'd never had an instant connection with a woman like this before, and he wanted to see where it led.

Tomorrow would be orientation and, even though he wasn't teaching, thinking about it had his mind racing. There was something about the energy of a busy university campus that fired him up.

He was thinking about going over to his lab for a couple of hours before bed when the phone rang. He picked it up.

'Lucas Valeroso.'

'Lucas, darling, guess who?'

Lucas almost dropped the phone. How the hell had she found him? 'What do you want?'

Holly's brittle laugh scratched in his ear. 'I wanted to see how you were settling in. I've always loved the idea of Australia, all those beaches and blue skies and bronzed lifesavers, like a movie. How is it?'

'Hot, dry and not a beach to be seen. Just lots of trees and cows and flies.' There, he thought. Hopefully that would turn her off.

She laughed again, rasping over his ragged nerves. 'Oh Lucas, you funny you. We tried to get hold of Glenn Rainman at that place you mentioned, but he said he couldn't help. You scientists really are a bunch of tightasses, aren't you?'

Lucas rolled his eyes. 'Goodbye, Holly.'

'Don't hang up on me, Lucas.' Holly's voice hardened. 'I've got your chancellor's number. John O'Hara. He sounds just darling on his phone message.'

Lucas smiled. Finally. 'Go ahead, Holly. Call him. He already knows, and he doesn't care.'

'Really? Did you tell him? Well, good for you, Lucas. Although I have to wonder if you told him the whole story.'

'He knows the facts, Holly. He's seen the police reports.'

'Ah, so he only knows about the things that you were charged with.'

Lucas frowned. Sure, there had been some stuff he'd gotten away with, but it was nothing compared to the carjacking that had landed him in juvie. 'What the hell are you talking about, Holly?'

'About that terrible night, Lucas. You remember. You'd gotten out of juvie, we were celebrating, we got a bit drunk, in a fight, you picked up a knife ...'

'Bullshit. I don't drink, Holly. It didn't happen.'

'Will your precious professor believe that? Especially when I show him the scar?'

A chill rolled over him. 'What scar?' he whispered.

'On my stomach. The doctors said I was lucky — an inch either way and it would have hit something important and I would have died. Luckily for me, it was just an inconvenience more than anything else. It has since proved very useful.'

Nausea rose in his throat. 'Fuck.'

'I didn't report it because I loved you, and I hoped that we could get over it. But then you abandoned me, and it's taken me all this time to track you down.'

Every word of the lie was like a knife piercing his heart. He could easily see how someone would believe the story. O'Hara didn't mind his childhood mistakes, but this? This was too much for any man to stomach.

'What do you want, Holly?'

'Another name, Lucas.'

'Jesus. Just a moment.' He put the phone down and fired up his computer. He got online, Googled a few ideas and then came back to her. 'Why don't you try one of the Japanese firms? Okyo Pan at Risctronic has a good reputation.' He read out the phone number he'd got from the web page.

'Thank you, Lucas, you're so helpful.' Holly was now purring. 'And thank you too for the money. James isn't sure it's enough, but I know you'll help if we need more. Bye!'

Lucas hung up the phone, feeling physically ill. There had to be a way he could escape her. He closed his eyes and hoped the answer would come soon.

CHAPTER THIRTEEN

Lucas hadn't been aware that time was passing until he heard a knock on the door and looked up to see Maggie's face. He checked his watch. Five already. She'd come by earlier that day to check on his requirements, but he'd been consumed by his experiment and asked her to come back later. He signalled for her to come in and bent back over the platform, positioning the edges to join them.

He was grateful that she didn't immediately start chatting, but waited while he concentrated on what he was doing. It gave him the opportunity to go over his plans once more. It had been a week since that first date and tonight, he intended to get a little closer to Ms Shaunessy and see what else he could work out.

He clamped the two pieces of metal in place to solder them together, then stood and turned around to acknowledge her. As he did, the sweetness of her perfume struck him, as it had that morning. It wasn't overpowering — more like a manifestation of her essence.

She'd changed her clothes. Then, she'd been wearing a university-appropriate straight skirt, with a floral blouse and high-heeled wedges that made her legs look fantastic. Now, she was in a floor-length sun dress with tiny straps. Her hair was pulled back from her face and the ends still dripped, as though she'd just been for a swim.

She looked fresh and summery and altogether delicious.

'Finished your list?' She smiled.

'No.' Lucas's smile was sheepish. 'Sorry, I got a bit carried away with the experiment.'

'No problem. We can finish it together.' She went over and pulled a stool out.

Lucas grabbed the notes he'd already made and then joined her. It started as a general conversation on items for his laboratory, and turned into a discussion on science texts.

'I'm sure they're the same texts I was studying in high school,' Maggie said as she explained the paperwork she'd been doing for her grandfather. 'Have you got any ideas for something more appropriate?'

'A friend of mine started up a company a few years ago to publish interesting and easily updatable science texts,' Lucas said. 'I can give you his web address, if you like.'

'Please. I mean, the kids deserve better, don't you think?'

'I'm surprised your grandfather let things get that bad. He's struck me as being very capable.'

'At some things, yes. At others, not so much. He's going to have to find someone to replace me when I start work, because he can't let things go on like this. Now, another question for you. Did your descent into the world of physics today mean you missed lunch?'

On cue, his stomach rumbled. She laughed. 'Agreed, Dr Valeroso's intestines. It's been too long since I ate as well. You aren't one of those irresponsible scientists who run themselves into the ground, never eating or sleeping, are you?'

Lucas wiped the back of his hand across his forehead and acknowledged he was beat. 'I learnt a long time ago that you need a strong, healthy body to get anywhere in this life.' He reached up and stretched, then bent down and put his hands on the floor, his head on his knees.

'Impressive.' He could hear the smile in her voice. 'Can you twist yourself like a pretzel?'

'Only after a bottle of bourbon.' He straightened up and looked at her. 'I take it you enjoy a healthy lifestyle yourself.'

'I'm not sure enjoy is the right word. I'd like nothing more than to live my life sitting on a sofa, watching daytime soaps and eating chips and potato scallops. Tell you what: how about you come and have dinner at our place? Grandpa will have made plenty of food, and you can tell me how you manage to be both healthy and a genius physicist.'

'Gee, no one told me it was supposed to be hard. Dinner sounds good, though,' As did a sojourn into the inner sanctum of the O'Haras.

They tidied up, or rather Maggie watched him tidy up. 'I'm willing to bet those scabby-looking piles are in rather specific places and misplacing one would cause a worldwide catastrophe,' she said. He lifted an eyebrow and she grinned. 'Grandpa is exactly the same.'

He smiled and then pulled the door open. 'After you.'

They walked up the hill, through the olive grove. There was no one in the kitchen but a pot of stew was gently simmering and the smell of freshly baked bread set his mouth watering.

'Take a seat and I'll serve up. What do you want to drink?' Maggie began to bustle around the kitchen.

'Water, thanks. Mind if I wash my hands?'

'Go ahead. There's soap at the sink.' As Lucas washed and sat down, Maggie ladled the stew into two large bowls. Then she took some loaves from the oven and brought them over to the table. Lucas took hold of one and broke it apart, steam rising from the interior. He couldn't remember anything smelling this good.

Maggie put a glass of water in front of him and sat down across the table. He looked up and watched her lift a glass of white wine to her mouth. 'Very healthy of you.'

'A glass of wine each day is supposed to be good for you.'

'I'm sure that's red wine.'

She shrugged. 'That's what Mum said, so I started putting red food colouring in it. She soon shut up.'

Lucas laughed. 'Your grandfather's blackmailing me into going to see her tomorrow for a check-up.' Something he wasn't too upset about. It would be interesting to see if he had the same reaction to her touch as he did her father and daughter's.

'I can assure you, her check-ups are generally quite gentle. Unless you're a hypochondriac.'

'We should get on just fine, then.'

'Tell her about the teleporter. You'll bore her to tears and she'll have you out of there quick smart.

Mum doesn't have a great deal of time for anything that isn't alive.'

Lucas stuck his fork into the stew and lifted a piece of lamb, putting it into his mouth. It melted on his tongue, the spices and gravy sheer perfection.

He looked at Maggie. Even though she was sitting, a normal woman eating a normal meal, she seemed lit from within.

Margaret smiled before forking some of her stew into her mouth. A little of the juice dribbled down her chin and Lucas turned away, telling himself he didn't want to lick it.

Maggie picked up her wine glass, swishing the last of its contents around. 'How did you get into physics?'

Lucas felt his back stiffen and forced himself to relax. 'The usual story, I guess. Fantastic teacher in high school.'

Luckily, she didn't question any further but nodded her head. 'I'd imagine the ranks of the scientific community would be severely thinned if it weren't for inspirational high school science teachers.' Then she caught sight of something over his shoulder and frowned. 'Excuse me for a moment.'

Before he could reply, she stood and walked over to the large glass doors that led onto the terrace. He turned and watched over his shoulder: there was a tall man outside. He watched the man bend to whisper something in Maggie's ear and wrap his hand around her arm.

Lucas stood, picked up his coat and left via the front of the house. Damn, he thought as he made his way down the hill. They had been making some great headway. He needed to find out more about her background, about the relationship with Flaherty, to judge what was going on. He was upset about missing out on more information, he told himself. Not the fact she could right now be making out with some local Adonis.

CHAPTER FOURTEEN

Maggie walked through the university on her way to her father's, enjoying the soft breeze that tickled away the worst of the day's heat. Her body still hadn't fully adjusted to the sudden move from winter to summer, and from time to time all she could do was lie in the air-conditioning and curse herself for the stupid story.

She rounded the science block and stopped when she saw a tall man with dark hair step out of the door. Her heart thudded and she smiled ruefully. She'd been disappointed when, after getting rid of Scott and his determination to take her out, she'd gone back inside to find Lucas gone.

That had been two nights ago. Time to find out what had happened and whether she'd somehow ruined things with him.

'Lucas.' She sped up.

He stopped and turned around, the setting sun painting his face in gold. 'Maggie.'

She stopped in front of him. 'You left awfully suddenly the other night.'

He shrugged. 'You seemed occupied. I didn't want to interrupt.'

'Scott was the one interrupting, not you.' She waggled her finger. 'Never walk out on me again, understand?'

He smiled, and her heart fluttered again. 'I won't. I swear.'

'Good. Now, I'm going to have dinner with my father, but I think you should at least walk me to the uni gates. As punishment for abandoning me.'

'A very sweet punishment, I think.' He hooked his elbow, inviting her to wind her arm through his.

He was right, Maggie thought as she put her hand on his forearm and they started to walk across the lawn. Walking arm in arm at sunset with a man you find very attractive is sweet. And hella sexy too.

She looked toward the administration block, saw a light in one of the upstairs windows and sighed. Her grandfather was still at work. 'Doesn't he ever stop working?'

Lucas looked up and shrugged. 'It'd be a big job, running a university.'

'He won't be in any condition to run it if he works himself into the ground.' Maggie changed direction, heading toward the admin building. She wasn't leaving until Grandpa went home.

Then she noticed a shadow pass in front of the window. A shadow that was much too large to be her grandfather's. She quickened her step.

The front door was locked, but a simple touch of her power had it swinging open. She marched across the tiled entrance way and up the wooden staircase. At the top, she turned to walk down the corridor. A blue light flashed in her grandfather's office and she recognised it instantly. Grandpa was using his power full-bore and he would only do that at the university if he were in danger. 'Grandpa.' She ran down the corridor and stopped in the open doorway.

A huge beast towered over her grandfather. She recognised it as a fuiparra, a medium-level beast that was even stronger than its size warranted. It was seven feet tall, slender and whiplike, with a pointed chin, nose and teeth. Its skin was grey with an oily sheen, and pulled tight over the long muscles in its thighs and arms. A sour smell of over-boiled cabbage wafted from the room. As she watched, a thin extension of an arm flicked out, lashing her grandfather and, thanks to the burst of power behind it, sending him flying across the room, crashing into a bookcase. Heavy texts cascaded down on the crumpled old man.

She stepped into the office, lifted her hands and sent a bolt of power, an energetic dark pink, toward the creature. The power hit the fuiparra and sent it sideways, crashing into the wall. The creature saw her and screamed, the sound almost splitting her eardrums, before moving toward her.

She sent another bolt, this time trying to hold the creature. For a moment, it halted. She took advantage of the reprieve to look at her grandfather. He wasn't moving. Blood dripped down from a wound in the side of his face and his arm wasn't straight where it should have been.

How could that have happened? He was sixth order; taking care of a fuiparra, while challenging, shouldn't have been a major problem. Had the creature surprised him and managed to injure him before he was ready to fight back?

Her concentration wavered, and the fuiparra pushed through her hold and continued toward her.

She gulped. As a second level gadda, she didn't have the skills to fight a beast this powerful. She prepared to send power out to hold it again, but the fuiparra lifted one arm and swung at her. She flew through the air, back out the door and crashed into the wall on the other side of the hall before hitting the floor.

Pain rocked through her and she quickly sent her power through her body, healing the minor bruises and nerve damage the fall had caused. For a moment, she was dazed and then she shook her head. She stood and moved over to the door and then stopped in shock. Lucas was taking on the beast, wielding a lamp in one hand and one of her grandfather's awards in the other. He stabbed at the creature with one hand, slashed with the other, moving gracefully around his opponent. The fuiparra seemed unsure how to handle this unique form of attack and rather than whipping at Lucas was trying to push him away.

Maggie stepped forward, gathered her power into the strongest hold she could muster and fired it at the fuiparra. The beast screamed, but she held it.

'Check Grandpa,' she yelled at Lucas, then mentally called for her mother. Lucas didn't listen and used the hold Maggie had to attack the beast frenetically. The fuiparra screamed and pushed against Maggie's power and she could feel the edges fraying.

'Leave it alone, Lucas,' she shouted. 'I can't hold it while you're upsetting it.'

Then a stream of pale lavender power flashed past her shoulder and struck the fuiparra, pushing it back and pinning it against the wall. 'Get out of the way, Lucas,' Siobhan shouted as she came to stand next to Maggie.

Maggie was miffed that he instantly obeyed her mother. Siobhan pulled back one hand, gave it a whirl and then sent a beating pulse of power at the creature. The fuiparra roared and pushed away from the wall, breaking through the hold and staggering toward the two women.

'Shit,' Siobhan said before reinforcing the hold and pushing the fuiparra back against the wall. 'That should have worked.'

Maggie quickly looked over at her grandfather. He hadn't moved, hadn't regained consciousness. Her mind battled with the concept that her grandfather had failed. She shook her head to focus on the situation at hand. 'What do we do now?'

The fuiparra struggled and started to move slowly from the wall, slowly against their power, slowly breaking through. They only had seconds.

'Lucas,' her mother shouted. 'The head, that's where it's most vulnerable.'

Lucas nodded, dropped the lamp, held the award in two hands and lifted it high above his own head. Then he brought it crashing down upon the fuiparra.

The creature stilled and Maggie swore an expression of astonishment flickered over its features. Then it collapsed onto the floor.

Lucas knelt down next to it, grabbing the lamp as he did so. 'Check on John,' he said as he began to use the lamp's cord to tie up the fuiparra.

Maggie and Siobhan pulled back their power. Siobhan turned, gasped and rushed over to her father.

Maggie stood in the middle of the trashed office, panting, unable to think. Lucas stood and walked over to her. He put his hands on her shoulders and gave her a gentle shake. She focussed what little attention she could muster on him.

'Are you OK? That was quite a flight you took out into the hall,' he said.

Maggie blinked and then she smiled. 'I'm fine. And I guess you have more pressing questions.'

Lucas released her and took a step back. He narrowed his eyes. 'I must be going mad. I thought I saw you using magic.'

'Not magic. Power.' Then a groan caught her attention. She turned and saw that her grandfather was sitting up, with her mother's help. 'Grandpa.' She rushed over and knelt down next to him. 'Are you all right?'

'I'm fine,' he said, shaking his head. 'Just fine.'

'I've taken care of the worst of the damage,' Siobhan said, with a nod that said it wasn't the whole truth. 'But I've summoned the Heasimir and the Sabhamir.'

John groaned. 'You shouldn't have done that, Shevvy,' he said, resting his head in his hands.

'Are you mad, old man? You have to stop trying to save the world yourself,' Siobhan said.

Maggie felt a pressure in the air and turned as the Sabhamir and Heasimir appeared. She started to bow, but then noticed the pallor in Lucas's face. He was staring at the two gadma, and his body was trembling.

Maggie went over and touched his hand. 'It's OK,' she said softly. 'We'll explain everything. It all makes sense, you'll see.'

He looked down at her and she couldn't tell if her words were registering. She guided him to a chair, pushing off some debris before pushing him onto it, then she turned to greet the gadma. Like it or not, it appeared that Lucas Valeroso was about to find out all about the gadda.

Lucas sat and looked at the disaster that was now John O'Hara's office. Nearly every bookcase and shelf in the room had been emptied of objects and books; awards, statues and piles of paper were strewn across the floor. On the top of John's desk he could see a splash of blood.

Adrenalin drained from him. He looked down at the strange creature lying on the floor. He had never seen anything like it in his life. It was slender, pale, limp and seemed quite peaceful. But he'd hit it, felt its strength, seen it lift both Maggie and John O'Hara with a flick of its whip-like hands and send them flying.

And Maggie and her mother had been holding it with some form of energy coming from their hands.

Lucas turned his attention to where Maggie was greeting the two strangers who had just appeared from nowhere. One was a tall, slender man, dressed from head to foot in black – black trousers, black shirt, black jumper, black shoes. He even had black hair. The other was a woman wearing a long white robe.

The woman simply nodded to acknowledge Maggie's greeting. She was beautiful, with ruby red lips and a cascade of shining white-gold hair. But she had an aura of coldness. The woman turned and made her way over to John and Siobhan and crouched down next to them.

The man shook Maggie's hand with a small smile twisting his lips, a smile that twisted something in Lucas's gut.

The guy started to turn toward the creature but stopped when he caught sight of Lucas. Looking into the other man's black eyes, Lucas was swept with the knowledge that this man was power. Dangerous. That he shouldn't be messed with.

'Who is this?' His voice was deep but flowed like a smooth melody.

'This is Lucas Valeroso.' The man frowned, then he lifted his hand and Lucas had a sensation of stillness washing over him.

With the next blink, Maggie was over by the window, pouring what appeared to be whiskey into four glasses. John was sitting at his desk, Siobhan perched on the edge and both were watching him. The two strangers, and the beast, were gone.

'How do you feel?' Siobhan said.

Lucas shook his head. 'Like I'm in a movie. Where did they go?'

'No after-effects, then.' O'Hara smiled. 'Now, let's all have a drink, and we'll explain everything to you.'

Maggie walked toward him, two glasses in her hand. Maybe she really was a goddess, as well as looking like one. But then he pushed that aside. There would be a rational explanation for this. There had to be.

'Here.' She smiled down at him as she held out a glass. 'You look a little pale. Are you sure you're OK?'

'Sure. I mean, I battle imaginary beasts oh, every second day at least.' He looked at the carpet, where moments before the creature had lain, then at her again. She didn't seem rattled. 'Who are you, Buffy?'

She smiled. 'Did that look like a vampire?' She sat down next to him and took a sip from her own snifter.

'Then what was it?' Lucas's mind prepared to organise the information.

'That was a fuiparra.' O'Hara answered the question. 'It is a creature of power, conjured by someone who doesn't like me.'

'Conjured.' Lucas's mind fought to stay open. 'You mean magic?'

'That is what humans call it,' O'Hara agreed, sipping on his whiskey.

'Humans?' None of this made any sense.

Maggie sighed. 'I'll explain. You're just confusing him more.' She turned to Lucas. 'You've been brought up believing that Earth is inhabited by humans alone. But there are also the gadda, who came from other ancestors. The gadda appear human in every way, except for access to a well of power. Some have a little, some have a lot, but all gadda are trained to access and control this energy. We can then –'

'We?' Lucas leant forward in his seat. 'You think you are one of these gadda?'

'I don't think, I know,' Maggie said with admirable calmness. She sat next to him, in the office of the chancellor of Winton University, perfect as always, spinning this implausible story with aplomb, while he felt like the world had started spinning on a different axis. 'You witnessed us using that energy tonight. That energy created the fuiparra. And it was that energy that brought the Sabhamir and the Heasimir here from Ireland in a matter of seconds.'

The implication of that hit him immediately. 'Teleportation,' he said softly.

She nodded. 'We've already got it. But it would be useful for humans, so don't give up on finding a way to give it to them.'

'And they've gone back to Ireland? With the, what did you call it, fuiparra?'

'The Sabhamir put a stillness resolution on you, so you couldn't witness what happened, just in case.' Maggie's comforting smile became a little strained and Lucas wondered what had happened while he was out of it. 'Don't worry, it hasn't hurt you or anything.'

Lucas's thinking was muddied, slow, something that had never happened to him before. 'I don't understand,' he muttered.

Maggie smiled at Lucas. 'You should go home, have a good sleep. When you're ready, call us and we'll talk.' She laid a hand on his shoulder and her warmth and concern soaked into him.

He suddenly felt very, very tired. 'You're right.' He stood and looked down at her.

'It will be all right, Lucas. Just give yourself time.'

He nodded, bowed his head in farewell to the chancellor and then went home.

CHAPTER FIFTEEN

The moment Lucas left the room, Maggie dropped the calm act. 'Bloody hell.' She drained her whiskey.

'My thoughts exactly.' John held his empty glass up to Siobhan. 'Another, please, Shevvy.'

'No,' she said. 'You went through quite a bit of trauma tonight, Dad. No more drink until we know for certain that you're OK.'

'I'm fine. More than fine. Fit as a fiddle.'

'Except you can't move your legs,' Siobhan said, taking the glass from him.

Maggie stared at her grandfather. He'd always been indefatigable – unbeatable. And for a fuiparra to have caused him so much pain ... it didn't seem possible. But then, as the Sabhamir had said, no one was safe from the use of power. He should know – he'd inherited his title and position from his father, who had been killed by a stupid mistake.

'Temporary problem. I can't believe I was outsmarted by a fuiparra. My ego is bruised, my girls, but it will recover. No, it's Lucas we need to worry about. I was hoping the bardria wouldn't find out about him yet, that we'd have more time with him.'

'Yes, about that,' Siobhan said. 'I thought that you had agreed to tell the bardria about Lucas.'

'Got busy,' John said. Siobhan snorted. 'I just thought —'

'With all the focus on this family, did you really think it would be a smart thing to hide the presence of an unknown gadda from the bardria?'

'They still wouldn't know if you hadn't over-reacted and summoned the guardians.'

Maggie didn't think her mother's actions had been an over-reaction. She thought back on the moment the Sabhamir had realised Lucas wasn't human.

After freezing him, the protector of the gadda had walked over and touched Lucas. Then he'd turned and frowned at her.

'Please tell me you haven't touched him yet, that you don't know he's gadda.'

Maggie had frowned. 'Well, yes. Didn't —' She stopped, realising before she said the words that her grandfather hadn't told anyone about Lucas.

The Sabhamir frowned over his shoulder at John, then looked back at Lucas. 'What did you say his name was?'

'Lucas Valeroso. Don't you recognise him?'

The Sabhamir shook his head. He placed his hand on Lucas's shoulder. 'His essence isn't instantly recognisable. There are hints of various families, which I can probably tease out with some experimentation, but at this moment I can safely say that Lucas Valeroso is unknown to the gadda bardria.'

Maggie came round to stand next to the Sabhamir. 'He doesn't know about us. I'd stake real money on that. He was surprised by the fuiparra, surprised by what Mum and I were doing and he attacked it in a human way. Could he be from one of the lost families?'

Centuries earlier, when the original six formed the rules and structure of gadda society, a group of families hadn't agreed with the plans and had left. Nothing had been heard of them for so long that most gadda thought they were a myth.

'I don't know.' The Sabhamir studied Lucas a bit longer, then shook his head. 'I'll think on it. Now, let's look at this fuiparra.' He walked over and knelt beside it. He put his hand on the creature and instantly frowned. He looked up at Maggie. 'Tell me what happened.'

'I didn't see it arrive. I was coming to fetch Grandpa home and I noticed he was using his power. By the time I got here, the fuiparra had beaten him senseless.' Maggie looked over her shoulder, to reassure herself that her grandfather was fine. She quickly recounted the rest of the attack to the Sabhamir.

He nodded, stood and walked over to where John was attempting to wave away the ministrations of his daughter.

'I'm fine, I tell you,' he grumbled. 'I don't need nursemaids, that's for certain.'

'Then stand up,' Siobhan said in the practical tone healers adopted with their own families. John scowled at her and Maggie rushed across the room.

'Grandpa?' Something was wrong. Her grandfather was still just sitting by the bookcase, his legs stretched out in front of him.

The Heasimir delivered the news in a deadpan voice. 'John O'Hara has damaged his back in the fight with the fuiparra, and as a result has no feeling or motion in his legs.' She looked at John. 'I must take you back to the healers' wing.'

Maggie nodded. A wing of the gadda bardria building was set aside for the most difficult cases of healing. Her grandfather's injury certainly warranted admittance there.

John shook his head. 'I can't just up and go to Sclossin for god knows how long. How would we explain my absence to the university and town, especially at the beginning of the teaching year? Besides, it's just a temporary glitch. No, Siobhan can look after me and summon you if I get beyond the pale.' He crossed his arms over his chest and glared up at the Heasimir.

Maggie shook her head. Once her grandfather's stubbornness kicked in, there was no changing his mind.

'How will you explain your injury if you remain?' the Sabhamir asked.

'I'll be right as rain tomorrow, and if not I'll just sit in bed and tell people I've got a bit of a cold. Humans expect this sort of stuff at my age. I can still see them, still do my work, so it won't be questioned.'

'And if you don't get better in a day or two, if this is a permanent injury?'

'I had a stroke or something. Look, it's my choice and I'm not going. Now, get me over to that chair.' He pointed to his office chair.

'Dad, at the very least we should get you home,' Siobhan said.

'I'm not leaving until Lucas is released and I know he's OK.' John quirked an eyebrow at the Sabhamir.

The gadma looked at the old man for a moment, then lifted his hand. John rose in the air; his legs remained stuck out from his body at a ninety degree angle. The Sabhamir drifted him across the room and settled him in the chair behind his desk. 'Better?'

John used his arms to squirm into position and then nodded. 'Much better, thank you.'

'In that case, you can tell me what happened.' The Sabhamir crossed his arms over his chest.

'I was going over the monthly budgets, and I had some music playing.' John nodded to one corner, where a smashed CD player lay among the ruins of a table. 'I didn't hear a thing, wasn't aware of anything unusual until the whip hit the side of my head. I slumped onto the table and it picked me up and hurled me against the wall. I got to my feet and tried to fight back, but I took a couple more good hits and then I succumbed. I don't know the rest.'

Maggie's heart skipped a beat. For all his bravado, her grandfather was suffering. She hoped that he was right, that this was just a knock to his spine and tomorrow he'd be fine. Please, god, goddess, whoever, she thought.

'I've heard Maggie's version. Siobhan, what can you tell me?' the Sabhamir said.

Siobhan explained how Maggie had summoned her and then told of the few brief moments she had been involved, including the failure of the spell she had used.

'That's no surprise, Siobhan. The amount of power that was floating around this room at that point would have been like fuel for the fuiparra. Few could have made that spell work.' The Sabhamir tapped his chin for a moment. 'This makes my discovery all the more interesting. It would seem on first inspection that the fuiparra was created from your essence, John.'

'Impossible.' The weariness and despair dropped from him and his eyes glittered. Maggie thought he'd be on his feet and confronting the Sabhamir if he could. 'I expended a great deal of power in controlling it, you must be feeling that.'

'I can feel that, as I can feel Margaret's and Siobhan's power, yet below that, at the core, is your essence.'

'Never.' John shook his head so viciously that Maggie was scared he'd give himself a headache. 'I would never do this, and why the hell would I send it to attack myself?'

'There's another essence as well, one that I'm a little surprised to find here – Oswald Flaherty's.'

'What?' Maggie realised she had screeched before the Sabhamir frowned at her.

'I would hazard a guess that someone has tried to make this look like you made it and were trying to disguise it as a creation of Oswald Flaherty.' The Sabhamir walked over to the fuiparra, knelt and touched it again. 'It's very clumsily done.'

'Let me see that.' The Heasimir finally spoke. She strode forward and knelt on the other side of the fuiparra, touching it herself. Maggie moved closer, wondering how the healer of the gadda thought she could know better than the protector did.

A brief frown crossed the white brow, then the Heasimir looked at the Sabhamir. 'You are correct.' Her mouth was tight.

Maggie looked at the Sabhamir and saw a brief smile touch his lips. 'I thank you for your confirmation, Heasimir.'

Maggie watched the two for a moment. They were the two most powerful gadda alive, and it seemed they hated each other. She was sure that couldn't be a good thing.

'Could it have something to do with –' The Heasimir stopped suddenly and looked at the O'Haras. It was obvious to Maggie that she'd been about to say something.

'Perhaps,' the Sabhamir said calmly, as if he didn't notice that she had cut off her words. He moved over, lifted the fuiparra in his arms and stood. 'I will study the creature back in Sclossin. Expect a report from me in a day or two. And John, next time, call me rather than try to deal with things yourself.'

'I am perfectly capable of taking care of little problems like this,' O'Hara said.

The Sabhamir actually winked at Maggie before he continued. 'As for him ...' He nodded at Lucas. 'I'd take him with me, if his sudden disappearance from Winton wouldn't be an issue. As it is, his presence and lack of identity will be reported to the bardria. Be prepared to hear from them.' Then he disappeared.

'Margaret, I need to check you.' The Heasimir moved toward her. Maggie suffered the woman's touch, glad when she was finally given the all-clear. Then she went over and touched Lucas. She frowned for just a moment, turned, nodded her head to them all and left. The moment she was gone, Lucas was released.

Thinking back over it all, Maggie frowned at her grandfather. 'Is the Flaherty trying to set you up?'

John shook his head. 'He's a much more polished performer than this. No, someone appears to be trying to set us both up.'

'A common enemy?' Siobhan said. 'I wouldn't have thought that possible.'

'Neither would I.' John yawned. 'I'm too tired to think about this. Let's go home. The Sabhamir will bring us the answer soon enough.' He put his hands on the desk as if to push himself to his feet, and then stopped. He shook his head and then looked up at his family and there were tears in his eyes. 'It appears I need a bit of a hand, girls.'

'I'll go back to the house and get the car. Maggie, stay here with your grandfather.' Siobhan nodded but before she could transfer, there was a knock on the door.

Everyone frowned. 'Siobhan, go. Maggie, open the door.' John plastered a smile on his face, ready to greet whoever would come in. Siobhan transferred and Maggie crossed to the door and pulled it open, ready to delay whoever stood on the other side.

'Dad!' She stepped back and Peter walked into the room.

'I felt a disturbance.' He looked around. 'I see I was right. Are you two hurt?'

Maggie looked over her shoulder at her grandfather, who smiled. 'Just fine, Peter. Sit down, I'll tell you what's going on.' He gestured to Peter to find a seat among the broken furniture, which both he and Maggie did. Then John quickly explained what had happened. By the end, Peter was scowling.

'Oswald Flaherty wouldn't do something like this,'

he said. 'I know that the two of you have had your differences over the years, John, but he would never attack another gadda like this.'

John nodded. 'I agree, it isn't his usual method, but the Sabhamir was sure it was his essence.'

Peter scratched his chin. 'What did the Sabhamir say about Valeroso?'

'He's reporting his presence to the bardria,' Maggie said. Perhaps if they could convince the bardria that Lucas needed to stay here, all would be well. 'He didn't recognise him at all, or his essence, so his identity is a real mystery.'

'That's probably for the best,' Peter said. 'We really can't have rogue gadda just marching around the place unrecorded.'

'I doubt Lucas is a rogue,' John said. 'We'll have to wait and see what they decide to do about him. Now, is Maggie at your place tonight?'

'No, Grandpa.' Maggie sat forward on her chair. Mentally, she said to him, *'I have to come home with you, to look after you.'*

'It's your father's turn, Maggie,' John said.

Maggie frowned. 'I feel like a five-year-old, being shuffled from parent to parent,' she said aloud. *'Please, Grandpa, Dad would understand.'*

'Yes, I think Maggie should come with me tonight. I'm going to give Oswald a call, and I would like her opinion.'

'Just don't mention Valeroso,' John said. His expression remained calm, and he didn't respond to Maggie's mental urgings. She wanted to shake him; he wasn't going to give in.

'I had no intention of doing so. I want to know what Oswald will let slip. Come, Maggie.'

Maggie got up and gave her grandfather a quick kiss on the cheek. 'Are you sure?' she whispered.

'I'm fine, Mags. Go and spy on Flaherty for me.'

Maggie nodded and followed her father out of the building. They started to walk through the darkening streets.

'I'm guessing that Valeroso now knows about the gadda,' Peter said. 'How did he take the news?'

'Very well, I thought. I daresay I'll have to prove it to him tomorrow, but tonight he seemed to accept everything we had to say.'

'You took a risk, assuming he won't go running to the media about this.'

'What proof does he have? And he has his reputation as a scientist to protect. Besides, I really do think that Lucas Valeroso is one of the good guys.' Keep saying it and it might end up true, she thought to herself.

Time to change the subject. 'Dad, Grandpa wouldn't want you to know this, but the fuiparra really hurt him. He can't move his legs.'

Peter stopped and his mouth dropped open. 'You are joking me, right?'

Maggie shook her head. 'He's keeping up appearances, says it's just temporary, but I'm worried. I'm wondering –'

Peter nodded. 'Once we talk to Oswald, I'll walk you home.'

'Thanks, Dad. I'm sorry, but –'

'No need to explain, Margaret,' Peter cut in. 'I want to make sure he's all right myself.'

At his home, Peter wasted no time in taking her into his laboratory. Once inside, he opened up the star of gulagh, created a message ball and sent it to Oswald Flaherty. Within moments, Oswald replied, a green glow flooding the space between the star and the ceiling.

'Peter, wonderful to hear from you. I've just got in from a meeting at the bardria. The zoning problem we've been having between our properties looks like it will be settled in a matter of days.'

Peter signalled Maggie to silence before replying. 'I'm pleased to hear of that, Oswald. I've felt a little cut off from things, here in Australia.'

'Of course you have. The sooner we shut down mad experiments like O'Hara's, the better for us all.'

Maggie's jaw dropped open. She hadn't realised the Flaherty was so open in his opposition to her grandfather's work. Peter lifted a finger to his lips to remind her to remain silent. 'What do you suggest we do, to make that happen?'

'Continue as usual, Peter: periodically bringing the dangers of the situation to the bardria's attention. Your daughter helped a great deal in that respect.' Maggie's fists clenched by her side. 'The bardria will soon see sense, will call O'Hara back to Sclossin for good and we will be much safer.'

'I could do something a little more active, while I'm here.'

Maggie stared at her father. He was in league with Flaherty?

'No. Thank you for the offer, Peter, but I won't condone anything that breaks bardria regulations. You know that.'

Peter nodded. 'Well, you can't rely on any more help from Maggie, no matter how inadvertent. She's going to be keeping her nose out of trouble from here on.' Maggie rolled her eyes.

'Has she told you the good news? About her and Sean?'

Peter frowned. 'She told me that she and Sean got together before she left Sclossin. But Oswald, she has no intention of it going any further than that. If Sean has plans for a relationship with her, you'd best talk him out of them.'

'That isn't what Sean is saying, Peter.' Anger was clear in Flaherty's voice.

'I can't speak for Sean, Oswald, but I can speak for Maggie, and she's convinced it won't go anywhere. I'm as disappointed as you, for I would like a connection between our families, but we can't look for it with Sean and Maggie.'

'The girl is there in Winton, Peter. Of course she can't admit to loving Sean with her family around. But do not give up hope, because my son certainly won't. Now, I must go.' And the green stream of light disappeared.

'He's demented,' Maggie gasped. Then she scowled at her father. 'And what was with that "how can I help you destroy O'Hara" crap?'

'Why do you think I'm friends with Flaherty? It isn't for his conversation. I'm keeping an eye on his obsession with destroying your grandfather, so I can stop it if things get too bad, if I can. I'll keep working on Oswald, trying to make him understand he shouldn't encourage Sean. You need to get to bed.'

Maggie didn't have the energy to argue. They walked through the town and up the hill to the O'Hara house. There, the only light on was in the kitchen. Siobhan sat with her hands wrapped around a mug. She looked up as they walked in and managed a wan smile, even at Peter.

'I'm pleased to see you two,' she said. 'I just made a pot of coffee.'

'Maggie, you sit down, I'll make you a cup. Siobhan, can I refresh you?'

'Thank you, Peter.' She held the cup up to him. Maggie was pleased they were being polite, although she also noticed how meticulously they avoided touching each other as the mug was passed over.

'How's Grandpa?' Maggie sat down and rested her head on her mother's shoulder. Siobhan leant over and kissed her crown.

'Still saying it's no big deal, he'll be fine tomorrow morning. He's sleeping now. I put a little something in his drink so he should sleep away most of tomorrow too. But he's kidding himself. The Heasimir is extremely concerned; the damage to his spine, in both our opinions, appears to be substantial.'

Maggie shivered, and Siobhan shifted to put her arm around her shoulders. 'What if he never walks again?' Maggie whispered.

'Physically, we'll all adjust. Mentally, I'm more concerned. Dad's never been good at admitting he wasn't good at something.'

Peter came back to the table with three coffees. 'I'm here to help in any way I can, Siobhan.'

'I'm sure Dad will appreciate your assistance,' Siobhan said. They sat in silence for a while, sipping on their drinks.

Maggie tried to imagine a world where her grandfather couldn't walk. Here in the privacy of the house it wouldn't be such an issue – he could use his power to get around. But in the real world it would be a life of wheelchairs and frustration.

And her mother was right, that was the easy part of it all. John O'Hara was a very proud man. Accepting what had happened, how it had happened, was going to be the hardest part.

'What will we do about Valeroso?' Peter cut into her thoughts. 'I know John had dreams of teaching him here, but will that be possible, even if the bardria allow it?'

'Dad will still be capable of teaching Lucas, but whether he'll allow Lucas to see him this way is another matter,' Siobhan said.

'He'll be after answers tomorrow. Best to give them to him here,' Peter said. 'Maggie, you should go see him first thing in the morning.'

'Shit.' Siobhan shook her head. 'I've got a full roster tomorrow. Maggie can't deal with Lucas and look after Dad.'

'You said he would sleep most of the day. I can stay here with him,' Peter said. 'What time do you have to leave for work, Siobhan?'

'Seven. And Peter, thank you.' Another wan smile. Hope, Maggie thought. Not that they would get back together, but that they could be civil to each other.

'I'll be here about a quarter to so you can fill me in on what John will need. Now, both of you, go to bed and try to sleep.' He stood, nodded and then walked out the door.

Maggie snuggled against her mother, scared, tired, excited, and warmed by her father's care and concern. Siobhan kissed her head.

'Bed, Mags. For us both.'

Maggie nodded, stood and shuffled to her room. She stripped off her clothes and curled up in the sheets. She rested her fist against her cheek and closed her eyes. Faces flitted through her mind – her family, Lucas, Sean.

There was a Chinese curse – may you live in interesting times. These times certainly seemed cursed, and she couldn't help wondering how responsible for it she was.

It was some time before she went to sleep.

Lucas walked into his apartment but knew immediately that he wasn't going to gain any comfort from staying there or resting. When he was this agitated, there was only one thing that would work. He got changed into shorts and a T-shirt, pulled on his runners and hit the streets.

He ran down the main drag, through the town and onto the highway. He ran until his muscles burnt, his lungs were at their limit and his eyesight blurred. Then he stopped, panting, his mind finally clear.

Maggie and her family were members of a mysterious race called gadda, a race with magical powers. He waited for his intellect to reject the summation, but nothing happened. Unfortunately, the summation made a whole lot of sense.

He turned and started to walk back toward the town. There was still a lot to figure out. What was the story with the monster? And what happened in that office while that Saveloy guy had him on lockdown? Still many questions, and he was going to get the answers. Tomorrow.

CHAPTER SIXTEEN

Maggie had stepped out from the shade of the olive trees and was about to climb over the fence when she saw Lucas walking across the sporting fields toward her. She took a deep breath to calm herself. Even from hundreds of metres away, Lucas's tension was obvious in the strong stamp of his stride and the straightness of his spine.

He stopped on the other side of the fence, his expression blank. 'Ms Shaunessy.'

'Lucas.' She smiled. 'I was coming to see you. There's a lot we need to talk about.'

'There is.'

'Would you like to come up to the house?' He shook his head. 'OK, let it rip.'

'How many of you are there?'

The question surprised her. She had been prepared to have to prove to him that she wasn't human. She searched her mind for the answer. 'Around a million. We aren't the most prolific breeders on Earth. No one has more than two kids, and it's more common to just have one. Something about power gone awry a few centuries ago, I don't know why.'

'Do you all live and work as humans?'

'Ah, now that is a loaded question.' She smiled, hoping for a lightening of his expression. There was none. 'Some gadda are very much involved in human society, like my family. We believe that we should use our skills to help humans. It's the main reason Grandpa founded the university. Others keep their distance as much as any isolated minority can. In Ireland, there are entire villages of gadda and, in America, there is a group that have formed their own enclave and will admit none but gadda.'

'But you look human? Act human?'

'There are physiological differences, which mean we have to be careful not to end up in the human health care system. It's becoming more difficult, with technology and the development of genetic databases. Otherwise, we have the same needs as humans – we need to eat, sleep, have shelter, love and be loved.'

'So gadda society is just like human society?'

'Generally, yes. There are the haves and the have nots, although the differences are not as marked as in human society. We follow human laws, but we have special rules regarding the power and how it is to be used. These are created by the bardria, the gadda council, and policed by the guardians.'

'How is the bardria formed?'

Maggie decided his rapid-fire questioning was going to continue until he had satisfied his curiosity. 'Please, come up to the house,' she said. 'Grandpa's up there, along with my father. They can help answer your questions.' She waved her hand at the olives and smiled.

Lucas stared at her as if he hadn't understood a

word she had said. Then he nodded and climbed over the fence.

'You asked how the bardria was formed,' she said as they entered the cool of the shade. 'Well, the first one was made up of the first six families. They were the most powerful of the early gadda. Those six families still provide representatives to the bardria. As our numbers expanded, so did the size of the bardria. It now numbers twenty. They are lifetime appointments, elected by a majority of gadda. You can vote once you become eighteen, just as humans can.'

'So the bardria knows every gadda in existence.'

Maggie realised where his questions were headed. 'I think so. Although there are legends of the lost gadda, and no one knows who they are. That would explain why we didn't know you were gadda before now.'

His eyes widened. 'You think I'm gadda?'

She nodded. 'I felt it when we shook hands at the staff welcome. And what's more, you felt it in me.'

He looked down at her, then tipped his head back and began laughing. Maggie stepped away. Maybe Lucas wasn't going to be able to handle it. She was aware of a tingling in the air and realised his power was beginning to escape him. It would appear he did have access, but did he have control?

'Lucas, you need to calm down.' She looked around, wondering if the flow of energy was affecting anything in their surrounds.

He looked at her again and shook his head, grinning. 'No. It's not possible. An entire race of humanoids that no one knows about, a race that has magical powers? It's just not possible.'

Maggie frowned. 'You don't believe me?'

His smile disappeared and he sighed. As he spoke, the energy flow disappeared. 'Unfortunately, yes. I was trying to convince myself it's all a great joke, but it isn't, is it?'

Maggie walked over to him and put a hand on his arm. 'I know it's difficult to accept you are so different from everyone else, but there are plusses to the situation. Once you learn to unlock and then control your power, you will feel so much more alive and directed than you ever have before.'

He looked at her and she saw that he was calm again. 'How do you learn to control it?'

'There are exercises to access and gain control of your power. The lessons start when you're thirteen and usually take a year full time at the school in Sclossin. Then you are tested and, if you pass, you become a member of the first order. If you wish, you can remain first order forever, or you can move up the orders. Do you want me to tell you about them?' She half hoped he would say no. She didn't want him to lose control again.

'Yes please. Tell me everything. I await the knowledge that will, apparently, save me.'

She rolled her eyes but was pleased that his sense of humour had been restored. That was a good sign. They started to walk again. 'Well, first you need to know that once you reach first order, a female gadda is called a dath and a male gadda is called an oman. Once you become first order, you need to spend at least five years working on control of your power which you do yourself. There's no more formal education. Then you can sit another set of exams and if you pass those, become second order. Around ninety per cent of people who sit it become second order. Then it starts to become more difficult. After another five years, you can attempt the third order exams. Only about fifty per cent pass those. Once you are third order, you have a choice. You can continue up the normal levels, or opt to move to the gadma levels. Gadma are much more specialised practitioners of the power and only the strongest make it. The Sabhamir and the Heasimir, who you met last night, are third order gadma. That makes them two of the most powerful gadda alive.'

'Interesting.'

Maggie hid a smile. She could picture Lucas taking the gadma route. He seemed the type to choose the most challenging thing he could find. 'There's no time limit between the rest of the orders. You decide when you are ready to be tested and then you go before the bardria. There are three more levels to attain, whether you follow the normal path or the gadma path. Very few people ever reach sixth order, let alone third-order gadma.'

Lucas nodded. 'So, you're what, a third- or fourth-order dath, right?'

Maggie shook her head. 'Second order.'

'Why haven't you sat the third-order exam yet?'

Maggie laughed. 'I appreciate the fact you automatically assume I'm not third order because I failed the exam.'

'You, fail an exam?' Lucas waved his hand dismissively. 'So, why haven't you?'

'Because I don't qualify. I only became second order six months ago.'

A frown creased his forehead. 'I don't understand. According to what you said, you should easily qualify for third order. Even fourth.'

'If I had started my training at thirteen and had only taken five years to get to second order, that would be true, but I was almost eighteen when I began and no, I'm not going to tell you why. That story can wait until another day. And it took me nine years to get to second order because I was at uni and working at the same time. Any more questions?'

Lucas opened his mouth to speak but stopped as they reached the paved area around the house and Peter stepped from the sliding doors.

'I see you made it with no mishaps.' He smiled at Maggie and then nodded at Lucas. 'Peter Shaunessy. Pleased to finally meet you, Lucas. John is awake and looking forward to talking to you,' Peter said shaking Lucas's hand.

'I wouldn't want to disturb him,' Lucas said.

'He is well enough to talk, and discuss with you what should be done next. He is, however, still in bed so we'll try not to tire him out.'

Maggie's heart sank. If John was still in bed, then feeling was yet to return to his legs.

Peter led them through the house and into John's bedroom. Maggie quickly looked over her grandfather. The long sleep appeared to have done him good: there was colour in his cheeks and his eyes were bright. But his legs were straight and still under his duvet.

'*Grandpa?*'

'*Don't fret, my girl, it's just going to take a little longer than I had hoped. I'll be fine,*' John told her. Then he opened his mouth and addressed Lucas.

'Lucas my boy, I guess Maggie's told you a great deal about us all.'

'A great deal, and not nearly enough.'

John nodded. 'In time. First, there's something I need to check. Come, sit beside me.' He patted the bed next to his hip.

Lucas flicked a quick glance at Maggie before he did as he was asked. Maggie went to stand next to him. She felt she needed to protect someone, although exactly who and from what, she didn't know.

The old man put his hands on the young man's shoulders. He frowned with concentration for a moment, then smiled at Lucas. 'I'm very impressed with how well you've learnt to control your emotions over the years. I'll admit, I was a little concerned that what Maggie had to tell you would upset you so much that your power would explode out, but I see I needn't have been concerned. Nevertheless, I'd like to put a temporary block on you, since there is still a great deal to learn and some of it might upset you. Then, when we talk, you can lose your temper all you like and your power will not escape you. Is that all right?'

'Fine.'

A light glow around her grandfather's hands caught her attention. It lasted for only a moment, then John dropped his hands and moved away from Lucas. 'Now, I suggest a good cup of coffee and a neenish tart. Always does the body good after a shock, I've found.'

Maggie rolled her eyes. 'You'd force-feed the entire world neenish tarts if you could.' Now that her grandfather was involved and apart from his legs seemed well, she felt much more confident about a positive outcome.

Lucas nodded. 'That coffee sounds a great idea, although I'm more an apple pie man myself.'

John grinned. 'Maggie, my girl, serve up. We'll eat here, if you don't mind, Lucas. Doctor's orders, and you don't disobey the doctor, especially when she's your daughter.'

Lucas sat in one of the chairs brought to John O'Hara's bedside and sipped at his coffee. The coffee still looked and tasted the same, its bitterness calming him. Even the chair he sat on was familiar; it was the chair he'd used when he'd had dinner here with Maggie. In short, he was still apparently the same person and all his senses were in perfect working order.

Yet he wasn't human. All the facts pointed to him being gadda, despite his mind's refusal to admit it. Maggie had perfectly described the way it felt when he touched the O'Haras and Peter Shaunessy. He had felt it when he had shaken hands with Sean Flaherty on the plane. In Maggie's case, he might be able to write the sensation off as extreme sexual attraction, but the other four?

Part of his mind was screaming at him to get out, that he was obviously developing schizophrenia and he needed to seek help before it overtook him. His sensible, logical mind was saying he couldn't possibly be delusional, since he was questioning the delusion.

The same sensible, logical mind that was telling him he had irrefutable proof. He wasn't human. He was gadda. And the most important fact of all was that knowledge gave him a sense of relief. All his life, he'd struggled to fit in with the world, to belong. Now, he knew why he never had.

He looked at the three of them, watching him and waiting for him to speak. John O'Hara was sitting with his fingers pressed together and touching his chin. He was struggling to hide a smug smile. Peter Shaunessy was watching with polite detachment, as if still forming his judgement. And Maggie was looking at him with great concern and sadness in her big eyes.

He put his coffee down and looked at John. 'So, now what?'

'Now, we must begin to train you,' John said. 'You can't possibly go to the academy in Ireland. It'd be ridiculous — a thirty-five-year-old over-educated man with a bunch of thirteen-year-olds. They'd drive you demented. I'll petition the bardria for permission for us to train you ourselves. With your intelligence and skills, we should get you to first order before the end of the semester. Has Maggie explained about the orders?'

Lucas nodded. He felt like he'd been hit by a train.

'Good, good. So, I can work with you between classes and first thing in the morning, Maggie can take the afternoons and Siobhan will work with you at night on healing. I'll work on control, Peter if you could do the bardria and Maggie, you can handle the rest. You've got more of an idea about what's taught nowadays than the rest of us.'

Maggie took her eyes from him to frown at John. 'Grandpa, I'm only second order. I can't possibly take on a student.'

'Rubbish. I'll supervise you. It'll be fine. Now, I suggest the two of you take the day off uni. Stay here, you won't be disturbed. See how much you can get done in the next few hours. The faster we begin, the faster we can finish and Lucas will be ready to control his own life. Good? Good. Let's get to work then.'

Lucas looked over in time to see Maggie roll her eyes. 'Yes, Grandpa,' she said.

She put down her coffee and touched his arm. Lucas hid a smile. In the past couple of hours, they'd touched more than they had the entire rest of their time together. He liked it. A lot.

She nodded her head at the door and, after lifting his hand to John and Peter, Lucas got up and followed her from the room. Out in the hallway, she closed the door, then turned and again put her hand on his arm.

'I agree you should have a day off, but I don't think you should work,' she said. 'You've had a dreadful shock and you need time to get used to it.'

Lucas fought to ignore her scent and listen to her words. 'And what better way to get used to it than to learn about it?' Truth was, Lucas could have happily lain down and had a rest, but he didn't want to miss an opportunity to spend the day with Maggie.

'If you're sure.' The concern in her eyes warmed his heart.

'I'm a scientist, Maggie. I need facts.'

She sighed. 'That's what Grandpa said. Seems stereotypical to me.'

He smiled down at her. 'Just teach me how to be me.'

'If you insist.' She led him down the hall into the loungeroom. 'Make yourself comfortable, and I'll get some books for you to read.' Then she went back down the hall.

Lucas looked around. At first glance it was a typical loungeroom. There was a comfortable lounge suite, a three-seater and a couple of armchairs, covered in an Aztec pattern in red and cream. In the centre of the floor was a rug with a matching pattern, and on top of it a coffee table with magazines and a TV guide. The television itself was a flatscreen mounted on the wall, with a DVD player and a cable television box on a shelf below it. To the side was a bookcase with DVDs and CDs.

He moved closer to study it. The top shelf was classics, westerns and old sci fi and he decided that was probably John's. The next shelf was thought-provoking documentaries and art-house movies – undoubtedly Siobhan's. Below that was a mixed group, ranging from modern fantasy and comedy to some of the old musicals. He grinned as he traced his finger down the spine of a copy of *Moulin Rouge*. He hated musicals.

But then there was another shelf, which he had to crouch to look at, and he'd never heard of these DVDs before. A couple of words in the titles were familiar: words he'd just heard from Maggie. One was called *The Gadma Force*, and when he pulled it from the shelf it seemed to be a super-hero style of movie, men and women in heroic poses, though two of the figures illustrated were obvious representations of the Thingy-mir people he'd met last night.

So, the gadda make their own movies. Makes sense, he thought. That way, you could have your own stories sitting alongside the human ones in your cabinets and bookshelves, and they would be similar enough to escape notice.

A piece of art hanging above the sofa caught his eye. It showed some sort of magic ceremony. The O'Haras were broadcasting what they were right here on their loungeroom wall.

He stepped closer to the painting. A shadowy figure held a knife out over a star, and red liquid dripped from the point into the centre of the star. Around the edge the paint glimmered, as though an invisible power was gathering.

'It's wine.' Maggie's voice cut into his thoughts so suddenly that he jumped. He spun around to stare at her. She walked toward him, holding four books. 'A lot of people assume it's blood, but it's red wine. It's not a gadda ceremony either, but Wiccan. Some of the gadda follow human religions, since some of them speak so deeply to the emotions that are the basis of all gadda power. Wicca is Mum's chosen belief.'

'Your mother is Wiccan?' He looked over his shoulder at the DVD collection. Had he completely misjudged the doctor?

'She is, although I suspect it's mainly to get exactly that reaction.' Maggie put the books down on the coffee table. 'Unfortunately, my books aren't back from Ireland yet. One of the problems of living in a world majority-populated by humans. We have to stick to their timetables, so our ships still have to take a certain time to cross the ocean. Of course, they don't have to know few of our crew are actually *on* those ships twenty-four seven.' She sat down on the lounge and pulled the table toward her. 'You'll have to start on Mum's books, I'm afraid. She made me read this one heaps. I hated it.' She tossed it over and Lucas caught it. 'You're going to regret refusing my offer of a sleep.'

As she looked through the other books, Lucas looked at the cover of the one she had given him. *The History of the Gadda*. He opened it and read the first few lines. It was written in a light, narrative style.

'This doesn't read like any history book I've ever read,' he murmured as his eyes skimmed over the words 'antsy bugger'.

'Most gadda books are written in a fiction-style voice, so if a human picks them up they won't realise what they've got. Don't be fooled, they are as accurate as any human history book. More so, because they are printed on a special type of paper that prevents any sort of deliberate misrepresentation or inaccurate analysis.'

'I take it you don't write your fiction on that paper then.' Lucas sat down next to her and leant over to look at the other three books: *The Power Theory*, *Transference*, and *What the Gadma really think of the Oman*.

'Some do. They believe literature can only be great if it is true. Give me a good Stephen King any day.' Maggie leant back into the lounge. 'I'd better start with the power. Just as in physics, there's a fixed amount of energy in the world. Gadda have quite a store of it, although the amount and the ability to control it varies from person to person. Learning to control it is really important, otherwise you will give out your power too easily.'

Lucas hoped he had managed to keep his expression neutral as he nodded. If he'd only known all this in his teens, it would have saved him a great deal of angst.

Still, if he hadn't done what he had, he might not have discovered the joy of physics and therefore might never have met Maggie. 'How long does it take to learn control?'

'It depends. Some people are much better at it than others are. You being so much older than a usual student might mean you learn it easily.'

'Good.' He looked down at the books in front of him. Then he looked at Maggie again. 'Does this mean the gadda eventually run out of power?'

Maggie shook her head. 'Once you learn to control your power, you learn how to gather it. Most living things contain stores of power, particularly plant life. As you expend power in doing something, you take in the same amount of power to replace it. It's one of the reasons for the levels. You get to practise and refine your control and take in energy before you do more difficult tasks and use more intricate skills.'

'So, when you and your mother were holding the fuiparra last night, you were taking power from it as you were expending your own.'

'Exactly.'

'Fascinating.' Lucas flipped open the book on power theory. Within moments, the ideas and theories pulled him in.

He was vaguely aware that Maggie left the room, but wasn't aware of the time passing, or of anyone else moving around him. He was focussed entirely on the words before him. Every phrase, every piece of information, seemed to reach a place deep within him, making sense entirely. It felt right, as if he knew it all along, just hadn't realised it.

One phrase in particular resonated with him: Life, power, all is about balance and without it, life and power are nothing.

He nodded. Striving for a balanced life had always served him well, now it would make him what he was meant to be — gadda.

ASARLAI

'Fantastic news.' Helen O'Docherty ran into the room, her eyes gleaming. 'Oswald Flaherty is going to back us. We've got the money we need to finally show up the Humanists.'

She was followed by Sean Flaherty, who sauntered in with a flick of his hair. He looked around the dozen people gathered in the small room with a triumphant smile. 'I told you Father would come through.'

While three people jumped up to hug and congratulate Sean, Asarlai sat quietly in the corner. She'd learnt that these energetic young warriors were more likely to be open about their plans if she kept as much out of view as possible. She knew some of them were still uncomfortable with her presence.

Helen gestured everyone back into his or her place. 'Sean needs to tell us what's happened. It's vital information and I think guides our future plans.'

Everyone but Sean sat down. The air was buzzing with anticipation. Sean looked at everyone. His only acknowledgement to Asarlai was a slight tilt of his head.

'The Sabhamir came to see my father last night,' Sean said. 'It seems that John O'Hara's mind has been truly twisted by his time with the humans. He's actually accused my father of creating a beast and sending it to Australia to attack him.'

'Crazy,' someone said.

'Unfathomable,' said another.

Asarlai nodded her agreement. There wasn't anyone she could think of who was more concerned with obeying the law than Oswald Flaherty. Still, this was an interesting development. She'd never heard of a gadda conjuring a beast and sending it to attack another. If it continued, it could give her some cover under which to begin her activities with the Forbidden Texts.

Thinking about them made her fingers tingle. It had been hard to drag herself away to attend this meeting. For the first few days after she liberated them, she hadn't bothered to go about her daily routine; she'd been obsessed with the books.

When people had begun to comment on her absence, she had realised that she needed to continue living her normal life. So she came to events like this, even though she could feel the texts pulling on her soul.

'The Sabhamir said he'd been summoned to O'Hara's office in the university and had found the creature there, disabled. He said at its base was both O'Hara's essence, and my father's. Obviously, someone was trying to make it look as though Father made it, and that someone has to be O'Hara. After Father proved to the Sabhamir that it couldn't have been him and sent the guardian away, he was furious. He ranted and raved and stormed up and down the library, cursing John O'Hara and all Humanists to banishment.' Sean's face glowed. 'I told my father that now, more than ever, it was vital that I did everything I could to save Margaret from her family.' The group had heard all about the new love affair and agreed it would be a marvellous thing, to have an O'Hara become a Purist. 'I told him I had friends to help me, friends who had connections with O'Hara's circle and could bring pressure to bear. I guided him, and soon he was telling me I had access to all the family accounts. "I don't care how expensive it is, Sean, just find a way to save that girl and show the bardria O'Hara's foolishness once and for all." So I swore I would, and he gave me access and now we have all the money we need.'

Asarlai could understand his excitement. Helen had brought Sean to a meeting of the League of Purification just a few days after he'd arrived back in Sclossin. He'd been enthusiastic about joining them, but other members of the club had been less certain. They all knew that if Oswald Flaherty found out about them, he'd report them to the Sabhamir and their mission to destroy the Humanist agenda would be over. It didn't matter that he was a staunch Purist — he was a stickler for the rules.

This group broke a lot of rules. Such as when they'd spied on Margaret Shaunessy, broken into the university and stolen her story. They considered the result more important than the actions.

Although the thing with Ms Shaunessy hadn't worked out for them. They'd expected the bardria to ban her from working with humans. Her return to Australia and her Humanist family had been a deep disappointment.

'This isn't just about money, my friends,' Helen said. 'What O'Hara has done has shown me the way forward. We must force him to use his power, particularly in his human workplace. We must put pressure on him, make him put the secret at risk. Then the bardria will recall him and we will deal a serious blow to the Humanist cranks.'

'It's the beginning of the end.' One of the young girls was so excited, her voice squeaked.

'We must be careful, and plan diligently,' Helen said. 'With the money of the Flahertys, we've got all the resources we need.'

Asarlai bent her head to hide her smile. This group's idea of diligent planning paled in comparison to the years she'd spent researching and planning to liberate the texts.

Her palms itched. She needed to get back to them.

'We will meet again in two days. We will all come with ideas of what we can do. Remember, money is no longer an object. Dream big, and dream strong.'

The meeting subsided into individual chatter. Asarlai transferred into her laboratory, glad that Sean seemed not to have noticed her. There, on the silk platform, were the texts. She breathed out a sigh. Each time she left, she had a fear they would be gone when she returned. Every day, she wondered when their loss would be discovered and the search begun. She'd been listening carefully as she walked around the bardria building, but had heard nothing.

She reached out and traced a finger lovingly down the spine of one of the books. They couldn't take them away. The books were hers. She had almost unlocked all their secrets and, once she had, Helen, Sean and the rest of the League would watch on in amazement as she helped the gadda take over the world.

CHAPTER SEVENTEEN

'How's it going?' Siobhan put down her handbag and her briefcase.

Maggie handed her mother a glass of wine before pouring one for herself. 'Grandpa's resting before dinner. He seems fine, except there isn't any movement in his legs. Lucas has been devouring your books at a ferocious rate. I've never seen anyone so intent for this length of time. If he keeps that concentration up, he'll have no problems reaching first order by Grandpa's deadline.'

'Not a surprise. Either of them. Your grandfather is as stubborn as a bloody mule, and Lucas is the personification of dedication and control.' Siobhan sat down on a stool and stretched her neck from side to side. 'What a hell of a day. If I have to look down the throat of one more child and tell its over-protective mother that antibiotics don't cure colds, I'm going to scream.' She took a sip of the wine.

'How worried about Grandpa should we be?' Maggie sat down across the table from her mother. 'It's been more than a week now.'

Siobhan was quiet for a minute, then said, 'The problem with all these things, be they severe injury, chronic illness — or psychosomatic attack — is that the only person who can do anything is the person with the condition.' Siobhan shook her head. 'That's a very easy thing to believe, until you're the one trying to make her father look after himself. I'm worried sick over it, Maggie. He won't accept what's happening — or realise that his cure is in his own hands — and we can't help him until he does.'

'So he won't walk again?'

Siobhan sighed. 'The Heasimir and I discussed it at some length today. Can I just say? Cold fish. Ugh.' She shook her head. 'Anyway, you can never say never, particularly with spinal injuries. Remarkable things can happen, especially with the extra help he can get from gadda healings. And that's *if* the injury is a physical one. But he won't let us work on him because he refuses to believe how bad it could be, physical or not. You and I need to get through to him. Actually, it occurred to me that having Lucas to teach will be good for that. It's going to bring home his limitations so much faster.'

Maggie shook her head. 'I can't believe we found someone from a missing family. At least now we know they all must have forgotten they're gadda. We should probably make a concerted effort to find them.'

'I think we've got enough to worry about ourselves,' Siobhan said. 'Let's leave the lost families to the bardria.' Then she stood. 'I want to see how Lucas is going.'

Lucas was leaning on the coffee table, speed-reading a book while he wrote page after page of notes. He looked up and smiled at the two women.

'Fascinating,' he said. 'A whole race of people, with complex rules and ideologies, that the human race does not suspect exists.'

'Indeed,' Siobhan said, sitting with her arms crossed on one of the armchairs.

Maggie frowned at her mother then smiled at Lucas. 'We're not so sure they don't suspect. Mum thinks a lot of the alien sightings could be because of gadda working their power, don't you?'

'It's possible.' Siobhan's eyes never left Lucas.

Thankfully, Lucas seemed unaware of her mother's shortness. 'I would never have dreamed there was another history of Earth.' He leant back on the lounge. 'Why do you think humans don't have a store of power?'

When Siobhan wouldn't answer, Maggie spoke for her again. 'Mum's got a theory about that too, don't you, Mum?'

'Domestication.'

Maggie clenched her fists, wondering why Siobhan didn't trust Lucas. 'I've got a fascinating treatise by Maeve O'Halloran that postulates humans don't have a store of power because they aren't actually native to Earth. Once my books get here, I'll show it to you, if you like.'

'Yes, please. So, if humans don't have a store of power, that would make relationships between gadda and humans quite difficult, wouldn't it?'

To Maggie's surprise, Siobhan did answer this question. 'Gadda must gain incredible control over their power to not give it to humans at, ah, moments of abandon. It is difficult but it's not unknown.'

Lucas nodded. 'Why do you think I've not had a problem with my power until now?'

'I couldn't absolutely say that you haven't. Certainly, the regimen of scientific research and study, in keeping your life quite ordered, would have helped you control yourself. But I'm willing to bet that when you were young that control was much harder to maintain. I imagine that things occasionally happened – things you really couldn't understand.'

It was as though a shutter went down over Lucas's face. 'I wouldn't have taken you for a gambler.'

'Only on a sure bet.' Siobhan leant forward and studied him for a moment. Then she stood. 'You should stay for dinner, so Dad can work with you.'

Lucas looked back down at the book and picked up the pen. 'Call me when it's ready.'

Siobhan nodded to Maggie and they left the loungeroom, moving back to the kitchen. There, Siobhan started leafing through restaurant pamphlets. Yet another affect of John's injury was a lack of fresh food – neither Maggie nor Siobhan liked cooking.

'That boy has had a terrible life,' Siobhan announced.

Maggie sat down at the stool. 'What makes you say that?'

'He's incredibly controlled, almost absurdly so. Only great pain brings about that type of control. You need to be prepared, Maggie. The training may bring out all sorts of old memories and pain and his reaction could be violent.'

Maggie considered her mother's words as she sipped her wine. She'd never considered Lucas that controlled – he wasn't effusive, but he'd always seemed quite open with her. Maybe that's a good thing, she thought. She might be genuinely helpful.

Lucas barely tasted the Thai food Siobhan served him. His mind was full of the information he had taken in that day and his body was tense with the expectation of the night to come. Once he learnt to control his power, the sky was the limit.

He mechanically took another forkful of food, knowing he had to keep his body fuelled, and ruminated on what he had learnt about the gadda. His people. Where he belonged.

The idea sent warmth spiralling through him. After all this time, after all he'd been through, to finally find common ground with others was thrilling – and unnerving. What if they found him unworthy? No one had yet mentioned what happened to gadda who didn't make the grade.

Deep within him, a ten-year-old boy was staring at a leather belt and trying to figure out what he'd done wrong this time.

'Shevvy!' John O'Hara's voice boomed out from his bedroom. 'Great meal. Don't suppose you ordered lychees?'

Lucas hoped John's injury would be sorted out soon. Maggie and her mom were trying not to let on, but he knew they were worried. Sounded like the old terror was going to be a really shitty patient.

Siobhan rolled her eyes. 'I wasn't aware I'd become a maid in my spare time,' she murmured as she stood. 'Excuse me.' She left the room.

Lucas felt pressure on his arm and turned to see Maggie leaning toward him.

'Don't mind them,' she whispered. 'They're never happier than when they're arguing.'

She smiled at him and Lucas couldn't help but smile back at her. She was the best part of this news.

He tried to pinpoint when he'd fallen for her. Nearest he could figure was the moment she had smiled and welcomed him to visit the olive grove. He was a total cliché – but the best one: in love at first sight.

Siobhan came back into the room. 'Lucas, Dad wants to do some work with you. Come with me.'

Lucas stood and followed her to a door in the hallway, opened to reveal a set of stairs leading down. 'Dad's waiting for you.'

Lucas walked down and into the room. It was made of stone – walls, floors and ceiling. There was a six-pointed star painted on the floor, with a heart in the middle.

'The star of gulagh,' John said. Lucas looked around and saw he was sitting in a comfortable chair at one end of the room, a rug over his legs. Next to him was a long, tall bookcase full of books, jars and statues.

'It's the sign of the gadda. Six points for the six founding families, a heart for the emotion that is at the centre of all gadda power. I know this isn't the most comfortable room, but underground's the best place for this. Can't do too much damage. I was down here all the time leading up to my sixth-order exams.'

Lucas gave a small whistle. Sixth order, huh? No wonder John O'Hara didn't doubt his ability to teach him.

'Now, I'm going to teach you the meditation techniques you need to use to locate and get to know your power before I take the block from you. You haven't felt unwell, have you?'

Lucas shook his head. 'Just fine.'

'Good, good. Blocks can make some people feel dreadfully ill. It's a reaction to not being able to use their power. Once you get used to having your power, you'll hate it as well. Now, make yourself comfortable.'

Lucas placed his feet hip width apart and let his hands hang down by his side.

'Pull your shoulder blades back and down. That's it. Now, close your eyes until you can just see through your eyelashes. Make sure your jaw is relaxed and press your tongue gently to the top of your mouth. Focus on your breath going in and out your nose. Begin counting your breaths, starting at thirty-four and moving backwards. When you get to zero, go back to thirty-four. If you lose track of the counting, go back to thirty-four and start again.'

Lucas followed John's instructions and his body became very still, his mind focussed on his breathing. There was silence in the room for a time, then John spoke again.

'Focus your attention on your chest. Feel your lungs and ribs expand and contract. Again, begin counting from thirty-four, going back to thirty-four if you need to.'

Lucas did, and his awareness expanded a fraction.

'Now, focus your attention on your stomach. Feel your stomach rise and fall as you breathe. Again, count from thirty-four.'

Lucas became aware of his internal organs, the blood swishing though his ears and the thud of his heart resounding in his head.

'Draw your focus inward until you are aware of a tiny spot of light. Focus on that light.'

Lucas's world shrank until it was just his mind and that spot. His power.

'Open your eyes, Lucas,' John demanded.

Lucas opened his eyes and looked at the old man. John nodded. 'You did well, very well. Now, come over here. I'm going to release the block.' John laid his hand on Lucas's and a tingle moved through him.

'I want you to follow the same meditation until you get to your power. Don't do anything, just look at it.'

Lucas went back to the middle of the room and slowly worked through the pattern until the time came to see the spot. Instead of a spot, however, he found himself staring at a ball of white light that spun in the middle of infinite blackness. He reached toward it, but remembered he was only to look. So he watched it for a time, then he opened his eyes and looked at John …

But he didn't lose his awareness of his power. It sat within him, ready to access in an instant.

John smiled and nodded his head. 'Welcome to the gadda. Now, we just need to teach you to control it. You're going to do the same again, but this time you are going to reach forward and enfold it in your hand. Hold it tightly because once you touch it, it will want to react to your every command and whim.'

Lucas nodded and quickly found himself facing his power again. Slowly, he reached his hand out and the moment his fingertip touched the ball of light it flared, blinding him. He pulled his hand back quickly and opened his eyes.

John was watching him, arms folded across his chest and forehead creased in a frown. 'Take control of it, Lucas. Don't be scared of it.'

Lucas nodded, closed his eyes and focussed on his power again. He took a deep breath out, then reached forward and wrapped his hand around his power. Again, it flared brilliantly but its bright light stayed within his hand. It looked like his skin was glowing, the gaps between his fingers and thumb translucent. He could feel his physical hand cupped around air, the movement helping him focus the imaginative work he was doing inside his body.

The power hummed within his grasp, sending little tickles of sensation over his body. It was intoxicating, he realised. Now he had touched it, realised what he was capable of, he didn't want to let it go.

'Keep hold of your power, Lucas, and open your eyes.' John's voice barely registered within his euphoria. Lucas frowned.

'Trust me, Lucas. Open your eyes.'

He nodded. He had to trust John. Slowly, he opened his eyes.

John smiled. 'Still in control?'

Lucas realised he was. The wonderful warmth of his power filled him, and he was comfortable holding it. He nodded, mildly sad about all the years he'd lived without this.

'Well done. You now have basic control over your power. Very impressive, Lucas.' John grinned.

Lucas pulled his shoulders back and held his hand out. 'Thank you.'

John took the offered hand and shook it. 'You're welcome, my boy. You're very welcome.'

The door at the top of the stairs opened and a voice called down, 'Is it safe?'

'Come on down, Peter.'

Peter was more obviously Maggie's parent than Siobhan was. He had the same golden hair and arresting blue eyes. 'Maggie told me you two were working down here. I hope it's all going well.'

'Touch the boy.' John almost crowed. 'He's very impressive.'

Peter held out his hand and Lucas took hold of it. He could feel Peter's power immediately, glowing deep within him. He didn't know how to judge potential, but Shaunessy felt strong enough to him.

Peter nodded as he released Lucas's hand. 'You're right. It *is* impressive. And perhaps a little worrying.' Peter looked at John. 'We don't know what the bardria will do with him. Unlocking his power may not have been wise.'

A deep, sonorous chime echoed in the air. Lucas spun around, trying to see the source.

John waved his hand. 'Step out of the circle, Lucas. You don't want anyone transferring into you, believe me.'

Lucas scrambled over to the wall and moments later the man in black had appeared exactly where he'd been standing. Lucas found himself wondering exactly how the gadda power of transference worked and whether it could help him with his work before he realised he had more important things to worry about.

'John. Peter.' The Sabhamir nodded to each of them, then looked at Lucas. 'Mr Valeroso.'

Lucas decided the smartest thing to do right now was to stay very still, and keep his mouth shut. The man's lips twisted, and he looked back at John.

'I come with news from the bardria. They have decided they wish to do some further research before they come to speak to you about Lucas Valeroso. The Coiremir will be here tomorrow to speak with him, and the caelleach and two other councillors will come in the afternoon to meet with you all, although the caelleach has requested that Ms Shaunessy not be involved.'

All three men smiled, and Lucas wondered what the secret joke was. 'Do they wish us to keep Lucas here until then?' John said.

'I think that would be the smartest move.' The man looked at Lucas again, and then frowned. He marched over and grabbed Lucas's arm before Lucas had time to react. Then he swore and turned to John. 'You unblocked him?'

'You know that uncontrolled power can be dangerous. Star only knows how Lucas has survived so far. He needed access in order to learn.'

'Well, consider him locked again.' The man waved his hand and Lucas felt the warmth from his power disappear. 'Please, John, for the sake of my sanity if nothing else, try to keep out of trouble for the next day.' Then he was gone.

'I told you,' Peter said, shaking his head.

'I did what was best for Lucas, and will wear any punishment the bardria decree,' John said. 'Now, it's been quite a day, and I think we should all rest up for tomorrow. Lucas, we have a spare room here that you can use. Maggie will get you towels and so on.'

'I'll need clothes for tomorrow.'

'Give Peter your key, he can get them for you. Peter, if you see anyone, tell them that Lucas and I are neck-deep in an experiment. That should keep them from bugging us for a while. They're all a bit scared of me when I'm working.' John grinned at Lucas.

'You're having too much fun with this,' Peter muttered as he held his hand out to Lucas.

Lucas handed over the keys, then looked at John. 'I'd rather keep studying for a while. I want to know everything I can before I face the bardria tomorrow.'

John nodded. 'Here, try these.' Three books left the shelves and hovered in the air in front of Lucas's face. Lucas touched them and their weight fell into his hands. He barely managed to hold onto them.

'Now, I have some work to do down here, my boy, so I suggest you retire to the loungeroom to read.'

Lucas started up the stairs. He stepped into the hallway and stopped at the glare on Maggie's face.

'Will you tell me what the Sabhamir said?'

'The bardria want to investigate me further, so they won't come to see me until tomorrow. In the meantime, my power is blocked and I'm going to study up a storm.' He shifted the books in his hands.

Maggie put her hand on his arm. 'Are you OK? I hear being locked feels terrible.'

He had liked the warmth of feeling his power, but

hadn't known it long enough to really miss it. 'No different from when I thought I was human.'

'I guess not. So, are you a coffee addict when you study?'

'Absolutely.'

'Then go into the loungeroom. I'll make us up a pot and together, we'll make sure you pass the bardria test.'

Lucas walked away feeling confident that things were going to be fine.

CHAPTER EIGHTEEN

Maggie woke suddenly and lay in bed, trying to decide what had disturbed her. Then she heard a crash from somewhere inside the house. She sat up, and strained for a clue as to where and what was happening. She heard panting, and another crash.

Grandpa's trying to get up, she thought as she climbed out of bed. He'd probably fallen onto his bedroom floor and would need some help.

As she opened her bedroom door, the hallway was lit by a blue flash, followed by another crash and a moan.

'*Mum!*' she screamed, hoping her mother was already partly awake, as she ran down the hall and stopped in the doorway to her grandfather's room. John lay across the bed, blood pouring from a gash in his forehead. He had his power wrapped around a briarracht, a translucent concoction of bones and rotting flesh that barely formed arms, legs and a head. The stench of decay hit Maggie with such force that she staggered back out of the room and into the hallway.

Her grandfather apparently had control of the beast — it wasn't fighting, but being flung around the room, crashing into the walls and throwing photographs and prints to the floor. Whether this was by her grandfather's will or the briarracht's own struggles, she couldn't say.

But then the balance changed: the creature stilled and then it was John who flew into the air, hitting the ceiling and showering plaster down onto the bed before falling back onto the mattress with a scream of pain. The briarracht screeched and then started to scramble across the duvet.

Maggie lifted her hands and sent a bolt of her power out. It bounced off the briarracht and flew back at her, knocking her against the doorframe then to the ground.

She was winded and her chest squeezed and pulsed as she struggled to draw breath.

'Maggie!' She looked up at Lucas, surprised before she remembered he was staying there. 'Are you OK?'

'Can't ... breathe.'

'Here.' Siobhan shouldered her way between the two of them. She put her arms around Maggie and her power flowed. The pressure on Maggie's lungs eased and the breath returned.

Siobhan released Maggie, stood and stepped over her into the bedroom. Lucas leant back in and swept some hair from Maggie's forehead.

'Is that all? You're not hurt?'

Maggie shook her head, still breathing raggedly. She tried to pull herself to sit against the doorframe, but Lucas reached around her back and supported her against his chest.

They both looked into the room.

The briarracht was kneeling over her grandfather, its sort-of hands resting on his chest.

Blue power wrapped around the creature and it slowly started to float back away from John, who was raising his hands.

'How are you going, Dad?' Siobhan said, positioning herself at the end of the bed.

'I've ... been ... better,' he panted. 'Keeps ... getting ... away.'

'Time to call the Sabhamir, I'd say,' Siobhan said, with only a hint of I-told-you-so colouring her voice.

'I ... yes.'

Siobhan nodded, and Maggie waited for the stir of power in the air that would signal the Sabhamir had arrived. When nothing happened, Maggie looked at her mother.

'Shit,' Siobhan muttered. 'I can't reach him.'

'What, as in can't send the message, or can't find him?' Maggie asked.

'Does ... it ... matter?' John panted. As he spoke, his power faded and the briarracht started to move toward him again.

Siobhan lifted her hands and sent her power out. Maggie watched her mother's power wrap around her grandfather's. The briarracht began to struggle again, and soon was thrashing about the room, crashing into the walls with such impact that it left indentations.

'Fuck,' Lucas said.

'How long can you two hold it?' Maggie called, struggling to her feet with Lucas's help.

'Not long,' Siobhan said.

Maggie thought frantically. If not the Sabhamir, then who? The Hammonds. Her face lit up. She'd call Ione, get her to send two or three of her sixth-order relatives over.

Maggie pushed Lucas away and ran to the phone. Her finger shook as she punched the numbers, and she miscued and hit a five instead of a six.

'Fuck, fuck, fuck, fuck.' She banged the receiver down and picked it up again, but there was no dial tone. 'Fuck!' The sounds of impact from the bedroom were decreasing. The briarracht was starting to gain the upper hand. What was *with* these low-level creatures and their super fucking powers? She slammed the receiver down, counted to two and picked it up again.

'Yes.' She dialled the number, this time getting it right. Then she waited. And waited. And heard Ione's voice.

'Io, shut up, I need –' Maggie stopped as she realised what the voice was saying.

'Hi, you've reached the cool place that is home to Ione and Jack, but we're out having a life so –' Maggie slammed the phone down and screamed in frustration.

From the bedroom there was an ominous silence. Maggie started to run down the hall. 'Sabhamir!' She shouted the word, sending it flying towards Sclossin, hoping, praying that whatever had kept him from answering her mother was no longer in force.

'*Coming, Margaret.*' His calm voice, echoing in her mind, was such a relief that she let out a sob. She stopped in the doorway and another sob escaped her. Her mother had collapsed and was lying on the floor on one side of the bed. John had managed to drag himself across his mattress to sit against the wall but his power was only a thin stream: the briarracht was crawling toward him, almost using the stream of power to pull itself to its intended victim. Lucas was trying to grab hold of the creature's legs and pull it away.

'Lucas, don't.' Maggie darted forward. 'The Sabhamir's coming, he'll deal with it.' She grabbed his arm and tried to yank him away.

'It never stops with you O'Haras, does it?' the Sabhamir said as he appeared in the doorway. 'Margaret, Lucas, out of the room, please. What have you used, John?' He walked to the end of John's bed.

'Macresie's ... curse ...'

'Old fashioned, but effective enough, you'd think,' the Sabhamir said and John glared at him. Maggie smiled as relief swamped through her. It was going to be OK. 'On the count of three I want you to release it and I'll take over. One, two, three.'

From the doorway Maggie clutched Lucas's arm and watched with bated breath. Briarracht could move very quickly; if the Sabhamir wasn't careful he could miss and the creature would be free.

For a second it seemed he had. John's blue power suddenly ceased as a stream of blackness that glowed silver flew from the Sabhamir's hands. The black looked like it touched the briarracht, but then it seemed to disappear around it. The creature rushed up to the ceiling and gave itself a shake, as if freeing itself of the last of its imprisonment and readying for the attack. But then the shaking increased and the creature began to moan. Maggie realised the Sabhamir did have it.

'This is interesting, John,' the Sabhamir said. He sounded as though controlling the beast was requiring little of his attention. 'Yet again, it would seem you've been conjuring beasts to attack yourself.'

'Bloody hell.' John slouched against the wall, obviously exhausted. 'What is going on here?'

'A good question. I'm going to try to send the creature back from where it came and follow it. The Heasimir will be here any moment to help Siobhan. Margaret, Lucas, can you help John to the kitchen?'

Maggie clenched her hands together as she stared at the still form of her mother.

John started to drag himself across the bed, his limp legs trailing through the covers. When he got to the edge of the bed, he looked down at Siobhan and moaned, closing his eyes.

'Grandpa,' Maggie whispered, feeling his pain. As hard as it was for her to see her mother like that, how much worse for him to see his child in trouble?

'Margaret, let me past.' The Heasimir barely gave Maggie time to respond, pushing between her and Lucas to kneel next to Siobhan.

'Margaret, take John out of here,' the Sabhamir said.

Maggie looked at her grandfather then turned to Lucas. 'Can you carry him?'

'What?'

'Grandpa hurt his legs the other night. He didn't want you to know. His power would now be too drained for him to move himself.'

Lucas opened his mouth, then shut it, nodded and walked over to John.

'No,' John whispered but Lucas bent and picked him up.

'Where to?'

'The kitchen.' Maggie led the way.

As Lucas put John into a chair, power roiled through the air, thickening it, making it difficult to breathe. John frowned in the direction of his bedroom. 'Shouldn't be that hard,' he muttered to himself. 'But then, what would I know?' He buried his head in his hands.

Then the pressure eased and Maggie breathed a sigh of relief. It appeared that this attack was over, for the time being.

She leant over and put her hand on her grandfather's shoulder. 'Grandpa, none of this is your fault. You've been attacked twice this month, you've been badly injured, you can't expect to just deal with it and go on as though nothing had happened. Most other gadda couldn't have held that briarracht as long as you did.'

'I should have summoned him, as soon as it came, but oh no, thought I could deal with it myself.' John's voice was barely audible between his hands. 'Now Shevvy —' His voice broke.

'I'll make some coffee,' Lucas said, moving over to the kettle.

'Grandpa.' Maggie put her arms around him. 'It's going to be OK.'

'Is it?'

Maggie sighed. 'Grandpa, what's going on? Why are you suddenly being attacked?'

'I don't know. It doesn't make sense. I wonder if Flaherty's involved in this one as well. Perhaps I've done something to —' He stopped, looked at Maggie then shook his head.

She quickly followed his thought process. 'My rejection of Sean has ramped up the feud,' she said.

The Sabhamir walked into the kitchen and stood at the end of the table. 'I wasn't able to follow it back, but once again there's the touch of the Flaherty in it. You've not been in contact with him, have you?'

John shook his head. 'What did he say about the last one?'

'He denied making it, and had a water-tight alibi. No doubt he will again.' The Sabhamir scratched his chin. 'It doesn't make sense: the Flaherty always acts well within the gadda law. This is so far out that it's ridiculous. Oh, and the Heasimir said that Siobhan should make a full recovery. She's going to keep her in Sclossin for a couple of days to make sure. You need to come up with a story here. Any troubles, give me a call.'

John's shoulders straightened at the news, and he focussed his attention on the Sabhamir. 'We've always had something ready, just in case she had to suddenly go over to Sclossin for Maggie. She's come and gone from the town suddenly for some time now, so people won't really notice. Knew she'd be fine.' He nodded his head. 'These attacks, however, they're not so easy to solve. It must be someone else, someone who wants to see both the Flaherty and me in trouble.'

Lucas put a coffee down in front of Maggie and John, and then looked at the Sabhamir. 'Would you like one?'

'No, thank you,' the Sabhamir said, then looked at John. 'I can't think of anyone who would want both you and Flaherty to get into trouble. Generally, people are on your side, or his. I would say that the person either wants it to look like you're trying to frame Oswald, or he's trying to frame you. I want you to think seriously about any supporters of yours who have seemed particularly agitated about the Purists. I'll come back in the morning to see what you think. Try to sleep, all of you.' He nodded, and then he was gone.

'Sleep. All right for him,' John muttered.

Maggie wished her mother was here. She'd know exactly what to do to soothe her grandfather.

Lucas sat down next to Maggie, a steaming mug of coffee in his hands. 'What was that about Purists?'

'Time for a bit of the political history of the gadda, my boy,' John said. 'Over the centuries since the codifying of the gadda orders, two distinct points of view have grown. One is that the gadda are a special, special little race of people and that specialness must be maintained by keeping themselves clean and away from the nasty, nasty humans. The other says that power is a privilege, and with it comes responsibility. In particular, we should use our special abilities for the advancement of life on the planet, in particular for humans.'

'Guess which point of view Grandpa subscribes to?' Maggie said.

'Was what I said inaccurate?'

'That depends on your definition of accuracy.'

'It suits mine.'

Maggie sighed and turned to Lucas. 'The Purists believe that there should be as little contact with humans as possible. Those enclaves I told you about? All Puritan. Humanists believe in working with humans. In Grandpa's case, he studied alongside humans and using his gadda powers managed to create a new formula for plastic that made him a fortune. He's now used that fortune to build the university. He and Mum continue to use their power in sly little ways — for example the water supply around here is always clean, never-ending. They never do anything to break the gadda laws — you can't use power on humans, for example, without bardria permission.'

'But they're clever enough to work around the edges of that,' Lucas said.

'Thank you.' John smiled.

'Grandpa's very strong Humanist leanings have made him a legend in some circles and a pariah in others.'

'And Sean Flaherty and his family are in the pariah section?' Lucas said.

'Exactly.'

'So, what's happening with the monsters?'

'Good question,' John said. 'When you use your power, you leave behind some of your essence. It's like a fingerprint, really. These monsters have both mine and Oswald Flaherty's fingerprint, making it hard to work out who the creator is.'

'And they seem to be linked to this Purist and Humanist fight?'

'That's the theory,' Maggie said. 'It will be up to the Sabhamir to prove or disprove it. Won't it, Grandpa?'

John snorted. 'Not that I can do much anyway.'

'How badly hurt are you?' Lucas said.

'Just a bit of a bump, my boy. I'll be fine. Now, I think the Sabhamir was right, we should try to sleep.

Lucas, would you be so good as to take me back to bed?'

'*Changing the subject much?*' Maggie sent the charge to her grandfather.

'*I'm tired, Mags.*'

She managed to restrain her own snort. She watched Lucas go over, pick her grandfather up and carry him away. She sat at the table and sipped her coffee until Lucas returned.

He sat back down next to her. 'How bad is he really?'

'Mum and the Heasimir are worried. Very worried. He refuses to go to Sclossin for proper treatment. As you saw, he's acting as though it's nothing.'

'And now your mum's hurt.' He lifted a hand and cupped her cheek. 'It's been a hell of a month for you, hasn't it?'

She leant into his touch. 'Hell of a year so far, really.'

'Anything you need, I'm here.'

It was undoubtedly the nicest thing anyone had ever said to her. As much as she just wanted to lean on him and have him hold her until it all went away, she was aware that this wasn't any easy time for him, either. So she just smiled, and said, 'Thank you. You'd better get to sleep. You'll need to be rested and ready to face the bardria.'

For a moment, she thought he would say no – and she wanted him to. Then he smiled. 'Good night, Maggie.' He leant forward, and pressed a gentle kiss to her forehead that sent shivers down her spine. Then he stood and walked out of the room.

Maggie closed her eyes and released a deep breath. How sweetly this attraction to Lucas was turning into something stronger.

With a slight smile twisting her lips, she washed up the cups. Then she started down the hallway to her bedroom. She peeked in her grandfather's room, and saw he had fallen asleep, and was snoring softly.

She stopped at the door to the basement. She knew Lucas and John were safe — now her thoughts were with her mother. She pushed open the door and tiptoed downstairs. She stood in the middle of the star and sent forth her message.

'*Maggie.*' The Sabhamir's voice rang in her mind. '*Siobhan is awake, and well on the way to recovery. The Heasimir and old Madge decided that since she was actually knocked unconscious, a night or two in Sclossin would do her the world of good. And Siobhan thinks that maybe without her around, your grandfather might come to admit to his problem sooner.*'

Maggie breathed a sigh of relief. '*I hope she's right, but he's as stubborn as a mule.*'

'*You don't become sixth order without a certain level of determination. Valeroso is fine?*'

'*He's sleeping. There don't seem to be any side effects. Have you learnt any more about him?*'

'*No. Try to keep your grandfather from teaching him too much. The less he knows, the easier the bardria will feel about him.*'

'*I'd do better trying to hold back the sunrise,*' Maggie said.

'*Well, if there's one thing I've learnt about the O'Haras, they're all blessed with stubbornness. If you need anything, don't hesitate to contact me, Margaret.*'

'I *won't*.' Maggie felt him disappear from her consciousness.

With the worry about her mother lifted, weariness started to wash over Maggie. What an incredible night it had been. Well, if there was one thing she'd learnt from this, it was to stop wasting time. She was going to tell Lucas how she felt. Life was too short, too precarious, to waste a moment wondering.

CHAPTER NINETEEN

Lucas woke the next morning and took a moment to orient himself.

He flopped onto his back and stared at the ceiling. So, he thought, what's going to be on today's schedule. How to make myself disappear, like the Sabhamir?

'Lucas, my boy, are you up?' John's voice bellowed through the morning air.

Lucas got up with a smile. He couldn't help but admire the fact that even from his sickbed, John O'Hara ruled the household. He went to his door and pulled it open. He was about to call out to John but then he was distracted by the sight of Maggie coming out of her bedroom. She was tousled and flushed and rubbing at her eyes.

She was wearing cotton shorts and a T-shirt and the sight of her was more than enough to get his hormones going.

'Good morning.' He smiled as she stopped and stared. Not a morning person, it would seem.

'Is it?' she muttered. 'You'd think after last night he'd let us sleep in a little.'

The smile dropped from his face. 'There's no need for you to get up. I can deal with your grandfather.'

She sighed. "'S' all right. Go have a shower. Spare towels are in the cupboard under the sink. I'll let Grandpa know you're up.' And she began to shuffle down the hall.

Lucas had a quick shower and, as he got out, there was a knock. He pulled a towel from the cupboard, slung it around his hips and then opened the door.

Maggie stood there, her arms full of men's clothing and her mouth open as if to speak. However, her eyes immediately riveted on his chest and she didn't utter anything more sensible than a squeak.

Thank you. Lucas sent a silent prayer to whoever was looking after him. 'Are those for me?'

She jumped and then looked at him, guilt flashing across her face. 'Um, yes.'

Lucas wanted to tell her she could touch as well, if she wanted. They weren't quite there yet, though. 'Could I have them?'

'Dad got them for you.' She thrust the clothing out at him.

He took it, careful to brush his hands over hers. Her eyes flicked to his, her breath caught and he thought that maybe they *were* at the point where he could suggest she join him. But then she said, 'I've put some coffee on,' and almost ran back down the hall.

Lucas closed the bathroom door and dried himself. Well, that was a nice start to the day, he thought.

He went into the kitchen. Maggie put a cup of coffee down in front of him — avoiding his gaze — and left the room.

Lucas leant back in his chair and sipped with a satisfied smile, feeling incredibly pleased with himself ... until the sound of running water reached him. He immediately pictured her under the shower, water cascading over her golden skin. Now he was the one suffering.

'Lucas? Ready to work?' O'Hara's shout cut into his fantasies.

'Sounds good,' Lucas called then downed the rest of his coffee. Anything to take his mind off her until he had the chance to put thoughts into action.

Then the work began. Lucas considered himself lucky to have well-honed study skills; otherwise he would have been overwhelmed. Peter and John spent two hours going over how to conjure and combat creatures. This was usually considered advanced, Peter said, but under the circumstances they thought it a wise extension on his pre-first-order curriculum.

Then it was supposed to be Maggie's turn — two hours on basic healing and conserving his power. He wondered how he was going to concentrate on what he needed to learn, not on her.

However, instead of coming down into the basement to start working, she stood at the top of the stairs.

'Lucas, let's go for a walk,' she said.

'Maggie.' There was a warning in John O'Hara's voice that surprised Lucas.

'I'll teach the way I want to teach, Grandpa,' she said. 'Coming, Lucas?'

Lucas walked up the stairs and followed her through the house and out into the olive grove. They started to walk through the trees, and across the hill away from the town.

Lucas allowed himself a few minutes to enjoy the daylight. The warmth of the flickering sunlight on his skin, the sweet scent of the olive trees. Great idea, he thought. They all needed a break from that basement. And he was alone with Maggie. That couldn't help but be a good thing.

'I'm not going to teach you anything,' she said.

Lucas stopped and stared at her. She took a couple of more steps then turned to face him. 'What do you mean?' he said.

'The Sabhamir thinks it would be for the best that you don't know too much before the bardria meet you, and I agree. They need to see that you aren't a threat.'

Lucas frowned. 'You think I'm a threat?'

'Anything new, or particularly human, is a threat. They consider me one, they'll certainly see you that way. Grandpa doesn't agree, and I can't stop him. We, however, are going to spend two hours wandering around the olives, and you're not going to learn a thing and hopefully when the bardria get here you won't intimidate them too much.' She started to walk again.

For a moment, Lucas was disappointed, but then he smiled. He caught up to her. 'So everything gadda is banned, right?'

'Absolutely.'

'Then I suppose we'll have to talk about us.' He grinned as Maggie almost tripped over an invisible stick. This was going to be a very enjoyable morning.

Then the sound of a machine reached his ears.

'Oh, shit.' Maggie grabbed his arm and swung him around. 'Back to the house, quickly, before Jeff finds us.'

She started to pull him back along the hill. 'You'd think he owns the bloody grove, not my mother,'

Maggie muttered. 'Just wait until I'm in charge, then he'll see some fireworks.'

'He'll be long gone before you own the grove,' Lucas said.

'I wouldn't count on it.' She stopped suddenly, listening to something he couldn't hear.

'What is it?' Lucas said.

'A message. Be prepared, Lucas, you're about to meet the teacher of all teachers, and we're already late for class. Come on.' She grabbed him again and this time began to run toward the house, dragging him behind her.

Lucas quickly overtook her, taking hold of her hand to propel her along. They were panting by the time they reached the back door.

Sitting with John and Peter at the dining table was a strong-faced woman, with a Roman nose and a cleft in her chin. Her brown hair was pulled back from her face and wrapped around her head. She wore a brown robe, rich and beautifully cut.

'Coiremir.' Maggie bowed her head. 'An honour, ma'am. May I present Lucas Valeroso? Lucas, this is the Coiremir, the teacher of the gadda.'

'Sit, Lucas,' the Coiremir said, nodding to one of the chairs. 'I'm here to decide if you should be educated here, or in Sclossin. I have spoken to John and Peter; I want to hear what you think you need.'

Lucas nodded as he sat down. That was a good approach. 'I don't know anything about Sclossin and I barely know anything about the gadda, so I can't comment on that. I can say — with obvious bias — that this whole thing is alien and amazing. I would prefer to be in a relatively familiar environment with people I am getting to know. There's also my work and my ordinary life, which give me time to process the gadda information and skills I'm being taught. And look, I have a reasonably high profile, in my circle at least. If I just disappear it would cause a lot of discussion. I understand you guys like a quiet life.'

The Coiremir nodded. 'The Ceamir told me that it would be difficult to take you from your human life altogether. However, there is the university in Galway, where Margaret studied. You could work there, and study in Sclossin.'

'That is a possibility, but in Scolossin I would be among complete strangers, and a lifestyle and culture that I do not know. Everyone else who goes there at least knows how to be gadda, and just needs to learn how to control their power. I know nothing. Doesn't sound like the best fit.'

'I agree,' the Coiremir said. Lucas's jaw dropped. 'I will recommend to the bardria that you remain here, under my supervision. Good day.' She stood, nodded her head to everyone and then disappeared.

'Not much of a one for conversation, but one hell of a teacher,' John said. 'Now, it's time for lunch, and then we need to start drilling you.'

'Grandpa —'

John waved his hand. 'None of that, Maggie. We have the go-ahead of the Coiremir, so let's get cracking. Now Lucas, I'm sorry the Coiremir's visit cut off what Maggie was telling you about healing, so I'll fill you in while she and her father get us lunch.'

Maggie wasn't happy as she got up from the table,

but she'd clearly decided it wasn't worth arguing. Then Lucas didn't have time to think any more, as John tried to pump as much information into him in the next fifteen minutes as he could.

Lucas's mind swam and he spent lunch in silence, organising the knowledge and storing it. The meal was followed by three hours of drills in using his power, teaching him control and finesse.

He was surprised at how difficult it was to use his power. He could hold it, but then making it do something was another matter. The main task was moving a piece of paper around. Sometimes it wouldn't move at all, other times it would shoot from his hand with the ferocity of a bullet and once, Peter had to jump out of the way to avoid it plastering his face.

By the end of the three hours, all Lucas could consistently do was lift the piece of paper onto its end and lay it back on the bench surface.

'Damn,' he muttered as it failed to lift into the air for the tenth time.

'Don't be too hard on yourself, my boy.' John said. 'You're doing amazingly well. Best I could do for the first couple of weeks was make the paper shake. Listen, I think it's time we all had a rest. Go and lie down; I bet when you come back to it, it will all seem much easier.'

Lucas lay down on the bed in the spare room and stared up at the ceiling, his hands clasped on his chest.

Thoughts were dashing about in his brain in an attempt to find a place to belong. He closed his eyes and focussed on his breathing, using his power-control exercise to try to order his thoughts. But his mind would not be silent; his brain wanted to work this out.

With a shrug, he gave up. As quietly as possible, he made his way down into the basement. Then he began practising the exercises.

He took his time, didn't hurry or worry about how pretty it all looked. As he worked, little linkages formed between different bits of knowledge and he felt it settle into place.

A footstep on the stair drew his attention and he opened his eyes to see Maggie walking toward him. Black shadows ringed her eyes and her shoulders stooped. Lucas wished he could whisk her away, find her a quiet spot where she could rest.

He smiled. 'Couldn't rest either, hey?'

She shrugged. 'Nope. Everything just keeps playing through my mind.' He walked over to her and they joined hands, a bit shy all of a sudden. He was still taken aback by the buzz that moved through him on contact. 'You're exhausted.' He began to rub her hand. 'You should try to sleep.'

She swayed a little and he stepped closer. She put her head on his chest. 'I'd much rather stay here with you.'

Lucas put his arms around her and she snuggled against him. He stood there for a moment, relishing finally having her in his arms. Then he put his enjoyment aside and thought of her. 'Bed, Ms Shaunessy.'

'Just what I was thinking, Dr Valeroso.' She smiled.

The temptation was irresistible. He bent his head and touched his lips to hers. He caught a little sigh escaping her mouth, and then desire rushed over him in a wave that astounded him. Bloody hell, nothing had ever felt this good.

One kiss, and he felt hotter than he ever had. Stop, he told himself, stop. He allowed himself another moment of bliss, then another, then with a willpower he was proud of, he pulled his lips from hers.

Maggie's lips were slightly parted, her eyes were shining; he almost forgot his resolve. 'Bed.' Wrong word, he thought. 'You need to sleep.'

She opened her mouth to argue, and he tried to simultaneously plan how to make her see sense and where the most comfortable place in the basement was so they could give in to their obvious desire for each other. Then a sharp ping rang through the air.

'What the hell?' He straightened and turned around. A purple globe hung in the air, above the star of gulagh.

'It's the bardria.' Maggie stepped forward and tapped it.

'This is Horatio Cormac. Who am I speaking to?'

'Maggie Shaunessy.'

The response took longer than Lucas thought it should. 'Where is your grandfather, Ms Shaunessy?' The tone was icy.

'He's sleeping. How can I help you, Caelleach?'

'Is your father there?'

Lucas looked at Maggie. She rolled her eyes. 'No, sir. Shall I tell him to contact you?'

'No, I'll contact him myself. Good day.'

'And to you, sir.' Then Maggie poked out her tongue.

'Was that the caelleach?' She nodded. 'Head of the bardria?' Another nod. 'If I had to guess, I'd say he doesn't like you.'

'Hard to believe, isn't it?' She shrugged, then smiled. 'Now, I think Caelleach Cormac interrupted something very nice.' She stepped closer to him.

Lucas liked the expectation in her eyes, but the message from the caelleach had reminded him of what was at stake. Work now, play later.

'That's right, a good nap. So come along, Ms Shaunessy.' He put his hand on her back and guided her towards the stair.

'Wouldn't you rather kiss me?' She batted her eyelids.

God, yes. 'Don't you want me to pass the bardria?'

'Damnit.'

Lucas smiled and pressed a quick kiss to her lips. Even so, it was enough to make his power hum. 'I'll make it up to you.'

'Too right you will.'

Lucas, John and Peter were in the basement. John sat in the armchair, Peter and Lucas on either side, all facing the star of gulagh. Somehow, John had convinced Maggie to stay out. Lucas had to admit he was glad. If this ended badly, he didn't want her to see it.

The air shimmered and two men and two women stood in the middle of the circle, along with the Sabhamir and the Coiremir. One of the men and the women were dressed in purple robes marked with a star like the one they stood on. The other man was dressed in a navy blue robe, plainer than the others, though he looked like he meant business.

'Caelleach Cormac, councillors Flaherty and Smyth, Sabhamir, Firimir, Coiremir, welcome to my home.' John bowed his head to them.

Lucas looked at the red-haired woman in purple — her resemblance to Sean Flaherty was clear. She was already looking at him like some sort of insect.

'John.' The man in the purple robe bowed and looked around the room. Lucas watched him closely and, while his eyes landed unerringly on each of them, they seemed not to focus. He was blind, Lucas realised with a shock. 'The Heasimir tells me that you are injured.'

John waved his hand. 'Temporary problem. I'm already feeling much better and I'll be right as rain in a day or two.'

'Humph.' The man continued to look around the room and stopped when he faced Lucas.

'Lucas Valeroso, come forward.'

Lucas tried to keep his breathing regular as he obeyed. The man extended his hand, and Lucas took it. Again that sensation, but this time a picture of amazing power and control formed in Lucas's mind. This was not a man to be trifled with.

The man dropped his hand and nodded at John. 'I suggest we take our seats and begin.' As he spoke, furniture suddenly appeared in the room. Three chairs behind a table, three in front.

The three in the purple robes took the seats behind the table. Peter assisted John to one of the three in front, then motioned Lucas to take the middle chair before sitting on his other side. Lucas was pleased that the two men were so obviously supporting him. The Sabhamir, Coiremir and the other man stood over to the side in a line.

'First, I want to state that having touched Lucas Valeroso, I confirm that he is gadda. But who is he exactly and what do we do with him?' the blind man said. 'Sabhamir, what have your investigations shown?' The way he took control made Lucas think he must be the caelleach.

The Sabhamir bowed. 'There is no record of anyone of Lucas Valeroso's description having been banished from the gadda. I have begun tests on his essence in an attempt to connect him to one of our families. So far, there is nothing clear.'

'Is this man a risk, Sabhamir?' said the Flaherty woman. 'What about his control of his power?'

'I have only had fleeting contact with Mr Valeroso, Councillor Flaherty. However, I can begin testing him right away, if you like.'

Councillor Flaherty nodded; Caelleach Cormac shook his head. 'Not at the moment, Sabhamir. I wish to hear more about Mr Valeroso and his background. John, perhaps you can take us through how you discovered that Mr Valeroso was gadda. Firimir, take your position please.'

The navy-robed man stood, bowed to the councillors, then walked to stand behind John's chair. He put his hands on either side of John's face, fingers pointing upward. Then he closed his eyes.

'You may begin, John,' Cormac said. As John recounted the story, including how Lucas himself learnt about the gadda and his own identity, Lucas tried to get a handle on how this might go. The caelleach seemed happy enough to hear information now, and make a decision later. Councillor Flaherty, on the other hand, appeared to have already made her decision, and it wasn't a good one. The other councillor was an older woman, who was sitting with her eyes closed. Lucas wondered if maybe she was sleeping.

He looked sideways at the Sabhamir, whose gaze was on John. The guardian's eyes flicked to Lucas and a slight smile tugged at his mouth before he turned his attention back to John. The Coiremir watched proceedings with what Lucas thought was probably her customary aloofness.

Then Lucas looked over his shoulder at the Firimir. His eyes were also closed, like the older councillor, but there was an aura of alertness about him. He was listening intently to every word that John said.

Lucas turned back to face the front and relaxed a little. It seemed a good balance to him.

Once John was finished, Cormac said, 'We've spoken to Siobhan Shaunessy, who is recovering well after the attack of the briarracht last night and should be home in a day or so. She told us the following about Lucas Valeroso.' He nodded to the Firimir, who closed his eyes and began to speak in Siobhan's voice.

'Lucas Valeroso is a very intelligent, controlled person. He's shown that he's determined to learn all he can about the gadda, and has accepted all that has been asked of him unquestioningly. He's very loyal and trustworthy, and would make a worthy addition to the ranks of the gadda.'

Lucas would never have expected such praise from Siobhan. And it looked as though he should be careful what he said in front of the gadda, if they could function as walking tape recorders.

The Firimir continued Siobhan's testimony. 'He is, like all gadda, very emotional and, having learnt to control his emotions so strongly during his life, will now have to loosen up and use them to his advantage. Whether he is capable of that is yet to be seen.'

Or maybe not such praise, he thought with a wry smile. He knew Siobhan didn't quite trust him yet. Hopefully, that would change.

'Peter, you've worked with the man, what do you think?' Cormac said. The Firimir took hold of Peter's face.

'I think he has the talent to take the gadma route,' Peter said.

Lucas looked at him. Wow, talk about compliments.

'Really?' Cormac stroked his chin.

'Indeed. He has amazing control of his power, thanks in no small part to the training already done here with him. He'll be ready to test for first order within a few weeks, and then who knows. But he's certainly too talented for us to give up, and he's too different to be treated and trained like other gadda, at least until he's first order.'

'I see.' Cormac stared blankly in Peter's direction for a moment, then tipped his face up to the Firimir. 'Firimir, do you have any questions?'

The listening man spoke. 'I'd like to hear from the O'Hara why he kept Mr Valeroso's presence a secret, and why he began training him without bardria permission.' His voice was soft, each word spoken precisely. As he spoke, he went back over to stand behind John.

'Yes, good question,' Flaherty said.

'Thank you, Councillor, I do try,' the Firimir murmured and Flaherty flushed. Lucas suddenly saw that the small man was, in his own way, as powerful as the Sabhamir.

'Certainly, Firimir. I intended to tell the bardria about Lucas as soon as I found out, but then my family was attacked. If he was involved or was a threat to us I needed to find out all I could before I turned him over to the bardria. We are entitled to protect ourselves, I believe.'

Lucas felt a sinking sensation in his stomach. John hadn't trusted him? It shouldn't have hurt him this much. Had Maggie not trusted him either?

'Once Lucas found out about the gadda, I thought it was important that we begin training immediately, particularly as he needed to get control of his power. And Sclossin would be an alien environment for him — he can't be expected to study with thirteen-year-olds.'

'That's for the bardria to decide, O'Hara,' Councillor Flaherty snapped.

'Of course,' John murmured, bowing his head to her.

'You seem to have been taking a great deal upon yourself lately, John. First, you try to fight monsters sent to you instead of calling for the Sabhamir, and now this. I think it's time to test this alleged control and training,' Cormac said. 'Sabhamir, if you please.'

225

'Certainly, Caelleach.' The Sabhamir stood and walked to the middle of the room, between the two groups. 'Stand, Valeroso.'

Lucas did. This was it, the moment it all came down to – fail this and he was a goner. Well, he'd not failed a test for more than eighteen years; he wasn't going to fail this one.

'I am going to attempt to take your power from you,' the Sabhamir said. 'Hold onto it as long as you can.'

Lucas reached within and took hold of his power, careful not to squash it. Then he felt something surround his control and it squeezed so strongly that his entire body spasmed with pain. He gasped and looked at the Sabhamir. Holy shit, so this was real gadda power.

Keep calm, he told himself, focus on your power, you'll be fine. His heart beat for a moment, than another, and he thought the balance was tentative but was holding. Then his power suddenly wrenched from him, was gone and he started to fall into the gaping blackness within.

Then his power was back and hands gripped his shoulders. 'Valeroso, look at me.' Lucas obeyed. The Sabhamir smiled reassuringly. 'Fine?'

Lucas nodded, feeling his power circling calmly within him. The Sabhamir released his hold and turned to the councillors.

'His control is extremely impressive, well beyond a lot of second-order gadda. I do not doubt Peter Shaunessy's contention that he could sit for first order in a few weeks. He has been well trained.'

Lucas went back to his seat, his knees a little wobbly.

He stared at the Sabhamir, who calmly took his seat as though nothing had happened. Holy shit.

'Coiremir, you believe that this is the best place for his training to continue?' Cormac asked.

'Yes, Caelleach, I do. I believe living in Sclossin would in fact hamper his training,' the Coiremir said.

'We have spoken to the Ceamir, and she tells us it would be extremely difficult to remove Valeroso from the human world suddenly. Coiremir, are you willing to come to Winton weekly to oversee the training?'

'I am, Caelleach.'

'While I am disappointed that the bardria was not informed about Mr Valeroso earlier, I understand the O'Hara's reasons for that. I am satisfied that Lucas Valeroso's training can be undertaken here in Winton,' Cormac said.

'What about the sentence? They are unable to use their powers!' Councillor Flaherty's eyes spat sparks.

'Not a great deal of power is needed for first order,' Cormac said. 'However, there is still the matter of exactly who Mr Valeroso is. If his origins prove contentious he will need to come to Sclossin immediately.'

'Well, I do not agree,' Flaherty said. 'We must take him back to Sclossin with us right now.'

'What say you, Councillor Smyth?' Cormac said.

The old woman opened her eyes and pinned Lucas with her gaze. Then she nodded. 'He is best here, for now.'

Lucas felt sweat bead on his forehead as though a fever had broken. He would stay in Winton, stay with Maggie.

'Firimir?' Cormac said.

There was a pause, and a sweet scent filled the room. Lucas felt wellbeing flood him.

'All have spoken truth,' the Firimir said.

'Then I declare this investigation closed, and the judgement will stand.' The finality of the words struck Lucas like a blow. He closed his eyes and let them sink in. It was OK. He was allowed to be gadda.

'Now, if you wouldn't mind leaving us, Mr Valeroso, there is something we need to discuss with John and Peter,' the caelleach said.

Lucas didn't need to be asked twice. He was overcome with the need to tell Maggie. Somehow, he managed to restrain himself, stand, and bow to the councillors. However, by the time he got to the top of the stairs he was running. He threw open the door and stopped when he saw her waiting.

She was wringing her hands, the knuckles white under the pressure. Her face was pale, her eyes wide. 'Is it over? What happened?'

Lucas smiled. 'It's OK. I'm going to train here.'

'Yes!' Maggie almost flew through the air to him. Wrapping his arms around her, Lucas swung her in a circle and laughed.

'Where are Grandpa and Dad? We should celebrate.'

'The bardria wanted to talk to them. Not about me, about something else,' he added when she looked at him, worried again.

'Ah. So, they're gonna be down there for a while, are they?' The smile that grew on Maggie's face, the heat that blossomed in her eyes made his heart thud.

'Indeed. The celebrations will have to start with just you and me.' He pulled her closer to him.

'My favourite type of celebrations.' They kissed and again, the desire and power flowed over him, an experience like nothing he'd ever known: the simplest kiss was a landscape of emotions and pleasure.

Life was starting to look goddamned fantastic.

CHAPTER TWENTY

Maggie was sure she'd never had a more horrible afternoon in her life. She'd wandered up and down the house. She'd felt the councillors arrive, but she hadn't heard a sound.

Several times she'd hovered by the door and considered busting in there, but decided her grandfather was right – she'd be a hindrance, not a help to Lucas. But when the door had opened and Lucas stepped out and smiled at her – that had been the sweetest moment of her life.

She'd wanted to spirit Lucas away so they could be alone, finally, so that they could begin to explore what was between them, but the few brief moments of celebration were all they got. Once the bardria had left, her father and grandfather had immediately sat Lucas down and started to organise his training schedule around his research routine, leaving her to organise dinner.

Apart from that delirious moment in his arms when he told her he was staying, Lucas had been irritatingly normal. Maggie waited to catch his eye, to see the heat there, the secret connection between the two of them. But he was as focussed and impassive as she had ever seen him.

If only Mum was here, Maggie thought as she waited to place her pizza order. She'd find a way to get Grandpa and Dad away, to give me time alone with Lucas, so we can find out what this is. Actually, Maggie thought, I know what this is. Lucas was caring, compassionate, intelligent and funny. It didn't hurt that he also had a killer body. She would never forget the moment he'd opened the bathroom door that morning and she'd seen nearly all of him. That wonderful expanse of chest, tinged gold after his weeks in Australia and sparsely covered with curling black hair. Muscles, hard and defined, dotted with droplets of water that she had immediately wanted to lick away.

And beyond any of that (she forced herself to move on from the physical) — was the genuine *rightness* of being with him. She remembered the flash of joy and relief she'd felt leaning into him during the briarracht attack. She knew exactly what this was — the start of the biggest thing in her life so far. And in Lucas's — she knew that just as clearly.

But then why had he all but ignored her once he was declared safe in Australia?

Maybe he was overwhelmed, she thought as she showered, dinner safely on its way. Maybe the feelings had been so intense, he hadn't known how to deal with them, and had gone back to his traditional method of dealing with anything — control.

Maybe it didn't mean that he wasn't interested, but he was scared by just how interested he was. Maggie smiled as she rinsed her hair. She'd suggest a night off for everyone, and that she and Lucas should just talk. She'd take him somewhere private, perhaps under the olive trees, and show him that overwhelming was the best thing in the world.

She dressed, choosing her clothing with care. A long, swinging skirt that moved around her calves, and her best top. She'd put her shoulders back, walk out and watch Lucas's reaction. If he showed one iota of interest, it would be on.

When she walked into the dining room, Lucas was talking to John while Peter got them drinks. Lucas's back was to her, but he swung around when John said, 'Feel better, cushla?'

Maggie watched Lucas carefully. His eyes darkened, and his nostrils flared.

'Fabulous. There's nothing like the feel of water on your skin to make you feel like new.'

'Absolutely.' Lucas said, looking at her unblinkingly. 'You look wonderful.'

While the heat in his eyes was obvious, there was a tenderness in his tone that warmed her heart. She couldn't stop the smile that spread across her face as she moved over to the table and sat down. John and Peter looked up from the whiskey bottle they'd been studiously examining, uncomfortable and amused in equal parts, by the look of it.

Maggie knew she carried on a conversation but didn't know what she said. All she was aware of was Lucas's body next to hers, the heat emanating from him, the occasional touches of skin as he leant over to get something.

Each accidental touch sent pleasure skittering across her skin, slowly but surely building her arousal. Every breath she took brought Lucas's scent to her —

warm and musky and overwhelmingly male. She had to concentrate to keep her breathing normal, to chew and swallow and chat.

It was the most exquisite torture she had ever undergone, and occasional glances into the blackness of Lucas's gaze seemed to suggest that he was suffering just as much. She couldn't wait for the meal to be over, so she could finally have him alone.

As dinner neared its conclusion, John gazumped Maggie's plan. 'No more work tonight. We've all worked like Trojans today, particularly you Lucas, and we deserve a break. I am going into the loungeroom, putting my feet up and watching the cricket. And you need to get out of the house. Take him for a walk under the olives, Maggie.' Then with a wink, he made Peter levitate him into the loungeroom.

Maggie knew she should be embarrassed that her grandfather was so aware of her plans, but she didn't have time for such insignificant emotions. Instead, she stood up.

Lucas took hold of her hand and they left the table and walked out onto the patio. Drenched in the red-gold of the setting sun, she fitted her body perfectly to his. Then she tipped back her head and kissed him.

Bliss flowered within, as her desire and power were met with his. Maggie wrapped her arms around his neck and pressed herself to him, opening her mouth to receive the thrust of Lucas's tongue.

Then all coherent thought ended. Her world focussed on Lucas: his scent teasing her, his lips pleasing her, his hands exploring her, his power enfolding her.

She wanted Lucas with a passion that she'd never known before and she didn't want anything to stop this. She could feel his arousal building, both in the press of his body against hers and in the pulses of his power. There was such a promise of pleasure in the moment that she decided some smooching on the verandah wasn't enough.

She pulled away from him. 'Come on.' She grabbed his hand and started to pull him along the house.

'Where are we going?'

'Somewhere private. I don't intend to put on a show for all of Winton to see.'

'But you do intend to put on a show?'

She stopped, spun around and gave him a kiss that sent his power soaring. 'Like nothing you've ever experienced before.'

'I can believe that.'

Along the driveway was the storage shed for the grove. It was mostly taken up with machinery but in one corner was the olive store. When the fruit was picked in April and May, it was stored here before being taken to the press near Tamworth. Most of the year, it was empty but even now as Maggie pushed the door open the sour-sweet scent of the olives hung in the air.

The room was small, but it was dry and smelt fantastic. In a corner was a pile of hessian sacks, ready to take the next crop.

'Now, where was I?' Maggie turned to Lucas with a smile. He wrapped his arm around her waist and pulled her tight against him.

'About here,' he said, and kissed her.

They ended up lying on the sacks. One of Maggie's

hands grasped Lucas's thick black hair while the other stroked up and down his back and sides, learning the contours of his body. She wrapped one leg around his thigh, pressing her pelvis into him and thrilling to the feel of his erection against her thigh.

One of Lucas's hands moved inside her top, cupping her breast. She felt it swell at his touch, her nipple hardening. He massaged her breast, and then began to tweak her nipple. Pleasure shot through her, gathering between her legs and tingling deep within her. Then he pushed her shirt out of the way and lowered his lips to her breast, kissing the plump mound before finding her nipple and sucking on it.

Maggie's back arched and she moaned. Nothing had ever, ever felt this good. Everything combined – their power, their desire, their friendship, their companionship. Everything combined to make this moment perfect.

He transferred his attention to her other breast. She began to squirm, needing his touch on her clitoris so much that she felt sure she would go mad.

Then his hand was under her skirt and Maggie opened her legs. He was there in her slickness, finding the sensitive spot, which responded with a burst of pleasure that had her gasping. She ground against his hand, wanting so much more.

Tension and bliss began to build within her, spiralling, until she realised she was close to coming – without even taking her clothes off. She strained, gasped and begged Lucas not to stop. He continued rubbing until her body stiffened and light burst within her.

Wave after wave of pleasure shook her, power streamed from her, meeting and joining with Lucas's more masculine power and she yelped, groaned, and gasped until finally, the last tremors melted away and her body collapsed into the sacks.

Lucas kissed her again, deeply and intimately, his tongue on hers. Maggie responded, her fingers on his cheeks. He pulled back a little and smiled down at her.

'You certainly have a way of telling a man how you feel, Maggie.'

The fire was still there, but banked under tenderness. The power that flowed from him was smooth and warming. Maggie could feel the evidence of his desire still pressing against her leg. His lips moved to nuzzle her neck and her earlobe.

Well, it didn't seem fair that she'd had all the fun. She began to trail one hand down his back, then his side, moving around to the front of his hip.

She felt his power throb, and knew how desperately he wanted her to touch him. 'My turn now.' She pushed at his shoulder.

'I think you mean my turn.' He rolled off her onto his back. Maggie sat up and straddled him, pressing her moistness against his straining zip.

'Can you feel it?' she whispered, twisting her hips to grind against him. 'Not just my body, but how I feel?'

His eyes were dark, his breathing heavy. 'Yes.'

'Tell me how I'm feeling.' She slipped her hands down to the bottom of his T-shirt and started to pull it up his torso. He pushed himself up so she could pull it over his head, and then flopped back onto the sacks.

'Tell me.' She bent down and flicked her tongue over his nipple.

He groaned. 'Turned on. You're really, really turned on.'

'And?' She nibbled her way over to his other nipple.

'Happy. Content.'

His voice trembled. Maggie smiled against the hair-roughened skin of his chest. There really was something special about testing a man's control like this, especially someone like Lucas.

She put her hands on his chest and pressed her lips against the edge of his jaw. Then she lightly took his earlobe between her teeth and pulled gently. His hips shook and he groaned.

'Tell me what else you feel.' She tugged his ear again.

'God, Maggie.'

'Can you feel how happy I am to be here with you? Can you feel how happy I am that you've come into my life? Can you feel how much I —'

There was a loud thud outside. 'Hey! Whoever you kids are, get out of my shed.'

Lucas sat up, wrapping his arms around Maggie and holding her tight. 'What the fuck was that?'

'Shit. Must be Jeff,' she whispered. 'Stay quiet, he'll go away.'

But he didn't. There was another thump, closer to the olive store. 'I know you're in there. I've got a gun.'

'Oh, crap.' Maggie got up, pulling her skirts down. She marched over to the door and flung it open, then put her hands up to hide her face from the sudden light that shone in it.

'Jeff, it's me.'

'What are you doing here, late at night?' She couldn't see him with the torch shining right in her face, but she heard him come closer. 'Who've you got with you?'

'Jeff, it's OK. Just go back to bed.'

'It's not OK. Your mother pays me good money to protect these olives, she does. I have a gun. I could've shot you.'

Maggie heard Lucas moving. She looked over her shoulder to see he was standing and pulling his T-shirt on. Damn, it seemed Jeff had ruined everything.

'Well, you didn't, so you can go back to bed and —'

'I'm not sleeping until I see you back to the house, and that's that.'

Lucas came and stood behind her. The torch flicked toward his face and then back to hers. 'Ah, so that's the way it is, is it?'

'No, it isn't, you disgusting old —' Lucas put his hand on her back, and with his touch she felt calmer.

'I'm sorry we disturbed you, Jeff,' Lucas said. 'Maggie and I will head back to the house now.'

Maggie spun around to look at him. 'But —'

He bent down and kissed her and she realised the moment was over. She was going to have to wait to get her chance to give Lucas the pleasure he'd shown her. 'It's OK, Maggie. There'll be other times. Plenty of them.'

It was a nice thought, and so she was smiling as she walked out of the shed. Not tonight, but next time. And the ones after that. Maybe for the rest of her life.

*

238

When Lucas woke the next morning, this time in his own bed, his smile threatened to split his face in half.

Feeling Maggie's power flood over him as she came was the most amazing thing he'd ever known. His heart had wrenched and his entire body had tingled, and he'd been desperate for her. When Jeff had arrived, his initial thought was that he wanted to kill the old man.

But as his arousal dimmed he'd been aware of her feelings. It was as though he had a view directly to her heart and what he saw there had amazed and humbled him. Maggie admired him. She liked him. She wanted him. She cared for him — not what he could do, not what he was, just him.

Now, he was glad Jeff had come. He didn't want their first time to be in a shed. Pure feelings like Maggie's deserved better than that.

He put his hands behind his head and happily considered the day ahead. John would no doubt keep them all busy, but tonight Lucas was going to bring Maggie back to his apartment for dinner. Here they could talk — finally voice all the things their bodies had said the night before. Then they could kiss again, and touch, and goddamnit, they could take off their clothes and she could show him how the gadda have fun.

His body bucked a little. Best stop thinking things like that. In fact, he grimaced, best take a long cold shower before he went to say good morning to anyone.

The cold shower did him the world of good and, as he stepped out of the apartment, he was ready to face the world and the myriad wonderful possibilities it held.

He made his way toward the university. He'd spent too much time away from his work – people would start to talk, and the gadda needed him to avoid that.

Once he got into his laboratory, however, he stood at the door and stared at the platforms, the metres of wiring, the tools and computers and felt – nothing. This had been his life's work for more than a decade, and now he felt nothing. Working here didn't fire his imagination, challenge him the way working through the gadda exercises did.

He scratched his head. He was going to have to keep working. The world wouldn't believe it if he just dropped out, not now he was the Julius Edgar Lilienfeld Fellow. They expected more papers, more discoveries, and he'd never felt less like providing them.

He walked into the middle of the room and crouched down by one of the platforms. He traced his fingers over the metal surface, remembering how once he'd imagined his experiments almost spoke to him. Now, it was just steel.

He shook his head. You need to get over this, Valeroso. He stood, went over to his computer and turned it on. Review, he decided. The moment he looked at existing results, ideas would start to flow and he'd get back into it.

There was a knock; Maggie opened the door and walked in. He leant back against the bench and watched her walk toward him with a smile.

'Hello,' he said. Mentally, he wondered how she'd react if he kissed her, here where anyone could see and where he knew it couldn't go further.

'Hi.' She stopped and smiled up at him and

while her smile was warm, it wasn't as wide or all-encompassing as he might have expected. 'We need to talk. Do you mind?'

He felt his heart sink a little. Surely she couldn't be regretting last night. No. He had seen into her: her feelings were no lie. He had to trust her. 'Sure, pull up a pew.'

Her smile widened a little, but he could tell something was wrong. She grabbed two stools and pulled them over, sitting down on one. He ignored the other and maintained his pose against the bench, fighting the impulse to take her into his arms and kiss away whatever was bothering her. Best he let her speak and then he could decide how to act.

The fact she had her hands clasped in front of her and the smile had disappeared from her face did not bode well. 'I've got some news for you, both good and bad I'm afraid. The Sabhamir has found out who your family is.'

'I'm not from one of the missing families, am I?'

Maggie shook her head. 'Your mother was Simone Harrington. My father knew her and said she was a lovely woman, very sweet and kind-natured.'

Lucas frowned as memories crowded into his mind. 'Dark haired?'

'I don't know. Why do you ask?'

'I have this image of a dark-haired woman who was very quiet and sweet. I never was sure who she was.' He shrugged. 'I take it she's dead?'

Maggie nodded. 'She died over thirty years ago, when you were a little boy. Your father died before you were born. His name was Rogan Connor.'

Finally, a name. Throughout his childhood, Lucas had dreamt of the nameless, faceless man who had fathered him. He had imagined him as a great man: kind, wise, full of laughter. And now, finally, he would know.

The shock was almost overwhelming. Lucas sat down on the stool with a thump. He was relieved that Maggie reached out and put her hands on his. 'Rogan Connor. So my name should really be Lucas Connor.' He heard the hope in his voice and smiled. Yesterday he had found Maggie, today his father. Could things get any better?

She squeezed his hands and Lucas focussed his attention on her. Her expression was very serious and the warmth within him began to chill. 'There's more, Lucas, and it's not good. The reason no one knew who you are is your father was banished from the gadda. Your mother followed him and cut her ties with the bardria.'

'Banished?' He frowned down at her, aware that his heart was now contracting.

She nodded and again squeezed his hand, her eyes brimming with compassion. 'He murdered another gadda. His power was blocked and they sent him away. His character was considered so black that an extra sentence was proclaimed upon him.' Then she smiled, but he could see the tears welling in her eyes. 'The bardria decreed that no child he fathered would be welcomed into the gadda.' She squeezed his hand as the words cascaded out of her mouth.

Lucas felt his entire body freeze. His blood iced up; his heart stopped. His gaze moved from Maggie's beautiful face to the floor. Not welcome. He wasn't welcome. Because he carried his father's bad blood.

'We're going to fight this. Lucas, are you listening to me?' Maggie was shaking his arm. 'They must know you're nothing like your father — it's going to be fine.'

Lucas nodded. No, nothing like him at all. Not a murderer. Just a thief and a gang member who'd been in juvie for assault. Even as a kid he'd been capable of —

It began to close in on him, as it had the last time he had gone to court. Well, he knew one thing. He was never going to stand and be judged by anyone else ever again. He stood and walked out of the lab, down the halls and out onto the lawn. He saw people passing by, their faces a blur, as if part of a world he couldn't connect to. He was vaguely aware of Maggie pursuing him, begging him to talk to her. Part of him wanted to turn to her, to accept the comfort she would offer, to drown in her love. But the voice was back, shouting at him. How could she love him? Once she knew the truth, she would turn from him.

So he stayed calm. Control was the only thing that would save him. He felt the coolness of the air and understood he was walking up the stairs to his apartment. But he was on autopilot while he forced his mind and his heart to prepare for the end of the dream.

He opened his front door, stepped inside, closed and locked it, then leant against it. He had barely begun to think what to do next when a figure appeared in front of him. Lucas blinked once, blinked again, then focussed on the Sabhamir.

'Lucas Connor,' the gadma said. 'The —'

'Valeroso.' The Sabhamir frowned. 'My name is Lucas Valeroso.'

'Lucas Valeroso, the bardria of the gadda demands your presence in the bardria chamber in Sclossin in a week's time, on 28 March, at 10 am.' The Sabhamir spoke politely, but Lucas felt the protector was less than happy with him.

'And if I don't go?'

The Sabhamir pulled his shoulders back and looked down his nose. Lucas remembered the power within this man, recognised his control of that power and decided to be more diplomatic. 'The choice is, of course, up to you. The consequence of non-attendance in this case will be instant banishment and I will come to block your powers. If that is what you want, then stay here, by all means. But I suggest you consider what your actions will mean to the O'Haras.'

Lucas frowned. 'What do you mean?'

'There are some in the bardria who do not like John O'Hara. The fact he went ahead and began to train the son of Rogan Connor will be all the excuse they need to destroy him. It will be nothing compared to what you have seen over the past few days. And Siobhan and Margaret will be the ones to really suffer.' The Sabhamir stepped forward and Lucas was aware that the slender man topped him by a good two inches. 'My impression of you is that you are a good man, Lucas Valeroso. I hope I am right, because if your actions destroy the O'Haras, I will come for you. I will find you. You don't want that to happen.' The air wavered and he was gone.

Lucas had heard many threats in his life, but none delivered so politely. He'd never been as scared by one, either.

It appeared, whether he liked it or not, he was going to face the bardria of the gadda. He shook his head and wondered why his stepfather hadn't managed to beat his conscience out of him.

CHAPTER TWENTY-ONE

'Mum!' Maggie flung herself into her mother's arms as Siobhan appeared in the star.

'Careful, darling.' Siobhan stumbled and then regained her balance before she hugged her daughter.

'I've missed you so much.' Maggie pulled back to look at her. 'Are you sure you're OK? You're still a little pale.'

'I'm fine, Maggie. Really. Now, I need a good dose of sun. Even in the middle of the bardria building, I could feel how cold it was outside.' Siobhan took hold of Maggie's elbow and led her from the cellar.

They stopped at John's bedroom and Siobhan put her head in, then turned to Maggie. 'Sleeping. I won't disturb him. How is he going?'

'Not well.' Now it was Maggie who led her mother down the hall. 'He's still telling everyone that it's temporary, and he'll be out of bed in a day or two. But I've not noticed his movement get any better.'

Siobhan shook her head as she leant against the table. 'Save us from stubborn old men,' she said. 'I'm going to have to just force it on him. You know what I really feel like? A cold beer, drunk in the hot sun.'

'Cold beer it is.' Maggie got them a stubby each from

the fridge, then they went outside and sat down on the lounge chairs. 'I am so, so glad that you're back.'

'I know.' Siobhan reached over and put her hand on Maggie's. 'I heard about Lucas. The gossip is all over Sclossin, that Rogan Connor's son has been found. Is he OK?'

'I don't know.' Maggie slumped into the chair. 'He won't talk to me. He went straight to his flat, refused to let me in, packed and left yesterday afternoon. He's probably already on a flight to America, running as far from the gadda as he can.'

'I heard he was going to face the bardria.'

'And do what, beg to be allowed to be gadda? Can you see Lucas doing that?'

'I don't know,' Siobhan said slowly. 'He never struck me as someone who would give up on what he wanted, and there's no doubting he wanted to be gadda.' Then Siobhan glanced at Maggie. 'There are other things for him to fight for here as well, if I'm not mistaken.'

Maggie blushed but looked her mother in the eye. 'I love him, Mum, and I'm sure he loves me.'

'Well, as I said, your taste in men *is* improving, although it would appear you're destined to be with a Flaherty.' Siobhan sipped on her beer.

'What?' Maggie snapped forward, her bottom precariously perched on the edge of the chair. 'What are you talking about?'

Siobhan grinned. 'You mean your father didn't tell you? Shame on you, Peter. My darling, Lucas is to all intents and purposes a Flaherty. His paternal grandmother was Oswald Flaherty's sister. Up until the banishment, Rogan Connor was in line to be the great Flaherty heir. In fact, I think it was his shame that forced Old Man Flaherty to put aside his obsession with Mum in order to have a son with another woman. The Flahertys must continue, you know.'

Maggie flopped against the back of the chair. 'I don't believe it.'

'Believe it, darling. It's destiny. It just took you a while to find the right one.'

Maggie shook her head. 'Grandpa's going to die when he realises this.'

'Oh, I don't know. I think he'll quite like the idea of having an insider in the Flaherty family. And if Lucas can convince the Flahertys that he wants to be part of the clan, they'll make sure he becomes gadda. So it could actually be a good thing.'

'Maggie!' Her grandfather's voice rocked through the house.

'Shame it wasn't his vocal chords that were paralysed,' Siobhan said, putting the beer down and getting up.

Maggie shook her head, grinning as she followed her mother inside. Siobhan pushed open John's door and then put her hands on her hips.

'Still in bed, I see. It's been more than a couple of days, hasn't it?'

'Oh! Shevvy, Shevvy, I'm so happy to see that you're OK.' John opened his arms and Siobhan went to him, sitting on the side of the bed and wrapping her arms around her father. After a long hug, they pulled back.

'Now, you're not to worry about me,' John said. 'Instead, we need to worry about Lucas. Poor boy, we need to find him and —'

'Of course I'm going to worry about you, since you don't have the sense to worry about yourself,' Siobhan cut in. 'But fine, let's ignore the fact you've not been able to move your legs for weeks now and pretend that's just temporary and move on to discussing Lucas.' John's eyes narrowed and Maggie smothered a smile.

'I heard that Lucas is going to face the bardria, so my guess is that he's on his way to Ireland,' Siobhan continued. 'He's going to need support there. Now, Maggie can't go and I won't be allowed to since I've just been sick, so you're going to have to get better so you can go.'

'Damn you,' John growled. 'Don't you think I want to get better?'

'No, actually, I don't,' Siobhan said. 'I had time to think about this in Sclossin. I think as long as you remain injured, you have an excuse for the fact you were beaten by a fuiparra.'

John sat bolt upright. 'What kind of cock-a-mamie bloody psychological crap is that?'

'Crap that's hit the mark, apparently,' Siobhan said, standing. 'So, there are your choices, Dad. If you admit that you're injured and it's permanent, then you'll go back to Sclossin to be fully checked over and for aids to be created to enable you to get around and be independent. You can then easily go to help Lucas. Or, it's just temporary and it's all in your mind and you get off your backside, admit that for once in your life you were beaten, chalk it up to experience and then get ready to go to Sclossin to help Lucas.' Siobhan tipped her head to one side. 'Of course, Lucas does have his family to turn to now, so I guess we can leave it to the Flahertys to help him remain gadda. So you can probably just continue to lie here and be a pain in the arse, if you want.'

'The Flahertys? What the hell are you talking about, girl?'

Siobhan sighed. 'You really don't pay much attention to what happens in Sclossin, do you? Lucas's father is Rogan Connor, and Rogan's mother was —'

'Eliza Flaherty.' John's body began to quiver, including his legs. Then he swung himself over to the side of the bed and glared at Siobhan. 'Flaherty will no more accept the truth of his past than the bardria will. They'll think he's just like his father.'

Maggie stumbled forward, her eyes wide. What was her grandfather talking about? What truth?

Siobhan frowned. 'Lucas's past? You aren't telling me we've had a murderer in our house, are you?'

'Of course not.' John got to his feet. 'Would I hire a bloody murderer? No, he just stole a car at knife-point when he was a stupid kid, but he's done nothing wrong since — not that the bardria will care about that, will they?'

Maggie put her hand to her mouth. Lucas had threatened someone with a knife? She tried to make that information fit with the vision in her mind, and it wouldn't. She turned and slumped down onto her grandfather's bed. She barely registered that her family were still talking.

'Well, it's a good thing you seem to have regained the use of your legs so you can go help him, then, isn't it?' Siobhan said. 'Now, I think we need to help Maggie deal with this news.'

'Oh shit, Mags.' John shuffled his way around the

bed to sit on one side of her, and Siobhan took the other. John patted her hand. 'I thought Lucas would have told you by now. He was brought up in the Bronx, by an abusive step-father, and the only chance he had to survive was to join the local gang. He did a few petty things until the carjacking, and that's what put him in detention. He was fifteen, sixteen. But then he discovered physics, and he's not put a foot wrong since. I think his story is actually a benefit to him, as it proves his ability to control what little blackness he might have inherited from his father.'

'Actually, it's no surprise that he got into trouble, with his power building through puberty,' Siobhan said. 'I wonder if we went through the prisons of the world, how many of the inmates would be gadda who didn't know they were?'

Their words helped Maggie to meld Lucas's past with the man he had become. They were right; rather than being a mark against him, the fact Lucas had overcome his bad childhood was a huge mark in his favour. Pride in him, in his courage and dedication, bloomed within her. She leant against her mother and sighed. 'I just wish he'd had the chance to tell me himself.'

'I'm sure he will as well.' Siobhan kissed her forehead. 'Now that Dad's mobile again, let's go and have lunch and we'll plan how to help Lucas.'

Maggie sat up and smiled at her grandfather. 'Grandpa. You can walk again.'

'Fat lot it'll do me, failure that I am,' he muttered.

Maggie shook her head. 'Not a failure. Just old.' Then she smiled at his obvious anger. 'But you can redeem yourself by saving Lucas.'

John looked at the two of them and shook his head. 'Save me from stubborn women.'

By that night, Maggie was feeling quietly confident that Lucas would be fine. Her family had done marvellously – they'd called and contacted heaps of connections in Sclossin, getting as much support for Lucas as possible. And John was planning to transfer over there to be by Lucas's side during the actual hearing.

She sat on the patio watching the sunset and allowed herself the luxury of considering the future. When Lucas came back next week, decisions would have to be made. It all felt so right. She knew he wanted what she did – or close to it. He'd be OK once he'd faced the bardria, wouldn't he? Even though he'd been so shut down when she told him about his father – he still wanted her, right? They'd be together. Should they move in together? His apartment in Winton would do for now, cosy and sweet enough for a loved-up couple, but if things worked out, at some point they'd need a home of their own.

Maggie closed her eyes and sighed as she pictured the rest of her life making love to Lucas. If their one night together was evidence, the two of them were amazingly compatible.

Her mother came out and sat down next to her. 'You OK?'

Maggie nodded. 'As OK as I can be until Lucas is back.'

Siobhan patted her hand. 'Hopefully we'll get the whole thing over and done with quickly. There are other things happening, Maggie, that could have a much bigger impact.'

Maggie frowned. 'What sort of other things?'

'When I was in the healer's wing, the Ceamir was brought in. I don't think she has long to live.'

'Poor Ceamir.' Maggie remembered how the old woman had saved her from the punishment she probably deserved over her children's story.

'She's been a good Ceamir, particularly for us O'Haras. She's been very understanding of our desire to work closely with humans. But if the next one isn't ...' Siobhan's voice trailed off.

'They can't pick a Ceamir who isn't sympathetic to humans, can they?'

'The Ceamir and the other guardians will have a big say, and I'd imagine they'll want to retain the balance, but the bardria may not let it happen, particularly in light of recent events.'

'The fucking story.' Maggie slumped back onto the lounge.

'And the attacks. And Lucas's discovery. And there are rumours circulating the bardria building that something important has been stolen: apparently the Sabhamir is going crazy looking for it and all the bardria are on tenterhooks. It would seem this isn't the most placid of times for the gadda and, while that's a good argument for keeping the balance, it's also an argument for change. So pray, Maggie, that we do end up with a good Ceamir.'

Maggie closed her eyes and began to do just that.

CHAPTER TWENTY-TWO

By the time Lucas's hearing came around, Maggie was a nervous wreck. What if her family's work wasn't enough? What if Lucas was banished anyway? Somehow, she felt sure there was something she could do, if only she could get over to Sclossin. Just holding Lucas's hand, and letting him know that regardless she loved him and he had a home in Winton.

Damn the bloody sentence, she thought as she paced up and down the loungeroom. Why had she made such a stupid, foolish mistake? It wasn't fair if it robbed Lucas of his place in the gadda.

She looked at the clock and shuddered. It was half-past eight on the evening of 28 March in Winton. In half an hour's time, on the other side of the world, Lucas was going to face the bardria and try to prove he deserved to be gadda.

At least, that's what she thought he was going to prove. Maggie's pacing slowed and she began chewing on her fingernail. She had no idea what Lucas was thinking. She could only imagine how scared he was. He had finally found his home, where he belonged and they were threatening to take it away from him.

She stopped and stamped her foot. She wouldn't allow it. She wouldn't.

She turned to pick up the phone, to defy her sentence in order to save Lucas, but the peal of the doorbell stilled her hand. She took a deep breath to control her emotions, then went over and pulled the door open. Her eyes widened when she saw a woman standing on the doorstep. Maggie's first impression of the woman was that she was hard. Thick make-up tried to hide the impact of thirty-five years and managed pretty well. Her hair was piled on top of her head, small tendrils left to curl prettily but precisely around her ears and neck. Her slender body was encased in black linen, with a floral print silk blouse adding a feminine touch.

'Excuse me?' The woman's voice was husky and drawled with a thick American accent. 'I'm looking for Professor John O'Hara?'

Oh great, Maggie thought. Perfect bloody timing. 'I'm afraid he's not in at the moment.'

'Do you know when he'll be back?' The woman's smile was wide but unconvincing.

'He should be back later tonight. If you come by tomorrow, he will be able to see you.'

'Actually, it's not really Professor O'Hara I want to see. It's just, I was told that my fiancé was with him.'

American accent. Wanting her fiancé. A terrible suspicion began to occur to Maggie. 'Who is your fiancé?'

The woman smiled and pulled her shoulders back. 'Dr Lucas Valeroso. Have you heard of him?'

For a moment, her heartbeats shuddered through her body and Maggie was unable to think. Then her brain clicked into gear. 'Have you just arrived from America?'

'Just this hour, to find my fiancé gone from his apartment and me with nowhere to stay. This really is a long way from anywhere, isn't it? Still, it's quite lovely, in its own way.'

Maggie just couldn't see Lucas and this woman together. 'Please, come in, and I'll get you some coffee.' She stepped back.

The woman smiled and nodded. 'Thank you. I'd appreciate that.' She stepped into the house and closed the door.

'This way.' Maggie led the woman up the hallway, sending a mental message to her mother in the cellar. She offered her visitor a seat, then went into the kitchen and turned the kettle on. By the time she turned back to face her guest, Siobhan was walking into the room.

'Maggie, you didn't tell me we had a guest.' She smiled at the stranger. 'How do you do? I'm Siobhan Shaunessy.'

'Holly Faulkner.' The woman held out a perfectly manicured hand.

'Of course! So lovely to finally meet you. You've just arrived?' Siobhan sat down, apparently fascinated.

As Maggie, confused, got out the cups, milk, sugar and biscuits, she listened to Holly Faulkner repeat that she was Lucas's fiancée.

'Of course,' Siobhan said with a smile. 'Lucas has told us all about you.'

Maggie dropped a spoon but caught it with a pulse of power before it hit the bench.

'Really? I am surprised.' Holly grinned. 'I was a little concerned when I had to let him come out here alone. Lucas can be a bit of a lad, you know.' She looked pointedly at Maggie as she spoke.

Maggie gritted her teeth and smiled.

The kettle's whistle saved her from Holly's scrutiny and she put the coffee in the container, filling it with water and pushing the plunger down to release the wonderful aroma. Then she put it on the tray and carried it to the table.

'I was quite disappointed to learn Lucas wasn't home. I can't imagine what could have possessed him to leave when he knew I was coming.' Holly pouted.

'I'm sure it was something that couldn't be avoided. When my father returns, he'll be able to fill you in.'

'Ah, so you're Professor O'Hara's daughter? And you?' Holly looked at Maggie.

'His granddaughter.' Maggie hoped her smile appeared more natural than the last one. She was sorely tempted to knock this woman's teeth out. And then Lucas's.

She turned her attention to pouring the coffee. She was at war with herself. Half of her was furious at him for betraying her and his fiancée. The other half couldn't believe it was real. She could have sworn Lucas was as faithful as they come. But then, she'd have sworn he'd never stolen cars, too.

'Oh, I see.' Holly put a wealth of emphasis into the three words and Maggie was determined not to respond. Instead, she carefully handed Holly her coffee and passed one to her mother.

'I do hope Lucas hasn't been making a nuisance of himself.' Holly poured herself some milk and put several teaspoons of sugar into her coffee.

'I doubt Lucas is capable of making a nuisance of himself,' Siobhan said, taking a sip of her black coffee.

'Yes, he is the very personification of charm, isn't he?' Holly smiled conspiratorially. 'And then, when he tires of you ...' She sighed, as if she were carrying a terrible load.

Maggie nearly choked on her drink and had to swallow it quickly. Holly was laying it on a bit thick.

'You make it sound as though Lucas is hard work.' Siobhan reached forward for a biscuit. Maggie silently cheered her mother's technique.

'He is. Of course, I think it's worth it.' This time, Holly's smile was the smile of a sexually satisfied woman.

The idea of Lucas with this woman made Maggie feel nauseated.

Holly continued. 'I love him, but I'm not blind to his faults. Still, I live in hope that one day, he'll turn around and then all that wonderful intelligence and strength will turn to the good. How much freedom does Professor O'Hara give Lucas, do you know?'

'I would imagine the same freedoms as any of his staff. What do you think, Maggie?'

Maggie fought for an answer. 'More, I would say, since Lucas doesn't have to teach like the rest.'

'Excuse me, but you work at the university?'

Maggie smiled, glad she had discomfited the woman a little. 'Yes. Lucas is a brilliant scientist. You must be extremely proud of him.'

'As long as he keeps all his chemicals at work and doesn't stink up the apartment, I'm very proud.' Holly waved a hand in the air.

For a moment, Maggie's anger almost overcame her confusion. How could Holly be Lucas's fiancé and not know what he did?

'Well, it's too late for you to get a room in town tonight, so I think you should stay with us,' Siobhan announced, pushing her chair back and standing. 'Maggie, come and help me set up the spare room, will you?'

Maggie was glad to escape their visitor's presence. She followed Siobhan down to the spare room and the moment they were inside, hissed, 'Who the hell is this woman? How could Lucas's fiancée not know the difference —'

'Hush.' Siobhan frowned. 'We won't discuss our guest like that. Now, help me with this sheet.' Then, mentally, she said, '*I don't know, darling. Though I don't trust this Holly Faulkner as far as I can throw her.*'

'*It's just one thing after another, isn't it?*' Maggie tucked in her side of the sheet.

'*We wouldn't want things to be boring. Now, you and I are going to be nice to this Holly, understand?*'

'*Yes, Mother.*' They finished the bed, and returned to the dining area to find Holly had polished off the rest of the coffee and the biscuits. 'I don't suppose you have anything more fiery to drink, hmmm?' She smiled at them.

Maggie looked at the woman's smug face and fought the unworthy urge to offer her a makeover. 'Irish whiskey?'

259

'Only if you've got the good stuff.' Holly reached into her bag and pulled out a cigarette case and a lighter.

'Certainly.' Maggie walked over to the bar and poured Holly a good stiff shot of whiskey.

'Thanks.' Holly blew a plume of smoke toward Maggie. She looked at her mother, hoping Siobhan would tell the American to put the cigarette out. 'Do you mind if I speak plainly?'

Better than the lies you have been telling, Maggie thought as she sat down. 'Not a problem. Go ahead.'

Holly leant forward. 'I think maybe there might be something going on between you and Lucas. I've got a nose for the kinds of girls he likes. Don't worry, I don't blame you, not one little bit. I mean, I know full well just how easy it is to love him.' She smiled. 'But I should tell you that while I'm around, I keep Lucas far too busy to bother with other women. So my advice to you is to forget about him. Perhaps you need to get out, see the world. After all, there can't be much action here.'

It struck Maggie she should introduce Holly to Scott, if she was worried about a lack of action in Winton. 'I thank you for thinking of me, when you must be so hurt yourself.'

Holly frowned. 'I beg your pardon?'

Maggie realised she couldn't spend another moment with Holly. True, the woman didn't *seem* upset by the betrayal she was alleging, but perhaps she was just a really pragmatic person, like those sportsmen's wives who stuck around no matter what their husbands did. Maggie was tense with trying to give Lucas the benefit of the doubt. 'Forgive me. It's late and I'm tired.' She got to her feet. 'I hope you will excuse me. Good night, Mum.' She kissed Siobhan on the cheek, then walked away.

She heard Holly say, 'I hope I didn't hurt her feelings by speaking so bluntly, but it's best she knows the truth now, don'tcha think?' Maggie could only pray that it was Holly Faulkner who was clinging to false hope.

Determined to wait up until her grandfather and hopefully Lucas returned, Maggie got herself a romance novel and sat down on her bed to read and wait.

Lucas looked around him and, even after his experiences in the human justice system, was intimidated by the gadda bardria room. It was simple, plain even, but he didn't mistake that simplicity for a lack of power. If anything, the fact the bardria of the gadda didn't feel the need for podiums and lecterns showed just how powerful they truly were.

The room was crowded with around fifty people. They had come to see the son of the infamous Rogan Connor, and to see what the bardria would do with a newly discovered gadda. On Lucas's left sat John O'Hara, ready to defend his recruit. Lucas wished John hadn't come. Until the moment he walked into the room and saw the older man talking with someone else, Lucas had been doing a great job of forgetting about the O'Haras, Maggie in particular. At least, he'd convinced himself he was doing a great job, considering last night he'd only lain awake for an hour thinking of her and how her mouth tasted before he fell into a disturbed, dream-filled sleep.

Then he'd seen John and realised he was fooling himself. He missed O'Hara's relentless determination. He missed Siobhan's practicality and concern for others. He even missed Peter and his overbearing dedication to correctness. Most of all, he missed Maggie: her smile, her intelligence, the way her body felt pressed against his.

And now they were going to take it all away from him. He tried not to tell himself that he should have expected it, but that dark voice was enjoying its freedom. *As if you could have a woman like that*, it whispered in his mind. *As if you deserve any happiness.*

A door at the far end of the room opened and twenty men and women walked in – the bardria, including Caelleach Cormac, Flaherty and Smyth. He looked at the three familiar faces. Flaherty wore a smirk of triumph, Smyth one of disappointment. Cormac's expression was calm, and Lucas felt a tiny flicker of hope. They all sat. The first man to speak sat to Cormac's right.

'This hearing, dealing with the future of the son of a banished one, is now open. We all know what has happened: John O'Hara found an unknown gadda. After some investigation, we know he is the son of a banished one: Rogan Connor. At the time of the banishment, the bardria decided that no child of Connor's would be admitted to the orders of the gadda. This decision stands, and we are here to decide whether to rescind it.'

Lucas raised an eyebrow. Guilty until proven innocent, hey? At least that was a variation on the theme.

The man focussed his attention on Lucas, and the depth of his black eyes struck home. 'Lucas Connor, you may speak in your defence.'

Lucas folded his arms across his chest. 'I am not Lucas Connor.'

A small crease formed between the man's eyebrows. 'I beg your pardon?'

'I am not Lucas Connor. My name is Lucas Valeroso.'

Lucas was aware of shuffling and whispers coming from the crowd behind him. He guessed no one spoke to this man in this manner.

The man leant forward, his eyes narrowing. 'Your birth name is Connor.'

'So you say.' Lucas shrugged. 'But I know myself as Valeroso and that is the only name I will answer to.'

The man's face flushed and he opened his mouth, but Cormac leant forward and put a hand on the man's arm. The man looked at Cormac, and desisted.

Cormac nodded at Lucas. 'Mr Valeroso, if I ask you some questions, will you answer them truthfully?'

Lucas nodded. 'With pleasure, Caelleach Cormac.'

'Then please, take the seat.' Cormac gestured to a chair placed in isolation before the bardria. Lucas flicked a quick glance at John, but the older man appeared unconcerned. As Lucas sat, the Firimir came to stand behind him, placing his hands on Lucas's face.

Lucas felt pressure against his mind and his jaw clenched.

'Relax, I mean you no harm,' the Firimir murmured. Lucas took a deep breath and then forced his body and his mind to relax. He felt ease flood over him, and his awareness of anything except Caelleach Cormac and the man behind him disappeared.

The sudden loss of his senses threw him and he tried to fight it, but then he heard the Firimir's voice inside his mind. *'Relax, Lucas Valeroso. I seek only to discover if you speak truth.'*

I really don't have a choice, Lucas thought as he relaxed.

'Mr Valeroso, how long have you known you are gadda?' The caelleach's voice was loud and clear in his mind.

Lucas calculated quickly. 'A few weeks.'

'And how do you feel about being gadda?'

Lucas smiled. 'I feel wonderful, sir. I never felt I belonged anywhere in human society. The moment I knew I was gadda and was shown my power, I knew that this was what I had been missing all my life.'

There was a murmur, noise trying to intrude into his consciousness, then suddenly it broke through. 'Considering your past, it's really no surprise you were not welcomed anywhere, is it?' The first man spoke again, his eyes flashing hatred at Lucas.

Lucas had no idea who this man could be. He realised that he couldn't afford to respond to his anger, no matter what its cause. 'I did not say I was not welcomed. I have almost always been warmly received and admired by the scientific community, for example. But I never felt that I belonged. The closest I ever got to feeling peace was when I was lost in an experiment but the moment it was over, the loneliness and pain would return.' Amazingly, Lucas felt his eyes begin to water. He took a deep breath and hoped he wouldn't end up crying.

'You speak eloquently, Mr Valeroso, and certainly your words echo those of gadda who are late in controlling their powers.' The caelleach nodded.

'Let him address the facts of his convictions,' the first man broke in. 'Let him prove he does not carry the bad blood of his father. Is it true that at the age of eleven, you were arrested for shoplifting, at twelve for car theft and at fifteen you were sentenced to gaol time for stealing another car and knifing its owner as you got away?'

And there it was. The truth, in all its ugliness. His truth, not Holly's. He could only be grateful that she was safely in the US, where her dangerous 'proof' couldn't hurt him. His spine straightened; he held his head high. 'All those things are true.'

'And so he condemns himself.' The man threw his hands triumphantly in the air.

'Councillor Halloran, your words do you no credit. Henry, please.' Cormac's voice was barely audible to Lucas. Henry subsided, but with a smile. The caelleach turned to Lucas. 'Why did you do these things?'

Lucas blinked. 'It was what you did to survive. I grew up in the Bronx. You joined a gang and did what you had to do to stay alive. If you were lucky, eventually, you escaped. If not, you stayed until you were shot or you shot someone.'

Cormac shook his head. 'A terrible life for a boy.' He turned his head to look at his fellow councillors, an act Lucas thought designed to show he was addressing them even though he couldn't see them. 'It's quite possible that had he had a safer childhood, with greater opportunity, he wouldn't have behaved as he did and we would be considering overturning the decision.'

'How can you say that?' Henry jumped to his feet. 'He is a hardened criminal. He's been in gaol. It's only a matter of time before he returns to his old tricks.'

'Since he has had no contact with the law since he was eighteen, I find it hard to believe that he will suddenly be a threat now.' Cormac tilted his head to one side and frowned. 'I wish to question John O'Hara now. Lucas Valeroso, thank you. You may return to your seat.'

The pressure left Lucas, and little bits of noise, sights and smells flooded into him. He looked around, his body shivering. Then he looked over his shoulder at the Firimir, and the man nodded slightly.

Lucas stood and walked back to his chair on wobbly legs. John took his place in the hot seat. The Firimir took hold of O'Hara and then Cormac began the questioning. 'John, you hired the man for your university. Why?'

'Because he is one of the most brilliant scientific minds in the world. Because he is renowned as a hard worker and a loyal employee. I have found him to be a man of incredible self-control. We have nothing to fear from admitting Lucas Valeroso to the ranks of the order.'

Lucas bowed his head. The dark voice told him he didn't deserve such praise. He told the voice to shut up.

To Henry's evident disgust, the caelleach dismissed O'Hara with thanks. 'Firimir, your thoughts?'

'Both Lucas Valeroso and John O'Hara spoke truth.' Again, Lucas breathed in that wonderful smell. 'And I sense no darkness in Lucas Valeroso, nor a desire to do wrong.'

Lucas gripped his knees. No darkness? He carried no darkness?

'Thank you.' Cormac bowed his head to the gadma, who returned to his position by the wall. 'The bardria will now retire to consider its decision. We will return in an hour.' He stood and the rest of the bardria followed suit, filing out the door.

Once the door closed behind them, John let out a sigh of relief. 'That went well,' he said with a grin.

Lucas rolled his eyes. 'If that Henry has his way, they'll hang, draw and quarter me before they banish me.'

'Yes, he was a little intense. To be expected, for it was Halloran's wife your father murdered.'

Lucas began to shake. 'Jesus.'

John patted his hand. 'The rest of the bardria will be swung by rational thought, not emotion. Don't worry. Come along, I'll buy you a Guinness. We need it.' John stood.

Lucas looked around. 'Won't I need to stay here? In custody?'

John laughed. 'Crikey, no. I mean, if you do run away, do you think the Sabhamir won't find you?'

Lucas shook his head. 'There are advantages to having magic, aren't there?'

'Shhh, don't let anyone hear you use that word. Some people are a little touchy about human labels. Now, I can feel a pint calling me. Come along.'

When the Caelleach announced the bardria's decision, it was brief.

'We do not have enough evidence to decide whether Lucas Valeroso would be worthy to be admitted to the orders or not. The impression of this bardria is that he seems a worthy man, but they cannot judge whether he would be a worthy gadda. His age counts against training him. There is also concern he has spent too long immersed in human society to ever fully understand being gadda. Therefore, the decision of this bardria is that the sentence stands. In two days, Lucas Valeroso will come before this bardria where his powers will be blocked and he will be banished from the gadda.'

Lucas waited for the thud of the gavel. It never came, but he had never heard a more final decision in his life.

CHAPTER TWENTY-THREE

Maggie was struggling to stay awake. She sat on a bench in the basement, a large mug of coffee next to her, the romance novel on her lap. Both the caffeine and the romance had worked for a while, but the late hour was starting to take its toll.

After several hours, Holly Faulkner had finally gone to bed and Siobhan had put a lock on her door so she wouldn't disturb them. Then the two women had taken up positions in the basement to await John and news about Lucas.

Maggie's head drooped down, and then it shot backward as she forced herself awake again. She looked at her grandfather, blinked a couple of times then realised she wasn't dreaming. 'Well?'

John walked over to her, picked up her coffee and took a long draught. Then he looked at her and Siobhan. 'He will be banished. The ceremony will take place in two days.'

'*No.*' Maggie's heart refused to beat, her mind refused to work. She swallowed and found something like her voice. 'They can't banish him. He's done nothing wrong. He's innocent.'

'He's got the wrong father. And his past got in the

way.' John's head flopped back to rest on the back of the chair. 'How many times must a man pay for his mistakes? May I have a whiskey, Shevvy?'

'If we've got any left,' Maggie said as her mother left the room. Her grandfather frowned. 'There's a woman here. Holly Faulkner. Claims to be Lucas's fiancée.' Oh please, please, please don't let it be true.

'Ah, so she finally turned up, did she? Lucas and I were wondering. Interesting she should come now, when all this is partly her fault. It was she who egged Lucas on to steal that car.'

Maggie knew she'd worry about Holly until Lucas himself explained her. But her grandfather's unconcern was reassuring.

'How did the bardria find out about it?'

'It wouldn't have been that hard.' John shook his head. 'It's ridiculous, but they're too scared of the slightest possibility of another Rogan Connor to give him a chance.'

Maggie considered life without Lucas. It looked grey and meaningless. But without his power, he may as well be human, and being with him would be impossible. No, she thought. Just harder. And she'd spend the rest of her life working out how to make it happen. 'You'll have him back here to work, won't you?'

'Of course, but I doubt Lucas will come. Imagine how difficult it would be for him, surrounded by gadda.' John sighed, but then looked up with a smile as Siobhan came into the basement, carrying a glass of golden liquor. He took the glass and had a mouthful, then stared down at it as he sloshed the liquid around the sides. 'I might start calling round, see if I can find somewhere for him.'

'This whole thing's a joke.' Siobhan leant against the bench. 'The boy never had any contact with his father and has shown he can control whatever streak of restlessness he might have inherited.'

'There's nothing we can do.' The lack of hope in John's voice was shattering.

'There must be something.' Siobhan began pacing up and down the room. 'We just need to appeal to the bardria from another angle. They can't possibly want to get rid of a potentially powerful gadda. What if we promise he will take the gadma route?'

'We can't promise that. We have no idea that he will be suitable,' John said.

Siobhan snorted. 'What rot. He's eminently suitable, and you know it. I think we should try that argument.'

'If we're going to go the "he's too valuable" route, why not just go with the fact we need all the fertile men we can get?'

'Don't you think that's a tad insulting to Lucas?'

Maggie sat deep in thought. Whatever the truth of Lucas's relationship with Holly Faulkner, the one thing Maggie knew for sure was that he desperately wanted to be gadda. And if he is gadda, said a small voice she tried to ignore, Holly can't have him anyway. But Maggie had to at least give him a chance at a life with power. If the bardria couldn't be convinced, why not use a little blackmail? After all, a big concern of all gadda was the fact they bred so slowly.

She stood and made her way up the kitchen. Picking up the phone, she ordered a ticket on the next afternoon's flight from Sydney to Ireland. Then she went to her room and began packing. She had to risk the censure of the bardria, even her own possible banishment. She had to save Lucas.

Lucas sat in the same chair he had used two days earlier. This time, over a hundred people had squeezed into the room. Obviously a banishment was a sight to see.

He wondered what would happen. Would there be huge flashes of lightning as his power was blocked? Would he be magically lifted and cast from the room? Surely they'd have to do something dramatic, to draw a crowd like this.

The seats around him were empty. Strangers weren't game to sit near him, it seemed. And there was no one here to support him. He'd banned John from coming again, and he'd been quite surprised when the other man had quietly acquiesced. It had hurt, the idea that maybe now the sentence had been passed, John was giving up on him.

Had Maggie? He hadn't heard from her, but then she wasn't allowed to contact anyone in Sclossin. Was she sitting in Winton, wishing, hoping for him? Or had she decided he was too much work and moved on?

The door opened and the bardria filed in. He avoided looking at Henry, not wanting to see the satisfaction on the other man's face. Instead, he focussed his attention on the caelleach and noticed the aura of sadness the man carried. At least someone was on his side.

The bardria sat and Cormac spoke. 'We have gathered here to banish Lucas Connor. Before we go ahead with the ceremony, is there anyone who wishes to speak?'

Lucas folded his arms over his chest. He couldn't think of anything he particularly wanted to say. He just wanted this over and done with, so he could leave and try to forget the gadda and the glittering future he had once had.

'I'd like to speak.'

Lucas froze then swung around. Maggie was pushing her way through the crowd. The lights of the room glowed in her golden hair. She looked like an angel. An avenging angel, he corrected himself, when he noted the hardness of her expression. She stopped next to him, looked down and gave him a smile. Then she faced the bardria. 'Good day, councillors.'

'Margaret Shaunessy. I must say I'm surprised to see you here, since the last time you appeared before this bardria, you were directed not to return to Sclossin for two years.' Cormac's voice was hard.

Shit, Maggie, what have you done? Lucas thought.

Maggie flushed. 'I am aware of that, Caelleach, and am willing to accept the consequences of my disobedience. They are nothing compared with what you're about to do.'

Lucas thought the caelleach would have rolled his eyes if he could. 'Ms Shaunessy, I admit that your loyalty to your friends and family is one of the few shining points of your personality, however –'

'Have *you* thought through the consequences of *your* decision?' Maggie cut in.

Cormac frowned. 'I'm sure we have.'

'So you accept that by banishing Lucas Valeroso from the gadda, you are condemning me to childlessness?'

There were gasps from all around the room. Lucas looked up at Maggie, wondering what she was playing at. She was smiling broadly at the bardria.

Cormac and the rest of the bardria were frowning. 'I cannot see how this decision impacts on your ability to have children,' Cormac said.

'Easily. If you banish Lucas, I swear to never fall pregnant. I've looked up the words of the curse of barrenness. Interesting reading.'

Silence fell on the room. Lucas grabbed Maggie's hand and pulled until she bent down to put her face by his, though she wouldn't look any higher than his chin. 'Are you crazy? You can't do this.'

'Don't sweat,' she whispered. 'They'll let ten children of Rogan Connor enter the orders before they let a young gadda woman swear barrenness.' She smiled sadly. 'Besides, I'll do anything to see you happy.'

Lucas released her and fought the urge to shout out his sudden hope. Maggie dropped the smile and presented a straight face to the bardria. 'Well?'

The councillors all wore expressions of varying degrees of shock and horror. 'Firimir!' Cormac almost screamed.

The gadma walked over to Maggie and stood in front of her to put his hands on her face. He looked at her for a long moment, then released her and turned to the bardria. 'Margaret Shaunessy speaks truth.'

Cormac blinked, then addressed the room. 'We

will need to discuss this recent development. We will return in an hour.' The bardria stood and they all hurried from the room.

'Fuck.' Lucas stared at the empty table.

'See? I told you it would work.' They stared at each other. Lucas was desperate for contact.

'I really shouldn't let you risk this kind of sacrifice,' said Lucas, his voice hoarse with relief and the effort not to touch her.

'It's not up to you what I do, Lucas.' Her voice was cool, and her eyes full of love and pain. 'Who's Holly? Why does she say you're going to marry her?'

Lucas's heart sank. 'And you think it's true? That I would —'

'I don't know. But surely you didn't think I was going to stand by and let them do this to you without a fight?' Maggie's eyes were glittering with tears.

'Thank god you didn't. But Maggie: please, *please* believe that Holly is a long time in my past.'

She nodded, and swallowed, and gave him a more genuine smile than she had thus far. He thought it was time to talk about something else.

'The caelleach didn't seem glad to see you.'

'Caelleach Cormac and I have had a few run-ins over the years. Can you believe he thinks I'm hard to handle?' Her voice was hers again too, firm and full of laughter. She knew he was telling the truth.

Lucas laughed with relief. 'Life's never quiet around you gadda, is it?'

'It's not the gadda, it's the O'Haras. And by the way, if this doesn't work and they banish you, don't think you're going anywhere but back to Winton.

Apart from anything else, you've got a teleporter to finish and Nobel prize to win.'

'I knew you just wanted me for my brain.'

'Among other things.' She looked directly into his eyes, and he could practically see the smorgasbord of evil sex she was imagining. His hand lifted, of its own volition, to her face, but a voice from the door stopped him cold.

'Ms Shaunessy, the caelleach wishes to see you.'

CHAPTER TWENTY-FOUR

Maggie stood in the doorway of the caelleach's office and admired the wood panelling, rich red velvet curtains and mahogany furnishings. Then she recognised the red-haired man who stood behind Cormac's seat.

A chill went down her spine. Sean. How the hell had he got a job here? Wasn't he being disciplined after his jaunt to Australia?

The caelleach sat behind the desk, his fingers steepled in front of him. He had worn that exact expression of pained exasperation on their previous encounters. 'I know you O'Haras too well to assume that you were not serious in your threat.'

'I will do whatever it takes to stop you banishing Lucas.'

'If I were to give Lucas Valeroso a month to prove himself to the bardria, would that be sufficient to remove your threat?'

Maggie smiled. 'Two months?'

'Do not press your luck, Ms Shaunessy.'

Quit while you're ahead. 'A month, then.' She stood and leant over the table to touch the caelleach's hand.

Cormac turned to Sean. 'Bring Lucas Valeroso to me, please.' Sean scowled, obviously not wanting to leave. 'You have been directed to do something, Mr Flaherty. You will do it.'

Sean stormed from the room, glaring at Maggie as he did so. Maggie relaxed into her seat.

Cormac looked in her direction and then sighed. 'What am I supposed to do with you, Margaret Shaunessy? You seem to take delight in disobeying my every direction.'

Maggie opened her mouth to defend herself, but decided that right now, words probably wouldn't help.

'At least you've learnt when to be quiet,' Cormac murmured.

The door opened and Lucas came in, followed by Sean, who took up his position behind the caelleach again. The Sabhamir was last in the room, closing the door behind him.

Cormac turned his face to Lucas. 'Ms Shaunessy's — shall we say, intriguing? — proposition has ensured a reprieve for you. The bardria will withhold your sentence for one month. During that time, you will remain here in Sclossin. We will —'

'Hang on.' Maggie frowned. 'You never mentioned he would have to stay here.'

'Didn't I? How remiss of me.' A smile crossed Cormac's lips. 'We will be watching you closely. Should you prove yourself a man of strength and virtue, then you can train for and sit the first order test. However, should your character be revealed to be akin to your father's, you will be banished and blocked and no threat from any gadda will stop that.'

'Thank you, sir,' said Lucas. 'You will not regret this decision.'

'I certainly hope not.' Cormac smiled. Then his attention turned to Maggie and he frowned. 'If you could teach Ms Shaunessy some self-discipline, you will go a long way toward achieving your aims. The Sabhamir will now place a block on your power. It is a non-negotiable part of the bargain, Ms Shaunessy,' he added, frowning at Maggie.

The Sabhamir stepped forward and put his hand on Lucas's forehead. His face went blank, and then he nodded and stood back. 'It is done.'

'I thank you for this opportunity, Caelleach Cormac, and I will prove you have nothing to fear from me,' Lucas said.

'I hope you are right. Now, Ms Shaunessy, say your goodbyes. The Sabhamir will be returning you to Australia. There, you will find your father is feigning an illness. You will be spending all your time with him, nursing him back to health. Your work, I'm afraid, will have to be sacrificed for the good of your family.'

Maggie's mouth dropped open. But the caelleach wasn't finished with her yet.

'While with your father, you will study for and pass your third-order test. We have granted special dispensation for you to complete it within the five years, courtesy of your advanced age. Hopefully the discipline needed will teach you some sort of loyalty to the gadda and the bardria.'

Maggie tried to speak, but stopped when a sharp alarm rang through the air. The caelleach jumped to his feet and stabbed a finger at Maggie.

'Stay there.' Then he pointed at Lucas. 'Don't let her move.' Then he and the Sabhamir disappeared.

'What's going on?' Maggie looked around.

Lucas shrugged. 'You'd have more of an idea than I would.'

'Why bother asking him at all, Margaret?' Sean cut in. 'He is not gadda.'

Maggie frowned. 'He certainly is.'

Sean smiled. 'He isn't, and he won't be. I don't know what the man has said to you, Margaret, but look deep within and you'll know the truth. You are a committed gadda, as am I. He is not.'

Maggie rolled her eyes. 'Sean, shut up.' She turned to Lucas and put her hands in his. 'Can you believe they won't let me work?' Lucas rubbed her hands and warm tingles spread over her body.

She leant closer. 'I guess you'll just have to find other ways to keep me occupied.' Visions of all the delicious ways Lucas could keep her busy flowed through her mind. Her desire began to swell, and she waited for the corresponding response from Lucas, but there was nothing. She looked up at him and he grimaced. Sean, whose face had been purpling with rage, cackled.

'Power block,' Lucas said, ignoring the Flaherty heir. 'Must be.'

'We'll just have to work out a way around it.' Maggie leant in to kiss him, but an invisible force hit her. It threw her back into her chair, covered her and then pushed inside her, wrapping itself around her power.

'Fuck.' She pressed her hands to her chest. The presence was integrating itself within her, becoming part of her power. 'Sabhamir!' she shrieked.

The protector appeared, and walked around the desk to put a hand on her shoulder. He was followed by the other guardians of the gadda: the Heasimir, the Coiremir, the Firimir, and the Garramir, the gardener, all in green. *I've never met him before,* some part of her was able to think.

'It's all right, Margaret,' the Sabhamir said. 'Don't panic. At least, not until I tell you what's happening.'

'Don't tease the girl, Hampton,' the Garramir said with a frown. Then he smiled at Maggie. 'We've got some news for you, Margaret.'

Maggie looked at the five guardians, her eyes wide. She wasn't sure what surprised her more — that they were all here, that they were all looking at her, or how casual they were being with each other, and with her.

'What news? What is happening to me? This thing came, and now it's in me, and what the hell is going on?' Her voice dwindled to an embarrassing squeak.

'Sean, Lucas, you need to leave,' the Sabhamir said.

'No.' Maggie squeezed Lucas's hand.

'I'm sorry, Margaret, but this is a private conversation. Gentlemen.'

To Maggie's amazement, both Sean and Lucas left without an argument, although Lucas looked back at the last with strength and love in his gaze. He trusted her to survive whatever this turned out to be.

The Sabhamir took Lucas's seat. 'Margaret, I'm afraid I have to inform you that the Ceamir has died.'

Maggie's own problems were temporarily washed away in a flood of sadness. 'That's terrible news.'

'It is indeed. She was a good woman. However, we do not yet have time to mourn her. We must find a new Ceamir, and that must happen quickly. For some time, the last Ceamir was quite clear about whom she believed should replace her, and we are all in agreement.' The Firimir and Garramir both nodded. The Heasimir and Coiremir didn't demur.

'And now, the Ceamir's spirit has also chosen.'

It took a moment for the words to make sense, then Maggie pressed her hand against her chest, where her power was changing, shifting, evolving. 'Me?'

The Sabhamir nodded. 'You, Margaret Shaunessy, are the one the guardians have chosen to be the Ceamir.'

Maggie lurched to her feet. 'But I can't be! I'm not a third-order gadma, I've only just made second-order dath, and I'm a troublemaker, and I'm too young!' The words rushed from her, even as the news settled within her and began to feel right.

'Arguments the bardria will undoubtedly use against you.' The Sabhamir leant back in his chair and smiled at her. His apparent lack of concern calmed her a little. She was able to squash her panic and pay attention to his words. 'However, few guardians are third-order gadma when they take on their role and you certainly have the capability to reach that level. Is that not so, Coiremir?'

'Yes,' the teacher said.

'You're certainly not too young — I myself was younger, as was the Garramir.' The gardener grinned. 'As for being a troublemaker, I'd say that's because you've not had enough responsibility to match your intelligence and abilities,' the Sabhamir continued. 'Once you're Ceamir, you won't have time to think up ways of annoying the caelleach. And there's no doubting there's no one in the gadda better suited to overseeing human and gadda relations than you.'

Now there was an argument with an easy answer. 'Yes, there is. My grandfather, my mother, Lucas – they're much more experienced and capable than I am.'

'Your family are gadda, first and foremost, and Lucas Valeroso is ready to throw away his humanness to join us. You are the only gadda who has actually wanted to be human, who truly knows and loves them. That is your gift, Margaret.'

'Shit.' Maggie stared at the floor as the reality hit her. They meant it. They really thought she should be the next Ceamir.

'Now, you can refuse, Margaret, and then we will search for someone else. But you need to understand the seriousness of that situation. It isn't just a matter of us hoping humans and gadda keep getting along until we find a new Ceamir.' He looked at the door, then came to stand in front of her. She looked up and when their eyes met he continued. 'The Forbidden Texts have been stolen and, if they are used, then the balance of power in the world will be disrupted and life will be endangered, for both humans and gadda alike. We can't risk not having a Ceamir, not at this time.'

'Fuck.' Maggie closed her eyes. She didn't know what to say, didn't know what to do. Her power was calling to her that saying yes was the right thing, it was who she was meant to be. Intellectually, she was screaming at herself to start running and never stop.

Then the Heasimir spoke. 'Of course, we'll understand if you think you are incapable and say no.' The message was clear — *she* thought Maggie was incapable.

Maggie's eyes snapped open and she glared at the Heasimir. 'It's not that I'm not capable,' she said. 'It's just that others are better qualified.'

'No, they're not,' the Sabhamir said.

'We've been watching you, Margaret, studying you, helping you,' the Firimir said. 'We all know you can do it. Why do you think we ensured you got an easy sentence over the story? Believe me, the caelleach was ready to banish you. And you can't think that the Sabhamir constantly drops everything to transfer to the side of just any dath in trouble, can you? We've needed you safe for this day.'

Maggie forced herself to look at the situation rationally. The guardians wouldn't put the gadda at risk by supporting an unworthy candidate.

'If Ms Shaunessy believes she will fail at this, we shouldn't force her,' the Heasimir said.

Maggie's eyes narrowed. Never in her life had she failed at anything she set her mind to — except being human, and this was the closest thing the gadda had. No ice-queen was going to tell her what to do.

'You've got yourself a Ceamir,' she growled. Her power flared within her and the invisible star of gulagh tattooed on her chest burned.

All the guardians smiled. Even the Heasimir's mouth bent a little, and Maggie realised she'd been played. 'Shit,' she muttered.

'We're going to have to do something about all the swearing,' the Coiremir said.

The door flew open and the caelleach burst in,

slamming it shut again. He looked at the guardians. 'Dare I hope she said no?'

The Sabhamir stood and faced Cormac. 'Margaret Shaunessy has agreed to take on the burden of Ceamir.'

'Shit,' the caelleach muttered then looked around in consternation as all six guardians laughed.

The moment the door closed behind them, Sean Flaherty stopped and faced Lucas. 'Do yourself a favour, Valeroso. Leave, now. Accept your banishment and be gone.'

Lucas leant against the wall of the caelleach's PA's office and folded his arms across his chest. 'Just why would I want to do that, Flaherty?'

Sean's eyes narrowed. 'Because you aren't going to be accepted, whichever way it happens, and I think you'd prefer it to be the easy way, not the hard way.'

'The hard way being?'

'All sorts of things will start happening around here, things that have not happened in Sclossin since Rogan Connor's day, and guess who everyone will blame.'

Lucas nodded. It would work. No one here knew him; no one would vouch for him. It would be much easier for the gadda to believe he did it, than accept one of their own was capable of such actions.

'I can't see that working, Flaherty. I'll probably be living here in the bardria building, people will be watching me all the time.' I hope, Lucas added to himself.

Sean smiled. 'I'll make sure you're put out in the community, in a flat by yourself. I have some influence here now, you know.'

Not so much relatively sane as completely demented, Lucas thought. Well, if Sean wanted to think he had the ear of the caelleach, let him. He'd trip up eventually.

'I'd have thought you'd rather me stay in Sclossin for the month, Flaherty. Otherwise, I'm back in Winton, with Maggie.' And working with her on making a human-gadda connection work. He smiled at the possibilities.

Sean snorted. 'As if she'd have anything to do with you once you're human.'

Lucas shook his head. 'You really don't know her, do you, Flaherty?'

Sean took a step forward, his face flushing red and clashing badly with his hair. 'Oh, I know her, Valeroso. I know how good she feels beneath me, I know how much she likes –'

'Boys.' Lucas turned his head to see Helga Flaherty walking into the room. 'Play nice.'

Lucas closed his eyes. It seemed he was fated to be forever plagued by Flahertys.

'Of course, Aunt Helga.' Sean's voice was dripping with the need to please. 'I was just wishing Valeroso all the best in his quest to become gadda. I'm sure he'd make a worthy addition to our great race.'

The man probably can't lie straight in bed, Lucas thought. He heard Helga stop next to the two of them, and opened his eyes to look at her.

'Of course he will,' she said, looking Lucas up and down. 'With the family behind you, you'll go places.'

Lucas frowned. 'What family?'

Helga's eyes widened. 'Haven't you been told? You're a Flaherty. Your paternal grandmother was Oswald's sister.'

Lucas laughed. It was all just too ridiculous – him, a Flaherty? Then he looked at Helga and realised it wasn't a joke. 'I'm a Flaherty?'

'Surely you saw the resemblance between you and Sean – although he's got Flaherty colouring, whereas you take after your paternal grandfather's side. On the whole, the Connors are good people, albeit a bit ineffectual, but then the Flahertys have always married for love.'

'Mutual love, I hope.' Lucas looked sideways at Sean.

'Indeed.' Then Helga frowned. 'You two aren't fighting over the Shaunessy girl, are you? Because if what I think is happening actually is, neither of you stands a chance with her.'

'Margaret loves me,' Sean declared.

Helga rolled her eyes and Lucas realised that while Sean might have her loyalty as a Flaherty, she knew he was an idiot. 'I know your father is encouraging your attachment, but I'm telling you to give it up. Margaret Shaunessy is about to pass beyond the reach of either of you.'

Lucas opened his mouth to ask what she meant but was stopped by the amazing sight of the caelleach, running full-bore into the room. Helga grabbed Lucas and Sean and pushed them back.

'Helga, glad you're here, just wait a moment please.' Cormac didn't stop, but threw the door open and slammed it shut behind him. Lucas thought he heard the faint sound of laughter. Then the door re-opened and Cormac stepped into the outer office.

'Sean, summon the bardria to meet in the preparation room in fifteen minutes,' he said.

'Has it happened?' Helga said.

'It has, gulagh save us.'

'She will do well, Horatio.'

'We'll see.' The caelleach looked at Lucas. 'You'd better come in, Valeroso. Ms Shaunessy has some news for you.'

'I'm coming in too.' Sean stepped forward.

'You will do what you're told, or I'll forget your family's honour and blast you to smithereens.' The caelleach was obviously at the end of his patience. 'Go.' Then he turned and walked back into his office.

'Do not argue, Sean.' Helga touched her nephew's arm. 'Go.'

Lucas grinned at Sean as he stepped into the caelleach's office. The only one of the guardians still there was the Sabhamir. Maggie was sitting in the chair, her face pale, her hands clasped so tightly that her knuckles were white.

She jumped to her feet as Lucas walked in and extended her hands. 'Lucas, save me,' she said, tears welling in her eyes.

Lucas rushed over and pulled her into his arms. He glared at the Sabhamir. 'What have you done to her?'

'Nothing.' The Sabhamir's smile was less than innocent. 'Ms Shaunessy is naturally regretting a hastily made decision. It is the right decision, however, and she'll soon come to understand that.'

'I'm never going to forgive you,' Maggie mumbled into Lucas's chest.

'Would someone like to tell me what's going on?'

'The Ceamir has died, and Ms Shaunessy has been chosen as her replacement.'

Lucas wasn't sure what he was expecting to hear, but he was damn sure that wasn't it. He held Maggie away from him a little and looked down at her. 'Is this true?'

'They tricked me,' Maggie said. 'She sent me her spirit and then they came and tricked me. Don't trust the guardians, Lucas. I can't do this.'

He could see the panic in her eyes. He looked at the Sabhamir and saw the calmness in his. It appeared that Maggie was going to be the Ceamir, whether she currently wanted to be or not.

'Of course you can do it.' Lucas searched his brain for information about the Ceamir. 'The Ceamir is the guardian of gadda–human relations, right? Well, no one knows more about trying to be gadda and living with humans than you, right?'

Maggie frowned. 'You aren't supposed to be supporting them, you're supposed to be supporting me.'

Lucas smiled and pulled her back into his arms. 'I am. You will be Ceamir, and you'll be wonderful. And look, here I am, your first task, so it can't be that bad.'

Maggie pulled back, her eyes wide. 'I'll have to stay in Sclossin.'

Lucas rubbed her arms. 'And you'll have to guide me in my endeavours to leave my human life behind and become gadda.'

She smiled, and to Lucas it was as though the sun had suddenly appeared. 'That sounds wonderful.'

'So, are we decided?' The Sabhamir cut in. 'We need to start preparing for the ceremony of commitment.'

Maggie looked over her shoulder and frowned at the protector. 'The bardria could still say no,' she said.

'They won't. They know you're the best one for the job, even if some wish you weren't.' He grinned. 'So after the bardria ratify you, I'll take you back to Winton and you can wind up your life there, then I'll fetch you later tonight for the commitment ceremony.'

Maggie looked at Lucas. 'I guess I'm going to be Ceamir.'

In that moment, Helga Flaherty's meaning hit Lucas. Maggie was about to become one of the six most powerful gadda alive. He wasn't even gadda yet. Could they have a future?

Then she pushed herself onto her toes and pressed a light kiss onto Lucas's mouth. 'Just a few hours, then I'll be back here in Sclossin and we can be together.'

Lucas smiled as he kissed her back. She obviously thought they had a future together, and she was proving to be very good at pursuing what she wanted. There was hope, and for now that was enough.

Maggie looked around the bardria room, unable to fully comprehend that she was back here again and under such different circumstances. Was it really barely two months since she'd faced banishment?

Then, she'd stood here with just the Sabhamir by her side for support. Now, all the guardians were with her, ready to prove to the bardria if need be that she was the right choice as the new Ceamir.

The councillors began to silently stream into the room, each one casting a glance at her as he or she took a seat. Some expressions seemed curious; some were definitely disapproving. Only a few gave her the brief glimpse of a smile.

It seemed that feelings about her elevation were mixed. Well, whose aren't? she thought.

Last in was the caelleach, and he didn't attempt to hide his dismay. Cormac's mouth was drawn into a thin line and there was a vein throbbing on his temple. His eyes were narrowed as he focussed his unseeing attention on Maggie. He didn't sit, but instead put his hands on the back of his chair and leant forward.

'This special meeting of the bardria of the gadda is called to order.' He was forcing the words out from between his teeth. 'We are here to discuss the elevation of Margaret Shaunessy to the role of Ceamir.'

Interesting choice of words, Maggie thought. Discuss, not approve.

'I know there are several members of the bardria who wish to speak on this matter. Councillor O'Meara, you may begin.'

A grizzled old man from the far right put his hand on the table to help himself to his feet.

'The girl has been nothing but a troublemaker, and has no real love for the gadda. How can she possibly be a suitable guardian?' He thumped back into his chair, this speech obviously as much as he could manage.

'She is young.' Councillor Clara Kinnard, a well-known supporter of her grandfather, spoke up. 'I do not doubt that Margaret will grow and develop in her dedication to the gadda through this role.'

'What evidence do you base that on?' Henry Halloran spoke up. 'On her desire to unlock her power? On her determination to move through the orders and prove herself? On her devotion to her duty to further our race through the sacred state of motherhood? She's displayed none of these, and in fact tried to be human.'

'Something which could make her a very good Ceamir,' Kinnard retorted.

'I think a better question is: do we want the O'Haras to have this much power?' Councillor Robert Yarrow, a close friend of the Flahertys, put in.

Maggie looked at Helga Flaherty, and was surprised when she kept her mouth closed. Interesting. Very interesting.

'Margaret's father is one of the most upstanding citizens of the gadda, and her mother is extremely well regarded,' Clara said.

'The general gadda population think her grandfather is a nutter,' Yarrow shot back. 'And how can Siobhan Shaunessy be regarded at all? She only comes to Sclossin when her human medicine fails her.'

The Firimir's voice sounded in Maggie's mind. '*You might want to think about speaking up soon.*'

'*Not sure I want to get involved,*' Maggie thought back to him as she swung her head to watch the comments ping-pong back and forth. Purist versus Humanist.

'*You've got no choice, Margaret.*'

Maggie watched Yarrow's face get increasingly red as he raged about her grandfather and the danger he posed to gadda society.

It was the caelleach who stopped his diatribe. 'I myself am not concerned about John O'Hara's influence, as I believe John has no ambitions beyond his university. The choice of Margaret Shaunessy, however, concerns me deeply. You are right, Councillor O'Meara, Councillor Halloran, in bringing up her lack of commitment to the gadda. Then there is the fact that she does not respect authority. How are we to work with a Ceamir whom we do not trust?' This last question was directed at the Sabhamir, who was standing on Maggie's right.

'Is trust necessary?'

Maggie thought the caelleach's sightless eyes might pop out of his head. 'Is it necessary? Of course it is. How are we to trust her to do her job, when we don't trust her?'

'The oath of office will see to that.'

'*What do you mean?*' Maggie sent the question to him mentally.

'*You don't do the job properly, you'll die. Literally.*' Then he continued aloud. 'Trust is not the issue here. The issue is whether Margaret Shaunessy is capable of fulfilling the role of Ceamir, and the answer to that is a resounding yes. What you have painted as her flaws are in fact the reasons she will succeed. She made trouble because she is a woman of supremely developed intellect who has never been fully challenged. Her desire to be human gives her an insight into human behaviour and motivations that no other gadda has. We guardians are quite satisfied with the choice of Margaret Shaunessy.'

'*Now,*' the Firimir hissed in her mind.

Maggie took a step forward. 'If I might speak?' The caelleach frowned, then nodded. 'I first want to apologise to you all. You are right — in the past, I did not give my heritage as a gadda the respect that it deserved. But since working with Lucas Valeroso, I've come to realise what a privilege – and a responsibility – our power is. I promise you all that I will take the oath of office solemnly, and that I will always put the good of the gadda before all else.'

'*Well done,*' the Firimir thought as she stepped back into the line.

'*I hope it was enough,*' she sent back.

'One more point before you vote,' the Sabhamir said. 'I must remind you of the precarious position in which we find ourselves. Until the Forbidden Texts are retrieved and any damage done neutralised, we cannot afford to be without any of the guardians. Say no to an eminently suitable candidate like Margaret Shaunessy and you put all the gadda at risk.'

If Maggie had thought the caelleach looked unimpressed before, it was nothing compared to the darkness that covered his face now. 'Thank you for pointing out the obvious, Sabhamir,' he snapped.

Maggie got the distinct impression that relations between the bardria and the guardians weren't all they should be.

For his part, the Sabhamir calmly inclined his head. 'I exist to serve the gadda and the elected bardria,' he said.

After that, Maggie's ratification was a mere formality. While there were many of the bardria who didn't want Maggie as the Ceamir, they wanted to be down a guardian even less.

The caelleach's voice was even harsher than before. 'I announce that the bardria has approved Margaret Shaunessy's appointment as Ceamir. The ceremony will take place at midnight, as we apparently do not have time to wait. May the star of gulagh bless us all.'

Maggie lifted her chin, and then bowed her head to the bardria. Silently, she swore that she would be the best damn Ceamir to ever have lived.

ASARLAI

The long, sonorous chime shocked Asarlai out of her reverie. She sat forward and squinted. The laboratory was dark. Ridiculously dark. How long had she been sitting there?

She waved a hand and a candle fluttered into flame. She set three more alight, and then looked over at the clock. It had been ten hours since she'd finished reading the texts. Ten hours while she'd just sat in her armchair and allowed the darkness and energy of the books to swim through her. Ten hours that she didn't have to waste.

Yesterday, she'd finally heard the whispers she'd been waiting for — the Sabhamir was in a flap over something that had gone missing. The search was on.

She'd come back home, picked up the last book and read it, determined to finish as quickly as possible. She had thought she would then start making some decisions about what to do next.

She hadn't expected to while away the day basking in the glory of the texts.

She leant forward, smiling, her attention focussed on the five tomes in front of her. Beautiful, stunning masterpieces. Who could have thought the power could be used like that, bent to such wonderful forms?

The chime sounded again, and she looked at her star. A purple message ball hung there. The bardria had something to say.

Her heart thudded. Did this mean they'd worked it out? Was she discovered? She shook her head. If they knew she had the texts, it would be the Sabhamir standing in front of her, not a simple message.

Asarlai went over and touched the ·ball. It peeled away into nothingness and the caelleach's voice resonated.

'People of the star, it is with great sadness that I inform you that the Ceamir has passed away. Patricia O'Donnell was a great and true servant of the gadda and her work was much appreciated. Margaret Shaunessy has agreed to fill the role, and we welcome her. She will be sworn in tonight.'

Asarlai tapped her chin. So, there was a new guardian. That would mean there was a weakness, albeit temporary, something that she could undoubtedly use.

She turned toward the book. Margaret Shaunessy, she thought as she walked over to the table. An interesting choice. The League will be upset. John O'Hara wasn't just a stupid Humanist any more – he was the relative of a guardian of the gadda. That made him all but untouchable.

Still, Maggie would be back here in Sclossin now, so Sean Flaherty would be happy.

Asarlai reached out and put her hand on the books. Words began to form in her mind, voices with different pitches and tones.

Take me. Take me. Take me. Take me.

She nodded. With the guardians focussed on their newest member, now was the perfect time to get the texts out of Sclossin. She would use the human way — the new Ceamir wouldn't be ready for her yet.

From the corner cupboard, she pulled out a mobile phone and called for a taxi. Asarlai packed the Forbidden Texts away. The voices in her head jabbered, excited, overjoyed to be moving. Then she packed some clothes and potions for herself.

The taxi arrived and she got in. 'Take me to the train station at Carrick-on-Shannon,' she said.

The driver pulled away and Asarlai settled into her seat and watched the thatched roofs and stone walls of Sclossin pass by. Just like that, she would take the Forbidden Texts through the centre of the village, right past the bardria and away and they would never know.

It made her giddy.

As they left the village, the excited chatter died, and the voices began to mumble and then whine. Asarlai shook her head to clear them away. She had a right to be nervous, she thought, but this was the thing to do.

Her stomach heaved and she swallowed against a sudden rise of nausea. Damn human transport, she thought. How do they stand this, travelling in a manner that made them ill?

She hugged the texts to her chest and breathed slowly, hoping to control the churning of her stomach until her journey was ended.

CHAPTER TWENTY-FIVE

The Sabhamir deposited Maggie in her family's laboratory.

'I'd warn you to be careful about letting humans see you back here so suddenly, but you're the last person I need to say that to,' he said with a grin. 'I'll be back for you in three hours.' Then he was gone.

The door to the basement opened, and her grandfather appeared. 'What the —' He started to walk down the stairs and stopped when he saw her. 'Maggie. What are you doing here?'

'Hush, Grandpa. There are things we need to discuss. Where are Mum and Dad?'

'Up in the kitchen, waiting to hear about Lucas. Is he OK?'

'Can you bring them down?' Maggie said.

Her grandfather gave her a strange look, but did as she asked. Within moments, her entire family was gathered. John sat in the armchair, Siobhan pulled up a stool and sat by his side while Peter leant against the wall behind the two of them.

Maggie began. 'First, Lucas. He has been granted a reprieve by the bardria. He will be given a month to prove himself worthy to be gadda.'

'Yes.' John punched the air. 'Justice prevails. Good work.'

'You said first,' Siobhan said. 'If Lucas is just first, what's second?'

'The Ceamir has died.' Maggie bowed her head as she said the words. With the melding of the Ceamir's spirit and her power, Maggie was feeling more personal sadness over the loss.

'Gulagh save us,' John gasped.

'Terrible news,' Peter said. 'She did a great deal for gadda–human relations; she helped to curb the worst excesses of the Purists.'

'She will be sorely missed,' Siobhan agreed. 'Has a replacement been chosen?'

'Yes. Me.'

There was silence as her family stared at her, then they all shouted at once.

'I don't believe it,' said Siobhan.

'Way to go, Maggie!' said John.

'Unbelievable,' said Peter.

'Believe it,' Maggie said. 'The guardians have known for some time.'

'Hence the light sentence over the story.' John nodded. 'Very clever.'

'I wouldn't call a two-year non-contact sentence light, Dad,' Siobhan said. 'Look at the hassles it has caused.'

'That's the fault of whoever is conjuring the beasts. The guardians weren't to foresee that. And it's very light compared with what Cormac probably wanted to do to her.' John frowned at Maggie. 'How is he with this?'

'Disappointed, but he will come to be proud of me.'

The three of them looked at each other, then Siobhan stepped forward. 'He could never be as proud as I am right now.' Then she pulled Maggie into her arms for a hug.

Maggie hugged her mother back hard, knowing this would be the last time they met as mother and daughter. From now on, they would be dath and Ceamir.

She hugged her father and grandfather, then pulled back. 'We need to consider how to end my life here in Winton and begin it again in Sclossin.

'I've given some thought to this and here's my suggestion. After a couple of months here in Australia, I've decided that I miss my life in Ireland too much and I've returned. You'll need to pack up all my stuff and send it to me. Lucas, who is supposedly away at a conference, realises that he misses me and wants to be with me so rather than return here, he follows me to Sclossin. You'll need to send him his stuff too. We'll get him a position at NUI — no problem for the Julius Edgar Lilienfeld Fellow. You, Grandpa, are going to be terribly pissed that I've stolen him away from you but you're going to just shrug and say what can you do, young love and all, and move on.'

'I'm going to just shrug that I've lost him?'

'You will if you know what's good for you. Besides, it will probably enhance your reputation as a good employer who understands that there's more to life than chalk.'

'There isn't any chalk in my university; we're a whiteboard town.' John scuffed the toe of his shoe against the stone floor. Maggie kissed the top of his head, knowing that he was disappointed but not altogether upset.

'Now, my commitment ceremony will take place in a couple of hours. I assume you all want to be there.'

'Absolutely,' her mother declared, and the others nodded.

'Good.' As she looked at them, tears began to well in her eyes. This was it. From now on, her life would be irretrievably changed. She would never live here, in Winton, in Australia, ever again.

There was a moment of panic, then it subsided. With each passing moment, her confidence in her decision grew.

'I love you all,' she whispered, and they enfolded her in a family hug.

The commitment ceremony took place in the bardria chamber as it was the centre-most room in the building. When Maggie entered with her family, the only other people there were the councillors and the guardians.

All the furniture had been removed, and the room was illuminated by the light of the moon coming in through the glass ceiling. Each guardian stood at one of the points of the star of gulagh reflected on the floor, leaving one free for her. The councillors stood around the edges of the room.

Her family joined the councillors against the wall. Maggie hesitated halfway between the two groups. Once she stepped forward, she would never belong back there again. It was a responsibility, a challenge, and a job that would be neverending.

She saw herself clearly for the first time. Nearly all her life, she'd turned from what she was meant to be. First, she'd tried to be human rather than gadda. Then, she'd turned from her abilities with her power to concentrate on teaching. Now was the final test – would she turn from being the Ceamir?

She closed her eyes, smoothed her hands against the red robe she wore, then opened them slowly and stepped forward until she stood at the sixth point of the star. To her right was the Coiremir, to her left the Sabhamir. The Firimir was directly opposite her, with the Heasimir to his right, the Garramir to his left.

As she took her place she could feel energy rising from the star. It was humming, ready to burst into life. Only once before had she stood inside a living star – when she'd finished her studies, passed first order and become truly connected to her powers. The energy of the star, the way it burst to life and seemed almost to consume her, had been terrifying. Now, she was going to have to welcome it.

The Firimir moved into the centre of the star. 'Margaret Shaunessy, step forward,' he said.

Maggie took a deep breath, and then joined him. He lifted his hands and put them on either side of her face and she felt him reach into her mind, and touch her heart.

'*Say these words aloud*,' his voice whispered into her mind. '*I, Margaret Shaunessy, accept the role and responsibility of Ceamir. I commit myself first to the guardianship of the gadda and its secrets, and to the welfare of humanity. I promise to serve the bardria of the gadda, and all dath, oman and gadma with diligence and pride. This is my oath and my vow and may my life be forfeit should I break it.'*

As Maggie spoke the words aloud, each one seared itself into her soul, becoming a part of her life-force. The truth of the last words was clear to her.

After she completed the vow, the Firimir released her and stepped back into position. Then the star of gulagh flared blindingly to life around her.

There was nothing to be seen, heard, felt but the power of the gadda, swirling around and within her. She closed her eyes and opened herself to it – if she was to do everything she had just sworn to, she needed every bit of help she could get.

Then she was aware of something there, with her, within the star. She opened her eyes and saw a gold cup, hovering in the air in front of her face. She brought it close. It was filled with a red liquid – bright and warm, with tiny flecks of other colours swimming within it.

She brought the cup to her lips and drank. Countless images of faces and places from every age flashed through her mind. Each lasted only a part of a moment, but she saw and recognised all of them.

The cup disappeared from her hands, the star flared one last time and her tattoo burned. Then it was gone, and she was standing in the bardria chamber, the light of the moon bathing her face.

She stepped back to the star point that now belonged to her, and stood in silent union with her fellow guardians. She was the Ceamir, and it felt good.

CHAPTER TWENTY-SIX

Lucas put down the book he had been reading and looked at the clock. It was three in the morning. The caelleach had told him that Maggie's commitment ceremony would take place that night, and that she might well be able to see him afterward. So here he was, fighting off sleep and waiting for a visit that might not happen.

He got up, walked across his small loungeroom to the kitchenette, and put the kettle on. The one-bedroom apartment the bardria had provided for him was comfortable enough – the bed was a perfect firmness, the lounge comfortable, and even the bath looked like it would be big enough to encompass his large frame. But it wasn't home. He began to wonder if he would ever know what that felt like.

There was a knock; he went to the door and flung it open. Maggie leapt straight into his arms.

'Bloody hell, you feel good,' she cried in his ear.

Lucas kicked the door closed and pulled her to him, planting his lips on hers. Passion started to rise inside him, but then stopped. Shit, the block. He stepped forward, pressing her against the door, pressing himself against her, willing his power to rise as it had before.

Maggie pulled back and looked at him. 'Are you all right?' Then she smiled. 'Ah, the block. I forgot about that.'

Then his power flooded from him, so intense that she gasped and shivered. He barely got control of it before it overwhelmed both of them. He gaped at her. 'Did you do that?'

Maggie responded by wrapping her legs around his waist. 'Don't you think we've done enough talking?' Then she kissed him, opening her mouth to him. Lucas plunged his tongue into her, groaning as the taste of her filled him.

He'd barely touched her, but already he was erect to the point of aching. He ground his hips against hers, enjoying both the sensation and the anticipation of what was to come.

'Too many clothes,' Maggie muttered and then he felt the softness of her skin against his, and the head of his penis was suddenly pressed against her moistness.

'Damn, I love power.' He rocked against her, sliding himself between her labia.

She moaned. 'Now, Lucas, please. I need you.'

Her words, the intense throbbing of her power, took the last of Lucas's rational thought from his mind. He reached down to position himself then pushed inside.

Sweet mercy, she felt good — hot and slick and tight. He moaned against her throat as he pressed his hipbone against hers, pushing as far into her as he could. Then he pulled back and thrust in again.

'Lucas. Yes.'

The friction was intense; the throbbing pleasure stunned his every nerve. Their power danced, met and mated in time to the rhythm of his thrusts. Lucas moved against her — within her — over and over, unable to think beyond the rising tension he could feel in them both.

Maggie dug her fingernails into his back, squeezed his hips between her thighs and begged for more and he gave her everything he had.

He shouted as he came — his body locked in ecstasy, sandwiching Maggie between his chest and the door. Seconds after his own orgasm began, he was hit by an incredible wave of pleasure that buckled his knees. He barely kept his balance, holding Maggie to him as she cried out and her power screamed her pleasure.

They stayed against the door, panting, neither of them talking but waiting out the last shivers of satisfaction. Then he was aware of Maggie's feelings — deeper, stronger than last time.

God, he didn't know what he'd done to deserve those emotions, but he was going to make sure he never lost them.

'I love you too,' Maggie whispered in his ear. He lifted his face from the crook of her shoulder and looked at her. Her face glowed and her eyes were lit with such happiness that it made him feel the strongest man alive.

'Now,' she said, leaning forward and kissing his throat. 'Now that that's out of the way, I think it's time you took me to bed and we did this properly, don't you think?'

Lucas realised what he'd just done — fucked her against a door, as if she were nothing to him. 'Shit, I'm sorry.' He started to release her, but she tightened her grip on him.

'Sorry about what?'

'This.' He hit the door. 'You deserve better than this.'

'You can *do* better than that? Lordy, take me to bed now.'

He frowned. 'That wasn't –'

'I know, but what you were thinking is so ridiculous, I decided to ignore it. Do you really think I wouldn't have stopped it if I didn't want it?'

'No.'

'Good. Now, for the third time, take me to bed. And may I point out that I now seriously, seriously outrank you and can make your life miserable if you don't do as I want? On the other hand, do what I want and I will make you very, very happy.'

With a smile, Lucas grabbed her buttocks, held her tight to him and turned, striding to the bedroom. Maggie kept her legs wrapped around his waist and one arm around his neck. She kissed his throat while her free hand moved across his chest, branding him, before one finger touched and circled his nipple.

Lucas reached the bed and threw them both down onto it. Then he pulled back and looked at her. Maggie's skin was flushed, her lips full and her golden curls strewn across his pillow. Every fantasy he'd ever had come true.

She held her arms out to him. 'You aren't going to just look for the rest of the night, are you?'

He smiled. 'No, I think there will be some tasting as well.' He pressed kisses onto her face then against her lips, dipping his tongue into her again and again. With the excess of the passion curbed, he could focus more on the power. Maggie's power was different from his: it was lighter, possibly more fragrant. And feeling her love for him — and knowing she felt his for her — was profound and overwhelming. He cupped her breast and began to learn its contours: to learn just how he should squeeze it to make Maggie moan. Each pulse of passion through her brought a pulse of power as well, so he could really feel what she liked and didn't like.

Her back arched a little. He concentrated on her nipple, rolling it between his fingers and then gently tugging on it until her body strained up toward him and she was panting into his mouth.

He kissed his way down her throat, to take her nipple into his mouth, moving his hand to her other breast.

Maggie gasped and moaned and her hips began to twist, the flood of her power a sure sign that again pleasure was building in her. Lucas sucked and licked her nipple until she was panting, her hands twisting in his hair while she mumbled incoherently. Then he moved over to lavish affection on her other nipple.

He stroked every inch of her skin, over her face, her shoulders, her arms, her chest, her stomach. She gasped, and tried to press herself against him. His lips tasted all of her, learning all the curves of her body. He liked her softness, the fleshiness of her body. He loved the contrast between her hips and her waist.

He went down to her ankles, stroking and kissing his way up her legs. At the top of her thighs, he bit her softly, and she squirmed and muttered and pulled on his hair. Then he lightly stroked his tongue up her wetness, lying it lightly on her clitoris.

Maggie froze. 'Yes.' It sent a spasm of joy through him and he felt his power push into her. Then he bent his head and pressed his tongue against her clitoris.

Within moments, Maggie had returned to the brink of climax. Her pubic bone pressed against him. She was losing control. He liked that.

He found the right rhythm and used it, pressing his tongue against her, flicking the head of her clitoris. Her rising groans were the most wonderful music he had ever known. He wished he could do this and watch her at the same time. She looked so beautiful when she came.

Then she cried out: he felt her thighs tremble and he plunged a finger into her vagina, feeling it squeeze him as her orgasm echoed through her. He remembered feeling that around his erection and almost lost control again himself.

Her breathing began to slow and he moved up her body again. It was taking every ounce of control he had not to slide back inside her.

He kissed her, knowing she could taste herself in his mouth. Maggie wrapped her legs around him and turned, flipping him onto his back.

'Now I get to taste you.' She bent down and began kissing along his jaw.

It was torture. Maggie took her time, learning his body as thoroughly as he had learnt hers. She stroked his skin, tracing the contours of the muscles in his arms, shoulders, and chest. She kissed him and licked him and took tiny bites from him. Every touch of her fingers, lips, teeth and tongue sent shivers through him and power pulsing into her. And with every pulse of power he sent into her, he felt one in return. He was hard and throbbing, his cock begging for release, begging to be inside her. Maggie seemed to know this, for her every movement sent part of her body rubbing against his erection.

She licked and teased his nipples, then dipped her tongue into his belly button. Then, finally, her hands reached for his erection.

Lightly, she ran a finger up and down the length of his penis. He fought to not grab her and flip her over. Then she bent and ran her tongue up him.

Lucas went pretty much mad. He wanted to beg her to stop and beg her to never stop. She flicked her tongue across the head of his penis and he shuddered. He closed his eyes, trying to convince himself he could control his response.

And he opened his eyes to see Maggie straddle him. He felt himself nudging her heat and wetness and reached forward to grab her legs.

Then this time, agonisingly slowly, her slippery warmth surrounded him as she stretched to accommodate him.

Slowly, gently, she began to move on him. He bit the inside of his cheek to control himself as her breasts shifted with her movements. Her head fell back, her hands were on his chest as she angled herself so his penis was hitting the right spots, and her clitoris ground into his groin every time she sank onto him.

'Maggie,' he moaned. She leant forward and to his shock licked the tip of his nose. He stared as she grinned down at him.

'Let it go, baby,' she said. 'Stop thinking, and just let it go.'

As she spoke, she wriggled on him and her gasp was matched by a spike in her power. It was the last straw for Lucas. He grabbed her hips and strained up into her, coming harder than he ever had.

With the last spurt, his energy left him. Maggie's too, for she collapsed against his chest. Lucas wrapped his arms around her, hugging her tight.

After a while, Maggie's hand began to move across his back, lightly stroking. He felt a little trill of pleasure and wished he was seventeen, so he could roll her over and start all over again. Then the path of her fingers caught his attention and his blood stilled. She was slowly tracing his scars.

He waited for the response. The white ridges turned some women off. Others, like Holly, found them incredibly alluring.

'Where did you get these?' Her voice was soft, as though she didn't want to break the spell that surrounded them.

'My stepfather. His primary method of discipline was, ah, physical.'

Maggie lifted her head to look at him and he was surprised to see tears brewing in her eyes. 'Mum said you'd been hurt.'

He lifted his hand to her cheek. 'They don't hurt any more, sweetheart.'

She smiled. 'I know. I think it's wonderful, the way you've overcome your life and made something of yourself. I'm really proud of you. And I want you to know that you never have to worry about anyone hurting you again. I'll make sure of that.' Then she bent her head and kissed him.

Heat, warmth and love surged through Lucas. He moved, rolling them both over. Then he bent his head and kissed her, knowing that she was feeling every ounce of the love he felt for her.

He lifted his head and looked down at her. 'I'm going to spend the rest of my life making you happy.'

'If the past hour was an example of your work, I'm sure you'll be a roaring success.'

He laughed, and kissed her, then kissed her again because it felt so good. Then he rolled onto his side and pulled her tight against him. He was smiling when he fell asleep.

CHAPTER TWENTY-SEVEN

Something felt a little strange when Maggie woke the next morning. Then she realised that it was because she was draped over Lucas. He looked so peaceful; it was hard to believe he was facing the threat of losing everything. Her smile widened. She had done that for him.

She slowly sat up. Lucas mumbled a bit and she thought he would wake, but then he settled down. She nodded. Let him sleep. He deserved his rest.

She, on the other hand, had priorities now. She had to step up to her responsibilities as Ceamir.

She picked up her clothes and pulled them on on her way out to the loungeroom. She left a message for Lucas telling him she'd be in touch later, then let herself out of the apartment.

Out in the corridor, she realised she didn't know where she should go. The Sabhamir had mentioned an apartment for her here in the bardria building, but she had no idea where it was.

As embarrassing as it was, she needed to ask. '*Sabhamir? Where should I be?*'

His voice echoed in her mind. '*Here.*' He sent her a mental image of a rather old-fashioned loungeroom —

soft, curved sofas, covered with floral material and lace cushions. '*And please, Margaret, call me Hampton.*'

She focussed on the picture, then called on her power and, to her amazement, slipped through the air and into the room as easily as she would walk through a door.

'Wow,' she said as she looked around. Already, being Ceamir was affecting the powers she had. She'd never been that good at transferring. Then she smiled at the man in black sitting on her chaise. 'I'll call you Hampton if you call me Maggie.'

'Deal.' He stood. 'Let me show you around. You can redecorate, if you want.' Maggie wrinkled her nose and he laughed. 'She was a lovely woman, but old-fashioned in many respects. Now this, funnily enough, is the loungeroom, as is evidenced by the presence of lounges.'

Maggie's first impression was that her predecessor had had terrible taste – everything was pink and chintzy and just way, way too much. Her second impression was that this was a big apartment for just one person.

Adjoining the loungeroom was a formal dining room seating eight. The main bathroom held a bath big enough for her and Lucas to share and there were three bedrooms.

The last Ceamir had slept in one of the smaller bedrooms and, when Maggie looked at the single bed, she could see why she'd not wanted to use the massive master. Again, there was an overabundance of lace and overblown flowers.

The third bedroom was the laboratory, but it seemed the Ceamir hadn't used it for a while: there was a fine layer of dust across everything.

The last room the Sabhamir took her to was the office, which connected the apartment to the bardria building. Most of the gadda who came to see her wouldn't get any further than the office. Certainly, this was all Maggie had ever seen of the former Ceamir's space.

Maggie hadn't been here for a few years – in fact the last time had been when she'd informed the Ceamir she was commencing her studies for her Master's degree. As she had remembered, it was very sparsely decorated – a desk and a couple of chairs.

'This was never a particularly inviting room,' Maggie said. 'I never liked coming here. You're not going to convince gadda to come and have a chat and find out more about humans if this is where they're supposed to do it.'

'I knew you were right for the job,' the Sabhamir said with a smile. 'Why don't you do something about it?'

Maggie cocked an eyebrow, then shook her head. 'I'm gonna have to get used to this actually being able to use my power,' she said.

'Being Ceamir means being in contact with a lot of humans, but it also means being a very powerful gadda. This is as good a place as any to start.'

'Hmmm.' Maggie tapped her chin as she thought. To her, inviting meant warm, comfortable, cosy. It needed to be somewhere a gadda would like to be, but also somewhere that spoke of her strong connection with humans.

An image came to her and she smiled. Perfect. She closed her eyes, called on her power and sent it flooding out of her. She felt the room, the furniture, the air around her shifting, forming, changing.

When she opened her eyes, she was standing in a replica of her mother's loungeroom. Siobhan's picture of a Wiccan ceremony was replaced by a rendering of the star of gulagh. Otherwise, it was a modern and comfortable loungeroom — complete with human electrical appliances tucked tactfully away — that wasn't entirely Sclossin, but not so alien that people would be uncomfortable here.

'Nice choice,' the Sabhamir said, looking around. 'This looks good.'

'Maybe I'll hire myself out as a decorator,' Maggie said.

'First things first. We need to get you up to speed on what's going on around here.' He took her arm and led her over to the other side of the room. Then one by one the other guardians appeared.

'Hey, like what you've done with the place,' the Garramir said, looking around.

'Very nice, Margaret,' said the Firimir.

'It's Maggie, please,' Maggie said.

'Sit, everyone. We've undoubtedly all got things to do, so let's get this done as quickly as possible,' the Sabhamir said. Everyone except him took a seat. 'Now, first the introductions. Margaret has made it clear she prefers to be called Maggie. We all use our first names. So the Firimir is Owen, the Garramir Kenyon, the Coiremir is Wilma and the Heasimir —'

'I'm happy with Heasimir,' she interrupted.

'As you wish, Sarah,' Hampton said. 'Now, as I mentioned yesterday, the Forbidden Texts have been stolen. Do you know anything about them?'

Maggie shook her head. 'I didn't even know they were real.'

'Unfortunately, they are. The Forbidden Texts detail ceremonies and potions that twist the emotions, take power to places it shouldn't go. They were created around five hundred years ago, and almost wiped out the gadda. Many people trace our inability to have more than one or two children back to that time. The then-Sabhamir tried to destroy them but died in the attempt, so the texts were placed in a vault here in the bardria, where all the most dangerous possessions of the gadda are kept. Over the years, the responsibility for guarding the texts was passed down from Sabhamir to Sabhamir. Initially, there were many attempts to regain possession of the texts but gradually, as your comment proves, they faded into folklore and were forgotten.'

'But now they've been remembered,' Maggie said.

Hampton nodded. 'Remembered and taken. I check the vault every week and happened to be due to check it the day you got in trouble for your story.' Maggie gulped, but he waved her guilt away. 'I could feel they were gone as soon as I walked into the room, but I've been unable to track them since.' As he spoke, his shoulders tensed and Maggie realised he blamed himself for their loss.

He'd been searching for them, and dealing with her family and its troubles, and no one had suspected anything was wrong. Her admiration of him grew. 'Have they been used yet?'

'We think possibly they have. I'm firmly of the belief that the Forbidden Texts are somehow linked to the monsters that were sent to Winton. When your mother was here, we found a darkness within her that was hard to combat. None of us had seen anything like it before.'

Maggie frowned. 'So whoever made the monsters has been using the Forbidden Texts to replace his or her essence with Grandpa's and Oswald Flaherty's?'

'Apparently,' Hampton said.

'But why us?'

He shrugged. 'I'm still working on that. But the fact that your family is so closely aligned to humans may be a clue. That's why it was so important that we maintain continuity in the line of the Ceamir. Patricia was watching the humans for any sign of the Forbidden Texts at work. She swore by newspapers.'

Maggie scoffed. 'It's all online now. We'll need an internet connection.'

Owen sat forward. 'The internet. That's something to do with computers, right?'

Maggie nodded. 'I'll get Ione Gorton to help set me up. Looks like the guardians are about to get connected.'

The Heasimir stood. 'If that is all, I have things to do.' And she disappeared.

Maggie blinked and looked at Hampton, who shrugged. He didn't look surprised, so she decided not to take it personally.

'We'll get together again tomorrow to see what progress we've made,' Hampton said.

The others nodded and disappeared, leaving Hampton and Maggie alone. He stood and nodded to her. 'Get in touch with Ione as soon as possible. And you'd better get the rest of the apartment sorted out before you move Lucas in here.' Maggie bit her lip and he laughed. 'Try to be a little less obvious if you don't want people to know.'

'I don't have a problem with people knowing.' She scrambled to her feet. 'I just wasn't sure it was possible for guardians to have relationships.'

'Sure, so long as they know the job comes first. Not many partners will stand for that. Certainly, the Coiremir's couldn't. My parents were very happy, however. Don't judge it by the current crop. We're a sad and sorry lot, we are.' He smiled, but it didn't reach his eyes. 'Make sure Lucas realises exactly what he's getting into before you both get too involved.' And then he was gone.

Maggie flopped back down on the sofa. In the space of twenty-four hours, she'd become a guardian of the gadda, made love for the first time with the man she felt was the love of her life – and now she was in a position to make a home for them both.

She snapped out of her daydream. Internet connection was priority number one. And that meant letting Ione know she was staying in Sclossin.

Maggie grinned. She stood and sent a request to Ione for admittance, and felt Ione's assent. Then she transferred.

'Mags! Or should I say, your most gracious Caemirness?' Ione bowed low, her paisley scarf drifting on the floor.

'Shut up and give me a hug.' Ione laughed and did.

Then a small weight flung itself at Maggie's legs.

'Auntie Maggie, you're back,' Jack squealed.

Maggie released Ione to kneel down and hug Jack. 'I am back, although not to live here, I'm afraid, Jacky.'

'Pooh.'

'But you can come visit me in the bardria.'

'You live there? Cool. Maybe Mum and I can come live with you, so you won't be lonely.' Jack looked at her with wide eyes.

'Sorry, scamp. Already have a roommate.'

'Not the dishy and mysterious Lucas Valeroso? I heard all about your extreme method of saving him yesterday.'

Was that just yesterday? 'The same.'

'Drink.' Ione pointed to the bar. 'I don't care what the time is. I need alcohol. And you need to talk.'

Maggie poured them each a glass of whiskey (Jack got a juice), then sat down and pulled the little boy onto her lap for a cuddle before telling Ione everything that had happened since she'd left Sclossin.

Ione interjected many times: 'Bloody Flaherty'; 'Unknown gadda, whatever — is he hot?'; 'What's a fuiparra?'; 'It's all very *West Side Story*, if you ask me'; 'And she just, what? Jumped inside you when she died? Ick'; 'Good in bed as *well*? Shut *up*! (Sorry, Jack.)'

At the end, she sighed. 'And here was me thinking things would quiet down once you got to Winton. Should have known better.'

'Well, that's it so far, but now I've got something for you to do, Io. I need a computer and internet connection in my apartment in the bardria building. I'm guessing we'll have to go wireless.'

'First things first — a computer.' Ione stood. 'Time to go shopping.'

'While we're at it, we need to look at furnishings. The last Ceamir's taste was oldmaidish, to say the least.'

'Oooh, so I get to decorate too? God love ya, Mags. I know I do.'

Maggie laughed and hugged her friend and decided that accepting the position of Ceamir was possibly the best decision she'd ever made.

Maggie, Ione and Jack were singing along with the latest human number one hit as the car turned into Creoghan Road in Carrick-on-Shannon.

'What's that?' Ione slowed the car right down.

Maggie looked and saw a crowd of people walking across the road from the train station. They seemed disoriented – as if they were drunk. A strange sight in the middle of the day.

'Hey, Mum. Are those people high?' Jack leant over between the front seats, peering out the window.

'I have to stop letting him watch TV,' Ione said to Maggie as she eased the car to a halt, then frowned at her son. 'Back in your seat, Jack, and put your belt back on.'

'Ah, but Mum –'

Maggie ignored the two of them and stared at the crowd. People were stumbling, some were fighting, others were slumping down onto the middle of the road with pale faces. On the other side of the crowd, a car started to sound its horn. The gathering on the road ignored them.

She looked at the train station. People were coming out – obviously a train had just been through. They seemed fine as they walked out of the gates, but then as they moved closer to the road, they were shaking their heads and putting their hands to their faces, as if smelling something terrible.

She opened the door and started to get out, but Ione grabbed her arm. 'Mags, what are you doing?'

'I don't like this.'

'Spidey sense tingling, is it?'

Maggie pulled her arm free, got out and started to walk over to the nearest person. She was a young girl, barely in her teens, sitting in a gutter, and her eyes were rolling as if she were drunk.

'Hey, are you OK?' She crouched down and touched the girl's arm. There was something dark there, just beneath the surface, energy buzzing.

Power, but not like anything she'd ever felt before.

The girl looked up at her. 'I don't feel so good,' she whispered.

'Hampton?'

'Yes, Maggie.'

'Something weird's going on at Carrick-on-Shannon, at the train station. Humans are acting strangely, and I can feel a weird type of power.'

'Is there somewhere I can transfer?'

Maggie looked around. 'The front passenger seat of Ione's car. Can you get a fix on her?'

'I'll be right there.'

Maggie patted the girl on the arm, and went over to enquire as to another person's health. Again, she felt the darkness.

She looked over her shoulder and saw Hampton getting out of the car. He walked over to her casually. 'Hey, Maggie.'

'Hey. There's some sick people here.'

Hampton helped a young man sitting on the road to his feet. The man wobbled, and Hampton helped him sit down again. *'Maggie, I think this might be the texts.'*

Her eyes widened. She hadn't considered that.

'I'll get the others here. You start doing what you can to make this look ... normal.'

Maggie started to walk over toward the railway station. As she got closer, she saw that there was something in the gutter that people seemed to be recoiling from. Closer to it, she wanted to walk away, but she kept going. Vomit. And not only was there that awful sour stench, but there was also a chill in the air that set her nerves tingling.

'Hampton, I think I've found the source.'

He came over and to her disgust, crouched down and actually touched the vomit. He looked at her and nodded. *'Kenyon and I will deal with this. Sarah, Wilma and Owen can help the humans. You need to find a way to hide this.'*

She turned away from him and saw that Sarah was stepping out of Ione's car and heading over to the group. Ione's windows appeared darker than usual — Hampton must have done it to hide the people appearing in it.

Maggie turned in a slow circle. In the distance, she could hear sirens. And if the message was out, the media would probably be here soon too.

She needed something to explain what was going on, without it being linked to the six people who were fixing it. An idea from the classroom came to her, and she grinned. Perfect solution.

She walked over to where a group of men and women in business suits stood, pinching their noses closed. It seemed they hadn't been affected by whatever was in the vomit.

'Isn't it terrible?' She said as she joined them. 'That new cleaning product they've put in the street cleaner is foul. I've complained, I'll tell you.'

'Is that what it is?' One of the women said. 'It's foul.' The group stumbled away. Maggie went over to where a middle-aged man was holding his head and moaning.

'So sick,' he whispered.

'It's the spray,' Maggie said, putting her hand on his shoulder and giving him a quick pulse of power to take away the worst of the nausea. 'I saw the plane go over earlier, and I thought they hadn't turned off the sprayer after doing the crops.'

She came up with two more excuses – all based around the poisoning idea – and then sat back and let the Chinese whispers take care of the rest of the story. By the time the media or police started questioning the victims, there'd be so many stories that they'd never get anywhere close to the truth.

'Don't completely cure them.' She sent the message to the other guardians. *'There are police and ambulances on the way and they'll be curious if they arrive to find nothing wrong with anyone.'*

'Just take away the darkness,' Hampton said. *'Bring it to Kenyon to neutralise. Leave the symptoms. They'll be fine.'*

When the police and ambulance arrived a few minutes later, Wilma and Owen had already returned to Sclossin, the worst of the emergency over. Sarah healed the final few victims, then she, Hampton and Kenyon walked away to find somewhere else to transfer from.

Maggie leant against Ione's car and gave a statement to the police, but refused the media's request. Then she got back into the car and as the police shuffled people off the road, directed Ione to drive on.

'What the hell was that?' Ione said as they turned into Station Street and headed across the Shannon River into County Leitrim.

'I don't know,' Maggie said, hating that she was lying to her best friend. No one in the general gadda population knew about the theft of the Forbidden Texts and she wasn't going to be the one to break the news. 'Whatever it was, I did an awesome job handling it. I'm so going to be a kick-arse Ceamir.'

'Never doubted it,' Ione said.

'Now, onward. I need to get that computer set up and connected ASAP, to make sure news of this hasn't got out.' Maggie leant back in the seat and hoped that her first duty as Ceamir would prove to be as successful as she believed.

They'd only just left Carrick-on-Shannon when she heard Hampton's voice. *'Maggie, we need you back here now.'*

'Sorry, Io, gonna have to leave you to drive alone,' Maggie said. She undid her seatbelt and transferred to Hampton's office.

She took a seat on the couch between Owen and Sarah and watched Hampton pace up and down the room.

'Right,' he said. 'What the fuck was that? Any ideas?'

'Whoever vomited had the Forbidden Texts, or has been using them,' Owen said.

'I don't think anyone has been using them,' Kenyon said. 'I've been doing a lot of walking around town, and I haven't sensed any imbalance in the power.'

'So they have them. Were carrying them, perhaps. And the texts are making them sick.'

'Why were they in Carrick-on-Shannon?' Wilma said. 'And why outside a train station?'

'Because they were catching the train.' Hampton stopped and stared them. 'They were moving the texts, hiding them and they used human means so we couldn't track the power.'

'Clever,' Sarah murmured.

'How did they get to the train station?' Wilma said.

'Bus,' Maggie said. 'Car. Taxi.'

'They wouldn't have risked gadda–run transport, so that leaves out the bus and the Sclossin taxi service,' Hampton said.

'They they used a human taxi service. They called a taxi here to Sclossin, and used it to go to Carrick,' Maggie said. 'The car trip made them nauseated, and just outside the train station they vomited in the gutter. Then they went inside, jumped on a train and headed off to star knows where.'

'Or when,' Hampton said.

'Can't have been too long before I stumbled upon it,' Maggie said. 'A train had obviously just been through the station. It's possible that if Ione and I had turned into that street ten, fifteen minutes earlier, we would have seen another gadda there.'

'So whoever did this is comfortable using human ways. Other than car travel, of course,' Wilma said.

'We need to find out if anyone saw someone leave Sclossin today in a human taxi,' Hampton said. 'I'll go check anyone living along Ballycough Road – the taxi would have had to pass by there to get to Carrick.'

'Could we figure out their destination?' Owen asked. Maggie shook her head.

'There're eight stations between Carrick and Dublin, and in Dublin they could swap and catch a train to almost anywhere else in Ireland. It would be impossible to work out.'

'Let's hope that we get lucky with a witness and find out the identity of this person,' Hampton said. 'In the meantime, now we know they're moving the texts around. That means they could start making mistakes. We need to be ready to pounce. Maggie, how did things finish up in Carrick?'

'Pretty good. The police officer I spoke to seemed really confused about things. I've got Ione helping me with a computer, so I should be able to confirm that the secret is safe later today.'

'Good.' Hampton shook his head. 'Keep ears and eyes open, folks. And don't speak of this to anyone.'

Maggie left the meeting confident it wouldn't be long before they recovered the texts.

Lucas woke and stretched. It felt as though he'd slept for hours, then he remembered why he'd been so tired and slept so soundly. He smiled.

He could still feel Maggie's power within him, and her emotions too. At the moment she was feeling very happy, and that made him feel good.

He got up and went into the loungeroom, hoping that she might still be here. He wasn't surprised that she wasn't. He didn't really know what being Ceamir involved, but thought she'd probably have to get onto it straight away.

He found her note on the coffee table.

Hey gorgeous, I'm very sorry to be leaving. Very, very sorry. However, there are things I need to do. I'll be in touch later today, and hopefully we'll be able to pick up where we left off. I love you.

Maggie loved him. It was a very good world.

He'd turned to head to the kitchenette to scrounge up something for breakfast when there was a knock at the door. Maggie? Or not – and he didn't have any clothes on.

'Just a minute,' he shouted. He found his jeans and shirt in the bedroom and pulled them on. Then he pulled open the door.

A middle-aged woman stood there, conservatively dressed in a gadda robe of mauve, which fell from her neck to the floor. On her shoulder was one star, a sign that she had reached first-order gadma. That made her a formidable woman.

Lucas nodded. 'I am Lucas Valeroso.'

The woman bowed her head in return. 'Blair Callaghan. I am in charge of the gadda school here in Sclossin. The Coiremir has asked me to lecture you in the gadda and our way of life to better prepare you should you become gadda.'

'Thank you. Please, come in.' Lucas stood aside, so she could enter the room. He couldn't quite get a read on the woman. Her words and posture spoke of a woman of strong morals and harsh demeanour, but her voice was sweet and warm.

She walked in and gestured to the dining table. 'Come, sit, and tell me everything.' Lucas sat down and Blair took the seat opposite him, looking at him without a hint of a smile. 'I understand from the bardria that, like Maggie, you are highly educated in the human system. Tell me about that.'

Over the course of the next hour, Lucas went through his human education, and then what he had achieved so far in his gadda one. Blair asked many questions about his time at school and college, focussed mainly on styles of teaching and learning, and then listened as he went through the particulars of his time with the O'Haras in Winton.

At the end, she nodded. 'It seems that you have already had a well-rounded education in the history of the gadda. I have a test here that I give to all my first-orders at the end of their study, to see what they know. I would like you to take it, so I can see what gaps you have in your knowledge.'

Lucas nodded. 'Of course.'

A piece of paper suddenly appeared in front of him, and a pencil next to it. At first, it seemed blank, then words began to appear: an instruction to write his name. He did this, and then both the original writing and his disappeared, to be replaced by the first question, one about the history of the gadda. He searched his mind for the answer, and then began writing.

As always when he was involved in learning, Lucas was so caught up in the test that when he finished and lifted his head, he was surprised to find Blair there.

'Done?' she said.

He nodded and she leant over and picked up the paper. A pencil appeared in her hand and she began reading and making notes.

Lucas sat and watched her for a moment, but then his rumbling stomach reminded him she had interrupted breakfast preparations.

'I was going to get something to eat. Would you like anything?' He said. She shook her head, not lifting her eyes from the paper.

With a shrug, Lucas went over to the kitchenette. He fixed himself a coffee and some toast and took them back to the table. By the time he'd finished eating, Blair had finished marking the paper.

'You've done well, Lucas,' she said. 'Your knowledge of historical facts is comprehensive, although you're less clear on the realities of life with power and living alongside a world majority-populated by humans. Still, that's to be expected and is easily remedied. I'll come by every afternoon about three to work with you. Is that suitable?'

'Very,' Lucas said.

'Good.' And then she smiled and suddenly, she was approachable. Ah, thought Lucas, I should have known. She was just making sure of me. 'I look forward to working with you, Lucas.' Then she was gone.

So that's one thing on the schedule each day, he thought as he leant back in the chair. But he was used to having a packed timetable, each moment planned and accounted for. He couldn't spend the rest of the month in this room, reading books and spending a couple of hours a day with Blair. He'd go mad.

There was another knock at the door, and he went over to answer it, still pondering the weeks stretching before him.

All that disappeared from his mind the moment he saw Maggie's smiling face. 'Hi, you.'

'Hi.' She stepped toward him and the kiss she planted on him was sweet and much too short. Seeing her, touching her, smelling her had him instantly ready to sweep her back into the bedroom and return to the activities of the night before, just as she'd suggested.

However, she put a hand to his chest. 'Easy, tiger. I want that as much as you do, but there are some things we need to discuss first.'

It was enough to have the voice back. *See,* it crowed, *as if you could have a woman like this.*

Maggie thumped his chest. 'Whatever you're thinking, stop it. I can feel your doubt, and there's no reason for it. I am utterly yours.'

He grinned. 'This gadda stuff is weird.'

'And going to get weirder. Come, sit.' She took his hand and led him to the lounge. She pushed him down on it and then curled herself up on his lap.

He leant back and held her tight against his chest. She trusted him. That was nice.

'There's been so much going on that we've not really had a chance to talk about anything, about us, and we need to,' Maggie said, resting her cheek against his shoulder. 'After last night, we've covered how we feel, and what we want, but we need to discuss the realities of the situation, particularly since I'm Ceamir.'

'Fair enough.' He rested his cheek against her hair. For all that his body was screaming at him to do more than just hold her, this was a very peaceful place to be.

'As the Ceamir, my first priority is guardianship of the gadda. Any time, any place, any way, if I am needed, I must answer. Nothing can come in the way. No one can come in the way.' Then she lifted her head to look at him. 'Can you live with that?'

His automatic response was to say of course he could, but that was his emotions speaking. Maggie was asking him to look at this logically.

'You're saying that I'll always come second. That while you'll give me as much time and energy as you can, I'll always have to give way to your responsibilities.'

She nodded. 'It's a hell of a lot to ask someone. I mean if something had happened last night, some gadda had inadvertently shown himself or herself to a human, I would have had to leave, right there and then, in the middle of everything. And who knows how long I might have had to be gone. That's the reality of it all.'

He knew exactly what Maggie was doing – she was giving him the chance to walk away now if he thought it was too hard, before either of them got too invested. Except that it was already too late for that.

'Look, there will undoubtedly be moments that it pisses me off. But I can't see that those moments of being furious would wipe out the joy of moments like this – of holding you, talking to you, knowing that you love me. So if you have to go, fine. Just so long as you're coming back to me, it'll all work out.'

He felt Maggie shake, and he could feel both fear and hope warring within her.

'Are you sure? Because it's a hell of a lot –'

Too many words, he decided. He pulled her mouth to his and told her with his body that he was all hers, just as she was all his.

CHAPTER TWENTY-EIGHT

The reality of the situation imposed itself much sooner than Maggie wanted. Within moments of Lucas's declaration, clothes were strewn around the loungeroom and Maggie was giving herself up to the intense pleasure that only Lucas's touch could give.

Then a voice rang in her head. '*Ceamir, I need you. Chancellory office.*'

To add to the shock, it was John O'Hara calling. She pulled her mouth from Lucas's and leant back to minimise their physical contact.

He looked at her through passion-glazed eyes. 'What?' he said.

Damn. Bugger it. 'I have to go.' She leant forward and gave him one last kiss, then crawled off his lap and started to pull her clothes on.

'Shit, already?'

'Already, and what's more it's Grandpa. Where on earth did my bra go?'

Lucas shifted his body and pulled the bra from beneath him. 'Why would John be calling you? I wouldn't imagine he'd ever have need of the Ceamir.'

'Me either. I'll fill you in when I get back.' She pulled her shoes on, then leant over to kiss him again.

'Get someone to show you the way to the Ceamir's office. I'll meet you there when I'm done. Love you.'

Then she pictured her grandfather's office at the university, and transferred.

She turned around as the door opened. John came in with a young girl, probably only a first year. She was extremely pale, shaking, and her eyes were darting all over the place.

'Ah, Margaret, my apologies, I completely forgot about our meeting,' John said as he helped the girl to a chair. Mentally, he said, '*She was attacked by a taiboll. She thinks she's going mad, and the other students were just watching and laughing.*'

'Not at all, Professor,' Maggie said with a smile. 'I can see you had more important things on your mind. Is there anything I can do to help?' '*Where is the taiboll?*'

'If you could pour Ms Quong a drink of water, I would appreciate that.' '*It's on the front lawn.*'

'Certainly.' '*Go and fetch it. I'll have a chat with the girl.*' Maggie went over to the drinks cabinet and poured a glass of water. She wished she knew enough to put a calming draught in it, but it wasn't something she had studied.

'I need to go speak to the other students, but I'll leave you in Ms Smith's capable hands.' John patted the young girl's hand and then he walked out of the office.

'Here, drink this, it will make you feel much better.' Maggie held the glass out with a smile. The girl took it and sipped it, but she was obviously too upset to drink it properly.

Maggie sat down beside her and concocted her cover. 'I'm Margaret Smith, the Chancellor's assistant. You are?'

'I'm Lee Quong.' Lee was shivering, despite the warmth of an Australian autumn afternoon. Maggie gently laid a hand on hers and sent a soft wave of warm power over the girl. It warmed Lee, and the shivering subsided.

'What happened, Lee?'

'I don't know.' Lee shook her head. 'I was just standing and talking with my friends, and then suddenly, I could feel something cutting me, little cuts, like paper cuts, all over and it was so, so cold.' She shuddered.

'That sounds terrible.' Maggie patted Lee's hand while she considered what to say to her. 'It must have been very scary.'

'It was. I've never felt anything like that.'

Fuck, how should she handle this? 'Are you a local?'

'No, I'm from Melbourne.'

Inspiration began to blossom. 'It's much hotter up here, isn't it? Such a different environment. Maybe you're allergic to something up here?'

Lee frowned. 'I guess that's possible.'

Seeing her doubt, Maggie pushed harder. 'I think it's very likely. You're first year, right? Been studying hard, not eating too well? I bet you've strained your system to the point it's decided to tell you to slow down.'

'I have been feeling tired.'

'There. I bet if you just take a couple of days off and relax, you'll be back to normal in no time.'

'A couple of days off does sound good.' Lee slumped back into her chair and took a long sip of the water.

The door opened and John walked back in. Maggie could see he was dragging something that was visible only as a slight shimmer. The taiboll appeared to be about as big as a beagle.

'Chancellor, I was just telling Ms Quong that she probably is just a bit overworked and needs a few days off.'

'That sounds a great idea, Ms Smith.' As he spoke, John dragged the taiboll over and dropped it next to his desk. '*I didn't quite kill it, I thought the Sabhamir would prefer to investigate it as fresh as possible.*'

'Perhaps you should send her to see the doctor as well?' '*I'm sure he would. Be prepared to be summoned to Sclossin. The bardria obviously didn't have a problem with you handling things when the attacks were against the family, but this is an attack against humans.*' Maggie wondered if maybe this was another sign of the Forbidden Texts in action.

'That's a good idea. If you don't mind postponing our meeting, I'll catch up with you later.' '*I'll be ready.*'

'Not at all, Professor.' Maggie stood and watched her grandfather escort Lee from the room. Once the door was closed behind them, Maggie went over and crouched down to touch the taiboll. Her grandfather had done a good job of stopping the creature without killing it. Hampton would be pleased.

She grabbed hold of the creature and sent a message to the Sabhamir. '*Hampton, I have something for you.*'

'*I'm in my office.*' He sent her a mental image of the room. She noted that it was surprisingly normal for the workspace of the most powerful man alive. Then she transferred there.

Hampton was walking around the desk as she appeared in the middle of the room. He stopped and frowned down at her hand. 'Is that a taiboll?'

She nodded. 'Gran – John O'Hara summoned me. It attacked one of the students at the university. That situation has been dealt with and she is fine, but –'

'But now conjured creatures are being sent to Winton to attack humans.' Hampton came forward and took the taiboll from her. 'I'll start investigating this. You need to report to the caelleach.' He disappeared.

Maggie sent a message to the caelleach, and within moments was standing in his office. It was the first time she'd ever been here not in trouble. At least, she didn't think she'd done anything to get herself in trouble.

'Ceamir, what can I do for you?' Cormac stood and bowed to her, very stiffly.

'Caelleach Cormac, I'm afraid I have to inform you that there has been an attack against a human. Someone sent a taiboll to Winton University, where it attacked a young girl, a student there. I've spoken with her; she is fine and doesn't think it anything more than an allergic reaction or a breakdown brought on by overwork. The Sabhamir is investigating the taiboll.'

Cormac collapsed into his seat; she was surprised to see such a natural reaction from him. 'How much worse can this get?' he whispered.

'I expect that until we find the Forbidden Texts, it will get a whole lot worse,' Maggie said. Cormac shook his head.

'I can't believe I'm having this conversation with you.' He looked down at the desk for a moment, then lifted his head to look at her. 'Thank you, Ceamir.'

Maggie nodded, and transferred back to her office. She flopped down onto one of the lounges and thought through the events. Had she done everything she needed to do? Should she be helping Hampton?

Then her mind went back to events before she had been summoned. She'd told Lucas to get directions so he could meet her here. Obviously, he hadn't been able to find anyone.

She walked over to his apartment, thinking that this was going to be a good thing – having Lucas to talk things over with after each mission she went on. Someone objective to discuss possible ramifications and responses with. Really, the gadda are getting a two-for-one deal with this Ceamir, she thought, they should be bloody grateful.

He wasn't in his apartment, so she began searching the bardria building. She went everywhere she could think of – the restaurant, reception, and even outside – but couldn't find him anywhere.

She walked into her office, wondering if there was some way of finding him, but stopped just inside the doorway when Sean Flaherty jumped up from one of the lounges.

'Ceamir.' He bowed low and a tremor ran down Maggie's back. 'I had to come and tell you how absolutely thrilling your elevation is. I knew you were a remarkable woman.'

'Thank you, Flaherty. Now, you may leave.' Maggie

started across the room toward her apartment. But Sean stepped into her path.

'I want you to know that you need not be concerned that I will find it difficult to be with you, despite your power. I too am experiencing a surge of my own, thanks to our love. We are perfectly matched, as always.'

Maggie stepped backward, making sure he could not touch her. It was time to make Sean Flaherty see the truth.

'There is no *us*, Sean. There never was, there never will be. We had sex. It was a terrible mistake, and it is over, and that is all there is to it.'

Confusion flitted across his face. 'I don't understand, Margaret. You –'

'Please address me as Ceamir.' She was enjoying this.

'That's just it.' Sean stepped toward her. Maggie retreated, remembering how she'd hurt him last time. 'You are Ceamir, you need not be afraid of your family any more.'

'I'm not. I do not love you, Sean. I never loved you, that night was a mistake and I am now telling you to leave me alone.'

'No.' Sean shook his head, then pressed his fingers against his ears. 'No, I am not hearing this. You could not be saying this to me. You love me. Our night together was magical.' He sounded like he'd got all his lines from a C-grade chick-flick. It flitted across Maggie's mind that no one really talked like this. Was he mad, not just annoying?

'That night was crap.' Maggie put her hands on her hips. 'Here's a bit of advice for you, Sean. Next time you're with a woman, *she should come as well.* Now, leave my office and do not return here unless you are summoned to the Ceamir's presence. Is that understood?'

'But Margaret –' he whined, and stepped toward her yet again.

Patience exhausted, Maggie lifted her hands and blasted her power at him. She pushed him onto the floor.

Sean glared up at her: she'd finally convinced him that she didn't love him. And it looked like love wasn't flooding his heart either.

'That, Margaret, was a foolish mistake,' he said softly as he stood. 'You don't know what I am capable of. But you will see.' And then he vanished – a long-drawn-out affair where he gradually faded away.

Maggie went over to the space where he had stood. His essence lingered in the air, and it was very familiar. As if she had felt it recently ...

'*Hampton!*' The Sabhamir appeared in the middle of the office. 'Come here.'

He came and stood by her, and then frowned. 'Have you had the taiboll here?'

'No, Sean Flaherty.'

The two guardians looked at each other. 'Move aside, Maggie, I'm going to try to follow him.' Hampton shimmered, and then he disappeared, but was immediately back on the same spot.

'Fuck. He's protected wherever he is: I can't get in.' He started to stalk up and down the room. 'How is that possible? It's been a long while since I've seen Sean Flaherty, but he barely passed his third order. He shouldn't have the power to block me.'

'He said his power has been growing lately,' Maggie said. 'He said it was because of his love for me.'

Hampton snorted. 'Delusion, more likely.' Then he stopped and spun around. He stared at Maggie, then shook his head. 'It's not possible. He was back in Sclossin the day the Forbidden Texts were stolen, but only just – he'd been in England the whole time the robbery was being planned. He couldn't have been the one who stole them.'

'But perhaps he's in on it. The Flahertys are power-hungry enough.'

'But law abiding. Still, it makes sense. Stay here, I'm going to go talk to Oswald.' He was gone.

Maggie slumped on the lounge. Where was Lucas? She didn't like the idea of him out and about, not when Sean had turned malicious. She closed her eyes and offered a quick prayer to whoever was listening.

A deep tone rang in the air; she answered and Hampton appeared. 'Oswald hasn't seen Sean, said he was still at work. But there's a pressure in that house that I've not felt before. I think Sean's been at work there.'

'So? Did you check out the laboratory?'

'I did. There's nothing out of the ordinary. He's been working somewhere else in the house, but it's hidden from even his father and that makes me think that he's used the texts to hide his real laboratory.' Hampton shook his head. 'This will take time, and preparation. I'll call all the guardians together when I'm ready.' Then he disappeared.

Maggie slumped back on the lounge and closed her eyes. Lucas, wherever you are, come to me soon, she thought. I need you.

CHAPTER TWENTY-NINE

After Maggie left, Lucas closed his eyes and tried to hold onto her taste, her smell, the shift of her skin against his for as long as possible. But it all faded, and left him with the ache of unfulfilled arousal.

He'd better get used to this, he thought to himself as he got up and headed to the shower. A spray of cold water took the edge off his craving for her, and then he got dressed and stood in the middle of his loungeroom, wondering what to do next.

Ask for directions to my office, I'll meet you there, Maggie had said. He wondered what it would look like. Did she take after her grandfather and embrace organised chaos, or was she meticulous and clean like her mother? He was willing to bet she was more John than Siobhan.

That reminded him that he hadn't actually spoken to John, Siobhan or Peter since his sentence had been postponed. He found his mobile in his suitcase and was pleased to find he could still get a signal here in the bardria building. He dialled John's number. He got the message bank, so asked John to give him a call and hung up. Then he went out into the corridor to find someone to direct him to the Ceamir's office.

There wasn't anyone in the hall outside his apartment, so he picked a direction and started walking. He turned the first corner, but there was no one there. He walked to the next junction and looked down one side, then the other. To his disappointment, there was someone there, walking toward him – Sean Flaherty.

Lucas crossed his arms over his chest and waited to see what Sean would say this time.

'I'm surprised to see you, Valeroso,' Sean said in a friendly way as he approached. 'They told me you were intelligent, but I guess you're not smart enough to realise that your life is under threat every moment you spend in Sclossin.'

'I'm safe enough around you, aren't I? After all, I'm under the protection of the Flaherty name.'

Sean scoffed. 'I wouldn't put too much stock in what my aunt has to say, Valeroso. She's not the head of the family, my father is. And when he's gone I'll be the Flaherty.'

'Sure, but I'll be the one with Maggie.' Suck on that, Flaherty, Lucas thought. He needed something, anything to deflate the man's monstrous ego.

Sean's nostrils flared. 'She's the Ceamir now, and you'll treat her with respect, human.'

'I do, Flaherty. That's why she wants me, not you.'

'No she doesn't.' Before Lucas knew what was happening, Flaherty leapt forward and grabbed his arm. Then the air shimmered and pressure built around them, squeezing Lucas's lungs until he couldn't breathe. It felt like the top of him was being pulled somewhere, but his feet were glued to the floor. Shit, he thought, I'm going to die.

Then there was a loud pop, and he collapsed onto a stone floor; the bardria corridor had been wood. He tried to breathe, but pain racked his body. Then his arms were pulled behind his back and his wrists tied to his ankles, and his muscles screamed in protest.

He looked up through pain-hazed eyes at Sean Flaherty. The other man was flushed and breathing heavily, but otherwise seemed unaffected by whatever had just happened to them.

'I was able to transfer us here because of the great power that Margaret's love has given me. I am a worthy partner for a guardian, and she knows it. She's been toying with you to satisfy her family, but that is all over. I'm sorry if you've been deluding yourself that she loves you, but false love passes in time. You'll forget about her. That, or you'll die. Up to you which. Now, I'm going to leave you to think about the mistakes you've made, and I'm going to go and congratulate our new Ceamir.' Sean shimmered and stretched, and then he was gone.

Lucas lifted his head to look around the room, glad that his body wasn't protesting as much as it had been. He felt weak but not hurt, and his strength was returning.

He was lying on the floor of a small stone room. Piles of wooden boxes, covered with a thick layer of dust, were haphazardly pushed against the walls to create a space in the middle, where a star of gulagh had been painted on the floor. Some of the boxes had been covered with a cloth to form a bench, which held glass jars of chemicals and powders, mortar and pestle and dirty bowls encrusted with some sort of dried solution.

It smelt musty and tangy at the same time and,

despite the light glowing from a globe on top of one pile of boxes, the room was dark and cold. It was obviously a makeshift gadda laboratory. That couldn't be a good thing.

First things first, he told himself. He needed to get out of the ropes, then figure out how to get out of the room. He pulled with his ankles and arms and found that almost immediately the ropes loosened. He grinned. As if Sean would know how to tie someone up properly. He, on the other hand, hadn't done it for some time, but at least he knew how to.

Sean had used a thick rope, thinking that meant more strength, but instead it meant larger, easier knots to undo. Lucas wriggled and pulled and, within minutes, was hauling himself to his feet, the rope a pile on the floor.

Then he started to investigate the room. He quickly worked out there wasn't a door. Being effectively human was, frankly, a pain in the arse.

A beep resounded through the room, and he jumped. What was it? Another beep, and he located the sound in his pocket.

He cursed as he pulled his mobile phone out. How stupid, to forget he had it. He looked at the phone – the beeping meant it was running out of power. He picked a number and dialled it, but it went to a message bank.

'Hi, you've called Maggie Shaunessy, I can't take your call right now so leave a message and I'll get back to you.'

'It's me. Sean Flaherty has taken me somewhere, some sort of stone room, and I can't –' *Beep, beep, beep* and the phone was dead.

'Fuck!' Lucas threw the phone at the wall, then buried his face in his hands. He had no idea when Maggie would get the message. It could be hours.

Time for the next plan. Maybe there was something in the boxes? He turned to study the nearest box – it was a sturdy construction of thick planks of wood and nails. He wasn't going to be able to rip it open, but maybe there was something here he could use to jimmy it. He started to search the bench, but there were just a few spoons and a small knife – nothing substantial enough to open a box.

He eyed off the chemicals, appreciating the irony, given Holly's misunderstanding of what physics was all about. Right now, he was wishing he *had* majored in chemistry. He picked up one jar, hoping against hope that he'd recognise the contents, but wasn't surprised when it appeared to be nothing more specific than a foul-smelling brew.

Right, he thought to himself as he put it down, can't open any of the boxes, can't concoct any potions. Only hope is to overpower Flaherty when he comes back.

Lucas looked around the room. There were plenty of places to hide, but he needed somewhere small enough to hide him but large enough for an easy exit when Flaherty arrived. He'd seen a couple of guys knifed in fights because they hadn't been able to get completely out of their hidey-holes.

Sean would expect him to still be lying on the floor, so he'd likely reappear at one end of the room or the other, rather than in the middle, and Lucas guessed it would be the end away from the bench. As he built a screen of boxes in that area, he thought about how Sean had looked when he'd transferred out. Lucas had seen a few people transfer, and they'd all disappeared and reappeared cleanly. He'd never seen any of them take as long as Flaherty did. Did that mean that Flaherty actually wasn't that good at it?

He tested his hidey-hole and decided it would do. Then he hid himself and waited for a sign that Sean would reappear.

For a time it was comfortable — the effort of moving the boxes around had warmed his body up. But soon he was aware of the chill that seeped from the stones into his feet and then moved up his legs. He hoped Flaherty wouldn't take too long.

Lucas didn't know how long he'd waited before he saw the air shimmer. Shit, he thought: Sean was appearing at the other end of the room, near the bench. Lucas flew out of his shelter and across the floor, knowing he had to get to Flaherty the instant he fully transferred.

For a moment, he thought he wasn't going to be quick enough. He saw Flaherty lift a hand and a stream of dark grey power come out of it. But he dove at the man's legs, and the power passed over his back.

He crashed into Sean's thighs, driving the other man back against the table. Sean screamed, an ear-tearing sound that had Lucas thinking he'd done more damage than he intended.

Lucas landed on the floor next to the table, pulling the other man down on top of him. As Sean fell, Lucas rolled to ensure he wasn't pinned. He released Flaherty, surged into a crouch to again jump, and then looked at what he'd done.

Sean lay on the floor, moaning, his head shifting from side to side. His body, and in particular his hips and legs, were very still.

Holy shit, Lucas thought. I've broken his back.

He reached forward and touched Sean's leg. No response. Then he moved his hand up to Sean's hip. Nothing.

Fuck.

Lucas ran a hand through his hair. He'd intended to incapacitate Flaherty, hurt him even, but this was much worse than that.

Still, a part of his mind said, he's out, and you can get the secret of the room and escape and then get him some help.

Then Sean shifted, groaned. His entire body moved and he swore violently – and Lucas realised that he hadn't hurt the other man as much as he'd thought. Sean would be OK. That meant he was still dangerous.

Lucas grabbed the rope and quickly tied Sean's hands behind his back with much more effective knots than Flaherty had used on him.

Sean rolled onto his back, gasped as his clenched hands pushed into what was probably a very sore spot, and glared up at Lucas. He took a couple of deep breaths, then squeezed out, 'You're going to pay for that, Valeroso.'

'No more than you,' Lucas said, crouching down by Sean's shoulder. 'Now, tell me how to get out of this room, or I'll hurt you.'

'No point. You're not gadda, you can't get out. You can't fight this either.' Sean narrowed his eyes, his eyebrows drew together and Lucas didn't doubt a spell was being formed that would fire at him at any moment.

He acted instinctively. He lifted his fist and slammed it down onto Sean's temple. There was a flash of shock in Flaherty's eyes, then his body slumped. Out cold.

Lucas sat back down on the cold stones and stared at his captor, now captive. Well, this was one hell of a mess. Only Sean could get them out, but Sean was too dangerous conscious.

I'll just ... see what happens next, he thought ruefully, and settled in for a long wait.

Maggie's mobile rang. She scrambled through her handbag and answered it. 'Hello?'

'Maggie, it's your grandfather. Is Lucas there? He called earlier and left a message, but now he's not answering his calls.'

Maggie sat straight, ideas pummelling in her brain. 'Have to go, Grandpa, bye.' She hung up, then checked her messages. Sure enough, there was one from Lucas.

'Maggie, it's me, Sean Flaherty has taken me somewhere, some sort of stone room, and I can't –'

'*Hampton!*' One breath, two, and the Sabhamir was standing on her carpet, frowning at her.

'Maggie, this better be good, because –'

'He's got Lucas.' She thrust the phone at him. Hampton took the phone, looked at it, then at her. She pulled it from his hand, pushed '1' to replay, then pressed it to his ear.

The colour draining from the Sabhamir's face proved that he had heard every word. 'When was the last time you saw Lucas?'

'When I was summoned by John O'Hara to Winton. I told him to get directions here, that I'd meet him when I was done, but I haven't seen him since.' As she spoke, Maggie dialled Lucas's number, but there was no answer. 'His phone must have run out, damn it.'

'Maggie, remain calm. We can find him. We'll start with the blackness I felt at the Flaherty house. Let's gather the others.'

Within moments, the six guardians were all in Maggie's office. A request for entry was sent to and approved by Oswald Flaherty, and then all six appeared in his library.

Oswald Flaherty looked old and feeble, but Maggie knew he was incredibly powerful. Judging by his stooped shoulders and the deep lines on his face, his life hadn't been a happy or easy one – though she knew enough to guess this was mostly his own doing.

Sean was there in the sharpness of his features, but what had once been bright red hair had long been a white crop. His body hunched over, so it was hard to see if Sean had inherited his father's height. It was clear the old man had passed down rage and entitlement.

Hampton spoke. 'Oswald Flaherty, we thank you for allowing us entry into your home. We come pursuing Sean Flaherty, who we believe has detained Lucas Valeroso without authority.'

Flaherty shook his head. 'They're not here.' His voice was strong and resolute. 'They're my blood. I would know.'

'Are there any stone rooms in the house other than your laboratory?'

Flaherty's shoulders seemed to dip a little as he nodded. 'Yes, very old storage rooms. They're only able to be entered by the use of power. No one's used them in decades.' He looked at them all, and nodded to Maggie, then looked at the Sabhamir. 'I see all the guardians are here.'

'We are concerned, both for your son and for Lucas Valeroso. You will take us to these rooms, Oswald.'

'Of course. Flahertys have been conservators of the rules of the gadda throughout our existence. You will find nothing.' Flaherty led them from the library, across the hall to a sumptuous loungeroom. Then he pointed to the floor. 'The first is down there.'

Hampton knelt and touched the floor. 'It feels fine,' he said over his shoulder. 'Undo the lock, Oswald.'

Flaherty nodded and waved his hand. Then the Sabhamir transferred. He was back almost instantly. 'Next one,' he said.

The next room was under the dining room. Again, Flaherty unlocked it and again, Hampton found nothing.

The third room was under the tea room, and this time as he touched the floor Hampton's face darkened. 'There is something here,' he said.

The Heasimir crouched down next to him, and then nodded. 'This does not feel right. There is a chill.'

'Oswald, unlock it.'

Flaherty waved his hand, then frowned. He tried again. 'I cannot.'

The Sabhamir nodded as he stood. 'Oswald, I will borrow your power in order to break the lock. Ceamir, I will need your help as well. When it's ready, Heasimir,

I will give you the signal to break through. Firimir, Garramir, Coiremir, you will follow her.'

He planted his feet hip-width apart and then held out his hands. Maggie stepped forward and took hold of one. She had no idea what he was planning to do, but she trusted him.

He wiggled the other hand at Oswald Flaherty. 'Take my hand, Oswald.'

The old man shuffled forward and did as he was told. His brow was wrinkled and his lips thin.

'Both of you, think of your love, yours for Lucas, Ceamir and yours for Sean, Oswald. Meld it with your power, then send it out to me on the count of three.' Hampton nodded at the two of them, then he closed his eyes.

Maggie closed hers and, after some thought, chose the moment when she'd known Lucas was hers.

She melded her happiness, her desire, her love with her power, then on the count of three fed it to Hampton, hoping that Flaherty had done the same.

The floor beneath them shuddered, a wind tore at Maggie's hair and heat seared her face. Then there was a ripping sound, as though the air was tearing.

She opened her eyes to see first the Heasimir then the other guardians disappear. Hampton squeezed her hand and the two of them followed.

'Maggie!'

She barely had time to gather herself when she was pulled into Lucas's arms and held tight against his chest. She wrapped her arms around his waist and squeezed.

'Are you all right? Are you hurt?'

He leant his cheek against the top of her head. 'I'm fine.'

'Thank the star.'

There was a scream: she looked up to see Oswald Flaherty standing in the corner of the room. He was shivering, his hands clenched into fists and pressed against his chest.

'Is he dead?'

Maggie followed Oswald's gaze and saw both Sarah and Hampton kneeling over the supine figure of Sean Flaherty. There was blood oozing from a cut on his forehead and his hands were tied behind his back.

'No,' Hampton said, looking over his shoulder. 'Sean will live. Although he'll wish otherwise.'

Oswald stumbled forward. 'What do you mean?'

Hampton got to his feet and gestured to the debris on the makeshift bench. 'This, Oswald. If I'm not mistaken, that's the leftovers from the creation of a taiboll. And I won't be surprised to find fuiparra and briarracht traces here either.'

The old man looked around, and Maggie knew he couldn't dismiss the clear sign that this storeroom had been turned into a secret laboratory. 'That was Sean?'

She couldn't believe she was actually feeling sympathy for the Flaherty.

'Firimir, take Oswald upstairs. I've summoned Madge to come have a look at him. The Heasimir and I will take Sean to the healer's wing.'

Owen nodded, and put his hand on Oswald's shoulder. 'Come, sir, and I'll get you a whiskey.' They disappeared.

Hampton looked at Maggie. 'Take Lucas back to your apartment and make sure he gets a rest. He's going to be called up before the bardria over this, and it's not going to be pretty.'

Maggie felt fear run through Lucas's body and gave him a squeeze. Then they transferred to the apartment.

'Fuck.' Lucas held her so tight that she thought she might be bruised. 'I've fucked up, haven't I? They won't let me be gadda now.'

'You were protecting yourself.' She tried to send calming emotions to him. 'You have no power, and you were up against a third order. They'll understand.'

'But he's a Flaherty.'

'It will be all right. I promised no one would hurt you again, remember? I meant it.' Maggie pulled away from him. 'Now, you're under orders from the Sabhamir to rest, and even I won't go against him. Bed!'

She couldn't help but be a little dismayed by the new zombie version of Lucas. He didn't demur as she undressed him and helped him slide between the sheets. He laid his head on the pillow and closed his eyes.

She knew he wasn't sleeping, but she only pressed a kiss to his forehead, then went out into the loungeroom.

She couldn't help feeling that despite her assurances, Lucas was right. The bardria wasn't going to react well to the news that he'd assaulted a gadda, particularly one from the old families.

A plan. She had to devise a plan to again save Lucas, so he could have the life he deserved.

CHAPTER THIRTY

Lucas did try to rest as he was told. He lay there, he was sure, a whole ten minutes, and begged his body to relax so he could sleep.

But one part of his mind was intent on replaying the events of the day, over and over again, with the dark voice crowing *you've done it this time!* for a sound track. The other side, however, was slowly but surely getting angry.

Fuck this, it kept saying. *No one's going to control my life any more. Fuck this.*

That part of his mind was short on helpful advice, though. There was one thought that he should just get up, walk away, and start all over again. Abandon Lucas Valeroso. Abandon the sticky, destructive past.

The other thought was that really, he'd been running all his life, and he needed to stop. He'd made some dumb mistakes as a kid, but he'd been punished for that. Nothing he'd actually done was unaccounted for, whatever evil trolls like Holly might say. He'd now spent more of his life as a fucking ornament to society than he'd ever spent as a fucked-up little shit. Fucked if he was going to keep running.

This was the thought that took hold, the one that coalesced into a plan of action. He got out of bed, dressed, and then walked out into the loungeroom.

Maggie wasn't there. He breathed a sigh of relief — he knew she'd want to come along, and she could probably save him. But it was time for Lucas Valeroso to save himself.

He went over to what he thought was the front door of the apartment and threw it open. And walked into Siobhan Shaunessy's loungeroom.

He stopped and turned around. Had he somehow been spirited back to Australia, without knowing? Except this room didn't seem right. There wasn't a desk in the O'Hara loungeroom, and the big picture was different.

On the other side of the room was another door. Here, he found the corridor he'd been looking for. He looked back at the room behind him and shook his head. Then he set out in search of the caelleach.

He had to call upon a tall, skinny figure in a pale blue gown, who directed him with a smile. He stepped into the outer office and found himself facing the caelleach's personal assistant. The young woman, who bore a striking resemblance to Cormac, looked up from the book she was reading with a frown.

'Can I help you?'

'I'm Lucas Valeroso, and I'd like to see the caelleach.'

'You're Lucas Valeroso.' He watched her catalogue him. He tried not to squirm and guessed he'd have to get used to that reaction — he was something of a celebrity among the gadda now.

She looked up at him, nodded, and then smiled at him.

'Caelleach Cormac will see you now.'

Lucas turned to look at the door. He took a deep breath in, released it slowly and pulled his shoulders back slightly. You've done nothing wrong, he told himself. Now, go fight. Then he walked into the office.

The caelleach stood as he entered. 'Lucas. I hope you've settled in well.'

Lucas frowned. That wasn't the reaction he'd been expecting. 'I've had better welcomes. I'm wondering what you're going to do about it.'

Now it was Cormac who was frowning. 'Do about what?'

Lucas's eyes widened as he realised he'd managed to get to Cormac first. His timing was perfect. 'About the fact that I bashed Sean Flaherty unconscious.'

There was a pause, then the caelleach said quietly, 'I see. Would you like to explain to me why?'

'Because he kidnapped me and threatened to kill me.'

Cormac seemed to sway on his feet. 'I beg your pardon?'

'Flaherty and I met walking the corridors here in the bardria building. After an as usual riveting conversation, he transferred me to a stone room filled with boxes and laboratory stuff. I reacted badly to the transfer and by the time I recovered he'd tied me up. He said "This town ain't big enough for the both of us", then left. I managed to untie myself, tried to get out but couldn't, so hid away in order to neutralise him when he returned. When he did, I charged him, tied him up and tried to convince him to let me go, but when he tried to throw a spell at me, I clubbed him unconscious. Then after an hour or so the guardians came and found me.'

By the end of this speech, Cormac had dropped into his chair. His empty eyes stared up past Lucas, his mouth wide.

'He kidnapped you?'

Lucas opened his mouth to describe the events again, sure Cormac hadn't heard them the first time, but stopped when a deep knell rang in the room.

Cormac stood up. 'Lucas, sit down.' He gestured to one of the chairs off to the side of the desk.

'I'd prefer to stand, if you don't mind.'

Then a force pushed him, and Lucas stumbled across and leant against a chair. Seconds later, the Sabhamir was standing exactly where he had been.

All right, he told himself as he re-established his balance. Next time a gadda tells you to move, do it.

The Sabhamir looked at Lucas, then at Cormac and said, 'I see Valeroso has started to fill you in on what happened.'

'He says he was kidnapped.'

'He was.'

'Taken from the bardria building, by force?'

'Yes.'

'By a man who by my understanding barely passed third order and therefore should be incapable of it?'

'Yes.'

Cormac slumped down into his chair again. 'Star above. How is that possible?'

'The Forbidden Texts.'

Cormac surged to his feet again. 'Sean Flaherty has the texts?'

'That I'm not sure of. I've yet to find the texts themselves, but there is no doubt in my mind he's had contact with them.'

As Cormac sat back down again, Lucas looked from one man to the other, confused. 'What are the Forbidden Texts?'

Cormac spun around. 'Ah, Valeroso. Forgot you were here. Never mind, never mind. Thank you for coming to see me. I'm sure there won't be a problem. Kidnapping is strictly forbidden. No doubt you did what you had to do. Good day.'

Lucas looked at the Sabhamir, who gave him a twisted smile. 'I suggest again that you go rest.'

Lucas walked out through the outer office and into the corridor, trying to make sense of what had just happened. He wandered back to the apartment, he sat down in the real loungeroom, flopped against the back of the sofa and went over it all again. If Sean had used something weird to kidnap him, that would explain why his transferring had seemed so different.

These Forbidden Texts were obviously important if the caelleach wasn't even bothered by Lucas's confession. It appeared he was going to get away with his actions.

He thought he should be happier about that than he was. The vision of a scar in soft white skin appeared in his mind, and he dispelled it as he had been doing for days.

The air shimmered in front of him, and Maggie appeared. She sat close to him on the lounge.

'Hampton told me you'd been to see the caelleach.'

He gathered her close and took a deep breath, drawing her scent and warmth into him.

'Hampton?'

'The Sabhamir.'

'The Sabhamir's called Hampton?' He hadn't thought of the guardians as having real names, being real people.

'In answer to your question,' he said, 'I went to face the music. I'm sick of constantly apologising for stupid things I did when I was a kid. If I was going to be punished for what I did to Sean, I wanted to face it like a man.'

Maggie looked up at him. 'And?'

He saw the heat in her eyes and realised she was girding herself to go into battle. 'I think it's OK. I believe my transgression has been trumped by something called the Forbidden Texts. What are they?'

She sighed. 'The bane of our existence.' She leant against him. 'Terrible teachings that subvert the basis of gadda power and upset the balance. They were hidden, but now they've been stolen and it's up to us guardians to get them back.'

'The Sabhamir thinks Flaherty has them?'

Maggie sat bolt upright and stared at him. 'Sean?'

'That's how he thinks he was able to take me. I tell you, honey, I hope that never happens to me again. That transfer was terrible. I really thought I was going to die.'

Maggie squeezed him, hard. 'Thank the star you didn't. I can't believe it. Sean had the texts?'

'So they were saying.'

She shuddered, then leant back against him. 'Now I'm even happier you did what you did.'

Lucas closed his eyes. 'So my probationary month can continue.'

'Then everything will be fine.'

Lucas held her close and thought that maybe, just maybe, it would be.

The night passed surprisingly peacefully. Maggie got the message from Hampton that investigations were ongoing, and there was nothing she could do to help. So she and Lucas cooked dinner, and talked, and then went to bed, where she spent some time ensuring Sean hadn't hurt him, and that he was feeling fine. She fell asleep in a contented daze.

She was woken by an entrance request ringing through the apartment. She sat up and rubbed at her eyes.

'*What time of the bloody morning do you call this to wake someone up?*'

'*I call it 8 am,*' came Hampton's voice. '*Get up, Ceamir. We have work to do.*'

Maggie gave her head a shake, leant over and kissed the sound asleep Lucas, then crawled out of bed. '*Do I have time for breakfast?*' she asked, and pulled open the wardrobe door. Then she stopped and gaped at her clothes. Somehow, everything she'd put in the wardrobe, regardless of its initial colour, was now red. '*What have you done to my clothes?*'

'Not me, Ceamir, but you. And I'll give you something to eat when you get here. Now, hurry up.'

'Can't believe I actually thought you were nice,' Maggie grumbled as she pulled out a skirt and top. She showered, dressed, and then transferred over to the Sabhamir's office.

The rest of the guardians were already waiting.

'Good morning, Ceamir,' Kenyon said brightly. Maggie smiled at him.

'Nice to see you're finally in red,' Wilma said. Maggie thought she was very mature in not poking her tongue out.

'The bardria will be meeting at 9.30 am to consider the attack of the taiboll on Winton University. I wanted to talk to you all because it's clear there's a link between all the recent events at Winton and Sean Flaherty,' Hampton said as Maggie took a seat between Owen and the Heasimir.

'Sean Flaherty isn't capable of creating those creatures,' Wilma said. 'He barely passed third order.'

'For an ordinary third order, I agree,' Hampton said. 'But all the evidence points to those creatures having been created in that room at Flaherty House. I've done a lot of testing of the three of them, and there is no other essence there except Oswald Flaherty and John O'Hara, but neither man was involved. I think Sean's relationship to Oswald meant he could mask his own essence as his father's, and he got hold of John's during his brief trip to Australia.'

'So he's been using the Forbidden Texts,' the Heasimir said.

'Actually, I'm not so sure of that. He shouldn't have been able to do anything of what he has done recently — transfer Lucas Valeroso or set that lock being other examples — but none of that is forbidden. Just higher order. There is a darkness within his power. But there was no sign of the texts in his laboratory, and he's not using any of the spells and potions they contain, so I'm wondering if maybe he hasn't read them.'

Maggie began to mentally run through all her encounters with Sean. Maybe there was a clue there.

'Maybe he can't read them,' Kenyon said. 'Language was very different five hundred years ago, and Sean's not the brightest boy.'

'Possible, but then where has he hidden them? I've searched the house, and that room is definitely the only place that the darkness exists.'

'He said he thought his power increase was because of me.' Maggie spoke slowly, as the memory of the last encounter with Sean played through in her mind. 'You said the Forbidden Texts went missing the day that I got in trouble for the story, which was also the day that I met Sean. Maybe he had the texts without realising at some point around then, and they had an impact on him.' She looked up and saw the five other guardians staring at her, aghast.

'If that's the case — if even having them briefly can have this impact, then what could they be doing to the person who really has them?' Wilma asked. 'Vomiting could be the least of their problems.'

'I take it no one saw the taxi or its passenger?' Maggie said. Hampton shook his head.

'If we can relive Sean's movements during the time we believe the texts went missing, maybe we can see who has them now.'

'The only way we can do that is by scrying,' Owen said. 'Sean won't just tell us. Can we get a warrant from the bardria?'

'I'm sure we can.' Hampton stood. 'Come, it's time for us to be at the bardria.' He led the guardians from the room, across the corridor and into the bardria chamber. Maggie was surprised to see her mother and grandfather there. She gave them a nod as she took her position at the end of the line of guardians.

On the other side of the room were Oswald Flaherty and members of his family. The old man appeared to be pale but not unwell after yesterday's events.

The bardria filed in and took their seats and Cormac began.

'We are here to deal with an attack on a human, namely that at 11 am local time on 1 April, a taiboll was sent to Winton University in Australia, where it attacked a human student. Luckily, the creature was detained by John O'Hara before any real damage was done. First, we will hear from John O'Hara regarding the attack.' Cormac nodded, and John took the seat in the middle of the room. Owen took his customary position and connected and then John began.

'I was walking among the students when I noticed a group over to one side of the lawn gathered around a girl, who was reeling and swatting at the air. Looking closely I saw the faint outline of the taiboll. I ran over and sent enough power into the creature to disable it without killing it. I sent for the Ceamir, and she was waiting for me in my office when I got there with the girl, Lee Quong. She spoke to the girl while I fetched the taiboll. Thanks to the Ceamir and Siobhan the girl believes that she had an allergic reaction and is fine. I visited her before coming here. She is embarrassed by her reaction, but is none the wiser about the presence of the monster or the gadda.'

'Thank you, John.' Cormac nodded, and the Firimir released O'Hara. 'Ceamir, can you confirm John's description of your actions in this?'

Maggie stepped forward. Now she was a guardian, she didn't need Owen's truth-checking. She recapped her side of the story, then finished, 'I have been keeping an eye on local media and student blogs, and I can report that there has been no talk of anything strange.'

'Thank you, Ceamir. Sabhamir, can you tell us what you learnt from the creature?'

Hampton took Maggie's place. 'As per both the fuiparra and the briarracht, the taiboll bore the essences of John O'Hara and Oswald Flaherty. I remain sure that neither of those gentlemen created the creatures. In fact they were all created and sent by Sean Flaherty.'

Robert Yarrow jumped to his feet. 'Preposterous,' he roared. 'Sean Flaherty would never do such a thing.'

'Sit down, Robert,' Helga said. He stared at her, aghast, then did as he was bid. Helga turned to look at the Sabhamir. 'Sean is only third order and is not capable of these acts.'

'Ordinarily, I would agree,' Hampton said. 'But yesterday, in an unrelated matter, a hidden laboratory in the Flaherty home was discovered, and within it evidence of the creation of these creatures. All the investigation I've done leads to Sean Flaherty.'

'No!' Now Oswald jumped to his feet.

The Sabhamir looked at him. 'He broke a bardria ruling and visited Ms Shaunessy in Australia, Oswald. He has hurt people and deceived you. I am sorry.'

The Flaherty slumped back into his seat and his family began to stroke him and pat him, offering him comfort.

Hampton continued. 'I myself have been witness to uses of power far beyond the acknowledged potential Sean Flaherty usually exhibits, and above his third order level. He put such a stout lock on his laboratory's entrance that it took the combined force of the Ceamir, Oswald Flaherty and me to break it. This can be supported by all the guardians.'

Silence descended on the room. Then Maggie heard sobs. Someone was crying. Everyone looked at Oswald Flaherty.

'How can this be?' the old man whispered. 'Sean cannot *do* any of this.'

'Yes, Sabhamir. You've not explained how this is possible. The evidence must be false.' Helga looked at Oswald, concern clear on her face.

'The evidence is genuine, and I do know how it is possible. I believe Sean is involved in the disappearance of the Forbidden Texts.'

'No!' Oswald roared the word, although tears streamed down his cheeks. 'My son would never use the Forbidden Texts. Never.' He shuddered, then said softly, 'Perhaps he did send those beasts to Winton.

I know why. I'm sorry to say that I might even have encouraged it.'

'Why?' Cormac said.

'To save Margaret Shaunessy. Sean was in love and was concerned with her being in such close contact with humans. He wanted her back in Sclossin.'

'And so he broke gadda law and threatened the O'Haras and humans?'

Oswald looked at the Sabhamir. 'You are sure?' Hampton nodded. 'Then yes, he broke gadda law. I leave him to the mercy of the bardria.'

Maggie watched the old man shuffle from the room, his weight borne by his family. Looking at him, it was hard to believe he was the same age as her grandfather – his grief rendered him ancient.

'Sabhamir, bring Sean Flaherty here. We will hear his words on the allegations you bring. He must also face trial for what he did to Lucas Valeroso.'

'Certainly, Caelleach.' Hampton bowed, and disappeared. Maggie pressed her hands together to hide their trembling.

Hampton reappeared with Sean held in front of him. Sean's hands were bound behind him and the cut on his head was surrounded by a brilliant purple bruise, but otherwise he looked well. He walked with his head high, a half smile pulling at his lips.

The Sabhamir led Sean to the central chair and then stood beside him. The Firimir took his position and Cormac began proceedings.

'Sean Flaherty, you come before the bardria today to face several allegations. The first is that yesterday you kidnapped Lucas Valeroso from this building, took him to your own home and there imprisoned him. What say you?'

'Surely you aren't charging me for attempting to take care of a problem none of you is game to?' Sean said. 'Lucas Valeroso is a blight on the gadda. His father was nothing more than a thug and a murderer and Valeroso is no better, as his treatment of me shows. We would all have been better off if I'd succeeded in my plans. The purity and sanctity of the gadda must be maintained.'

How the hell did I ever find him attractive? Maggie thought. She looked at her fellow guardians. Kenyon and Wilma both looked embarrassed. The Heasimir had no reaction at all. Does she have no feelings, or does she agree with him?

'You are also charged with sending no fewer than three monsters, which you created without authorisation, to Winton with the intention of harming both gadda and humans. Finally, you stand accused of having contact with the Forbidden Texts. What say you to that?'

Maggie watched Sean closely. He had sat still and straight during the first exchange. Even mention of the beasts hadn't disturbed him. But at the words *the Forbidden Texts*, his entire body shuddered. He looked up at the Sabhamir, confusion writ large over his face.

'How could you think that?' he whispered.

'The increase in your power can only be explained by –'

'Not true.' Sean surged forward, but the hands of the Firimir pulled him back into the seat. 'It was my love for Margaret that made me strong, a love that was shamed and discarded. I have never seen the Forbidden Texts, never touched them. I would not! They are foul and terrible.'

'There must be another explanation for how he has come to have these extraordinary talents,' Helga said. 'Perhaps he is a ... a late bloomer, for example?'

The other councillors nodded at this flimsy excuse. Maggie couldn't blame them. The Forbidden Texts terrified everyone.

'Sabhamir, tell us more about the forbidden teachings and the impact you believe they have had on Sean Flaherty.'

'I discovered the texts missing on January 31, and I know they were in the room the week prior. I traced the thief to the outtran room, but by then so many essences had been traipsed in and out I was unable to track him – or her, of course – any further. Yesterday, Lucas Valeroso went missing and sent a message to the Ceamir saying Sean Flaherty had locked him in a stone room. I went to the Flaherty home to speak to Sean and realised there was a blackness there. The lock on his improvised laboratory proved that there had been a sudden improvement in his powers. It's not unusual in puberty, when powers can wax and wane, but the only time it's ever been noted in adults was during the time of the working of the forbidden. Sean has a darkness within him that speaks of touching the Forbidden Texts. I can conceive of no other rational explanation for what has happened to him.'

'Do any of my fellow councillors know of any other possible explanation for such a sudden increase in power?' Cormac turned to the councillors.

Most of them shook their heads. 'What of Sean's contention, that it is the love he shared with Margaret Shaunessy that has opened his powers to new possibilities?' Helga said.

'An unprecedented development and thus unlikely,' Hampton said.

'But not impossible,' Helga said.

'The love is unrequited,' Hampton said.

'Would you be prepared to agree that a love not shared cannot result in any impact on a person's powers?' Cormac said to Helga.

She bowed her head. 'He has shamed our family,' she whispered.

Cormac leant over and patted her hand. Then he addressed Sean. 'Did you create three beasts and send them to Winton, two to attack John O'Hara, one to attack a human?'

'No.' The smell of mildew and rotten fruit filled the air. The Firimir was detecting a lie.

'You lie, Sean Flaherty. Did you create three beasts and send them to Winton, using your father's essence to hide your identity?'

'No.' Maggie began to gag as the smell intensified.

'One last chance, Sean Flaherty, or the Sabhamir will compel you. Did you create the beasts?'

There was a pause, then Sean hissed, 'Yes. But I did what I had to do, to save Margaret, to save our love. You have to understand. It was our destiny.'

'Have you had contact with the Forbidden Texts?'

'No. No, I have not, I know nothing about them, it was my love that made me stronger, my love.'

Owen released Sean. 'Sean Flaherty speaks truth.'

'Very well. The bardria will retire, and we will return in one hour with our verdict. Sabhamir, escort Sean Flaherty back to the cells.'

Hampton nodded, put his hand on Sean's shoulder and the two of them disappeared.

Maggie avoided all conversation in the hour they waited for the verdict. She was embarrassed that Sean was talking about 'their' love in bardria, angry that he had considered he was right to treat Lucas that way and worried about the Forbidden Texts.

She was so distracted that she was shocked when the bardria door swung open and the councillors returned. She stood straight. Please let it be the end.

Hampton brought Sean in and sat him in the central chair. Cormac stood and delivered the sentence.

'Sean Flaherty, you have been found guilty of the charges of kidnapping Lucas Valeroso and sending monsters to Winton with the intention of harming both gadda and humans. As such, the Sabhamir will lock your power and you will no longer be considered gadda. However, we don't believe it is right to banish you, for your obsession with the Ceamir and your hatred of humans will not end with this, and you may cause more harm. So you will live out your days in a locked suite here, in the bardria building. We will take care of your every comfort, but you will never leave here again. Do you have something to say before your sentence is enacted?'

For once, Sean said nothing. His face was blank with shock.

'Sabhamir, lock his power.'

Hampton walked around the chair. 'Stand, Sean Flaherty.' Sean did as he told. Hampton put his hands on Sean's shoulders and became still. The air around the chamber swirled, and thickened, and Maggie's hair stood on end.

Then it cleared and Hampton released Sean. 'It is done.'

'Sabhamir, take Mr Flaherty to the cells until his suite can be readied for him,' Cormac said.

'One more thing, Caelleach,' Owen said. 'It would seem that Sean Flaherty has had some contact with the Forbidden Texts. We wish to scry him, to search his memories and see if we can identify the person who has the texts.'

Cormac frowned. 'Mr Flaherty is, to all intents and purposes, human. Scrying a human is illegal, Firimir.'

'And so it should be,' Owen said. 'But these are special circumstances, and Mr Flaherty is not really human.'

'I do not object,' Helga said. 'I wish to find out the truth of what Sean did. If it is possible that he unknowingly used the texts, the gadda should know that.'

'Mr Flaherty, do you agree?'

'I wish to prove my innocence,' Sean said.

'Very well. You may scry Mr Flaherty, but not mind-read him.'

'Thank you, Caelleach.' Owen bowed. He, Hampton and Sean disappeared.

'This session of the bardria of the gadda is ended.' Cormac stood and the other councillors followed him from the room.

The other guardians left. Maggie walked over to her family, putting aside her worries about the texts, and sat down next to her mother. 'It's over,' she whispered. No more attacks on her family. No more issues with Sean. It really was over.

'It should feel better than this,' Siobhan said.

'I can't believe I'm about to say this, but poor Oswald,' John said. 'No one deserves a son like that.'

'He was his father, Dad: he has to take some responsibility,' Siobhan said.

Maggie opened her mouth to reply when a voice echoed in her mind. '*Ceamir, I need you.*'

She sighed. 'Duty calls.' She kissed her mother and grandfather, then connected to the distressed gadda and transferred.

CHAPTER THIRTY-ONE

Lucas tried to pay attention to the book in his hand, but eventually he conceded defeat. Until he knew the bardria's decision about Sean, and thus himself, there was no way he was going to concentrate.

God, he wished he had access to his powers. He could speak mentally to Maggie, find out what was going on, not have to endure this endless wait.

Mind-talking was the first skill he would learn when he passed first order, he promised himself. The very first.

The second would be how to shield himself, so he'd never have to hurt someone about to cast a spell.

There was a knock and he spun around and stared at the door. Someone was in the Ceamir's office. Well, if they wanted the Ceamir, they would have to wait. Just like he did.

The knock re-sounded, this time accompanied by a voice calling his name.

Lucas went over to the door and stared at it. After everything that had happened, opening this was probably a damn stupid thing to do. But open it he did.

Standing in front of him was an old man with sharp

features and white hair. He looked like an ancient version of Lucas himself.

'I'm Oswald Flaherty, your great-uncle.'

Lucas hoped he wasn't staring at the old man. He couldn't tell. 'Mr Flaherty.'

'I wanted to apologise to you. You are a Flaherty, and we … support you. Sean had no right to attack you.'

Lucas fought down his surprise to focus on the old man's words, which sounded sincere, if hoarse with reluctance. 'Helga told me that the Flahertys were supporting me in my desire to be gadda. I appreciate it.'

Flaherty tutted. 'You'd be gadda already, were it not for the Shaunessy girl. Helga had plans to prevent your banishment, and the support of the majority of the bardria, but then that girl came in and ruined everything. Still, she is the Ceamir now, so the match has my approval.'

Lucas wanted desperately to laugh. Instead, he said, 'What will happen to Sean now?'

'I don't know, and I don't care. The boy has shamed me.' Oswald shook his head. 'What I can't understand is that I never saw it. Sean was a good boy. Not like your father. He was bad from the moment he was born.'

Lucas clenched his fists to fight the anger and grief welling within him. 'You knew my father.'

'Of course I did.' Then the Flaherty looked directly at him. 'Goodness, boy, you do know that your grandmother was my sister, don't you?'

'So I've heard.'

'You've got your hands full with Margaret Shaunessy. The O'Haras are mad.'

'I quite like mad,' Lucas said. He couldn't quite explain why it all seemed so much clearer, so much more positive, but it did.

'You should come to visit. You are family; you are welcome.'

'Thank you.' Lucas watched the old man turn and shuffle away. On the far side of the room stood a posse of people who surrounded him and ushered him into the corridor.

Lucas closed the connecting door. Had Oswald decided to replace Sean as favoured heir with Lucas? He laughed, but it was hollow.

After some more wandering around the apartment, he lay down on the bed to have a nap. When he woke, he found Maggie's beautiful face smiling down at him.

'Hi.'

'Hi.' He raised his hand to touch her cheek. 'Is it over?'

She lay down beside him and rested her cheek on his chest. Lucas started to stroke her hair.

'It is. Sean has had his power locked, and he'll be locked up for good here in the bardria building.'

'And me?'

'Nothing yet. Like you said earlier, your sins have been gazumped by the Forbidden Texts. So I guess this time I don't have to save you.'

'Apparently, you didn't have to last time either.'

She sat up and frowned down at him. 'What do you mean?'

'Helga had plans, what with me being a Flaherty and all.' He waited for her reaction. It was surprisingly modest.

She sighed. 'Of course she did. Underhanded, the whole lot of them.'

'So, you knew?'

She smiled at him. 'Grandpa's not that impressed. I'm still trying to decide whether I want to get involved with another Flaherty, since the last time went so badly.'

'Then allow me to point out the obvious advantages I have over Cousin Sean.' As he spoke, he pulled her back down onto his chest.

She snuggled against him. 'What advantages?'

'A, I'm not mentally ill, at least not that I know of. B, I don't have any hang-ups about those dastardly humans. C, I still have my power or I will when it's unlocked and D, I won't leave your bed until you're more than satisfied.'

Maggie wriggled and a shock of power and desire swam through him. 'I'm more than willing to believe A through to C, but I think you're going to have to prove D to me.'

'Great minds think alike,' Lucas said as he pulled her lips down to his.

The next morning, the guardians gathered again in Hampton's office to discuss the results of his and Owen's conversation with Sean Flaherty.

'You were right,' Owen said to Maggie. 'He does pinpoint the change in his powers to the day he met you. The scrying gave us more clues, but not the definitive identification we hoped for.'

Maggie frowned. 'Why not?'

'Scrying just shows us a person's memories, and they're not always accurate. In this case, I went through whom Sean saw that first day in Sclossin. There were a few faces, but he only remembered those he felt noteworthy. I did see the moment he touched the texts – someone was carrying them and one began to fall and he caught it before it hit the ground. He was so impressed with himself over that, he didn't pay attention to the person he gave the book to. All we've got is that it was a female, older and she was wearing a robe.'

'That's got us thinking that we are dealing with a dath who works here at the bardria,' Hampton said. 'Generally, gadda working elsewhere wear some form of human clothing. It's only here in the bardria building that most people choose to wear the robes.'

'So it's an inside job,' Maggie said.

'It would seem so, and that means we've got to be even more careful about what we say to whom. We don't know if by discussing things with staff, we might well be talking to the person with the texts,' Hampton said. 'That includes the bardria.'

'That's going to make life difficult, if we have to treat everyone with immediate distrust,' Sarah said.

'I think it's the safest route to take,' Hampton said.

'Unfortunately, the texts aren't the only thing we have to worry about,' Owen said. 'Hampton and I scried a little further, in case Sean had more than one encounter with the texts. A couple of days after he arrived, Sean was taken by an old friend to meet a group who call themselves the League of Purification. As the name suggests, their role is to rid the gadda of Humanists.'

'You're kidding. The League of Purification? What a stupid name,' Maggie said.

'Not a stupid group. Again, Sean didn't remember everyone in the group, but Hampton and I questioned a couple of people overnight. They've been prepared for this. Someone's messed with their minds, and they've had a lot of memories stripped. They came across to us as a Purist discussion group, but you don't need to strip your memories if that's all you are. They're refusing to take part in a mind-read, and the caelleach is taking his time to decide if the bardria will order them to.'

'So we've got a group of Purists who we suspect are involved in Sean's little plots,' Kenyon said.

'They existed before Sean, and may continue after him,' Hampton said. 'Hopefully we'll have more information later today.'

'No sign of the texts?' Wilma said.

'None. So, we're not only looking out for strange uses of power, we also need to keep an ear or eye open for whispers of Purist plots.'

'Is it always this hard?' Maggie whispered to Kenyon.

'Normally quite dull, really. This could be the most excitement you get for the rest of your life, so I'd enjoy it if I were you.' He grinned.

Maggie was sure that whatever happened, she wouldn't enjoy it.

*

As he and Maggie lay wrapped in each other's arms on sweat-soaked sheets, Lucas thought about the almost clear path ahead of them. Two days had passed since the incident with Sean, and he was starting to accept that his actions had been condoned. All he had to do was be admitted to the gadda, which a number of people seemed to think was a certainty, and then there would be no more obstacles, nothing to stand in the way of happily ever after.

Then Maggie sat bolt upright and turned to stare down at him. 'Oswald Flaherty needs me. You too.'

Lucas watched with both enjoyment and disappointment as she ran around the bedroom, gathering her clothes and pulling them on. 'What does he want me for?'

'I don't know, but as Ceamir I can't say no, so hurry up and get dressed.'

Once they were dressed, Maggie wrapped her arms around him and they transferred.

It was fluid and swift − a slight pull on him and then they were no longer in the bedroom but in a richly furnished loungeroom.

The door opened and Oswald Flaherty came in. 'Ceamir, Lucas, glad you could both come. You in particular, Lucas. There's a friend of yours in my library, someone I think you should talk to. She's, ah, human. And American. And, I think, determined.'

There was only one person Lucas could think of that would fit that description. 'Shit. Holly.' His heart froze. Who would they believe?

'How did she get here?' Maggie said.

'Plane, I'd imagine.'

'No, I mean, how did she know about Sclossin?'

Lucas was truly floored. Time to change the subject. 'What I'd like to know is how she ended up *here*?' He looked at Flaherty.

'Helga found her asking at every shop on the High Street whether anyone knew of you. She said she was your fiancée, and, once Helga realised the woman was human, she decided to bring her here.'

'Right,' Lucas said, perverse satisfaction swamping him. One way or another, he was in a position to deal with Holly for the last time.

He forced his heart-rate to slow down. No more Holly. Even if he threw away any chance at acceptance by the gadda, it would be worth it, just for that. Then he shook his head. No, he wanted to be gadda. Wanted it desperately. God, I hope they see through her.

Oswald led them from the room across the hallway and into the library. Holly was in a large armchair over by the fire. She looked around and jumped to her feet with a wide smile on her face.

'Lucas, darling, I'm so glad I found you. I've been so worried about you.' She started toward him with her hands stretched out before her.

'Can it, Holly,' Lucas growled and she stumbled. 'Everyone here knows you're not my fiancée, so quit the act.'

Holly stopped. 'You know you shouldn't talk to me like that, Lucas.'

'Actually, Holly, everyone here knows about the car-jacking, and they don't care. It's over.'

Holly tossed her head, her hair dancing around her shoulders. 'Car-jacking! Do they know about this?'

She lifted her shirt, pulled down the waistband of her skirt and there, on the curve of her belly, was a jagged scar. Lucas stared at it, transfixed. Not a knife, he thought to himself. Scar would be smoother, straighter if it was. Glass, perhaps?

'Star above.' Oswald's gasp barely penetrated his thoughts.

'Yes, this is what your precious Lucas is capable of,' Holly said. 'And this is just the external scar. There are internal ones, and mental ones. He ruined my life and abandoned me without a backward glance. I have a right to compensation for what he did.'

Lucas felt sick. God, it was a convincing act.

'What exactly did he do?' Maggie said. He cast her a quick glance. Her face was expressionless and he could barely feel any emotion in her. He didn't know if that was good or not.

'Ah, so you are involved with him.' Holly sneered at Maggie. 'You should know what you've gotten. Lucas Valeroso is a rapist. He's a murderer.'

Fuck, that was the worst thing she could have said. Lucas was aware of Oswald backing away and out the door.

'I don't believe you,' Maggie said.

'Believe this.' Holly pushed the scar. 'He raped me, often, because he was a drunk, like his father. Then when I fell pregnant, he stabbed me and killed my child. He also took away any chance of having children.' He could hear the tears building in Holly's voice and had to congratulate her for such a compelling performance.

'Holly, Holly, Holly.' Now he could feel an emotion from Maggie — satisfaction. 'You were going so well, and then you had to go just a step too far.' She put her hand in Lucas's. He looked down into her smiling face. 'I'm wondering how you managed to impregnate her, darling.'

A pulse of comforting power accompanied her words, a reminder of their gadda connection and he realised what Maggie meant. He was gadda. Holly was human. He couldn't father a child with her.

'So am I.' He grinned at Holly. 'Wrong move, Hols.'

'Young lady.' Lucas spun around to see Oswald Flaherty storm back into the room. Behind him was the Sabhamir. 'Repeat your story.'

Holly looked at Lucas and he didn't need telepathy to know what she was thinking – the old man believes, and he'll pay. 'Certainly, Mr Flaherty.' She repeated the allegation, making sure both Oswald and the Sabhamir had a clear view of her scar.

Lucas was watching Oswald closely, and saw the change sweep over his face when Holly said she'd been pregnant. The old man looked at Lucas and Lucas shrugged.

The Sabhamir waved his hand and Holly froze. 'Well, Valeroso, she tells a compelling story.'

'Holly always has,' Lucas said. 'Why do you think I ended up in that car with a knife?'

'If she hadn't added the part about the pregnancy, you'd have had a hard time convincing the bardria it wasn't true.'

'It isn't.'

The Sabhamir smiled. 'I believe you. However, we do have to deal with Ms ...'

'Faulkner. And don't worry, I can deal with her.'

'Very well.' Another gesture, and Holly kept speaking as though she hadn't been interrupted.

'Holly, shut up.' Lucas stepped forward. 'He doesn't believe you. No one here does. No one will. Your time of milking this cash cow is over.'

Holly looked at Oswald with a frown, then at Lucas. 'Maybe they don't, but the world at large will. How will your reputation survive that?'

'Probably wouldn't,' Lucas said. 'And if my reputation was all I had, that would concern me. But it isn't.' He held his hand out behind him, and smiled as Maggie took hold and came to snuggle against his side. 'You can't hurt me any more, Holly. Not where it really counts.'

Holly stared at him, then tossed her hair again and waved a hand at the others. 'Be it on your own heads if you believe him. Just don't come crying to me when his true colours are revealed.' With her back straight, she walked over to the chair, picked up a handbag and, without looking at anyone, walked out of the room.

'Well, well,' Lucas murmured as the door closed behind her. 'Holly does actually have a touch of class.'

Maggie threw her arms around Lucas's neck. 'She's gone. She's gone.'

Lucas laughed and hugged her tight. She was right — he could finally put his past behind him and move forward. With Maggie.

Maggie was bent over the computer, searching for signs of misuse of power in the human world when Hampton spoke to her.

'Guardians, the Firimir and I have just mind-read Helen O'Docherty and Paul Heffernan, the two members of the League of Purification identified by Sean Flaherty. Unfortunately, we didn't learn much more from the mind-read. Their memories have been so tampered with that we were unable to see the faces or hear the names of anyone else in the room, except, interestingly, for Sean. I believe he wasn't a fully fledged member yet, so hadn't been subject to the tampering. We were able to ascertain enough to fear that they've been doing some radical things – their passion for the cause is frightening. We don't have enough evidence to banish Helen or Paul, but we have detained them and so hopefully the League will be lost without them. But we need to keep watchful.'

'Is the tampering part of the texts?' Wilma said.

'I cannot feel the darkness in them, and unfortunately the knowledge to meddle with people's memories is not banned information. I think this is unrelated to the texts.'

'So, we have the texts on the loose, and potentially a terrorist group,' Maggie said. 'Great.'

'Remember, keep all these discussions between us,' Hampton said. 'The less other people know, the better.'

Her mind quietened, and Maggie frowned at the computer. It seemed impossible to her that the two things were unrelated – it was too coincidental that a seemingly extreme Purist group had arisen at the same time the Forbidden Texts were stolen.

She shook her head and focussed her attention back on the screen. She had work to do.

CHAPTER THIRTY-TWO

Maggie had never been so nervous. She was on her way to find out whether Lucas would be admitted into the gadda. He had the support of the Flaherty, and the caelleach, and all the guardians, and had well and truly proven himself over the past month. He'd passed Blair's lessons with high praise from the teacher (well, high for Blair), and there hadn't been a sniff of trouble attached to him. And he was the accepted partner of the Ceamir. Surely he would be admitted.

Except: he was Rogan Connor's son; he did have a criminal record; there was the incident with Sean; and he'd brought a human among them – and a truly terrifying one, too. Even though Holly's lies had been revealed, what if the bardria thought the risk of her return was too great – Stop. It will be all right. I have to believe that.

As she walked into the bardria chamber, she was surprised to see it was as packed as when she'd come to save Lucas. She looked around, trying to gauge if people were on his side or not. Had they come wanting to see the newest gadda, or see a banishment?

Ione and John waved; Siobhan and Peter nodded and smiled. Maggie nodded back, though she would have loved a hug or two to assure her it would be all right.

Luckily, over the past month she'd got a new family. Kenyon gave her a mental thumbs-up and Owen smiled. Even Wilma nodded her head in support. The only one who didn't give her any assurance was the Heasimir.

The door at the front of the room opened and the bardria entered. She quickly scanned the faces, and apart from the hatred searing Henry Halloran's features, they all looked passive. No clues there.

As the bardria took their seats, so too did most of the crowd, the rest standing around the walls. A hush descended over the room.

Then Cormac's voice boomed through the air. 'The bardria of the gadda calls on Lucas Valeroso.'

The door at the back of the room opened and in walked Lucas, escorted by the Sabhamir. Maggie's heart jumped. Lucas looked at her and winked and peace settled over her.

Lucas stood in front of the bardria desk and the Sabhamir hovered just behind him, as if he still wasn't trusted.

'Lucas Valeroso, you have been summoned to hear the bardria's decision as to whether the sentence against your father should be overturned and you should be given admittance to the gadda. The decision is not unanimous, but by an overwhelming majority the decision is that you would be a worthy addition to the ranks of the gadda.'

Tears welled in Maggie's eyes. Lucas looked over his shoulder and smiled his enormous love at her.

'Sabhamir, you may now release Mr Valeroso's binding,' Cormac said.

The Sabhamir came forward, touched Lucas's shoulder and then smiled. He leant forward and whispered something in Lucas's ear, and the two men nodded at each other.

'This meeting is adjourned. I would like to see Mr Valeroso and his family and friends in my office. Thank you.'

Maggie waited until they were in the caelleach's office, away from the eyes of the crowd, before she gave in to her true feelings and flew into Lucas's arms.

'You did it, you did it,' Maggie said.

'Of course I did. Did you doubt me?'

'Never.' She held his face and gazed at him, amazed that their last hurdle had finally fallen.

The caelleach's office was a tight squeeze for a gathering of this size. Cormac sat in his chair, the guardians standing behind him, while in the space in front of the desks all the available chairs and floor space were taken up by Lucas, John, Siobhan, Peter, Ione and Oswald and Helga Flaherty.

Cormac said, 'I believe we require something to mark this moment, but perhaps not the usual graduation ceremony. The Coiremir has supplied the perfect alternative. She has come across a now-unused ceremony for renewal of power and commitment to the gadda. She suggested combining it with the ceremony for the creation of Lucas's scent. May I suggest one week from now? I offer my home as venue since some councillors are against your admission; it would be disrespectful to hold the ceremony here.'

'No, it will take place in my home,' Oswald said. 'Lucas is a Flaherty.'

Maggie frowned at her grandfather. '*Don't,*' she told him mentally. Her grandfather looked at her.

'*Do you understand the strain you're putting on me, Maggie? And now I have to go to a party at the Flaherty's ridiculous mansion?*'

'*Yes. Don't.*'

He sighed and nodded sourly.

'Lucas, do you agree to that?' Cormac said.

'I do,' Lucas said.

'Then in one week, we gather at the Flaherty residence to welcome Lucas Valeroso into the gadda. Thank you.' Cormac nodded his head, dismissing them.

They all filed out of the room, Maggie clutching Lucas's hand.

'Let's celebrate,' John announced. 'Dinner at the bardria restaurant, my treat.'

'No, it should be at my home,' Oswald said.

Maggie sighed, seeing years of family-function bickering stretching before her. She put an arm around Lucas's waist and pulled him close to her.

The restaurant was finally agreed upon, with John and Oswald splitting the bill. Maggie thought it said a great deal for the joy felt by everyone there that even her grandfather and Oswald Flaherty were civil to each other for the length of the meal.

Dinner was brilliant but she became more and more impatient to get Lucas to herself ... and then realised she didn't have to wait for anything. She was a guardian. She waved at their families, grabbed his hand

and then they were in the bedroom of the Ceamir's apartment.

'You took your time thinking of that.' They rolled together onto her bed. 'I've been going mad with wanting you.' He began to nuzzle at her neck, and the inevitable passion swelled through Maggie.

But first, there was something she had to say. She grabbed his head and pulled it from her so she could look him in the eye.

'I'm so happy,' she whispered.

'I know.' He squeezed her tight. 'This is it, baby. This is our life. You, me, and the gadda. Just as it should be.'

She pushed his lips back down to her neck and forgot about everything but their perfect passion.

Lucas stared at himself in the mirror. Never in his life had he pictured himself wearing a long, white gown. It looked ridiculous — with his height and wide shoulders, there was so much material that he resembled a feather quilt rather than a powerful magician. Thank God the gadda didn't insist on wearing their ceremonial robes all the time.

The door opened and he heard a giggle quickly choked down. 'I see you're ready,' Maggie said.

He looked over his shoulder, frowning. 'Don't say it,' he growled.

'Say what?' Her smile was pure innocence.

'Don't think it either.' He started toward her.

'Now, that's not fair. You have to let me think it, otherwise I'll go mad.'

'Just because this works on you.' And it did. Somehow, the red gown of the Ceamir gave Maggie an earthiness and yet something ephemeral that spoke volumes of the power she now possessed.

She touched his cheek. 'Not long, my beloved, then you will be truly gadda and you can tear it off so we can celebrate in our now-traditional manner.'

Lucas smiled. 'Well, now, that's all I needed, something to look forward to.' Then he looked back at the mirror and pretended to gag. 'Shit.'

Maggie took his arm and they transferred to the Flaherty laboratory. Oswald was waiting for them.

'Ceamir, Lucas, welcome to my home.' He bowed to them.

'Oswald, thank you for this.' Lucas smiled at the old man. In the past few weeks, he'd decided to accept Oswald Flaherty's offers of friendship, even if he didn't support a lot of his uncle's extreme views. One day he'd maybe even like the intense character. Something Lucas would need to keep hidden from John O'Hara.

'We are having the ceremony in the library; it's the only room large enough. Come along.' He led them up the stone stairs and through the hidden door into the lounge.

Lucas was amazed that not only were his family and friends present, but also all the guardians and a number of the councillors.

'Let us begin,' Horatio Cormac announced.

Everyone formed a circle around the edge of the room, and then Oswald moved forward and waved his hands over the carpet. It shimmered and disappeared, revealing a star of gulagh painted onto the wooden floorboards. He stepped back into the circle and the Sabhamir stepped forward, stopping at one of the points of the star. Where Lucas's robe was ridiculous, the Sabhamir's black robe was sleek and well fitted.

'Lucas Valeroso, we are gathered here today to welcome you into the gadda, to offer you our support during your journey and to mark you as one of us,' he said. 'All gadda have their own particular scent, used as part of their ceremonies, created for them at their birth by their parents. As this counts as a birth for you, a scent has been created for you by the one who knows you best. Ceamir, step forward.'

Maggie brushed her hand against his as she made her way into the centre of the circle, stopping at the point of the star to the Sabhamir's right. She reached into her robe and pulled out a small vial that contained a deep red liquid.

'The scent must be mixed with blood in order to become one with the person it is intended for. Lucas Valeroso, step forward,' the Sabhamir said.

Lucas stopped on the point of the star opposite the Sabhamir and Ceamir.

'The blood must be drawn by the one destined to guide the newcomer. John O'Hara, step forward.'

John stepped to the point to Lucas's right. When Lucas looked at him, O'Hara winked.

'The blending must be witnessed by the head of the newcomer's family. Oswald Flaherty, step forward.'

Oswald took the point on Lucas's left. There was now just one left, between Maggie and John.

'There is usually a witness chosen by the family to support the carers of the child. In this case, Lucas has chosen his own supporter. Step forward, Siobhan Shaunessy.'

Siobhan took her position with a smile.

The Sabhamir nodded to John. The older man reached into his robe and pulled out a long, thin knife. He motioned to Maggie and Lucas. They all met in the centre of the star.

'Lucas Valeroso, you are given this scent, unique to you, a lasting symbol that you are born gadda,' John said, happiness ringing through his tone.

Maggie unstoppered the vial, and a strong and invigorating fragrance rose in the air. It instantly felt right to Lucas. He was awed. Is there anything she can't do?

Then he lifted his hand and Maggie held the vial under his middle finger. John reached forward and took hold of the finger, then pressed the tip of the knife into it. He put the knife away and squeezed one drop of blood from Lucas's finger into the vial.

As the blood and liquid met, a stream of red gas rose in the air and wrapped itself around Lucas, infusing him. He felt the scent move through him, settle within him until it was part of every fibre of his being.

'Lucas is now born gadda.' John nodded, and then he, Maggie and Lucas stepped back to the edge of the star. The six who surrounded it bowed, to each other and to the power symbolised and summoned by the star, and then retreated into the circle.

Lucas breathed in deeply, and the scent-tinged air rushed through him, bringing him peace and confidence. It was truly him.

'All gadda are intimately connected with and in control of their power,' the Sabhamir said. 'Join with Lucas as he contemplates. Feel your own power, reconnect with your soul and the essence of being gadda.'

Lucas closed his eyes and there was his power, deep within him, burning brightly. Since the binding had been lifted he had redoubled his efforts to learn about his power, running hourly over the focussing exercises until they – and his power – were as much part of him as the air he breathed. No more strange surges, no more sending cabs to a sudden halt in the middle of the road or losing his head in rage.

He didn't know how long he spent immersed in his power, and was only drawn from his reverie by the Sabhamir's voice.

'Now comes the final part of the ceremony, committing to life with the gadda.'

Lucas opened his eyes and forced his body to relax. He'd been most nervous about this bit. The Coiremir's instructions had simply said, *Lucas is marked with the star of gulagh.* He didn't think it meant a tattoo – he'd never seen one on Maggie. So what did it mean?

'Lucas Valeroso, return to the centre of the star,' the Sabhamir said.

In the centre, he felt a movement in the air. Shit, he thought. The star's alive.

The Sabhamir stepped to a point of the star and then bent down and touched it. A searing pain scorched across Lucas's chest; he thrust his hands against it but it was gone almost as soon as he realised it was there.

'Open your robe, Lucas, and see that you are truly one of us,' the Sabhamir said.

Lucas's hands were shaking as he reached up and pulled open the front of his robe. He looked down and saw a blazing white six-pointed star with a heart in the middle, seemingly burnt into his chest. There was no longer any pain involved, but there was no doubting he'd been branded. As he stared at it, trying to fathom how he felt, it faded from view.

'Holy shit,' he whispered.

'The star has judged you and considered you worthy. It has marked you, and you are now gadda. Welcome, Lucas.'

Wild applause broke out, and Lucas barely had time to gather himself before Maggie was in his arms. He hugged her tight, and accepted the congratulations of his family but he was focussed on the star, which might have disappeared from his chest but was now burning its way into his soul – and with the burn came a connectedness to everyone around him, and every gadda who had ever lived.

As it settled within him, he realised that this was what banishment was really about. It wasn't about losing your powers; it was about losing this connection, this sense of belonging. For a moment, he felt some sympathy for his father. But then he put that aside to focus on his new beginning, his new life, with Maggie.

ASARLAI

'May the Star burn their brains out. I knew bringing in Sean Flaherty was a mistake.' Jason O'Byrne stormed from one side of the room to the other. 'We had worked successfully and without being discovered for months. Damn Helen for her stupid ambition, she's put us all at risk.'

Everyone else in the League shouted his or her agreement. Asarlai relaxed in her chair, grateful that her foresight in ensuring their minds couldn't be read properly had saved them all from discovery.

How terrible it would have been for the Sabhamir to find her and maybe the texts because of this stupidity. She was glad she'd got the books out of Sclossin — regardless of the personal cost to her. However, the texts had proven to be very unsatisfied with their new home, and the few experiments she'd tried had been dismal failures.

The fact Sean Flaherty's simple touch of the texts had had such a profound affect worried her. She'd handled the books numerous times — what could they be doing to her? Had the terrible moment at the train station been about the texts and not discomfort from travelling in a car? What would they do to her apprentices?

She'd need to copy the texts, and have her apprentices work from them. She was close to deciding who to choose.

Asarlai looked over the gathering. The League now numbered nine, and of them she had four potential followers. They had the passion she was looking for, along with being at least third order so they could handle the texts.

They were also second children, so the family bloodlines would continue should Asarlai be forced to get rid of them. It was important that her plans only helped the gadda, not hinder them.

'What do we do now?' One of her potential apprentices, Shauna Connell, spoke. 'It would seem pointless to continue focussing on the O'Haras, since their relationship with the Ceamir provides extra protection.'

'There are many other options, and some much closer to home,' Jason said. 'I know Helen focussed on the O'Haras in order to ingratiate herself with the Flahertys, but I've always thought our main priority should be freeing Sclossin of human influence. Take the inn, for example. It's sacrilege that there's somewhere for humans to stay.'

'What about people like Ione Gorton?' Shauna said. 'Why is a good gadda making her living working exclusively with humans?'

'Exactly.' Jason smiled.

Asarlai was glad they were making new plans, especially ones so close to Sclossin. The more that was going on, the more the guardians would have to do and the less time they'd have to look for her.

She got up to leave, nodding before she transferred. The League wasn't the only group she was cultivating. Chaos would be her friend as her plans grew.

TURN THE PAGE
TO FIND OUT
WHAT HAPPENS NEXT ...

POWER UNBOUND

DREAM OF ASARLAI, BOOK TWO

For centuries, the gadda have worked to keep their identity secret from the rapidly expanding human race. All this is now at risk — the most terrible of gadda teachings, the Forbidden Texts, have been stolen and the race is on to find them.

Ione Gorton may have got her best friend back from Australia, but Maggie's elevation to the ranks of the guardians means that she's not around as much. And when Stephen O'Malley, almost the youngest (and definitely the hottest) ever candidate for the sixth order test, needs a place to stay after still more strange violence hits Sclossin, Ione is all too happy to lend a hand ...

But Ione, like Maggie before her, is soon a target for the forces behind the theft of the Forbidden Texts, and the now-urgent search for the artefact will change life for gadda and human alike.

NICOLE
MURPHY
POWER
UNBOUND

NICOLE MURPHY

ROGUE GADDA

www.ingramcontent.com/pod-product-compliance
Lightning Source LLC
Chambersburg PA
CBHW050611110726
47899CB00001B/70